Violet Flames

Primordial Gods Book One

P.S. Nail

Primordial Tree Publishing

Written by P.S. Nail

Illustrations by Diletta De Santis

Editing by L.M Wilkinson

ASIN: B0B1Z6R5NZ (E-Book) ISBN: 9780578377292

First Edition: January 2022

Primordial Tree Publishing

Dedication
To my aunt, Vicky Douglas
Dreams do come true!
And
To the readers
We all need a fantasy world to live in.

Note From The Author

I hope everyone enjoys the world I have built and I apologize in advance for any tears you may shed while reading—but not really. *wink*

I want ALL the emotions to come out of you!

You may fall in love, laugh, cry, or get horny, and if so, then I did my job right. I hope your self-pleasure item, if you need one, is rechargeable. ENJOY! *P.S. Nail*

Information

Content warning: This book contains profanity, blood, death or dying, alcohol consumption, animal hunting, casualties of war, murder, graphic violence, abduction, and imprisonment. There are also mentions of anxiety and depression.

It also contains explicit sexual content that includes unprotected sex and swapping of bodily fluids, e.g. semen and blood.

For information on this book, social media links, and more, please visit the author's website https://psnail.org/

To see a full colored version of the Primordial Realm world map, please visit https://inkarnate.com/p/RpLqpr--ps-nail/

To purchase officially licensed merchandise, please visit

https://www.primordialtree.com/

Contents

VIOLET FLAMES

PRIMORDIAL GODS
BOOK ONE

P.S. Nail

Hallowshade
Direbreak
Portal
Portal
Castleva
Berry Beach
Ashbern Crater
Amethyst Falls
Ashbern
Elderfall
Ethereal Pastures
Portal
Dazeth
Gailshire
Arnlean
Magecrest
Fairy Beach
Tessalone
Anahita
Cerulean
Portal

Angelcrest
Arcross Mountains
Portal
Valmeyer
Portal
Windcrest
Vanhall City
Portal
Blackveil Castle
Spellchild Castle
Arna Mountains
Pyreland
Portal
Winter's Peak
Mayhem
Mayhem Harbor
Wistar Isle
Mazuria
Nebulous Forest
Closed Portal
Nebulous Dungeon
Mistlaven

Primordial Gods

Voltarean: The God of Night, the maker of the Vampires, reigning from the country of Mayhem.

Toberon: The God of Day, the maker of the Fae, reigning from the country of Tessalone.

Reign: The God of the Sun, the Maker of the Angels, reigning from the country of Valmeyer.

Lykaon: The God of the Moon, the maker of Lycans, reigning from the country of Direbreak.

Ailwin: The God of the Forest, the maker of the Elven, reigning from the country of Dazeth.

Apothee: The God of the Earthen, the maker of Plants and Animals, reigning from the country of Ashbern.

Volcanis: The God of Fire, the maker of Fire Casters, reigning from the country of Mazuria.

Abzule: The God of Water, the maker of Water Casters, reigning from the country of Cerulean.

Zephyr: The God of Air, the maker of Air Casters, reigning from the country of Windcrest.

Tartarus: The God of Sulfur, the maker of Demons, reigning from the country of Mistlaven.

UNTIL DEATH, DISMISSAL, OR DISHONOR.

Music Playlist

To help me get into the mood of each book, I make playlists to match the theme and feelings.

Here is the one I listened to while writing Violet Flames.

Spotify:
https://open.spotify.com/playlist/4CJmKqwvUAjfacJYcj
Z7Ir?si=f6f140822e624922
iTunes:
https://music.apple.com/us/playlist/violet-flames/pl.u-8
aAVoo1UWdzDyV

Prologue

Two Years Ago

A loud bang coming from the dining room woke me from my sleep. Hopping out of bed, I threw my robe over my nightgown and made my way to the kitchen, slowly peeking around the corner before entering. Shadows of a person were flickering on the wall from an oil lamp someone had lit.

"Ember, why are you out of bed?" My body immediately relaxed when I heard my father's voice.

"I heard a noise, Father. I was making sure everything was okay."

"Everything is not okay. Come and sit down, dear." I did as he said and took a seat at the dining room table. "I have something I need to give you. I was going to wait until tomorrow, but since you are up . . . here." He pulled a dagger out of a leather sheath and held it toward me. It looked like a tiny sword.

Taking it from him, I turned it over in my hands, inspecting every inch of it. It had a handle made from braided leather and a silver pommel cap on the tip of the handle with a spiral configuration on it. The same spirals were also on the pommel that went across like a T and connected to the blade.

The blade was sharp and pointy. It flared out, getting bigger, then thinned again before connecting. It looked sharp—beautiful.

"Why are you giving me this?" I asked as I met his eyes.

"For protection, Ember."

My brows furrowed in confusion. "I don't understand."

"I have sad news, my dear. A Vampire took your mother tonight. We do not know why he wanted her, but he did." I threw my hand over my mouth. Air had completely escaped my lungs, making it impossible to speak. "She is no longer of this realm. There isn't a body left to be buried, but we will have a ceremony in her honor. I am deeply sorry to have to tell you this."

Gasping for air was all I could do. *How could he be so calm?* My entire body was exploding with pain, which ran through my veins like poison, threatening to eat me from the inside out. Tears rolled down my face as he continued talking, with no clue that I was dying inside.

"There will come a day that you will need to protect yourself and your sister from those blood-suckers, which is what the dagger is for. Remember, we were not born to be weak. Now, get to bed. It's late." He only had a tiny bit of sadness in his voice. He had become more emotionless with age. I nodded and my father left the dining room.

Emotions flooded through my body as my heart ripped open and exposed itself to the world. I'll never see her again—I didn't even get to say goodbye. I wanted to scream or punch something, but I couldn't. My father would be angry at me if I woke Cinder. Tears streamed down my face as the pain flooded through me.

Once I saw rays of sunlight coming through the window, I slowly made my way back to my room. Almost numb from the amount of pain I had just experienced, I was nothing but a shell of a person now. Gripping the dagger tightly, I slowly lowered myself down on my bed.

We were not born to be weak. My father had been telling me that since I was ten years old. He used to be a good man—a sweet and caring man—but throughout the years, he changed. The older I got, the colder he got. Tonight was the coldest I had seen him. He didn't shed a tear for my mother and I will never forget that.

Looking down at my new dagger, I realized that he was right. I glanced over to where Cinder was peacefully sleeping. I was going to learn to wield the dagger so I could protect her. She wouldn't suffer the same fate as our mother. I needed to get a job and hire someone to train us both to defend ourselves.

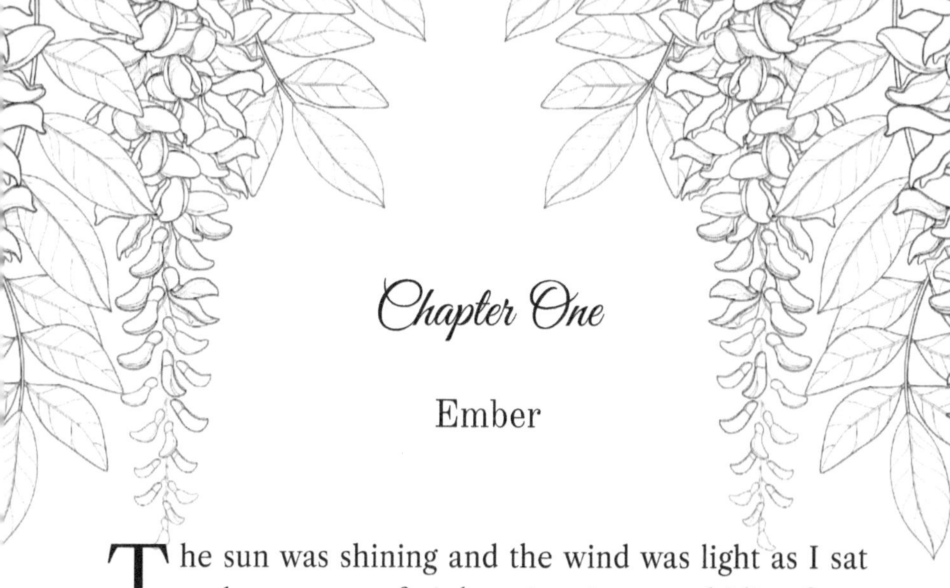

Chapter One

Ember

The sun was shining and the wind was light as I sat under a grove of violet wisteria trees, hiding from reality. Today was the day I had to leave because the king had summoned me. Yes, I would see my family and friends now and then, but I had never been outside of my country of Mazuria and the thought of leaving scared me.

Twenty-two years ago, I was born with the mark of a guardian—a black tattoo in the center of my chest. The guardian mark consisted of a double-headed battle axe with a fire burning under it. I was born to a family of Casters. Which meant I was born from the bloodline of Volcanis, the God of Fire, so I wielded fire as my element.

Each of the nine distinct species in our realm was born from a different God, but only those marked with a tattoo at birth were destined to serve the king and bc sworn in as a King's Guard. I would serve him and the realm for eternity.

Until death, dismissal, or dishonor.

Holding up my hand, I made a fireball and tossed it up and down without ever touching it, as I held a book in my other hand. I was lying against a tree, enjoying my reading, when I saw my sister strolling toward me with a glare on her face.

Father must be furious with me, I thought to myself as I extinguished my fireball.

"What are you doing, Ember?" She had a look of exasperation as her luminous emerald-green eyes watched me. "It's almost time to go."

"Is father angry?" I asked as I gave her my best fake worried face.

"He's going to be if we don't get back to the house right now!" She put her hands on her hips and furrowed her eyebrows. She was wearing a stunning, lightweight white dress. At that moment, she reminded me so much of our mother.

"I'm scared, Cin," I whispered.

"Why would you, of all people, be scared? You're the strongest, and might I add, the most peculiar person I know." She smiled teasingly, causing me to chuckle. I looked down at the book in my hand before closing it.

"I won't know anyone." My voice was small—vulnerable. "Who will I talk to about my book?" It was a lame excuse, but I didn't want her to know how scared I was about leaving her alone with our heartless father.

I don't want to make her cry today.

"It'll be fine, Em. You may even meet a hot Angel or Fae!"

I scrunched up my nose at her. "Finding a mate is *not* a top priority of mine." As I looked at her soft beige skin and her pretty face, I knew she would have no problem finding a mate when the time came. She had rosy-red cheeks with freckles sprayed upon them, just like I did. Her auburn hair, which was a lighter red than mine, was midway down her back. We looked similar, but she was more elegant than I dreamed of being.

"No need to mate them. Just occupy your mind with someone." She gave me a wink.

"To the Gods, Cinder! Bite your tongue!" I laughed and shook my head.

Cinder knew I had a male companion for a while, and she knew I had sex with him. But I didn't have those types of feelings. I didn't want to be mated to him, or anyone, for that matter. He was just a warm body when I felt lonely.

"I meant in conversation." My sister just shrugged it off. Unlike me, she was a virgin. "Let's go before father comes and gets us."

"You go ahead and gale there. I'm going to walk a bit first."

"Okay, but don't take too long." She sighed. After waving at me, she created a portal in her mind to teleport home, then disappeared.

I'm not ready for this. I'm not ready to leave my sister.

With a father as a tradesman and my mother gone, Cinder would be all alone. I'd been dreading this day since my mother passed.

I wish I didn't have to go. I'm all she has.

Grabbing my bag, I packed up my blanket and book, then picked up my bow and slung it over my shoulder. I walked for about five minutes on the sandy area of Wistar Isle, which was the peninsula I was on. Once I was well out of the shade of the wisteria trees, I decided to gale back to my home before my father reprimanded me.

Taking one final look behind me at my favorite place, I sighed. Tears filled my eyes, but they didn't break free.

Everyone born in our world could gale about to places we had been before. We could instantaneously transport ourselves by using our minds, as long as it was a place that we were familiar with.

I opened a portal in my mind by envisioning the beach at the edge of my town so I could gale home. It only took me about two seconds to do now that I was older. When I was younger, I could only gale about a foot away from where I was standing. Most people didn't bother practicing and couldn't gale far. Now I could gale across my entire country if I had been to that land enough to envision it.

I felt a light tingle of magic on my mind before I galed and landed on a beach next to the road, taking me into

Pyreland—my town. It was the last time I would see my hometown for a while.

Before I started walking, I took one last look at the snow-covered banks across the water. It was far away and so blurry that I could only see the whiteness at the edge of the land and on the mountains. Reading about snow but never seeing it up close or touching it intrigued me. Even though I was dying to see it, I also didn't want to visit Mayhem because that was the land of the Vampires.

I wonder if there is snow on other lands. With a sigh, I turned and strolled towards my house. Sadness filled me as I thought about leaving my entire world behind.

My house was the first one at the beginning of town. My father was at the edge of our property, glaring at me. Two King's Guards were standing behind him—the blonde one was chatting away with my sister. My father saved grace and smiled as I approached him, but I could tell he wasn't pleased.

"There's my beautiful daughter." He reached out to hug me. I gave him a side hug and moved away quickly before he could quietly scold me. I loved my father because . . . well, he was my father, but I despised him for how emotionless he had become. The way he was acting was a little show he was putting on in front of the company. "Cinder, go grab your sister's bags."

"Of course, Father." Cinder smiled at the guards and skipped off.

"Gentlemen, this is my beautiful daughter, Ember Lavaris." He gestured toward me like I was a prized pony. "Ember, I would like you to meet Zaynith Storm." He pointed to the brown-haired male. I extended my hand and shook his. "And this is Cashmere Voland." He turned toward the sandy-blonde male. As I shook his hand, I realized by their striking bright blue eyes that they were both Angels.

Angels were born from the bloodline of Reign, the God of the Sun.

My chest began to rise and fall as my breathing became heavy. I had only ever seen an Angel twice in my life. They came through town rarely, when they were on missions. I was much younger when I saw them and these weren't the same ones. These Angels were sexy with hard warrior bodies.

Both of them were over six feet tall, with lightly tanned skin like they spent time in the sun. The first Angel, named Zaynith, had scruffy, medium-length brown hair. He had a nice, well-kept, thin beard and was extremely fit, but not overly muscular. He donned a black shirt and trousers with matching boots. A pair of twin silver-handled swords was strapped to his back.

The taller one, Cashmere, had dark blonde hair that was just past his shoulders, with a single small braid on one side. He looked like he chopped wood for a living, but in a sexy way. He had a full thick beard, which was slightly long—four or five inches. His body was muscular, and he donned the same outfit as Zaynith, but his was deep brown. He had two battle axes hanging from his leather harness belt.

Oh, maybe he did chop wood, I thought to myself. I bit my lip to keep from giggling. "Nice to meet you both." *Don't panic. I can do this!*

"You can call him Zayn," the blonde one said with a grin. "And you can call me Cash. That's what all my friends call me." He had an attractive, rugged face.

"Oh, I didn't know we were friends." Zaynith chuckled at my joke. *He is gorgeous. Almost too perfect.*

"This girl is going to fit right in back at Castleva." Zaynith laughed as he clapped Cashmere on the shoulder. I gave him a wry smile.

"Maybe you should go help your sister with your bags." My father's voice was stern. He was displeased with what he would consider flirting—it wasn't. I just liked to make jokes to cover my nervousness.

"Indeed. It's probably best to keep Cinder away from blondie here," I said casually.

Zaynith busted out a laugh as my father's and Cashmere's mouths both plopped open. I couldn't help but smile as I strolled away.

That Angel isn't getting anywhere near my sister.

Cinder was smiling at me as I walked into the house. "Did you see the Angels?"

"Yes." I walked past her and headed to my room. As I readied the bags, she strolled in behind me.

"They're both so nice. I really like Cash!" Her excited grin and flushed cheeks had me furrowing my eyebrows.

"You're calling him Cash? You barely know him."

"I feel like I do. He's so easy to talk to and *really* cute."

"Those *cute men* kill for a living, Cinder." Her face paled at my seriousness.

"Only enemies." She shrugged and then smiled, recovering quickly.

A hard breath of exasperation escaped my lungs. I wasn't ready for my sister to have a love life, especially with someone in the King's Guard. Ignoring the feelings, I set my bow and quiver down and told them goodbye. We grabbed my luggage and dragged them outside to where the males stood waiting for us. About twenty feet behind them, I noticed a crowd gathering.

Great, I now have an audience watching my departure.

"Are you ready to go?" Zaynith asked with a huge smile.

Does he ever stop smiling? Do either of them?

"I'm ready when you are, but is it okay if I bring my dagger?" I pointed to the holster strapped to my right thigh and Zaynith glanced down. My father had gifted it to me and I didn't want to leave it behind. It was what motivated me . . . what kept me strong.

"Of course."

As I said my goodbyes to my father, I couldn't help but notice that he looked content. He didn't seem to care if I left.

My sister was teary-eyed, but she didn't cry. I knew it was only because the Angels were watching. That and how demanding my father was about us being strong. Cinder had been a blubbering mess last night, and her eyes were still puffy from all the crying she did.

"Em, you must send me a messenger Imp tomorrow to let me know how your first day went." She pulled me into a hug.

"I will, Cin."

"I'm going to miss you." She nuzzled her face into my hair as she sniffed back tears.

"I know." I quickly let the hug go before I cried.

The Angels said their goodbyes to my family, and each grabbed a bag before we turned away.

No one could gale across any open waters, we could only gale across whichever landmass we were currently on. There were ten different countries in our realm, all on separate continents, surrounded by the seas. Since we couldn't gale across the waters, we would have to take a land portal over to the country of Ashbern.

The ten different countries housed nine distinct species—one species per country. Nine Primordial Gods made one of those specific species from their blood. The tenth Primordial God, Apothee, The God of Earthen, made all plants and animals. Since his creatures were everywhere, the tenth country was where the current reigning king of our world resided. Ashbern South was where the king lived with his personal guard. The north was where the King's Guard trained and lived. That was where I was going . . . to a place called Castleva.

The townsfolk started cheering as the Angels and I walked toward the portals. Since I had never taken one before, I was uneasy.

As we walked quietly, I got curious and decided to ask something I probably shouldn't.

"Can I see your tattoo? I have never seen another species' tattoo in person before."

"Absolutely." Cashmere grinned as he pulled his shirt up, showing me his tattoo along with his stomach and chest. His guardian mark was gold—a sword with a pair of Angel wings. Staring at his chiseled chest, I peeped the tattoo and then quickly averted my eyes.

"Wow, very nice."

"Zayn has the same one. It's Strength in Emotions and Healing." I looked at Zayn and he smiled.

"Here we are," Zayn said as we approached the portal.

Two members of the King's Guard protected it. Both of them dressed in fighting leathers. Someone could only access the portals with a day pass signed by the king or if they had the tattoo of a King's Guard.

Fear filled me as we got closer. The guard immediately knew that Zaynith and Cashmere were King's Guards, so he stepped aside for us to enter the portal.

"Are you ready for this, Ember?" Zaynith asked.

"It's not much different from galing, just a little weirder. It may spin your head at first, but you will eventually get used to it." Cashmere had an empathetic face.

My heart sped up as I stepped onto the outside ring of the portal. I took a deep breath as I walked on to it. Nothing happened so I looked up at the dark-haired one.

"It's old magic so It won't go until one of us King's Guards wills it to," Zaynith said, meeting my eyes. "As soon as you are knighted in today, you will have full access to the portals and will then be able to wield them to go."

I glanced nervously at Cashmere, who smiled. "Ready?" I nodded in response, even though I wasn't ready.

It was like a thousand molecules burst through my body as warmth combined with a gust of cool air all hit me at once. Goosebumps stood up on my skin as I closed my eyes and saw hundreds of stars. I felt pleasure. Excitement. Happiness. Then it changed. It felt like waves were beating against the front of my body while I was swimming against the current. Nausea rose fast as I became dizzy. A hand grabbed my arm to steady me, and before I could even recognize which Angel it was, we landed in the north of the country of Ashbern, at the edge of Castleva grounds.

Nighttime came when we landed and I was confused because it was early morning when we left Mazuria.

"Are you okay?" a male asked.

"Open your eyes," said another male. "Look at me, Ember."

I did what I was told and Cashmere was in my face with his hands on my cheeks. It was indeed, not dark. Then I realized I was holding the shirt of the other Angel, who was still holding me steady. Panic and nausea were still present and I couldn't catch my breath.

I'm going to be sick. My knees felt like they were going to disappear as I swayed.

"Look at me." I glanced into a pair of bright blue eyes—Cashmere's eyes.

My symptoms started to lighten as my body relaxed. My knees were holding me up again and my nausea faded. He had used his magic to soothe me. Cash wasn't just an Angel—he was an Ornamental Angel, one who could control the emotions of others. Once I felt at ease, he let go of my cheeks. Then I got angry.

"How dare you use your emotional magic on me without my permission!"

Cashmere's face was empathetic as he took a couple of steps away from me.

Zaynith shook his head. "You held your breath in the portal, you panicked. If he hadn't used his powers, you would have thrown up or passed out. Cash did you a favor, so you should be thanking him."

"I don't need any Angel in shining armor to save this pathetic girl from vomiting!"

"I'm sorry." Cashmere's face showed he was utterly hurt. "I was trying to help."

"Don't apologize to her." Zaynith let go of my arm and patted blondie on the shoulder. "You did nothing wrong, buddy."

"I can manage by myself," I said angrily.

"Yeah, it didn't look like it to me," Zaynith snapped back and my mouth fell open.

How dare he talk to me like that!

"It's rough the first few times, but after that, it gets easier. I was making sure you were okay, Ember." Cashmere's voice was calmer than Zaynith's, but there was a slight sadness in his voice. "I'm sorry if you are to believe that my intentions were ill. They were not. I left my family two years ago, so I know how hard it can be."

Realizing how ridiculous I was being, I eased up a bit and relaxed my shoulders. It was hard for me to let my guard down and trust people. That and I was also still letting my nervousness get to me.

"The King's Guard is honorable." Zaynith had a proud look radiating across his face. "Sometimes we must do things when certain situations arise, even if that means using our powers without permission. I'm sorry if that offends you, but that's what we do."

"Don't be sorry, I'm sorry. This is just a lot of new things for me." I took a deep breath and slowly blew it out. "Thank you, Cashmere, for helping me."

"Call me Cash, and you're welcome." He politely smiled and patted my arm.

"We understand how you feel. We've all been there." Zaynith put his hand on my other shoulder. "Since you'll be living with us and are a part of the King's Guard now, we're your friends. We would never hurt you."

With a small smile, I nodded in agreement with his statement.

As I stood there staring at the two Angels, I realized they were just as caring as they were beautiful . . . and I was kind of an asshole.

Chapter Two

We strolled up to the large manor in Castleva and it was breathtaking. It seemed more like a small castle to me. The outside was gray brick with pointy spires at the top that were dark gray. The windows were massive, with arches above each one.

Two guards stood on either side of a large iron door that was the entrance to the manor and we stopped for introductions. One was a female—an Angel judging by her eye color. The other guard was a male. His eyes were . . .

No!

"Hey guys, this is Ember. This is my sister, Calista Storm," Zayn gestured to a brown-haired beauty who grabbed me in a full hug.

She was a couple of inches taller and had a thinner build than I did. Her brown hair was shoulder length and straight. There was a black leather corset over her blue, long-sleeved shirt. She paired it with black trousers and boots. She looked girly and adorable.

"It's so nice to meet you! Your red hair is gorgeous and so bright. I love it!" She smiled as she released me from the hug.

"Thank you. It's nice to meet you too." I gave her a kind smile and then looked in the direction of the male guard.

He has beautiful, deadly violet eyes, I thought to myself.

Those eyes were a dead giveaway that he was a Vampire. Born from the bloodline of Voltarean, the God of Night.

We do not associate with Vampires. I relived the words my father always said.

"And this here is Valarian." Zayn squeezed the Vampire's shoulder. He was the exact opposite of the Angels as he stared me down, no smile on his face.

"Hi," was all the stone-faced Vampire said and I was okay with it. Thank the Gods he didn't hug me like Calista.

Just breathe, I told myself.

Valarian shifted his stance, looking uneasy. He glanced away from me and locked eyes with the Angels.

"Ember . . . ahem." Cash cleared his throat, bringing me back to reality.

"Hi," I managed to muster back.

As if the Angels knew I was uncomfortable, Cash said, "Let's get going."

I'm perfectly content not getting to know the Vampire, I thought, as we walked away.

A small part of me told myself not to dare look back at the Vampire behind me, but I couldn't help it. I curiously glanced over my left shoulder at him. He had his arms crossed and was watching me walk away. As his eyes locked eyes with mine, his lips curled up. Sucking in a breath, I quickly looked away and continued following the Angels.

The inside of the manor was just as humongous as the exterior. Servants were running around preparing everything for lunch. We had barely gotten into the foyer when Cash stopped.

"I'm going to send a messenger Imp to let the king know we've arrived. Zayn will show you to your room." Cashmere headed down a hall to the right.

"It's this way, Red," Zayn said as he ascended the stairway. I followed behind him.

The wrought-iron railing going up both sides of the large, dark wood staircase was beautiful. We got to the top and turned right. The manor was impressive, to say the least. It was like a castle inside as well with corridors throughout. The hallway to my room was lined with hanging oil lamps, marble statues, and a couple of fancy paintings. I couldn't help but tense up, knowing that Castleva Manor was far more elegant than any home I had ever been in. I was too nervous to take in all the beauty as we walked.

"Each wing is separated into two sections. The west wing is for the servants and teachers, while the east is for guards and guards in training. That's where you will be staying," Zayn said as he stopped in front of a door.

I wonder if everyone is grouped by age, sex, or species?

"This is your new room." He opened the door and started dragging in one of my bags. "The bathroom is fully stocked with toiletries and anything else you need. There's a private bath in every room, as well as a fireplace. Val and Cash chop the wood and the servants keep the inside well-stocked with it. There's a large kitchen downstairs and a dining hall where we usually have meals together. Weapons storage is in the basement."

So, Cash is a lumberjack. I almost laughed aloud.

"There's a training facility in the building behind here. That's where you will spend a lot of time. There is also a huge outside training area past the gardens. I can show you those when you're ready. Oh, we have a library too!" He smiled while trying to catch his breath.

Yes, a library! At least that was exciting. "Thank you, Zayn."

"Since there are around-the-clock servants, you can get whatever you need, whenever you need it. You can call upon them any time for food, or you can go down and help yourself. Just make sure to take an oil lamp with you. The ones down the hall stay lit at night, but the stairs are dark. The only lamps you'll have to worry about keeping lit are the ones in your room. I'll be right back."

He headed back down the hall and I took the opportunity to examine the room. There was a lit fireplace along the outer wall and a huge bed that I was afraid to sit on because I didn't want to get it dirty. It had the most beautiful blanket on it—creamy white with gray flowers that matched the gray curtains on the wall. It was big and gorgeous—way more elegant than I was used to.

A thud brought back my attention as Zayn returned with the rest of my bags.

"You have at least an hour to clean up. Once the king sends a messenger, I'll find you. Until then, I'll give you some privacy."

"Wait," I said in a panic. Zayn turned and met my eyes. I was ashamed of what I was about to say, but I had no other choice. "I don't know what to wear. I own nothing regal and I don't have fighting leathers." That was a subtle way of saying that my father never bought us anything once we got older. I worked to pay for my bow and quiver.

"Ah, I see. Let me take over for my sister. She's on duty until lunch because the king is expecting other guests. I will send her up if that's okay with you, Red?"

Smiling at the nickname he kept using for me, I nodded my head.

After he left, I plopped down on the way-too-fancy gray chair and placed my face in my hands.

Don't cry. We were not born to be weak. My sister will be safe. She can protect herself.

Slowly, I inhaled deep breaths, trying hard to calm myself. I knew Cinder was trained in fighting like I was. She wasn't very good at it, but she at least tried. I had been protecting her since she was born so it was hard to stop. I knew all of this, yet I was still worried.

Hearing the wood of the floor creak, I looked up just as the door shut. My heart instantly sped up.

Oh, no. I don't have the strength in me to deal with this today, I thought as I stared into the Vampire's violet eyes. *His eyes are so beautiful.*

"Yes?" I squeaked out.

Silence. Standing there with his arms crossed in a sexy, lazy stance, I finally noticed how fit and tall he was.

He's at least six and a half feet of pure muscle.

His face was perfect with a hard jaw line, dusted with a thin beard like he hadn't shaved in two or three days. He had black hair that barely brushed his shoulders and a golden tan. He was absolutely gorgeous.

If he weren't so scary, he would be the most stunning male I have ever laid my eyes upon.

He was wearing a black shirt that buttoned up the front, but the top was unbuttoned just enough that I could see his tattoo perfectly in the center of his chest.

His tattoo was gold with one battle axe. There was a shield behind the axe that was shaped like a kite and a single drop of blood in the center. It was the symbol for a Vampire.

Man, I got screwed when I was born. His tattoo is better than mine.

"It's the symbol for Strength in Blood."

My eyes quickly met his when I heard him speak. My heart felt like it was trying to escape from my chest at the sound of his deep, sensual voice.

He shifted his stance and I glanced down as I noticed his weapon. It was a short sword sheathed in a holster. My eyes slowly followed down his body and stopped at his trousers—they were black and snug. I had a perfect view from where I was sitting.

His pants are tight-fitting. I can see the outline of his . . . oh my!

Averting my eyes quickly, they landed on his face. As I stared at him, his lips curled up ever so slightly with a sly grin.

Oh, Gods, he saw me staring at his chest, and his . . . I stopped my horrible thoughts immediately. As fear and embarrassment filled my body, I swallowed hard and quickly stood up from the chair.

"What can I help you with?" I asked.

"Nothing." His voice sent shivers through me.

He took two steps forward before looking me up and down. He started at my thighs, checking out my dagger. His head tilted more as he stared at it, before smiling. His eyes drifted up to my hips, then to my narrow waist. My breath caught as they landed on my breasts.

I wonder what his hands would feel like on me.

I didn't know if it was the fear or the fact that I was severely attracted to him, but I had never had a man make me react like this. I could barely move as my heart thundered in my chest.

His eyes stopped at my neck, and they stayed there much longer than I was comfortable with. As he locked eyes with me, he gave me a dominating grin.

Is this a challenge? I kept eye contact, not backing down. "I think you should leave." My breathing was heavy and my skin puckered as goosebumps crawled across my arms.

He said nothing as he stared at me like I was dinner. I narrowed my eyes on him.

I hope he doesn't want to eat me. I would stab him if he tried. I shivered at the thought as his eyes shot back to my weapon.

My instincts kicked in, so I reached down at the dagger strapped to my thigh.

Be careful, I told myself. *He's just as dangerous as he is sexy.* My traitorous nipples were hardening at the thought.

He threw his head back, breaking eye contact as he barked out a laugh. After he righted his head, his eyes met mine once more.

"Are you going to stab me with that if I don't leave?" he asked. He tilted his head again like I was an adorable baby rabbit.

No, but I'm going to punch you, I thought to myself. I let my hand fall from my dagger as I walked toward him and readied my fist.

He leveled his head back and looked into my eyes. Air had completely escaped my lungs as I stopped dead in my tracks, only three steps away from him.

How can someone so beautiful be so scary? A slow smirk crept across his face. He let out a small laugh and I could see his fangs. *He's a crazed animal.*

My body felt tingly beneath his stare as heat rushed over me. *I'm warm in places I have never been warm before.*

His breathing got heavy as if he could smell the lust on me, then he swallowed hard. The way he looked at me, at my body, made his stare primal. It was like he was the predator and I was his dinner. For some reason, it made me yearn to touch him, but I avoided that feeling.

We were in a standoff, neither of us moving. I quit breathing or forgot to breathe—I didn't know which. Shit, I wasn't sure if I even *had* lungs anymore.

I winced as the door flew open and Calista walked in. *Thank the Gods.*

"Hey, umm . . ." Her beautiful blue eyes looked back and forth between me and the Vampire. "Zayn said you needed me, Ember."

Valarian eyed me for a couple of seconds longer, giving me a seductive smile. The look on his face told me he thought he won. He winked at me before he strolled out of the room. I finally released the breath I had been holding. *Fuck.*

"Are you okay? Did I interrupt something?" Calista's face was confused.

Due to lack of air, I was panting. Taking a deep breath, I slowly blew it out. I had a million questions I wanted to ask her—one being if I had to worry about that Vampire—but I didn't know her at all. Asking to borrow clothes was already outside of my comfort zone.

"Gods, no. It was nothing. I'm fine, everything is fine. I just need something to wear to meet the king because I have nothing. I don't have fighting leathers or anything that's nice." I'm sure I sounded nervous since I said all that in one breath.

Calm yourself. My tense body relaxed slightly.

"I can help you! Let's go to my room." She smiled and turned, heading out the door. I followed close to her, still thinking about what had happened with Valarian.

Fifty minutes later, we headed down the hall. Calista had put me in a low-cut, emerald-green dress with gold embellishments on it. I was more top-heavy and a little thicker than her, so I was almost spilling out of it. It was a little long for me too, so I had to hold up the bottom when I walked. She'd also pinned up my hair nicely.

Even if the dress felt weird on my skin, I felt pretty. But I looked like I was going to a ball, so I couldn't help but feel overdressed as we headed toward the staircase.

Too late to turn back now.

We cascaded down the stairwell just as the front door opened. The two Angels came strolling in and both of their mouths dropped open when they looked up at us.

My cheeks flushed at the thought of two males staring at me. *I hope I look okay.* They both clamped their mouths shut as we stepped into the foyer.

"You clean up nice, Red," Zayn said. "You look beautiful." He ran his hand through his shaggy hair.

"Absolutely stunning, if I do say so myself." Cash grinned and bowed his head to me. I almost gasped. No one has ever spoken those words to me before.

Stunning? Me? I was too hard on that Angel earlier. I need to learn to control my emotions.

"Thank you both." I blushed at their words and their stares.

"The messenger Imp just arrived. The king is ready for you," Cash informed me.

"We're going to gale as far as we can, which is a few miles away from where we are going. Because the wards around the castle are larger than most, we cannot gale close," Zayn said as he opened the door.

"I will see you at lunch when you get back. I have a class to teach," Cash said to me. "I'll see you in a bit, Zayn."

A class? I wondered what class Cash taught as we exited the manor.

"Are we ready?" Valarian asked as he walked up.

Why is the Vampire coming with us? I would have been more comfortable if he wasn't.

Valarian's face was blank as he stared at me. He glanced down at what I was wearing and looked right back into my eyes with no changes in his facial expressions.

"Yes, we are going to gale to our usual spot just outside the castle wards. One of us will have to gale with her, since she doesn't know where we are going."

Valarian crossed his arms. "You can take her, Zayn."

What a relief and an insult. Asshole.

We walked about a hundred feet away from the manor and stopped. Zayn stood super close to me. "Are you ready?" he asked, and I nodded.

He put his hands around my waist, and with a blink of an eye, we were standing in a grassy area with bushes.

"That wasn't so bad," Zayn chuckled. "It's this way." He tilted his head in the direction of Castle Elderfall.

As we started our journey, Zayn was walking on one side of me and Valarian, surprisingly, on the other. Trying to get to know me, Zayn asked questions about my family and hometown.

He was a nice man who was always cheerful, it seemed. Valarian was completely the opposite—he was quiet and never looked happy. Well, unless he was trying to intimidate me and when he caught me looking at him. I'll never live that down.

As we walked, we eventually fell silent. I started thinking about what the king, the God, would be like. I met the current king when I was seven years old and he had given me a book, which I now live by. He seemed nice back then, but I was a child and didn't understand how people could be. My father used to be friendly when I was young. People change sometimes.

My mother taught me about the Primordial Gods when I was a kid. The ten Gods were born from the Primordial Tree of Life. The King was the only God that lived in our realm currently, as the other nine Gods were asleep. They switched off every five hundred years because of their age. It was also because it was safer that way. If the Gods got into a disagreement, they could destroy the land around us with nothing more than a nod.

The current reigning king wields the powers of all the Gods combined. I couldn't even imagine how amazing that would be.

Since the king was a God, he was considered an immortal—able to live for over ten thousand years, or forever, to my knowledge. I had no clue how old he was. Since I was a Caster, my life span was only about three hundred years. I was merely a blip in his long life.

We finally arrived at Castle Elderfall and I was at a loss for words. Any doubts I had about being overdressed slipped my mind. As I looked up at the castle, I couldn't believe how beautiful it was. Made of gray brick and immensely large, it was well fortified, with tall towers and battlements. Beautiful red maple trees surrounded the castle. The touch of color in front of the gray brick made it even more amazing. It was impressive and breathtaking, to say the least.

If only I knew a better word for beautiful. I tilted my head as I admired the castle.

"It's gorgeous, isn't it?" I about jumped out of my skin as Valarian spoke those words close to my left ear. "It's exceptionally captivating seeing it for the first time." His hot breath bounced off my skin and made chills run down my spine.

He managed to find some words better than beautiful. "Yes, it is captivating." I glanced up at his face.

He was looking at me like he wanted to devour me—like I was his lunch. His eyes trailed down to the tattoo in the middle of my chest. It was completely visible thanks to the low-cut dress Calista put me in. I blushed as I stared into his eyes.

He's so beautiful. His eyebrows furrowed together like he was confused.

"It's the symbol for Strength in Fire." I almost repeated his words back at him. His lips curled up in a smile and I immediately glanced away from his beautiful face.

Why did he have to be so damn sexy? Couldn't he be gross or disfigured or something? I was raised to hate Vampires, but here I was, severely attracted to one.

"Shall we?" Zayn interrupted my thoughts as he held out his arm for me to take. He escorted me up the stairs like a true gentleman and Valarian followed us.

I'm going to try my hardest to look comfortable. I cannot let my mouth fall open in shock while in this castle.

The enormous doors magically opened on both sides. My mouth dropped open as I saw the inside of the castle. I gasped and then snapped my mouth shut.

Damn it! I scolded myself. *Mission failed.*

Valarian let out a small laugh. Halting at the entryway, I glanced over my shoulder at him.

"Whatever is so funny?" I asked as I met his eyes.

He gave me a genuine smile and shook his head. "Just relax. You overthink."

My eyebrows furrowed as I shook my head at him. I'm glad he found my nervousness funny. I didn't.

It's hard to relax with a child of the Night God next to you.

Zayn started walking again, so I followed suit.

We strolled through the entryway, and the inside of the castle was astonishing. The walls were the same color as the gray wolves of the woods. There were stark white pillars throughout, white marble floors, marble statues—there was marble everywhere. Castleva Manor was aesthetically the same as Castle Elderfall.

Peering up, I noticed a gorgeous chandelier over my head. Above it was a mural painted on the ceiling depicting the ten Primordial Gods. Each of our tattooed symbols were also painted there. It was gorgeous.

Numerous things were marked in crimson red, from the chairs to the draperies—even the rugs. A servant dressed in all black with a crimson 'servant of the king' patch on his jacket met us in the foyer. He asked us to follow him and we obliged. It was about a ten-minute, quiet walk to the throne room. The halls were seemingly endless and I realized I could never find my way out if I was alone.

My breathing was labored from the walk and the anxiety of meeting a God. I tried hard not to breathe so loud in the quietness of the halls. Once we got to the double doors outside the throne room, I panicked. My arms shook as my knees became wobbly. Zayn still had his left arm still looped through my right one. He took his other hand and patted my arm, trying to comfort me. It didn't work.

I should ask him to use his magic to soothe my emotions.

Valarian reached up and grabbed my elbow to help lead me in and I froze at the small electric shock the little touch gave me. He let go at once. His breathing got a little heavy, as confusion settled on his face.

Valarian locked eyes with Zayn. *A silent conversation I wasn't invited to.*

"Would you like me to soothe your emotions?" Zayn asked. As I felt the bile rising in my throat, I realized it was my only choice. I gave him a quick nod of my head.

The Ornamental Angel looked into my eyes and I immediately felt the anxiety lessen.

I feel dirty letting him control my emotions, but I'm grateful.

"Thank you, Zayn." I tried to relax my shoulders.

"He only used a small amount of magic. Just enough to take the edge off." Valarian smiled, then slid his arm out and curled it around mine.

"Yes, we don't need you to be *too* euphoric when we walk in," Zayn said with a smile.

The doors opened wide, waiting for us to enter. Light spilled out onto the white marble floor we were standing on. I let out a breath and took a step forward. My male companions followed suit and the door closed behind us.

Chapter Three

The room was massive and even more stunning than the rest of the castle, if that was possible. The runner I was walking up was crimson, as was the throne the king sat upon. Lit torches lined the walls, casting shadows everywhere.

The God was not only handsome but enormous with arms bigger than my thighs and hands that equaled four of mine. Long black hair framed a pale face that was lit up by stunning, bright blue eyes.

He is the God of the Sun, the maker of Angels.

Even with him sitting leisurely with his ankles crossed out in front of him, I could tell he was over seven feet tall. His hands were on his thighs, patiently waiting for us to make it to him.

A short, light-skinned servant with gray hair stepped forward. "Welcome to Castle Elderfall. Currently residing is Your Majesty, King Reign, the God of the Sun."

All three of us bowed our heads in unison.

"Thank you, Meyers. You are dismissed until my guests arrive," the king said and Meyers quickly scurried off.

"Welcome to Ashbern South, Miss Lavaris. I hope you find your accommodations hospitable?" The king's voice was deep and soft. He spoke with demand, yet grace and elegance.

Valarian let go of my arm, but Zayn didn't.

"Tremendously so, Your Majesty. I am grateful for the opportunity to serve you and the realms." I spoke elegantly like I had practiced with my sister.

Use a strong, calm voice, I reminded myself.

"We had met once before when I visited your land. You were much younger. I'm not sure if you remember me."

"I remember, Your Majesty. You gave me a book about bows and arrows before I could even read." I smiled, willing my body to relax.

He let out a booming laugh and slapped his knee. He sat forward with a curious smile on his face. "Did you find the book beneficial? Can you shoot? Can you hunt?"

"I benefited from the book, sir. I can shoot and I can hunt. I have been told I am the best archer in my lands, Your Majesty." My voice had more pride than I intended it to.

His eyes went wide with surprise before he gave me a proud smile. "Well, that is great to hear. We will have to go hunting one of these days."

"Of course. I look forward to it, Your Majesty." I faked a smile back at him.

I'm not looking forward to it. The thought of going hunting with the king makes me nervous.

"While you are serving the realm, you will be granted with anything you need or want for your service. Your training starts tomorrow morning. In the afternoon, you will be fitted for fighting leathers and any other clothing you may need. You will have a variety of weapons to choose from as well."

"Thank you, Your Majesty."

"Being a part of the King's Guard means you will fight for the people and devote your life to protecting them. You may have to kill Demons or other species at some point in your life. Do you accept this role?"

I swallowed hard. "I do, Your Majesty."

"Kneel." Zayn let go of my arm. I kneeled to the ground and bowed my head as low as my body would allow me. "From this day forward, Ember Lavaris, you are officially a King's Guard. A warrior for the ten realms, a protector for the people. Until dismissal, death, or dishonor."

A gust of wind came through the room, whipping my hair around. With my head bowed low, I had a perfect view of my chest. I felt a slight tingle as my tattoo turned from black to gold—the mark of a warrior, the color of an official King's Guard. I was grateful for Calista choosing this dress because it was a fantastic thing to see.

"I am so glad you are finally where you belong," he said with pride. "You may rise."

Meyers returned and stood to the side with his hands crossed in front of him.

"I see it is time for my next meeting. My guests have arrived, so I must retire. You can request to see me anytime you feel you need to address something or would like to converse. You are free to get settled in. We will talk more at a later time." The king's voice was gentle.

"Thank you, Your Majesty." I bowed my head, as did the others.

We turned sharply and headed out at once. My breathing was back to normal by the time we got out the front doors.

"Well, that wasn't as bad as I thought it would be. Thank you, Zayn, for helping me. Thank you both." I was feeling bad about how I treated Cashmere for the same thing.

"No problem. I have a class to teach with Cash, so Val is going to take you back."

I froze. *He's leaving me alone with a Vampire.*

"I won't be home in time for lunch, but I'll see you this afternoon. I can take you for a walk around the grounds later to familiarize you with the surroundings. If you would like?"

"That would be wonderful, thank you." I smiled, trying not to frown.

"Alright, see you then." Zayn gave a nod to Valarian, then a gust of wind hit me as his wings sprung out of nowhere.

They were solid black and gorgeous, with lots of plush-looking feathers. They were similar to raven wings with hints of blue, green, and gold as the sun reflected off them. I had never seen an Angel's wings before, so it fascinated me. With a huge jump, he fluttered off into the sky. Nervousness filled me as I watched him until I no longer could. With a sigh, I turned toward Valarian.

"Come on." He headed the way we came in and I followed.

It was a quiet walk for a while. I enjoyed looking at the land and the animals scurrying around. My thoughts were going in a hundred different directions. I tried to calm myself from overthinking and settled on thoughts of the beautiful wisteria trees back home.

Under those trees was the only place I found peace, the only place I could escape this world—the sweet, musky scent of calm. I sighed.

Valarian stopped and as he turned toward me, my stomach instantly felt uneasy.

He's a King's Guard. I'm safe if the king trusts him, or so I hope. I swallowed hard.

"Would you like to see something beautiful?" he asked.

That's not what I expected to come out of his mouth. 'I want to eat you,' or something like that would have been closer. He laughed as he smiled.

"Why are you laughing?" I wasn't currently finding anything funny.

"You just always have this look on your face. Do you ever stop thinking?" He tilted his head like he was trying to figure me out.

"I don't have such a look." I sighed because I knew I had that look. My family had commented on it before.

"This place will make you stop thinking as much." He shifted from one leg to the other as if he were unsure of himself.

I'm not going anywhere that I don't have to with a Vampire. "I'm rather tired, maybe another time."

His eyebrows furrowed together. "Are you truly afraid of me?"

"No. I just don't know you." I was lying, but I didn't want to hurt his feelings . . . or show fear.

"And how will you *get* to know me if you don't even want to speak with me or be around me?"

Now I was the one furrowing their eyebrows. "I never said that."

"You don't think I know what you think about me? You've been distant since we met." His face was blank.

"I . . . umm." I was lost for words.

I was judging him by what he was. I took a deep breath and sighed.

"Do you want to go or not? I can take you back to your room if you would rather do that," he said bluntly.

Valarian thinking I was afraid of him made me want to challenge him.

I will not show fear around this Vampire. I took another deep breath.

"Okay, let's go to this place," I spoke the words as if they were my last.

"Really?" He laughed before relaxing.

One point for me . . . I think. I could have just signed up for my own murder.

"Really," I said with sheer confidence that I didn't feel on the inside. He gave me a half-grin as he prowled forward until he was a heartbeat away from my face. He was so close I could smell him.

He smells like the fresh scent of the woods, mixed with a sweet aroma of amber and a hint of a cool breeze. I was unsure what the lovely breeze scent was.

"May I?" He was asking my permission to gale us and it made me a little more comfortable. I nodded.

Flinching as he wrapped his arms around my waist, I felt that spark again. Since I was only five and a half feet tall and he had over a foot of height on me, I felt short next to him. He shifted slightly to look into my eyes. Afraid I would be bitten, I braced myself, but I kept eye contact so I didn't show fear.

My dagger.

My hand slipped to the dagger hidden in the folds of my dress out of instinct. Holding it made me feel safer.

My heart raced at the fact that a Vampire was touching me. It ran even faster at the fact that I liked it. He smiled, showing his fangs, mere inches from my face.

I wonder what it's like to kiss someone with fangs.

"Don't be afraid of me." We were so close that he almost spoke the words into my mouth. My breath caught as we galed away from the castle.

We landed on the edge of the land next to the water and I nervously glanced around. We were in a field of bushes, flowers, and *magic*. I looked back up at the Vampire, who met my eyes for a moment before letting me go.

He laughed. "Planning on stabbing me with that?"

I let go of my dagger and avoided the question. "What is this place?" I was standing exceptionally still, afraid I would scare the magic away.

"This is Ethereal Pastures." He waved his hand around.

I had never seen this much magic hovering in one place before. Teal, silver, and purple sparkles danced around the ground. They were like tiny bugs of light as they wove in and out between my ankles.

Valarian was right. This is beautiful.

Lifting my foot, I felt a subtle pushing against the bottom like the magic sparkles were trying to move me. Confused, I looked up at the Vampire.

"They want you to explore with them. They want to show you the lands."

Putting my foot back down, I slowly walked around the field, trying not to step on them.

"You can walk normally. You won't hurt them," he said. So, I did.

As I explored the fields, they pushed against my legs and arms. I could feel their excitement like they were begging to show me the lands.

This feels like my mother is hugging me. They feel so happy.

Looking down at my arms, I saw the magic dancing along my freckles. They were alive with exhilaration—pure joy. Something I had never experienced in my life. They seemed to have calmed me, to have made my emotions stable. The magic wanted me to be happy with them.

The closest thing I had to happiness was my spot under the trees—or staring at the snow-capped mountains over in the country of Mayhem. That was the land of the Vampires—where Valarian was from.

My curiosity was much stronger than my fear when I met his eyes. "Is there a lot of snow on your land?"

"There's some at the edge of the continent and by the mountains."

"I have never seen snow, not up close anyway. What's it like?"

He smirked. "It's cold."

"Funny." I rolled my eyes.

"Come on," he said with a slight amusement in his voice. "There are plenty of things to see here."

We seemed to have explored every inch of the field but I never got tired of seeing the magic dancing around me. We stumbled onto an area that had purple lavender stalks everywhere. They smelled amazing.

As I leaned down to get a deeper sniff of the flowers, the magic spiraled around me. As I smelled the flowers, it was like the magic smelled them too. They danced around the tops of the buds, glittering with happiness.

Eyeing a perfect spot in the middle of the lavender, I took a seat and crossed my ankles over one another.

The magic danced along my entire body.

Picking a bud, I held it out to them as an offering. Hundreds of them floated toward the flower. I laughed with pure joy, and some of the magic scattered away as if they were scared, but they soon started dancing their way back toward me.

"I have never seen this much magic before." I smiled as I held up my hand that was holding the flower. The magic on my arm danced down onto my hand and leaped off the flower as if they were diving into the ocean.

This is amazing.

Glancing up into Valarian's eyes, I saw him watching me intently. Like he was watching a small child playing in the sand for the first time.

"Come on. I want to show you something else." He extended a hand toward mine. Unsure if I should take it or not, I hesitated. He retracted his hand, and I stood up on my own, dusting off the bottom of my dress.

"We have to gale there," he said. I nodded my head, acknowledging that he was going to have to hug me again.

He wrapped his hands around my waist and I tried hard not to react—but my body didn't get the memo. My heart sped up and heat poured through me before he galed us away.

The sound of a waterfall close by fell upon my ears when we landed. As I smelled the familiar scent of my home, my eyes went wide and my mouth dropped open. A slow smile crept upon his face.

He dropped his hands. "Take a look."

I turned around and gasped. *I have never seen such beauty in one spot.*

We were in front of a canopy of trees and my heart jumped when I saw they were beautiful violet wisteria trees. Tears welled up in my eyes, thinking of my home, but I made sure none of them fell.

"This here is Amethyst Falls," he said. When I glanced back at him, he was watching me tentatively, I swallowed hard.

"These are like the wisteria trees back home. They're beautiful." If one tear escaped my eyes, I was ready to blame it on exhaustion.

Taking in the sights, there were a bunch of wisteria trees grouped together on each side of a cascading waterfall that was streaming down toward the ocean. My hand flew over my mouth when I saw chunks of amethyst rocks on each side of the waterfall. They were gorgeous.

There were still magic sparkles and lavender everywhere. With those, plus the wisteria trees and the waterfall, my senses were on fire.

This must be the most fantastic place that has ever existed.

Excitement filled me as I walked up to the biggest wisteria tree. The hanging branches were the longest I had ever seen, lightly brushing the ground. He smiled as he held back the hanging, bloom-filled branches of the tree, and I peeped inside.

The ground was covered in violet blooms and thousands of magic sparks. They danced up and down the tree and around the blanket of flowers on the ground. The magic made it so bright under the tree it was like it had its own sun hiding under the branches.

As Valarian held the branches back, I glanced up into his face. His eye color was the same as the violet wisteria tree. *Gorgeous.*

He gave me a nod of encouragement to go inside, under the tree. My heart skipped a couple of beats. The thought of being alone with him made me nervous. I was torn between running from him and ripping his clothes off.

He's just as sexy as he is terrifying. A deadly combo. I shivered at the thought of how evil he could be. *I can't go in there with a Vampire.*

He dropped the branches when he saw my hesitation. "Are you hungry?" Completely off subject from what was going through my mind.

I am hungry. I haven't eaten yet today.

"Come on." He nodded his head in the direction he wanted to go. "Lunch might be almost over, but there are always leftovers."

"Thank you for showing me this, Valarian."

His mood seemed to have completely changed as we stopped to gale back to the Castleva Manor. "May I?"

I nodded, allowing him to touch me.

His face was cold as he wrapped his arms around my waist, but his body wasn't. I only felt the warmth for a split second before we galed back to the compound . . . back to my new home.

Chapter Four

We landed about thirty feet from the front entrance of the manor. I dared to glance up at the Vampire still holding my waist. He was peering down at me, holding completely still. There was a look of frustration on his face and I held my breath. He finally let go of me like he remembered he was supposed to.

"The dining hall is this way." He walked away and I followed once more.

"Should I change first?" I asked, feeling uncomfortable in a dress that wasn't suited for a simple lunch.

"No, you look fine," he bluntly said.

Not beautiful, not stunning. Simply fine. I sighed.

He came to a quick stop and turned toward me. He leaned in mere inches from my face, and in a deep voice said, "What do you want me to say? That you're beautiful? Because you are, Ember. Is that what you want to hear?"

My mouth was agape as a realization finally hit me. He glanced around nervously at the guards standing in a group talking nearby.

"You have been reading my—"

He grabbed my waist and galed us away into a . . . *A forest? What the hell.*

"How dare you read my thoughts!" I shoved his hands off me as soon as we landed. "Why did you do that?" I pushed him but he didn't react. "Take me back now!"

I feel so betrayed. I should have known.

"What do you want from me?" he asked with a look of frustration on his face.

"I want nothing from you other than for you to take me back!" I was so angry that my fists were balled up and ready.

I'm going to punch him in the face.

He stiffened his chin, ready for the blow. "Go ahead if it'll make you feel better."

My eyes went wide as I replayed my memories. *Gods, what had he heard? I said he was creepy, I smelled him, I stared at his chest, his muscles, his . . . oh, Gods.*

"Don't forget that you don't associate with Vampires, yet you want me to tell you that you're beautiful."

"You're a traitor, a liar. Take me back!" I shoved him again, causing him to stumble this time. He quickly stepped closer and leaned into my face.

"Do you want me to tell you my favorite one?"

"Shut up," I snarled through gritted teeth.

"The one where you want to know what it feels like to kiss someone with fangs, to kiss me," he whispered and I stopped moving. "Yet you want to punch me in my face."

"You don't know what you're talking about!"

"You're so scared that you will like it, you have to fight for control." My lips parted slightly as I tried to suck in air and he noticed. "Even you know it's true."

"No, it's not! You know nothing!"

"I know you want to feel my touch, but you don't want to be alone with me." He spoke the words only inches from my lips, sending chills through me. "Let's not forget that one." When his hands rubbed down my arms, I didn't pull away and he noticed that, too. "See?" My heart threatened to beat itself to death as I felt his breath blow across my face. "So, what is it that you want, Ember?" My name fell beautifully from his lips and I stopped breathing. He tilted his head and dropped his hands. "Because I honestly don't even think *you* know what you want!"

My mouth fell open at his accusation and I took two steps away from him. The closeness of his body was calming me, making me want him, and I needed to be angry.

"You're an asshole!" I turned and stomped away.

"At least you called me an asshole to my face this time," he said, trailing behind me.

"Why gale us out here?" I asked as I stomped through the brush of the woods.

"For privacy since I knew you were going to yell."

"Obviously, traitorous Vampire!"

"You have no right to judge what I am, Ember," he said calmly. I stopped walking and whipped back around, facing him.

"How dare you even speak my name after what you did!" Angry tears threatened to consume me. I was mad at him for reading my thoughts, but I was even more furious at myself for liking the sound of my name falling from his lips.

Please don't say my name so beautifully. Shit. Stop thinking. I swallowed hard as I stared up at his beautiful violet eyes.

He smiled big. "Sorry, Ember." The way he drew my name out long on his lips was enticing me.

"Take me back, please," I tried to say calmly through gritted teeth.

"So confused and so mean." I shook my head as he glared at me. "And most definitely prejudiced."

His words were like venom to me and I was in his face in an instant. Well, about a foot down from it.

"Fuck you, Valarian and your words!"

"Oh, you don't like the words coming from an *asshole* like me?"

I straightened my spine, trying to make myself seem taller. "If you weren't so rudely listening to my thoughts, we wouldn't even be having this conversation!"

"I wasn't trying to listen! Please don't assume that it's my fault that *you* don't know how to shield yourself. Listening to you complain about how you don't want to be around me has put a damper on my mood. Not to mention how you send overly mixed signals."

"I do no such thing!"

"Oh, love, you most definitely do." He leaned in again and smiled arrogantly. "You may be rude as shit, but listening to you wanting me all day was a bonus."

Had I been rude? Yes. Do I want him? Also, yes. Do I care? No, I don't.

"You violated me. You betrayed me!" I yelled into his face. The fact that he wasn't screaming back made me even angrier.

"You have to be friends with someone to betray them, love. You don't stab friends with daggers, so you and I are *not* friends." His face suddenly whipped to the left, looking over his shoulder.

"We most definitely are not—"

Putting one hand around my waist while the other clamped over my mouth, my feet came off the ground as he yanked me up.

My dagger was up to his throat by the time he crushed me against his body. I pointed the tip of the blade into his neck just enough that a single drop of blood fell.

Dangling in the air, I was so close to him that I could smell his skin. With his hard body pressed up against mine, I was getting warm once more. My breasts touched his chest, causing my nipples to react and harden at the contact. My breathing was heavy as I stared at his face.

Why does he have to be so beautiful? He set me down on the ground slowly as his lips curled up.

My arm was stretched high since I hadn't withdrawn the dagger from his throat. He gently removed his hand from my mouth and put a finger up to his, quieting me. His eyes glanced back over at the dense part of the woods. I heard a branch crack and had a realization.

Something other than us is in these woods?

"Yes," he whispered.

I removed the dagger from his throat and the wound closed instantly. Turning away from him, I readied myself for whatever was coming.

With lightning speed, a large gray wolf jumped out, but Valarian was quicker. He caught it by its throat as it lunged for me, snapping its neck instantly. Fear and panic filled my body as I saw three more wolves headed for us.

My dagger was ready as I crouched down slightly, bracing myself for the impact as the first wolf lunged for my face. Valarian grabbed it by the fur on its back and yanked it away from me. The second wolf jumped at me so I whirled around and kicked it away. I didn't know where it landed, but I heard it yelp.

The third wolf lunged with its teeth bared, going for my leg. I pulled away and came down with a stab to the wolf's back. He barked out a yelp as I noticed two more wolves coming out of the forest. I stabbed him one more time before turning toward them. Wielding a fireball, I was ready to release it.

A large black wolf—three times the size of the others—came out of the woods and ran toward us. The fireball halted as I froze in shock, staring at the remarkable beast.

I'm going to die before I'm even fully trained. My fireball flew to the side wildly, almost hitting Valarian as pain radiated through my arm. I turned my dagger toward the wolf that bit me and slit its throat.

Looking over to check on Valarian, I saw him ripping a wolf's jaws open with his bare hands. My eyes widened with shock—and a significant amount of respect.

Glancing back, I noticed the large black wolf was entering the fight, and my heart raced at the thought of dying. But he didn't come for me. He went for the remaining wolf. They snarled and fought until the black wolf bit his throat and ended him quickly. The fight was over.

The black wolf tilted his head at me as we all stood, breathless. His eyes were dazzling silver and gray—like the moon. He wasn't a normal wolf of these woods. He was a Lycan—a person who could transform into a wolf—and I was mesmerized by the beast.

The Lycan was born from the bloodline of Lykaon, the God of the Moon.

"Are you okay, love?" Valarian asked as he grabbed my blood-soaked arm. "You're hurt."

I immediately yanked it away from him. "Don't touch me. I'm fine," I spat the words out, still furious.

Exhaustion from the day filled me as I watched the blood trail down my arm and land on my now ruined dress. With a sigh, I met the eyes of the others.

I don't know if the wolf can hear me in this form, but I should thank him. I should thank them both.

"You're welcome, and yes, they can hear you. Your words, not your thoughts, that is." Valarian's facial expression was pure frustration as he glared at me.

I'll have to learn to block my thoughts. "Thank you. What's his name?" I wiped my blade off with my dress and sheathed it.

"*Her* name is Zila."

The Lycan is a female?

"She is, indeed." Valarian answered my thoughts, angering me again.

"Stop doing that!" I strolled away, not knowing where I was going.

"Stop walking," he said as they both followed me.

"Why should I? You betrayed me by reading my thoughts, and you almost got me killed. I cannot trust you." My emotions were out of control.

"I would never let anything hurt you," he said and for some reason, I believed him.

Tears welled up in my eyes as I stopped walking. A single one broke free and I brushed it away before they saw how weak I was.

I cannot be weak. We were not born to be weak.

"You are far from weak, Ember." He sighed. "Come on. I'll take you back."

I turned around to face them and he slowly put his hands out. The Lycan watched curiously. I was unsure if my eyes were deceiving me, but I could have sworn the wolf looked sympathetic toward the situation.

"May I gale us?" Valarian asked and I nodded.

I just want to go home.

He put his hands around my waist. "I can't take you there," he whispered into the top of my head as he pulled me in close. "But I can take you back to your room."

Tears ran down my face as I closed my eyes. I sniffed back a cry as he galed us back to Castleva grounds. Glancing up at Valarian as soon as we landed, his eyes were filled with empathy. He hesitated to let me go before he dropped his hands from my waist. I quickly walked away and this time, I didn't look back over my shoulder at him. Even if I wanted to, I wouldn't give him the satisfaction.

Entering the manor, I quickly headed up the stairs and went to my room. The first thing I did was clean the wound from the wolf bite. Since I decided not to go down for lunch because I didn't want to see anyone, I drew myself a hot bath and sank into the tub. As I replayed the day's events in my head, I began to cry. Once the water turned cold, I got out and put on a white silk robe I found in the elegant bathroom.

There was a quiet knock at my door. I opened it to find Valarian. As he walked into the room, I glared at him.

Don't think about anything, I told myself.

"I was making sure you were okay. I brought you a healer for your arm."

His eyes slightly widened as he noticed my extra thin robe. The silk hugged my body in places, like my wide hips and chest. My breasts betrayed me when my nipples decided to harden at his stare. As if I was cold, I pulled the robe tighter and stayed quiet.

"She's in the hall when you're ready, Ember." The way he said my name sent shivers down my body. I focused hard on keeping my thoughts quiet as heat poured through me again. "Just so you know, I would never intentionally hurt you," he said as he turned toward the door. I didn't reply.

After he left, I took a deep breath and let it out with a long sigh. Once I assumed he was far enough away, I notified the healer that I was ready.

There were two types of Angels. The Ornamental Angels were trained guards who could control emotions, like Cash and Zayn. Then there were the Blessed Angels, which were physical healers. A healer had not blessed me since an accident I had when I was younger. I had broken my leg in multiple spots jumping from a tree.

The Blessed Angel strolled in, immensely serene, and asked me to sit in the chair. I obliged. She was tall, about six feet, with ivory skin, bright blue eyes, and long white hair.

"My name is Yevanicia. You can call me Yeva. Give me your hand, child." I held out my hand and she took it between hers. "Don't be nervous. Healing is a genuinely fast thing and it will be over before you know it."

A faint light radiated from her skin as her hands became warm around mine. As the heat traveled up my arm, I peered down at the wound and closed in seconds. The light on her skin faded and she released me.

"It is done." Her voice was gentle.

"Thank you."

"No need to thank me, it is my job. Just as fighting is yours." She bowed her head slightly before turning away. I noticed how long her hair was from behind—the white locks brushed the back of her knees as she strolled toward the door.

"Yeva, can I ask you a question?" She paused, nodding in acknowledgment. Zayn said they usually ate together in the dining hall and I was worried about having to see them at dinner. "Are the people here welcoming?"

"I was worried when I first came here many, many years ago. I knew no one. The people here are more welcoming than you can imagine. We have all been in your shoes." She spoke with refined elegance.

Many, many years ago? "If you don't mind me asking, how old are you?"

"I am a hundred and twenty-seven. Incredibly young for my kind." She smiled brightly before exiting the room.

This had been the longest day of my life and it was only early afternoon. Deciding to take a nap before dinner, I pulled the covers back on the huge bed and crawled into it. I laid my head against the soft pillow, barely able to hold myself together. Tears began to form so I tried to think about the good things I experienced today. The magic, the wisteria trees, and the waterfall were all amazing.

All things Valarian showed me. I was so confused.

As I slipped into a deep sleep, I dreamt of Amethyst Falls.

> *Sitting on a blanket of lavenders, right outside the wisteria trees, I looked up at the stars above us as the moonlight shone on my face. A man plucked a flower and put it behind my ear. I smiled as I felt his breath against my skin. He placed a gentle kiss upon my cheek and then on my neck. The magic danced and danced around us while he held me for eternity.*

Chapter Five

Awakened from my nap by a knock at the door, my eyes slid open. As I rubbed them, I realized the day hadn't been a dream, it was real.

"One second," my voice sounded sleepy. I hopped up and strolled toward the door.

This better not be Valarian.

I was not ready to accept his apology or give him mine. I opened the door to a smiling blonde-haired Angel.

"Come on in, Cashmere." I stifled a yawn.

"I told you to call me Cash." He shut the door, leaving it cracked open. For my comfort, I assumed. He was an honorable male, it seemed.

"Whoa, hold on." He immediately averted his eyes from me and headed toward the closet.

He grabbed a thick, plush robe and handed it to me.

"You may be more comfortable in this," he said.

Correction, he was an *extremely* honorable male.

"Thanks." I slid it on over my silk robe. "How can I help you?"

He raked his hand through his long beard. "I was just checking to see how you were doing."

"I'm faring well." Obviously, I was lying.

He gave me a sympathetic smile. "I heard you had a rough day today. Care to share?"

"It *has* been a rough and awfully long day, but I would rather not talk about it. Not right now, anyway."

"I completely understand. Are you coming down for dinner?"

"What time?"

"Now."

How long had I slept? "Oh, Gods, I have to get dressed. I'll head down in a few minutes." I hadn't eaten and I was hungry. Otherwise, I would have declined.

"There will be a servant at the bottom of the stairs waiting for you."

"Thank you."

He started to open the door and then stopped. "I don't know what happened today, but I really do hope that you're feeling better tomorrow." I nodded with a small smile and the Angel left the room.

Throwing on clothes as quickly as possible, I wondered what the others were wearing to dinner. I put on a white blouse, a pair of black slacks, and knee-high black boots. I ran a brush through my hair, pinned a piece back on one side, and headed out my door. A servant was waiting for me at the base of the stairs, as Cash had promised.

"Good evening, Miss Lavaris. Please follow me."

I followed the servant to the right, through a sitting room and down a hallway. I could hear silverware clinking on plates, talking, and laughter as he opened the door to the dining hall.

"There is a seat over there for you, miss." He gave me a nod of the head and quickly scurried off. I didn't even get to thank him.

"Hey, Ember, come and get some food!" Zayn shouted. "There's a seat right there."

As I looked at the table, I noticed that there were only six seats, and five were occupied. The only one left was between Valarian and a female I didn't know yet. I held my head high and walked with grace toward that end of the table.

"Hi, Ember," Calista said. I smiled at the brown-haired beauty on the right side of Zayn. Cash was sitting on the other side of him, shoveling food in his mouth. He nodded at me. I smiled at him as I pulled out my chair and sat down across from them.

"Did you have a good day today?" Calista asked me and Zayn elbowed her. "What? Did something happen?"

Zayn shook his head, warning her not to ask, then ran a hand through his hair.

"Today was fine. I met King Reign. He's genuinely nice."

"The king is authentically nice until he's angry," Cash said, bringing my attention to him. "Then not so much."

"Isn't that the truth!" Zayn laughed while grabbing a roll.

I made a mental note to never anger the king.

Looking around at the food on the table made my stomach happy. There was meat, potatoes, carrots, green beans, rolls, and wine.

"Dig in, Red," Zayn encouraged.

Grabbing a utensil, I started piling food on my plate.

"Would you like some rolls?" the beautiful tawny-skinned female with wavy black hair asked me. She was sitting to my left, and Valarian was on my right.

"Yes, please. Thank you."

"I'm Zila. It's nice to formally meet you."

Looking into her enchanting gray-silver eyes, she smiled widely.

Oh, she is the Lycan.

"Nice to meet you too," I said as I smiled back at her.

I took a roll from the platter and set it on my plate. Everyone was engaged in conversation, so I ate quietly. My eyes glanced at my empty wine glass.

I don't have a drink.

Looking around, I spotted the closest bottle of wine. Before I had a chance to grab it, Valarian snatched it up and filled my glass for me. I glanced at him, but he didn't make eye contact.

"Thank you," I said. He responded with a slight nod.

"Are you going to the bonfire tonight, Ember?" I turned toward Cash when I heard my name.

Great, I'm too tired to socialize. "What bonfire?"

"I told Val to invite you. We have them on the beach by the ocean."

"We get together at least twice a week to socialize," Zayn said

"It's a lot of fun," Zila added. "You should come."

Should I tell them I planned to cry myself to sleep tonight? Probably not.

"I'm tired," I decided to say instead.

Of course, Valarian didn't invite me. He hates me. I took a big swig of my wine as my thoughts got away from me. *I should stab him with this butter knife. He'll heal instantly, anyway.*

Something grazed my leg, getting my attention. I glanced under the table and immediately jerked my knee away from Valarian's. Glancing at his face, he kept eating, not making eye contact. As soon as I went back to my food, I noticed my butter knife was gone.

Did you swipe my butter knife? I asked, knowing he could hear it. He tried to keep from laughing as he grinned. *Good try, asshole. I still have my dagger.*

His proximity and demeanor made me nervous, so I took another big swig of my wine.

"You really should come." Calista smiled at me, her eyes longing for me to be her friend.

"She said she was tired," Valarian's stern voice silenced the room.

My head whipped toward the Vampire sitting too close to me. "Do *not* speak for me."

We locked eyes and my breathing became heavy. Everyone at the table remained quiet as I held his stare.

Don't test me, Valarian. He smiled and shook his head like I was amusing him. Grabbing the wine, he topped both our glasses before taking a swig.

Zayn tried to break the silence. "Well... if you want to go—"

"Actually, I will go." I was only going to get under Valarian's skin and the thought made me smile.

"Oh, yay!" Calista squealed as she clapped excitedly.

"Don't forget to grab me on your way down, Cali. I want to hang with the girls tonight." Zila smiled adorably.

"Me too," Cash said.

"You *are* a girl, buddy," Zayn said, laughing hard. Cash frowned, making his blue eyes look sad on purpose and everyone laughed.

The rest of the dinner was full of conversation. They asked questions about my boring life back home.

"Are there any cute boys in your town?" Calista asked me.

"Not really." I shrugged.

"Her sister is beautiful, looks just like her." Cash winked at me.

"Keep your eyes off my sister, Cashmere." Everyone laughed at my words. It made me feel a little more comfortable around all the strangers.

"Cash is a real ladies' man," Zila chimed in. "Or at least he thinks he is."

"Isn't that the truth?" Zayn rolled his eyes.

"Hey, why is everyone on me tonight?" Cash frowned, then shoved another big bite of food in his mouth.

"It's just your night, buddy." Zayn smiled at his friend and patted him on the shoulder.

Cash swatted his hand away and punched him in the arm. They started play fighting while everyone laughed.

When I finished eating, I took a big swig of my wine. I set the glass down, running my finger along the top edge of the glass while the others were still in discussion.

These people seem nice. Hopefully, I will get comfortable here. I still miss my family.

Well, I missed my sister. I had gotten accustomed to not seeing my father. Even before my mother died, he was always gone on trips. But after her death, he had been around even less. My eyes began to fill with tears.

I'm strong, I will show no fear. That's what he taught me. I cannot be weak.

A hand laid upon my leg and my breath caught since it was Valarian's.

He leaned in close to my face and whispered, "Fear and sadness are two different things, love." I blinked away tears as I swallowed hard. He gave me a sympathetic look before he got up and left the table.

Glancing up to see if anyone caught sight of what happened, I noticed something myself. Calista quickly excused herself from the table and followed Valarian out of the dining room.

"You look like you need a refill." Cash poured me another glass of wine, bringing me out of my daze.

"I do. Thank you."

Thinking about the day's events, I took a few more sips before I finally just chugged the rest. I excused myself from dinner before anyone had a chance to converse with me again. Everyone politely said their goodbyes before I headed to my room. The whole walk, I couldn't stop thinking about Valarian.

Why did he do that? Why did he comfort me? And why did I find him so irresistible? I was taught to not associate with Vampires unless I wanted my blood drained. My father said they are the reason my mother is gone.

Once I got to the top of the stairs, I turned into the hall and stopped dead in my tracks at the gorgeous Vampire before me.

"Your father is a liar!"

"You know nothing of my father. Stop listening to my thoughts!"

"I know more than you think. I know the things he says to keep you out of his business."

"And what business is that?"

He had a look of anger. "What he does for a living."

"He's a noble tradesman," I said, and he laughed at me.

"He isn't noble and I would use the word tradesman loosely."

"You don't know him or me for that matter."

"I knew who you were as soon as the king said Miss Lavaris. I knew you were Abraham's daughter."

"Is that why you let go of my arm in front of the king?"

"That and other reasons." His face showed no emotion.

People coming up the stairs pulled my attention away from Valarian. I turned my head and saw Zayn, Cash, and a young man who wasn't at dinner coming down the hall. I turned back around and Valarian was gone.

"Red, wait up." Zayn shouted. "We want to introduce you to someone!"

With a sigh, I waited for the three men to approach.

"Ember, this is Asher Whitlock."

The man walking toward me was sexy in an adorable way. He was light-skinned and had a nice muscular build. He wasn't as tall as Valarian, but he was still over six feet.

His hair was short on the sides and longer on the top and he had a clean-shaven face.

"Nice to meet you," he said as he extended his hand and I shook it.

His eyes were the same color as mine. I could feel my cheeks flush as my face lit up with excitement. "You're a Caster! What do you cast?"

He pulled his shirt down enough to show me his tattoo. It was a battle axe exactly like mine, but it had wind whipping around it instead of fire. He was an air-wielder from the country of Windcrest.

Air Casters were born from the bloodline of Zephyr, the God of Air.

"Strength in Wind. I cast air magic." He smiled proudly as a small gust of wind blew my hair back.

"Oh, that's wonderful!"

"And you?"

"Fire!" I proudly announced. I held up my hand, showing him a small fireball.

"Nice! Speaking of fire, are you coming to the bonfire tonight?"

"Yes, I am!" *Today may still get better.*

"I'll see you there. We can talk more magic." He gave me a handsome smile that I returned.

"I would like that."

"Let's change our attire, gentlemen," Cash said before strolling away.

Zayn gave me a kind smile. "We'll see you around eight, Red."

I waved. "Bye."

The men walked away and I hurried off to my room.

Chapter Six

After making it to my room, I plopped onto the bed, once again thinking about the day's events. The excitement was giving me butterflies. Even though the wine I drank had kicked in, I was still anxious.

I'm so excited that there's another caster. We can spar together and trade magic tips. He's cute, too! What am I going to wear tonight?

After a while, I decided I needed help so I headed down the hall toward Calista's room. I hadn't told her about the dress yet. I hoped she would still let me borrow something else after finding out I ruined it.

I knocked on her door and Valarian opened it.

Do I have the wrong room? I asked myself. It seemed like the right one to me.

"No, come in." He read my thoughts again. With a scowl, I squeezed past, making sure not to brush against him.

My heart raced as I locked eyes with him. *Why is he here?* I wondered not caring if he could hear me.

He sighed, then looked away. "We will talk later, Cali. I have to change."

"Bye, V," Cali called out as he shut the door.

"Am I the one that is now interrupting something?"

"He just needed advice." She smiled empathetically at me. "So, what's going on?"

Advice? Whatever. Not my concern. "I have some sad news about the dress."

"V just told me what happened. The dress isn't that important."

"He did?" I wondered how much he told her.

"Yeva said she healed you. She can sense things . . . people. She liked you and said you were remarkably nice."

"Well, she was incredibly nice, too." I strolled further into the room. "Why wasn't she at dinner?"

"She resides at the king's castle. She's his personal healer, in case one of his guards needs it."

"Oh, that makes sense."

Calista smiled mischievously. "So, you need another outfit for tonight?"

"I do, if you don't mind loaning me another."

"I was *so* excited when you said you would go," she jumped up and strolled across the room, "I already picked one out for you!"

She opened her closet and handed me a thin, black silk dress that had a slit up the left side. It also had the smallest straps I had ever seen.

I frowned at the dress. "I appreciate it, I really do, but I wanted to wear pants."

"You don't wear pants to a party. At least try it on!"

Knowing I should be grateful, I smiled kindly, headed into her bathroom, and put it on.

There was no way I was leaving my room dressed in such little clothing.

"Gods no, Calista! I cannot wear this."

She giggled. "Come on out and let me see you!"

"I can't. It's *too* embarrassing!"

"I'm sure you look beautiful." Her voice was genuinely kind. I sighed and came out of the bathroom.

Calista's hands shot up and covered her mouth. "Wow, I hope you don't mind me saying this but you look sexy."

"I look like a lady of the night, Calista." I looked down at the dress and pointed. "You can see one of my knees!"

She laughed. "You look gorgeous. Don't worry, Zila and I will be wearing this same type of dress."

I frowned and she gave me a look of empathy. "I can loan you a shawl to go over it if that would make you more comfortable?"

"Yes, please. I would like that."

She handed me a shawl and I slid it on. It didn't help that one of my knees was uncovered, but it did cover up more of my breasts. After thanking her, I went back to my room.

Removing the shawl, I threw it on the chair so I could wash the tiredness off my face. I brushed my hair and re-pinned a couple of pieces back. I fiddled with the dress, trying to cover my boobs more.

There was a knock on the door so I exited the bathroom. "Yes?"

"Zila and I are ready!" Calista squealed through the door. " Come out when you're done."

With a sigh, I grabbed my dagger off the dresser and strapped it to the bare leg that was hanging out of my dress.

The boots I wore came to the bottom of my knees, so at least my whole leg wasn't showing. With another sigh, I walked out my bedroom.

Calista, Zila, and I left the manor together. Both girls were wearing dresses. Cali had on a short, red dress that fit her outgoing personality. Zila had dressed more conservatively than Cali or me. Her long, gray dress complimented her eyes beautifully.

We headed to the edge of the grounds and I felt the magic tingle as we crossed the wards. Calista had to gale me since I didn't know where we were going. We landed on a beach and the smell of the sea hit my senses. Low rolling tides crashed against the shore as moonlight sparkled off the water. It was beautiful.

Around the bonfire were log stumps carved so that they could be used as seats. There were five servants in a small section to the left of me, playing music. One was playing the guitar, one a harp, one a violin, one a drum, and the fifth was singing. It was beautiful. They were exceptionally good and seemed to be enjoying themselves. There was another area to my right that had drinks and snacks.

"Take a seat on one of the stumps. I'm going to talk to my brother really quickly." Cali sauntered off toward the food table, where I saw Zayn talking to Cash.

"Would you like a drink?" Zila asked.

"Yes, thank you." She walked away, going toward the same table, leaving me alone.

It was cold next to the water at night and I wished I had worn pants.

Shit! I forgot my shawl!

With a sigh, I took a seat next to the fire, hoping to warm my legs. A shadow fell upon the ground, getting my attention. Glancing up, it was Asher. He had a drink in one hand and a big smile plastered on his face.

"Hey," he said as he took a seat next to me. "Nice to see you again. You look lovely tonight."

I gleamed at the compliment. "Thank you."

"How has your day been so far?"

"It's been good." I was forming a bad habit of lying.

"That's wonderful," he said with a smile. If he only knew the truth.

"Hey, Asher!" Cash called out. "Come here for a second."

"Sorry, I'll be right back." Asher got up and headed toward Cash. Apparently, the food table was the place to be. If I weren't so cold, I would have walked over there myself.

Sitting quietly with my thoughts, I watched the fire dance around the pit as the smell and the sound of the ocean filled my senses. It was serene. Hearing bursts of laughter, I glanced over and saw Asher using air magic to make sand fly. Cash was running and waving his hands in the air at the sand. I giggled to myself.

He is so cute and friendly, and he's a Caster. I wasn't going to worry about having a man in my life, but he seems like a perfect fit to me.

"He doesn't like you like that." Valarian appeared out of nowhere interrupting my thoughts. "He's just being nice, Ember."

I wish he wouldn't say my name. It sounded *too* beautiful coming off his lips. "How do you know? Did you steal his thoughts, too?" I asked, sarcasm lining my voice.

"No. He has learned to shield his thoughts." He grinned as he took a seat next to me. "Unlike some people."

"Oh, excuse me for never learning how. If I knew there were thought thieves around, I would have definitely learned!"

He smirked and even that was beautiful. "You'll learn this week since it's taught in my class."

"Why are you in class for thought shielding? Shouldn't you already know how to? Or did they put you in there so you can learn how not to steal other people's thoughts?" More sarcasm from me.

"I don't attend the class, I teach it." My eyes widened and he grinned, showing me his fangs. "And the king assigned it to you, so you are now one of *my* students."

Seriously? My heart raced at the thought of spending every day with him.

"Yes, seriously." He laughed as he leaned his elbows onto his knees. "I also teach hand-to-hand combat, along with weapons training. That will *also* be part of your curriculum."

I wonder what it's like sparring with him. Stop, stop! I tried to stop the thought, but it was too late. I winced.

"That was a good try. It didn't work."

"Stop doing that!" I shouted, a little louder than I intended.

He chuckled as he stood up. "Nice dress, by the way."

I swallowed hard under. "It's not mine."

His eyebrows rose as he looked down upon my breasts. "Obviously."

"What does that mean?" I shifted and pulled the dress higher.

"That's not something you would wear, love."

"How do you know?" I asked in a snotty tone.

"You aren't that type of girl."

"Oh, really now. What type of girl am I, then?"

"The type of girl that straps daggers to her leg and threatens to stab people." His arrogant grin was sexy and I hated that I thought that.

I swallowed hard again. "And what's wrong with that?"

"Nothing, it's fierce . . . and sexy."

I blushed at his words. *Does he think I am sexy?* I asked myself and immediately regretted it. I gasped and slammed a hand over my mouth like it would block the thoughts from coming out.

Valarian burst out laughing. "First class is at sunrise. Try to contain your thoughts until then, love." He was grinning uncontrollably when he turned away.

"Oh, I will!" I couldn't help but blush as I watched his hard body walk across the beach.

"Here you go, Ember," Zila said as she handed me a drink. "Sorry it took so long. I was talking to Zayn. Cash and Asher are crazy!"

"That's okay, thank you." I took the drink and chugged it, hoping to drown my feelings.

"Wow, difficult day?" she asked.

"Tremendously. I'm going to get another one."

She smiled nervously. "Okay."

The rest of the night started to get better. I was on my fifth, sixth . . . seventh drink? I couldn't remember but I was feeling good. The band's music sped up, filling me with excitement. I jumped up from where I was sitting and strolled out toward the dancing area.

Swaying my hips to the rhythm of the music, I realized that I didn't want to be the only one out there. "Calista, Zila, come dance with me." They wasted no time hurrying over. We danced, laughed, and had fun as we let loose.

The music changed tempo on the next song. It went from a fast pace to a sultry rhythm and I thought it would be a clever idea to put on a show.

My eyes wandered to the men. Asher was standing with Zayn and Cash. But this show wasn't for them. It was for the other person standing with them . . . Valarian. I turned toward the men, put my hands above my head, and started circling my hips. Valarian watched me attentively as I danced.

Looking away from him, I locked eyes with Asher as the band slowed down. I decided to grab his hand and pull him onto the dance floor. He smiled as he let me. He placed his hands high upon my hips, and I put mine on his shoulders.

"Do you have a girlfriend?" Apparently the alcohol had me being blunt.

"I do! She's back in my hometown. She's an Air Caster."

Judging by the look on his face, he loved her and was just being kind to me.

Valarian was right. I glanced over at him and he nodded. *Ugh!*

"That is lovely. I'm happy for you." I gave Asher a sweet smile. He danced with me like a gentleman would, never moving his hands away from where they should be.

The song was ending and I dared a peek over my shoulder at Valarian. His arms were crossed as he watched me brazenly. Our eyes locked like magnets. I wanted to look away, but I couldn't. His beautiful violet eyes held my focus. A few breaths later, the song ended, bringing my attention back to Asher.

"Thank you for the dance."

He let go of me and bowed. "The pleasure is all mine."

"I'm next, Red!" The Angel smiled at me while walking onto the dance floor. Zayn took my hand and danced with me appropriately. He stayed quiet for about a minute before he spoke. "I know it's only your first day and it was a rough one for you but other than that, how do you feel about being here?"

"I don't know yet. The people are nice—most of them."

"Most of them?" He glanced over at Valarian and chuckled.

"I do have a question, Zayn." He looked back at me and waited. "Why are there only a few guards here?"

"Well, once guards have been doing these missions for years, they usually want to transfer into quieter roles. Most of the older soldiers take on positions as portal guards. Some transfer to guard at duke's castles. It's less stressful and has shorter days. Then they can get mated and raise a family, since they get to go home at the end of every shift."

"That makes sense." I glanced at Val, who was still watching me. "I could get used to being here, I guess."

"It was weird for all of us at first. I have been here for four years and I couldn't imagine *not* being here now. Cali and I grew up with little family since our parents died when we were younger."

I tilted my head, giving him a sympathetic look because I knew what he was feeling all too well. Even though I was wondering what happened, now wasn't the appropriate time to have that conversation.

"I'm sorry, Zayn."

"It was a long time ago. It was rough for a while, but we managed. I was content with my life back home, but coming here fixed me. It made me genuinely happy having these people as family. Having my sister come the same day was the best part."

My eyes widened. "Are you twins?"

"We are."

"That is truly a miracle."

Letting out a slow breath, I suddenly felt lightheaded and nauseous. I wished the song would end because I needed to sit down. A shadow behind Zayn caught my attention.

"May I cut in?" Valarian asked.

"The pleasure is all mine, buddy." Zayn smiled as he bowed to me. "Thanks for the dance, Ember." He winked and walked away.

Not knowing what to do, I stood there like a fool with my hands hanging. Valarian stepped in close and placed his palms on my waist. Between his touch and scent, my senses were on fire.

Woods and cool breeze. I let out a slow breath. *I feel sick.*

He gently grabbed my chin, tilting my face toward him. His beautiful violet eyes were filled with concern. "Are you okay?"

With barely enough time to react, I pulled away and bolted toward the edge of the water. Stopping just shy of the ocean, I fell to my knees onto the sand. My head started spinning and I regretted my drinking decisions as I hurled.

This entire day is ruined . . . I will never live this down.

"Ember?"

My name coming out of his mouth sounds so sexy. What is wrong with me? How can I be attracted to a Vampire?

"Why did you take me to the pastures, to the trees?" I asked. "Were you trying to get me alone so you could use your mind games on me?" My stomach was still turning, and I tried to ignore it. "To take advantage of an innocent girl?" Before Valarian had a chance to answer, I started making disgusting sounds. He grabbed my hair and pulled it back right before I vomited again.

Valarian's hand was warm as he pressed it against my back and rubbed it in soothing circles. "Would you like to go back to your room?"

I sagged as my body gave up fighting. "Yes . . ." I vomited again.

He waited for my hurling to cease before he helped me off my knees.

His face was concerned as I stared at him. "You know, you're extremely sexy for a Vampire . . ." And that was the last thing I remembered.

Valarian

Enjoying the bonfire wasn't happening since I was thrown a curveball that I didn't handle well. Ember came to join the King's Guard and I had an instant attraction to her. She's like a magnet that was slowly pulling me to her.

The band's music sped up and Ember strolled out onto the dance floor. She started swaying her hips to the rhythm of the music. "Calista, Zila, come dance with me."

The girls joined her on the dance floor and she seemed to finally be having fun. It made me happy. I was concerned that she would hate it here because of me—because I was a Vampire.

When the music changed, Ember turned toward me and put her hands above her head. As she circled her hips, I couldn't help but watch her. I tried to look away, but I wasn't strong enough. My eyes and my cock were both betraying me tonight.

She locked eyes with Asher and a low growl left me. Zayn placed his hand on my shoulder.

"Val."

I shrugged his hand away and tried to steady my breathing. "I'm good, Zayn."

"Just checking, buddy."

The song slowed down and Ember strolled toward us. My heart soared in hopes that she would speak to me, but she didn't. She grabbed Asher's hand and dragged him onto the dance floor.

My jaw clenched as I waited to see where he was going to put his hands. When he placed them high on her hips, I smiled.

Good boy. I wouldn't want to rip his throat out—I kind of liked the guy. My eyes stayed locked on them as they engaged in light conversation.

Valarian was right. I smiled again when I heard her thoughts. She glanced over at me and I nodded. *Ugh!* When she looked away, I laughed to myself. I was happy she found out Asher had a girlfriend. I crossed my arms while I continued watching them.

Ember locked eyes with me again. The light from the bonfire flickered across her creamy light skin, making it glow. I couldn't help but admire her beautiful, freckled face and her emerald green eyes.

As the song ended, her attention went back to Asher. When she smiled, I growled again. I didn't mean to.

"Okay, that's enough, Val!" Zayn said before he strolled onto the dance floor. "I'm next, Red!"

When Zayn took Ember into his arms, I was a lot calmer. I trusted him with my life. He glanced over at me and laughed, and I immediately wondered what she'd said about me. Knowing that she didn't know Zayn was my best friend made me smile.

She glanced over at me again because she couldn't help herself. There was a visible struggle on her face—and in her head. She wanted me, but was fighting the feelings out of fear. I understood because the severe attraction I quickly developed also scared the shit out of me.

Come get your girl, Zayn wielded the thought to me.

Not being able to take it anymore, I decided to go get the girl I wanted. I took a deep breath and walked into the dancing area.

"May I cut in?"

"The pleasure is all mine, buddy." Zayn politely dropped his hands and I had never been more grateful for such a fantastic friend. He was like a brother to me. "Thank you for the dance, Ember." Zayn winked before walking away.

My attention was where it had been all day—completely on Ember. She was adorable, with her hands hanging like she didn't know what to do. I was going to continue being the brave one. She smelled delicious as I stepped in closer and laid my hands on her waist.

Woods and cool breeze. She looked down at the ground. *I feel sick.*

Out of instinct, I gently grabbed her chin and tipped her face up. "Are you okay?"

She took a couple deep breaths before she ran toward the water. Of course I followed. That was the moment I realized I always would. I would follow her anywhere.

She dropped to her knees on the sand and puked.

This entire day is ruined. I will never live this down.

I felt so bad for her. "Ember?"

My name coming out of his mouth sounds so sexy. What is wrong with me? How can I be attracted to a Vampire?

Hearing her thoughts did things to me, but hearing her say she was attracted to me sent shivers through my body.

"Why did you take me to the pastures, to the trees?" she asked in anger. "Were you trying to get me alone so you could use your mind games on me?" I wanted to tell her that I was trying to make her happy, but I couldn't. I stayed quiet as she continued. "To take advantage of an innocent girl?"

Her body spasmed, so I grabbed her hair and pulled it out of her face as she was sick again.

I hesitated to touch her, but I knew she needed comfort, so I placed my hand on her back and rubbed it in circles. "Would you like to go back to your room?"

Her body relaxed like she had given up. I hoped it wasn't me that she was giving up on.

"Yes," she said, before vomiting again.

Once she was done, I helped her off the ground.

The way her eyes locked on me like I was the most important thing in the world, made my heart skip a beat. "You know, you're extremely sexy for a Vampire . . ." She passed out mid-sentence and fell into me. I slid one arm under her legs and one behind her back and carried her away from the oceanfront.

Zayn's eyes widened as I got closer to him. "Wow, she went hard!"

"Anxiety gets to us all on our first couple of days." I shifted and pulled her close to me.

"You got her, Val?"

"Yeah. I'm going to take her to her room."

He clasped my shoulder. "Let me know if you need anything, buddy."

"Thanks, Zayn."

Even though I could gale home from where I was, I took my time heading back. I wanted to enjoy having her close to me and smelling her skin. She smelled delicious—lavender and vanilla.

For some reason, I was mesmerized by her. I didn't understand *why* I was attracted to someone who hated Vampires, but I was. She may hate my kind because of her mother's death, but she didn't hate me. She wanted me so bad it was almost impossible for her to fight it. She had no clue that I felt the same. It would be hard sparring with her every day. Touching her during practice, but not how I wanted to touch her, would kill me. I knew I wasn't strong enough to stay away from her.

She was the most beautiful girl I had ever met. But that wasn't the only reason I wanted her.

I loved her enthusiasm. The way she was mesmerized by the magic and the wisteria trees made me extremely happy. Seeing and hearing the love she had for all of it made her anger toward me completely worth it.

She was fierce, too—I saw it in the woods. I would have let her stab and kill me out there if that would have made her happy. She was perfect in my eyes.

After walking for a few minutes, I figured I should take her back home, so I stopped to gale us back to the manor. Heading to the door, I had to shift her to get it open. She groaned lightly, but didn't wake. I was glad because she needed the rest.

Continuing our journey, I went up the stairs and down to her room. I once again had to shift to get her door open. After we entered, I gently laid her down on the bed, took off her shoes, and covered her with a blanket. I wanted nothing more but to comfort her. To crawl next to her and hold her until she woke . . . but I didn't.

Pushing her hair out of her face, I watched her sleep. I wanted to kiss her forehead, but I would never do anything to her or any woman without permission. Especially something as intimate as a kiss.

Noticing her fireplace was burning low, I quietly added more wood before I headed toward the door. I turned to get just one more glimpse of her beauty.

"Goodnight, love," I said, even if she couldn't hear me. I sighed and left the room.

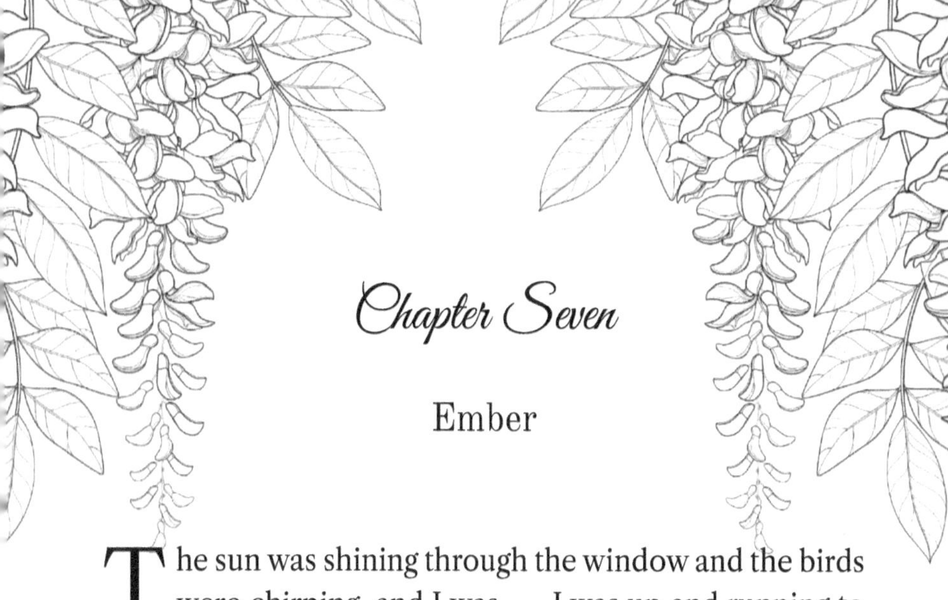

Chapter Seven

Ember

The sun was shining through the window and the birds were chirping, and I was . . . I was up and running to the bathroom. Blood pumped fast through my pounding head as I vomited.

What did I do last night? I sat by a fire, I talked to Asher, I danced, I puked. Oh no. I was mean to Valarian. I also called him sexy. I sighed. As I was skimming through my memories, there was a knock on the door.

"Ember?" Zayn called out.

"Yes."

"Class starts in ten minutes. I'll wait downstairs for you."

"Okay, I'll be there in a second!" I had no idea how I was going to get through practice.

Quickly getting off the bathroom floor, I washed my face and brushed my teeth. Then I threw on some black pants and a loose-fitting shirt before heading out the door. I sprinted down the hall and entered the stairwell.

"Ready," I said to Zayn as I skipped the last two steps. Bad idea. It made my head pound.

"Alright, follow me."

We left the manor and I wasn't paying any attention to where we were going because I didn't care. I felt like shit.

We stopped in front of a brick building and Zayn tilted his head at the door. "Your class is here with Val."

"Ugh!" I didn't mean to say that aloud.

"What is going on?" Zayn furrowed his eyebrows. "Why don't you like Val?"

"He read my thoughts without my permission." His blue eyes blinked with confusion, waiting for more info. "It's a violation of my privacy!"

"Why did you let your shield down? Did you get too drunk and forget?"

I shook my head. "I don't have a shield thing."

"Are you saying that you haven't been trained in shielding?"

Confusion was now filling me. "Valarian didn't tell you what happened yesterday?"

"He just said that you got bit by a wolf and was upset."

"Oh." That was surprising. "I assumed he told you."

Zayn shook his head. "He didn't."

A large breath escaped me and I tried to figure out what all I was going to tell him. "Well, I haven't been trained. I didn't even know that was a thing until yesterday. Regardless, he shouldn't have done it."

I knew Vampires could read minds if they wanted to, but I didn't know I could shield my thoughts before I came here.

"I don't think you understand how it works." He sighed and ran a hand through his hair. "Valarian can't hear your thoughts without your permission."

"But he did!"

"Yeah, but that was because you weren't shielding. You basically gave permission."

"But he didn't have to listen!"

"You're still not understanding. When a Vampire hears someone's thoughts, it's like a person is conversing with them. They can't block it or turn it off. It doesn't work like that."

Staring at him, the reality of me being wrong hit me as he continued.

"You telling him not to listen to your thoughts would be the same as me telling you *not* to listen to me speaking right now." He pointed toward the trees. "Or to not listen to the sound of those birds."

I'd heard the birds he was referring to the minute we stepped outside and during our entire walk. There was no way I could have blocked their sounds out. My mouth was agape in shock. I was so mean to Valarian and he didn't yell once.

I'm the asshole. "I understand what you are saying now, Zayn. I misunderstood the situation."

"Yeah, it's easy to do, I guess." His eyebrows furrowed with confusion. "I don't know why they didn't teach you at Mazuria Academy. Shielding is a required class that most learn by the time they're fourteen."

"My father didn't want to send us to the academy."

"You never went to the academy? What have you been doing with all your time?"

"Umm. Our mother taught us how to read and write, amongst other things. My father taught us how to fish and grow crops. After my mother died, I went to work at a local bakery so I could earn money to hire a mercenary to teach my sister and I how to defend ourselves. We trained every time our father was away on trips. I taught myself how to shoot a bow and to hunt."

"That is truly unheard of." Zayn's eyes were wide as he opened the door to the training center.

We fell silent as we walked down a couple of halls and came upon a door.

"Just for the record, Val is a good man. He would never do anything to hurt you, Ember."

I see that now. I smiled politely at him. "I appreciate you, Zayn."

He smiled at me as he opened the door. Valarian was standing with his arms crossed, making the muscles in his arms pop. He was dressed in leather pants and a black shirt with short sleeves. He didn't have any weapons strapped on him this time. Somehow, he was casually sexy.

"Val, buddy! Are you ready for your new student today?" Valarian's jaw clenched as he nodded. Then Zayn turned toward me. "I have a flying class to teach with Cash over at the elementary campus on Valmeyer. I'll be back this afternoon."

A flying class? So, that's what Zayn and Cash taught. The country of Valmeyer was the land of the Angels. I couldn't help but to think about how adorable it would be to watch young Angels learn to use their wings.

"Have fun, you two." Zayn was grinning when he strolled off, leaving me standing there looking helpless.

Valarian uncrossed his arms. "Are you ready to get started?"

"I would like to apologize first." I was ready to forgive and forget. Mainly forget.

"There truly is no need."

"I actually do *need* to apologize." *Please.*

"Go ahead." Valarian's violet eyes watched me as I struggled to collect my thoughts. I took a deep breath.

"Zayn told me that you didn't mean to hear my thoughts. I understand that it was my fault, since I was never trained to shield. So, I am terribly sorry for the way I acted toward you."

"Apology accepted. Let's get started." He turned and headed toward the middle of the room.

"That's it?" I asked as I followed him.

He had a look of confusion when we stopped. "What do you mean?"

"You aren't going to say anything else? Or apologize to me?"

He crossed his arms with a smirk. "For what?"

"I don't know, for . . ." *Shit, I don't know what for.*

"Should I apologize for trying to be nice to you and ease your mind when I heard you were sad? Maybe for ignoring your snide comments for as long as I could? Or how about holding your hair back and then putting you safely to bed? Which part should I be sorry for, Ember?"

I just blinked. *He was being kind to me the whole time and I was too ignorant to see it.*

"It's okay." He sighed. " Let's get started. Take a seat on the floor and cross your legs. We're going to work on shielding first, *obviously.*"

I laughed lightly at his sarcasm as I took a seat. As I peered up at the six and a half foot sexy man, I felt small.

"Close your eyes and listen to me while you focus on what I'm saying. Your mind and thoughts belong to you. You are the only one who can allow someone to hear them."

I wonder if Vampires are the only ones that can hear thoughts.

"No, we're not. Introspectors can too."

"What's that?" I asked.

"It's a certain breed of Demon. They're also called soul-searchers because they can get in your mind and make you do things. Which is the biggest reason shielding is so important. It's not just to hide your . . . um, specific feelings from others."

My eyes popped open and I glared up at him. "I don't have *specific* feelings to hide."

His eyebrows raised as he gave me a look that said he didn't believe me. I tried not to blush.

"Focus, Ember. Close your eyes again. Take a deep breath and relax. Try to build a barrier in your mind. Envision whatever it is you would like to protect your mind with. Most people use an invisible shield and others use brick walls. I trained a child one time that liked to use a grassy hedge."

I thought about what I'd like to use. *An invisible shield sounds like the best option for me.*

"Shield it is then." Instead of getting mad at him for hearing my thoughts, I focused hard on my shield. "Now, try to make it wrap around your mind."

Okay, I'll start the shield at the top and make it wrap around my brain.

"That looks good. Keep focusing."

It's getting thicker and unbreakable.

"Perfect. Now think of a color."

Violet. My favorite.

"Violet. The color of my eyes." I could practically hear the smile in his voice. "Try again."

Yellow.

"Yellow. Again. Keep it tight this time."

I focused hard on my shield and let out a slow breath.

Brown. When he said nothing, my eyes popped open. "Did you hear me?"

He smiled. "Nope."

"Is that it? Have I finished already?"

"Not even close but it's a great start. It's easier since you're older, but it'll take practice to keep it up without thinking about it."

So, I can say what I want and you can't hear me?

"Not when you immediately let your shield drop, you can't."

"Crap." I sighed and he laughed. The sound was beautiful.

He took a seat near me and crossed his legs. "Try putting your shield back up and then tell me the name of an animal. Keep your eyes open this time."

Raising my shield again, I locked eyes with him. *Sandmouse.*

"Eh, those things creep me out." I smiled at his confession. "Try again."

Woodrat.

His eyebrows furrowed. "What is it with you and rodents? Again."

Holding his stare, I focused as hard as I could.

Gray wolf. He said nothing as a smile crept across his face. "I got you, Valarian!"

"Good job. What did you say?"

"I can't tell you," I teased.

He shook his head with a chuckle. "It was probably some creepy rodent."

I giggled and shrugged. "Maybe."

"Okay, last one. Put your shield up, say something, take it down, say something, then put it back up again."

Shield up, *arrows.* Shield down, *biscuits.* Shield up, *books.*

"Are you hungry? Because all I heard was biscuits."

I did a little happy dance inside as he laughed.

"Okay, let's do some sparring." He hopped off the floor and I swallowed hard.

"Okay." *Keep my thoughts blank when he touches me.* I winced as soon as I thought the words because my shield wasn't up. *Shit.*

"Don't keep your thoughts blank, Ember. Keep your shield up."

"Okay." I bit my lip to keep myself from blushing.

"Do you know how to throw a proper punch?"

Getting up off the floor in one fluid motion, I walked up to him while looking him in the eye. I threw a punch just like I was trained and he effortlessly dodged it.

"Nice, considerably better than I expected." I smiled proudly. "But I want you to try a different stance." He held his hands out. "May I place my hands on you?"

"Yes, please." I immediately thought hard about my shield, trying to keep my thoughts blocked. *Why the hell did I say please? Could I possibly make a bigger fool of myself?*

He kneeled and slid his hand around my ankle. He grabbed it and lifted, placing my foot where he wanted it. His head was so close to the apex of my legs, my breathing got heavy. I kept focusing on how thick my shield was instead of the dirty thoughts trying to invade me.

Thick shield, thick shield.

After standing up, he went behind me and put his hands on multiple parts of my body. My heart raced as he touched my leg, ankle, hips, back, and shoulders, trying to get me in that stance.

By the time he came back in sight, I was already breathless.

"Let's do some sparring," he said with a grin.

I knew he could tell my cheeks were already flushed and we hadn't even started yet.

We threw punches and kicks until we were both sweaty and hot—in more ways than one for me. I regretted not grabbing a band for my hair as I waved my hand toward my face.

It's hot.

"Shield up and let's take a quick break."

As he walked over to the table, I threw my shield back up. He poured us both a cup of water. I sipped mine slowly, so I didn't get sick.

After a couple of minutes of catching our breath, he grabbed a dagger out of his bag and headed to the center of the room. I followed him.

"Okay, I want you to try to disarm me."

Being only a foot away had its advantages. I didn't hesitate as I lunged for him. Even though I had about a three-second jump on him, he was quick to dodge me. Lunging for him again, he quickly sidestepped and smiled at me. My pulse sped up when I saw his fangs.

Since my thoughts were about to be bad, I checked my shield. It was down again so I put it back up. I couldn't seem to keep it there for more than a few minutes.

It took me a while of lunging for him and dodging the swings of his dagger before I finally got an opening. I went for it, knocking the blade from his hand. Unfortunately, I had propelled myself so hard that I knocked him down and fell right on top of him.

It was an awfully intimate position we were in. My legs were on either side of his body as I straddled him. My chest was lying entirely against his as I struggled to catch my breath. Every part of me that was touching him yearned for more. All my senses were on fire from his scent.

"Great job." His breaths were as equally labored.

I pressed my palms on the floor and pushed up slightly. Meeting his face, I swallowed hard.

His eyes are gorgeous. His lips look soft.

As his violet irises searched my face, his breathing got even heavier. My lips parted, trying to get air into my body . . . or ready to meet his. I wasn't sure which.

I gasped when I felt something press between my legs. *Oh, I can feel his hard . . .*

"Shield!" he yelled while rolling me off him.

Tumbling away, I quickly scrambled to my knees as he jumped up from the floor.

My cheeks flushed as I stood up. I immediately snapped my shield back up as I died from embarrassment.

"We're done for today," Valarian said, while taking a towel and wiping his face. He met my eyes as he threw a towel at me. "I'm sorry about that."

"It was my fault. I'm sorry I made you—"

"Ah, no need. Just work on your shielding the rest of the day. Any time you think of it."

"I will." I nodded. His eyes locked on mine for a few more seconds like he was waiting for me to say more. "Umm, thanks for the lesson."

"You're welcome." He strolled out of the gym, leaving me standing there even more confused.

Chapter Eight

Now that practice was over and my adrenaline had worn off, my headache was back in full force. After I returned to the manor, I went to the kitchen and grabbed some food. Not wanting to run into anyone, I took it to my room and ate. My mind wasn't focused on what was important—I couldn't stop thinking about what had happened with Valarian during sparring class. And, of course, my reaction to him . . . once again.

Valarian is so sexy. Why am I attracted to him when he obviously has no interest in me? Well, a little interest, but I think any male in that situation would have had the same physical reaction. I had to stop thinking about him.

A little while later, a tailor showed up and took my measurements for my fighting leathers. She had a couple of sample pieces for women with her. I ordered a black leather corset that buckled down the front and laced up the back. I also ordered new casual clothes, some boots for fighting, and some for fun. But the best thing I ordered was a deep purple cloak. It was the end of spring, but I would use it this fall. The tailor said I would have my items in a few days. Once she left, I sat down at the desk to write a letter to my sister.

Hey Cin,

Day one was eventful, to say the least. I will elaborate more when I see you. Day two seems much better, kind of. I am safe and well. I have a lot to tell you already. I hope you are faring well.

Love, Em

I folded the letter and stuck it in an envelope, and as soon as I sealed it, there was a shiny silver circle in my room. It was a messenger Imp waiting for permission to enter.

"You may enter." A tiny, two-foot-tall Imp appeared. His exquisite orange eyes looked up at me from a happy face.

"Greetings." He held out his hand and I handed him the letter. "Salutations." He vanished.

About ten minutes later, the shiny circle reappeared.

"You may enter."

The Imp appeared and handed me a letter.

"Thank you," I said.

"Salutations." He bowed and, once again, disappeared. I opened the letter from my sister.

Dear Em,

I am missing you dearly. Father left as soon as you did, and I do not know when he shall return. It is lonely being in the house with no one. Ms. Delaney gave me your old job at the bakery this morning, so at least I will have work to occupy my mind. I cannot wait to hear about your first day. Take care.

Love, Cinder

I folded the note and put it away in the desk drawer.
Well, at least she has a job.
There was a knock on my door, drawing my attention.
"Yes?"
"Hey, how are you feeling today?" Cashmere asked as he peeked his head inside.
"Do you have to ask?" I said and his eyes turned empathetic. "My nausea is gone, but my head still hurts."
"I figured after last night, that's why I brought you a present." He pushed the door open further, and there stood Yeva. She strolled in gracefully.
"Give me your hand, my child." I gave her my hand. My whole body got warm in seconds as her skin glowed. My headache immediately disappeared.

"Thank you."

"I do not heal people who overindulge. This was just a welcoming gift in hopes that you adjust quickly. It will not happen again." She smiled and left the room. The residual feelings from drinking too much alcohol last night were gone entirely.

"Feel better?" He raked his hands through his beard.

"Much better!" I felt amazing.

Cash said his goodbyes, so I decided to get into a hot bath to soak. Time seemed to not exist while I was bathing . . . and, of course, thinking about Valarian. I had just gotten dressed when another knock came upon my door. When I opened it, another Angel was standing there. This time, it was Zayn.

"Are you ready to explore the grounds, Red?"

"Is this Angel visiting day?"

"Every day is." He winked a blue eye. "Get used to it."

I rolled my eyes. "Wonderful."

He laughed at my sarcasm as we headed downstairs. We left the manor and went around the back of the building.

"How do you like it here so far?" Zayn asked, drawing my gaze from the rabbit I was watching eating some clovers.

"The people seem nice. I just miss my sister a lot."

"That's expected. It's hard leaving home."

"I noticed." I rolled my eyes sarcastically and Zayn chuckled.

We continued walking around the grounds until we came upon the garden area. I gasped at the sights as my eyes widened. It was breathtaking, lighting all my senses on fire.

There were thousands of lilies in different colors. The smell of the flowers was intoxicating as the pops of color relaxed my entire body. I could curl up and read a book right here in the middle of them or lay upon them while stargazing.

We stopped at a huge water fountain in the center of the garden that was made of white marble. There was crystal clear water inside of it that cascaded down the top tier in the middle and splashed lightly into the pool at the bottom of the fountain.

"This is gorgeous! The fountain, the flowers . . . all of it!"

Zayn smiled at my excitement. With a sigh, I took a seat on the edge of the fountain. I had too many things on my mind that I had been thinking about during our stroll.

"Zayn, can I ask you something?"

"Of course." He took a seat next to me.

"I was mean to Valarian for listening to my thoughts before I knew it was my fault. Do you honestly think that he'll forgive me?"

"He already has."

"How do you know that? Did he say something?" I ran my hand lightly through the water of the fountain—it was colder than I expected it to be on such a warm day.

"No. That's just the type of man he is. He's exceptionally honorable, overly caring, and extremely forgiving. He understands that you were never taught to shield."

"I can tell he's all those things. He's far more kind to me than he ever should have been, considering how I acted. I was just concerned about what he thinks of me."

Zayn gave me an empathetic smile as he ran a hand through his hair. "Don't worry too much about how Val feels toward you. He forgives and forgets. He's a man of few words most of the time, but when he has something to say, you'll know."

"Thank you for easing my mind." For some reason, I was completely comfortable with Zayn. I smirked mischievously as I flicked the water from my fingers at him.

"You're mean for such a nice girl." I giggled. "Would you like to see the library?" he asked, making my eyes go wide with excitement.

"I truly would." *I hope they have romance books.* I blushed at the thought. I was grateful the Angel couldn't hear them. I threw my shield up anyway, remembering to practice.

"Come on." He stood up and I fell in step next to him.

Once inside the manor, we stopped in front of a large, deep brown wooden door with a wrought-iron handle. Zayn opened it and I threw a hand over my mouth in shock.

Dark wooden bookshelves were lined along the walls of the enormous room—each of them filled with books. There was a huge rectangular table in the middle of the room with a crimson velvet tablecloth on it. Not being able to contain myself, I walked up to a bookcase and ran my finger down the spine of a book.

"They're all categorized by genre. We have informational books over here." He walked to the left side of the room and pointed. "Next to these are other non-fiction books."

Not really caring about this side, I nodded my head in acknowledgment. Zayn walked toward the right side of the room, so I followed him.

"And this is my favorite side since all the fiction is over here. There's mystery, fantasy, and romance as well." He smiled at me, letting me take in the sights.

Excited to see my favorite genre, I walked up to the romance section and took a peep. I grabbed a couple of different books and read the first page. I quickly put a few of them back until one caught my attention.

"How do I borrow one? Is there a librarian?"

"Not technically, but Zila's on library duty. By her own choice, that is, since this is her favorite place. You can take whatever book you want and return it at your leisure. Just set it on the table there and she'll put it back where it goes. She's especially adamant about it staying organized."

"I want to read this one." I held the book close to me.

"Great book! I read it a few months ago."

I tried to keep the look of shock off my face. "You read romance?"

"Of course. How else will I know what the ladies like?"

I giggled at his revelation. "You're a softy," I teased.

"Sometimes." He smiled proudly. "Alright, I think you have seen almost everything. Are you ready to head back?"

Excitement filled me as we left the library. I was ready to engulf myself in this new book.

We parted ways by the stairs. I quickly went up to my room and plopped down on my bed. Now that I was alone, I put the book up to my nose and sniffed it. It smelled just like the books in the library back home. I sighed at the memory of me sitting in that library for hours on end.

The book was about a girl who inherited a castle and the rightful owner returned to claim it. He was a five hundred-year-old Vampire. I wondered for a second how old Valarian was. Removing the thought from my mind, I continued reading and completely forgot about the world around me as I was wrapped up in a world of lust, love, and danger.

Chapter Nine

Waking up to a beautiful, warm, sunny day was exhilarating. Since I had a later practice today, I spent most of the morning reading. It was my third day here and my second practice with Valarian. I was nervous to see him. After I braided my hair and threw on some comfortable clothes, I walked into the training center, where he was patiently waiting for me.

"You're not dressed in leathers." Odd choice of words, since he wasn't dressed in leathers either. He had on a short-sleeve shirt that showed off his sexy arm muscles. The pants he had on were dark and loose. Great for sparring. His hair was tied back in a bun that made him even hotter. As I reveled in his sexiness, I remembered to put my shield up.

"Nice to see you, too, Valarian." He narrowed his eyes on me, not finding my sarcasm funny. "I just got fitted for leathers, so I don't have any yet."

"You don't have to wear them anyway, unless you want to. Plus, we aren't sparring today, so I guess it doesn't matter."

I hope it wasn't because of the incident.

"Shield, and no, it wasn't. I have other plans for us today, Ember."

His deep, sensual voice saying my name lit a fire in me. I threw my shield up, willing it to be thick and tight. I would constantly have to remind myself of it today or die of embarrassment.

"Come on."

He strolled out of the building and I followed behind him as I watched his muscles move through his clothing. Not only did I have a perfect view of his back muscles, but also his butt.

He has such a nice ass. I blushed at the thought. With a sense of panic, I checked my shield and it was still up. *Oh, go me!*

We stayed quiet as we walked back to the manor. After going inside and through a few hallways, we came to a staircase that went downstairs. I remembered what Zayn told me about the basement.

"The armory?" I asked excitedly.

"Yep." He had a beaming smile plastered on his face as he descended the stairs. I had a feeling he loved working with weapons as much as I did.

As soon as we were downstairs, we turned down a few hallways until we came upon an iron door. It squeaked and groaned as he opened it.

The armory was bigger than I had imagined, filled with every weapon you could think of. Hanging on the walls were the larger weapons: battle-axes, swords, maces, staves, and spears. My face lit up the minute I saw bows.

Along the bottom of the wall and in the middle of the room were red velvet-lined shelves filled with smaller weapons: daggers, small axes, throwing daggers, nunchakus, throwing stars, sai, and a few others I didn't recognize.

Of course, my body was drawn toward the bows. After I approached them, I ran a finger down one, feeling the wood. Valarian was curiously watching me when I glanced over at him. I immediately dropped my hand from the bow like I'd been caught.

"You can take it off the wall if you want."

My eyes went back to the bows. There were about ten different ones to choose from. I picked up the first one, and it was a lot heavier than mine back home, so I put it back. Picking up another, I didn't like the feeling of the wood. I picked up the third one and it was too big. This went on for a while.

Finally, on the sixth bow I picked up, I decided it was perfect—the same size and weight as mine. Looking down at it, I smiled.

"Great choice." Valarian's voice brought me back from my admiration time with the bow.

"Thanks." I reached up to put it back.

"Don't. You're going to need it."

Oh, do I get to use it?

"Shield, and yes, you will."

Shit! I snapped my shield back into place.

"Shit?" He laughed. "That's not very ladylike."

"My sister's a lady. Not me."

He smirked. "I noticed. I heard worse come from you when you were mad."

I grinned. "Is that such a terrible thing?"

"Absolutely not." He gave me a genuine smile. "Grab a quiver and some arrows, and we'll do some unladylike shit." I couldn't help but giggle as I grabbed what I needed.

"Are you ready?"

"I'm not sure what we are doing, but yes."

"You'll see," he said with a wink.

We left the room and I stayed in step with him down the hallway. Once we got to the stairs, he stopped and gestured toward them.

"After you, love."

Knowing that my butt was now going to be at his eye level if he stayed right behind me made me nervous. If he was going to stare at my ass, I might as well feel good about it, so I climbed the stairs in a way that I hoped made my butt look good. He was, indeed, right behind me the whole way. We stayed quiet as we made our way back through the manor. When we got to the front door, a servant was waiting with a basket in his hand.

"Thank you," Valarian said as he took it.

We continued outside and strolled toward the back of the grounds. We went far enough to be out of the wards.

I wonder where we're going.

"We have to gale there. Unless you want to walk about ten miles?"

"Galing is fine."

Don't think about him touching me.

"You'll enjoy it, don't worry. Not the galing, I mean you'll enjoy what we're doing. Well, you might enjoy the galing too." He smiled at me mischievously. "Also, shield."

Throwing my shield back up, I blushed. After he hung the basket on his arm, he closed the distance between us.

"May I?" He held his hands out, politely asking permission to touch me.

"Yes."

The heat of his body felt good against mine as he wrapped his arms around my waist. I quickly checked my shield before I had a thought that embarrassed me . . . again. I was going to try hard *not* to think about him while managing to keep my shield in place. I knew I'd be mentally exhausted by the time we got back.

"Are you ready?" Since he was so much taller than I was, I felt his breath on the top of my head. Nervously, I nodded.

When we landed, he let go and I instantly missed the warmth of his hands. The forest was thick with trees, brush, and tiny yellow flowers. There were a couple of birds pecking around on the ground—looking for food, I assumed.

"What are we doing here?"

"We're going to hunt. I need to feed and you need to eat." He held up the basket. "It's almost lunchtime and Zayn told me you skipped breakfast."

"What?" I asked. *Like, feed?*

"Feed, like eat." He grinned arrogantly whilst showing me his fangs.

"I know what feed means." I rolled my eyes.

"You told the king that some people think you're the best archer on your lands. Since I need to feed, I figured you can catch the food and I can eat it."

My eyebrows furrowed. "Can't you catch it yourself?"

He laughed. "Of course. I just thought you might enjoy doing something you love. Plus, I wanted to see if you actually were the best." He gave me a doubtful face.

Game on.

"Shield. It dropped about a minute ago." He smiled and I sighed. "At least you weren't thinking, umm . . . your normal thoughts." He winked and I rolled my eyes. I tried to keep my mind quiet after that.

We hiked through the forest, making small talk while I looked for deer tracks. Valarian stayed close in front of me. We had been exploring for about twenty minutes when he suddenly stopped.

He put a finger to his mouth, silencing me.

Caster hearing was good, but it had nothing on Vampires. As I looked around the woods, I heard nothing and saw no movement. My face was confused as I glanced back at Valarian. Within a second, he galed mere inches from me and leaned in toward my neck. My heart raced with excitement as the air seemed to escape my lungs.

"Listen," he whispered in my ear. "It's coming."

I quickly checked my shield. Still intact. Thank the Gods because the thoughts that went through my head the moment he whispered *those words* would have been highly inappropriate—not to mention, embarrassing.

As we stood there in complete silence, only the sound of my racing heart was heard.

I wonder if he can hear my heart beating fast. As my eyes searched his face, he winked. I took that as a yes and threw my shield back up.

It was just up—I was doing well until he came near me.

A twig cracked, drawing my attention away from the sexy man in front of me. I immediately pulled an arrow from my quiver and nocked it as quietly as I could. Turning away from him, I crouched down. As I listened, another limb cracked loudly.

That sounded too large to be a deer. The moment I had that thought, I saw it. It was, in fact, not a deer.

A large bear crawled out of the dense forest and my breath caught. Valarian slowly kneeled beside me and nodded toward the bear. I shook my head no, a quiet answer. He nodded his head again toward the bear.

I dropped my shield. *I can't do it. I've killed nothing bigger than a deer.*

He leaned over and whispered, "I believe in you." My body got hot all over as my heart raced even faster.

After a few seconds, I took a deep breath and made my decision. If he had faith in me, I would have to have faith in myself as well.

Locking my eyes on the bear, he was facing away, so I needed to hit him on his side in the hopes that he would turn more toward me once he was injured.

Springing up from the ground, I immediately shot the bear. He let out a loud sound of pain as I grabbed another arrow and nocked it.

The bear caught sight of me and snarled. As his mouth opened, I could see his long fangs. He stood up on two legs, so I shot an arrow into his chest. He fell back down on all fours and snarled again. I nocked another one, waiting for him to stop moving.

This needed to end fast because he started charging toward me. I went with my instincts and used my magic to light the arrow I nocked. Pulling the bow tight, I took aim and shot the fire arrow right into his eye . . . when he was only a few feet away.

He was moving so fast that he was going to stumble right into us. I had mere seconds to block him, so I quickly turned my shoulder toward the direction of his body, knowing the impact was going to hurt.

Valarian threw his hands out and stopped the bear's skidding body from plowing into us. Shoving hard, the bear flew back about five feet and skidded to a halt. It didn't move—I had killed it. As my heart raced from an adrenaline rush, I bent down to the ground, trying to catch my breath.

He squatted next to me and grabbed my arms. "Are you okay?"

"That was . . ." I gasped for air, "that was . . ." *To the Gods.*

"Ember?" His hands moved to my cheeks as his eyes drifted over my face. "Are you okay?"

"That was amazing!" I smiled widely. My heart was racing from pure excitement.

Val blew out a hard breath. Pride was showing on his face as he grinned at me. "You did wonderfully. Nice touch with the fire arrow."

"Thanks," I said as I looked deeply into his violet eyes. *So beautiful.*

He let go of my cheeks and stood up—I immediately missed his touch. He lowered his hand down to me and I took it. I was still smiling as he helped me up.

"Put your shield back up and let's eat."

My adrenaline was pumping too hard to be embarrassed as I put my shield up.

He grabbed the basket he brought, pulled a blanket out, and laid it on the ground. "Take a seat," he said politely.

As he pulled out some plates and other things, I took a seat on the blanket, watching him curiously. He made a sandwich and put it on a plate with some strawberries on the side and a few slices of cheese. He also pulled out some wine and filled two glasses.

"Eat up, love." As he put a plate and a glass in front of me, I realized that he called me "love" randomly. It didn't bother me, but it did give me butterflies.

He walked over to the bear and kneeled on one knee. I watched him with curiosity as he opened his mouth. His fangs were sharp. I threw my hand over my mouth, not out of fear but out of wonder, as he sunk his teeth into the bear's neck. The sight of him feeding was intoxicating. Enthralling.

He drank for about a minute. When he was done, he wiped his mouth off and came back to me. Locking eyes with him, I quickly tried to remove the shocked look from my face.

"You haven't eaten your food, Ember. Do you not like it?"

I hadn't even looked at the food. I was still in shock from all the surprising things that had happened in the last five minutes.

"It's fine. Thank you."

He smiled and took a seat next to me. After he made himself a sandwich, he took a swig of his wine. "Do you like it here so far?" he asked before taking a bite.

"You just fed on a bear and now you're eating a sandwich. I have so many questions and you want to make small talk?"

He chuckled. "Ask away."

"So, you eat real food and drink blood?" That was a wasted question because I just saw both.

"Yep." He smiled because he also thought it was a wasted question.

"How often do you have to feed?"

"I can feed every day if I want, but I usually feed about once a week. It's too time consuming to hunt daily."

I turned my body toward him as my curiosity grew. "How long can you go without blood?"

"After about three months without feeding, Vampires get weaker. After six months, we start to go into bloodlust. After a year, we go insane."

My eyes widened. "Whoa."

"Yeah." He laughed before taking another bite of his sandwich.

"Do you prefer one animal over another?"

"Deer are my favorite but I do love a good bear occasionally. So, thank you for feeding me." He gave me an enchanting smile. It was so beautiful I had to quickly look away.

"You're very welcome and thank you for feeding me." I made sure my shield was up as I took a bite of my sandwich.

During our lunch, I noticed his leg was lying against my thigh. I couldn't believe how excited I got over something so small. I had been touched before in more sexual ways, yet this simple little touch through clothes had my brain scattered. After making sure my shield was up, I shifted to pour myself some more wine and made sure my leg didn't go near his again.

Once we were done eating, he packed everything up and we continued our journey. We strolled for about twenty minutes, enjoying the scenery before he spoke.

"Are you ready to go back?"

"Sure. Thank you for today, Valarian."

He prowled toward me as anxiety and lust ran through my body. "You're truly welcome. May I gale us?"

"Yes." *He is so sexy.*

He slid his arms around my body.

"Shield," he said as he locked eyes with me. "That one stayed up for a while." He grinned before we were swept away.

We landed back at the manor and he dropped his arms from around me.

"Can you take this?" He held the basket out, acting like I didn't just call him sexy.

"Sure." I also pretended like nothing happened as I took it.

"Be right back." He galed away as I stood there wondering what he was doing. He reappeared a minute later and had the large bear draped over his shoulders.

"How the . . . what are you doing, Valarian?"

"I'm not going to waste this good meat. The servants love to cook bear. They'll be ecstatic."

"How are you even carrying that?"

He grinned as blood dripped down onto the front of him. "I have muscles, Ember."

The sound of my name falling from his lips gave me chills *every damn time*. He indeed had muscles. With the bear over his shoulders and his arms in the air as he held it, his muscles were tight. Hard. Sexy.

His shirt was slightly up at the bottom, allowing me to see a small patch of hair that led into his pants. Trying to keep from staring too hard, I glanced up. He had that primal look on his face again as he watched me admire him.

I have never seen anything sexier in my life. I checked my shield. *Shit.*

"I'm not even going to tell you." He walked off with the bear over his shoulders, laughing hard.

With a sigh, I shamefully put my shield back up and headed to my room.

Chapter Ten

The following two weeks were a blur—nothing eventful happened. I received my clothes and my fighting leathers. Since Valarian said I only had to wear them if I wanted to, I hadn't yet. Every day at Castleva was easier and easier. I had gotten more comfortable and was kind of happy.

After I had finished writing a letter to Cinder, trying to explain how she could practice shielding, I was unsure if she would understand. So as I attempted to rewrite it, there was a knock on my door, bringing me from my thoughts.

A small part of me hoped it was Valarian as I opened the door. I was pleasantly surprised to see Calista and Zila smiling.

"Hey, Ember," Cali said as she strolled in. She was wearing a peach-colored shirt and some black trousers with her leather corset. Her hair was braided from her crown down. My eyes went wide when I saw a katana strapped to her back.

Whoa! Not what you would expect to see from such a girly female.

Zila's lovely, wavy hair was bouncing as she strolled in right behind Cali. She wore an ivory shirt with a black leather vest and matching trousers. My eyes went wider when I saw she had a sai strapped on both sides of her belt.

"Zila and I were wondering if you want to go with us on a mission?"

"Oh." I hadn't been on one yet and the thought made me nervous. "I don't know."

"It's nothing big. It's my and Cali's turn for the food run. We asked the king and he said you could go with us if you wanted to."

Immediately wanting to say no so I could stay home and read my book, I sighed. Both the women standing in my room were so lovely and so kind. I looked into Cali's dazzling blue eyes and her face was pleading.

"If you don't want to, you don't have to, but I kind of wanted to show you the cute Fae that Zila's crushing on."

"I am not! He's my friend." Zila blushed and looked down at her feet.

I couldn't miss the opportunity to meet Zila's crush. "I would love to go."

"Great!" Calista clapped her hands together in excitement.

"Wait, Fae? Does that mean we'll be going over to Tessalone?" *Oh no.*

"Yes, meet us outside by the portal and bring your dagger," Calista said, and they both left my room.

What have I gotten myself into?

With a sigh, I quickly dressed in my leathers for the first time and strapped my dagger to my thigh. I walked out the manor's front door, and looked around.

"Ember," I heard Cali call out from the side of the house. As I strolled toward them, I wondered what could be so exciting to catch their attention.

"Oh my," I said as soon as I saw what was so enchanting.

Cali smiled. "My thoughts exactly."

Right in front of us was a shirtless Cash glistening with sweat. His long hair was tied up in a bun as he chopped wood. He was an exceptionally good-looking male and quite sexy. As he turned away from us, I couldn't help but drool over the massive tattoo he had. It was a pair of angel wings that almost covered every inch of his sexy back muscles.

Clever. I laughed to myself. I found that there wasn't much that Angel would do to surprise me.

Then Valarian come around the corner carrying wood and my heart sped up. He was facing us—shirtless—with his hair also in a bun. As he started chopping wood, I bit my lip. His muscles tightened with every swing of the axe. They were very well defined under the sweat that shimmered on his body in the sun.

My eyes refused to look away from the pure sexiness before me. I couldn't help but wonder how often this occurred so I could make sure I was outside.

"Should we be staring?" I asked, my eyes never leaving Valarian's body.

"Oh, the males here know that we don't feel that way about them. It's just looking at some men that just happen to be shirtless," Cali said.

"And sexy," Zila added with a giggle.

"Have any of you ever . . ." I hoped they knew what I meant.

"Gods no. We don't mate where we live." Cali tilted her head, watching the men, and smiled. "It would be awkward afterward if we decided to part ways."

"We just like to look sometimes," Zila added.

"It can be just as fun!" Cali whistled at the males. "Looking good, gentlemen!" Both the girls laughed.

The men locked eyes on us. Cash tried to strike a sexy pose. He flexed his arm muscles, making the other two females giggle more.

Staying completely quiet and concentrating on my shield, I remained focused on Valarian. I'm sure I had a weird look on my face because his eyebrows squinted together as he tilted his head like he was trying to figure out what my facial expression was for. Realizing that I was working hard on my shield, the corner of my mouth pulled into a proud smile.

His gaze traveled down my body as he noticed my new leathers. His eyebrows rose and his smile grew. He gave me a nod of approval and winked, before continuing his job. His chest muscles tightened as he raised his arms in the air and swung down hard. Heat poured through me as I watched his hard body swing that axe like a professional.

"Okay, are we ready?" Cali asked, snapping my attention back to reality.

I took a deep breath and exhaled slowly.

"Ready as I will ever be."

Turning away, we headed toward the portal. I glanced over my shoulder, hoping to get one more sexy glimpse of Valarian. Shock filled me when I saw he was watching me walk away. As we met eyes, I whipped my head back around to face forward in embarrassment—excitement. Since I knew he was looking, I put a little more hip into my walk.

We made it to the portal and all three of us stepped onto it. I tried to make my body relax. Zila willed it to go and I was once again whipped through life.

The warm air mixed with a cool breeze hit me and I closed my eyes as I started to sway. My skin puckered as goosebumps formed all over my body. I felt pleasure, like when Valarian put his arms around me. My heart began to race as my stomach turned inside out. Nausea hit me and I got dizzy before we finally landed.

"To the Gods, Ember. Are you okay?"

"Yes, Cali." I lied. I was definitely feeling like I was going to hurl. The portal guards looked at me uneasily. I'm sure they weren't ready to clean up my sickness.

"Just breathe." Zila placed her hand on my arm and rubbed it up and down, trying to soothe me. "In through your nose and out your mouth slowly."

Cali looked upset. "I'm so sorry, Ember. I didn't even think to remember how bad portal rides used to be when I first came here."

"It's okay," I said, willing my body to relax. I contemplated asking if she could soothe my emotions, but I knew I had to get used to this on my own.

Once I was calm enough, we stepped off the portal. We were walking on a little sandy island that connected to the mainland, Cali told me. The country we were in was Tessalone, the land of the Fae. It was exceptionally green and incredibly scenic.

Since the girls didn't want to gale—they wanted to show me everything—we were going to walk most of the way to Magecrest. After strolling for about ten minutes, we crossed a bridge that covered the crystal blue waters of the sea.

"Isn't it beautiful here?" Cali swirled her hands around through the air, showing off the lands. She spun in a circle, dancing across the bridge.

"Undoubtedly," I said as I glanced around. The land was amazing.

"We love coming here for food runs because it's so beautiful and picturesque."

"You love coming here, Zila, because you like to see Natsu!" Cali winked at the Lycan. Zila blushed before quickly looking away.

We continued walking until we came across a vast portion of farmlands. There was any vegetable you can think of growing. Along its edge, the farmland was lined with fruit trees, and to the right of me was a vineyard.

"Beautiful," I whispered.

"It truly is." Zila had a longing look on her face as we continued walking.

We entered a large field of sunflowers. They were extremely tall—taller than any of us girls.

"The Fae are farmers. They have the best green thumbs and grow everything. We come here when needed and pick out whatever food we want. Then they load it up on the ship for us. It will arrive tomorrow morning." Cali sighed as she ran her hands down a sunflower, admiring its beauty. "It's still a long way from here, so let's go ahead and gale. My feet hurt."

I chuckled at her. She wrapped her hands around my waist and smiled as we galed right outside of Magecrest. The town was booming with shops upon shops down the main strip. Vendors were lined up with their produce, spices, and lots of other things for sale.

"Anything you want is paid for by the king. Let's do some shopping, ladies," Cali said as she strolled off ahead of Zila and I.

We walked around for a while, picking out the food we needed and some rare spices the servants asked for. Everything that was being sent back to Castleva. Once we were done with the list, we decided to do a little personal shopping.

The first place we stopped at was a vendor that sold little trinkets. As my eyes wandered the table, they landed on a little bear carved out of wood. It made me think of Valarian and I smiled. I decided to purchase it for him as a silly gift.

We were standing in a different boutique when a man approached us. He was over six feet tall with deep brown hair and sandy beige skin. His eyes were a radiant amber color, which meant he was a Fae.

He was wearing perfectly pressed black trousers and a green tunic that was untied at the top, leaving the Guardian Mark in the middle of his chest visible. His tattoo was similar to the Angel's. It was a sword with dragonfly wings on each side and vines wrapping around the sword. It was black, which meant he wasn't knighted yet, but he would be someday.

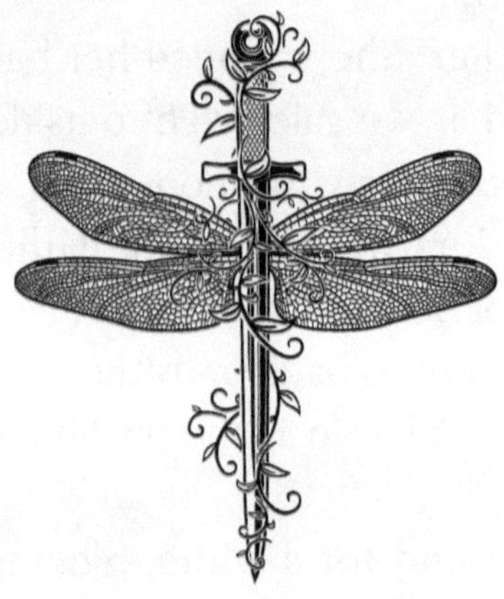

The Fae were born from the bloodline of Toberon, the God of the Sun.

I was used to seeing the Fae since they always unloaded the cargo ships back home when supplies were delivered and exchanged.

"Hello, Zila." He bowed to the beautiful Lycan. "Nice to see you once again." Her sparkling silver eyes met his as she blushed. She bowed her head to him elegantly. If she would have had a dress on instead of fighting leathers, I swear she would have curtsied.

"Hey, Natsu," Cali said with a huge, knowing smile on her face.

"Hi, Calista."

She gestured to me. "This is our new King's Guard, Ember Lavaris. She's a Fire Caster."

"Nice to meet you, I'm Natsu Amata. I'm a Fae, obviously, and a Weather Wielder." He smiled and extended his hand, and as I shook it, my eyes went wide.

"A Weather Wielder?"

"Yes, some of us Fae were blessed with the capabilities to wield weather elements and some of us can make plants grow tremendously in seconds."

"Wow. That's amazing!"

"Thank you, Ember." He immediately turned his attention toward Zila. "I must go for now. My father will have my head if I'm late. I'm one of the sailors loading up the ship with your supplies."

"We appreciate it." Zila smiled, her light gray eyes were longing to be with him. "Take care, Natsu."

"You take care as well." He bowed his head gallantly and briskly walked away.

"He was nice," I said, smiling at Zila.

"He was handsomely nice," Cali said, clapping her hands together.

Zila giggled while blushing. "Hush . . . both of you."

"Ember, you should come with us tomorrow night and meet some other nice guys!"

"Where at, Cali?"

"To Direbreak."

My eyes widened. "The Land of the Lycans?"

"Yep!" Zila said ecstatically.

After my portal ride today, I wasn't sure I wanted to go through hell again. "Why are you going there?"

"It's lonely being in the King's Guard, so every few months or so, we visit the other lands. Tonight just happens to be Zila's land. Next time it will be a different one."

"What will we do there?"

Calista smiled widely at my question. "We go to taverns and dance with men or women, drink, and have fun. Stop giving me that look, Ember!"

I tried to keep the anxiety-ridden look off my face. "I don't know if I'm up for that."

"Please come with us." Cali begged as she gave me her most perfect, sad face.

I sighed with defeat. "Fine. I'll go."

"Yay!" Cali clapped her hands together.

After we gathered our things, we galed back to the portal. I made sure not to hold my breath this time. Zila held my hand and I was grateful because it was intense.

Once we were back at the manor, I wanted to find Valarian. Cali told me which room he was in, down in the west wing, so I quickly found it. Taking a deep breath, I knocked.

Chapter Eleven

When Valarian opened the door, I couldn't help but wonder if I had made a mistake as I stared at his bare chest that was eye level to me. It was just as beautiful as he was. His muscles were even more well-defined up close. His arm was raised high in the air, stretching out his sexiness before me as he held the door. To say he was drop-dead gorgeous would have been an understatement.

"Oh. Sorry." I tried to swallow down the nervousness that hit me.

"Come on in. I just got out of the shower. I was sweaty from chopping wood." I quickly walked under his arm, checking my shield before I thought anything stupid. As he shut the door, my mouth dropped open at the sight of something marvelous. A huge skull tattoo completely covered his back.

Can he get any sexier? I had a vision of my tongue tracing his tattoo and had to put that thought out of my head quickly as he turned towards me.

"So, what's going on?"

"I got you something at the market today." I tried hard not to stare at his body.

"You did?" He gave me a surprised look as he tilted his head, like he was trying to figure me out. I hated the way he tilted his head. I'm lying, I actually loved it. I just hated that I loved it.

I held up the little bear with trembling hands. "Yes."

Reaching out, he took it from me. "Ha-ha, I'll have to buy a little bow and arrow to shoot him with."

I laughed and snorted at his words. To the Gods, I was so nervous. I was alone with him in his room and he was shirtless! The anxiety ridden part of me really wished he wasn't, but I was also grateful he was because it was glorious.

As he looked at the bear, my eyes went to his King's Guard tattoo. It was shiny gold—strong and beautiful, just like him. My eyes then drifted to the rock-hard muscles on his chest. I tried to force myself to stop looking, but I couldn't. Deep down, maybe I didn't want to. His body was a road map of beauty and I wanted to explore every inch of the land.

My eyes followed the trail down to the muscles on his stomach. They were well-defined—six muscles in the middle and smaller ones on each side. He had V-shaped cut lines going down the side of his stomach and into his pants.

V for Valarian, I thought. *Or valuables.* Since it led down to his valuables.

The small patch of hair that I had seen before trailed down his stomach to the edge of his loose gray lounge pants that were hanging low on his hips. I should stop before getting caught . . . or maybe I wanted him to catch me.

My eyes continued their journey south and I could see the outline of his . . . *Whoa.*

As the heat rose in my body, my breathing became heavy. My gaze darted up at his face. He was smiling seductively as he watched me. I most definitely got caught. I nervously bit my lip, trying *not* to react as I stared into his eyes.

Sexy, dangerous, violet eyes. I swallowed hard. *Nope, not looking there either.*

He laughed lightly and embarrassment filled me. I immediately threw my shield back up and pretended like that didn't just happen.

"So, this is your room?"

When he didn't answer, I met his eyes and he was smiling. "Yep."

That was a stupid question, of course it was his room. My emotions were too out of control to keep my shield up. I realized that I was the worst, stealthiest person ever born. I couldn't keep my eyes or my thoughts to myself. Trying to find something to focus on, my eyes landed on his massive bed. It had silky black sheets with a matching blanket.

Even his bed is sexy. Looking back at his face, he was grinning with amusement because he had heard me again. *I'm in deep here.*

As if my thoughts were turning him on, he lightly licked his lips and I about came unglued.

Shit. I threw my shield up as my nerves threatened to consume me.

My heart was racing and I had an aching between my legs that immediately needed to be attended to. I tried everything I could to avoid looking at his body, looking at him at all.

He knew exactly what he was doing to me, which made me want to rip his clothes off. Glancing down at his hips, he was big and hard now, right where it mattered. I let out a whimper as my lips parted.

Oh, Gods, so sexy. Look away. There's a chair.

"That's a nice chair," I said, avoiding him as much as possible. "I bet it's comfortable."

"Would you like to sit in the chair?"

Maybe I should sit. Do I want to sit? I don't know.

"You don't have to sit if you don't want to," he said, making my eyes meet his.

"Oh, I truly do want to sit. I just don't know if now is . . . if it is the right time to . . . sit."

"Are we still talking about the chair?" he asked and I blushed.

I am highly sure that the chair is not what I want to sit on.

He snickered before setting the bear on his dresser. I threw my shield back up . . . again. He took two steps toward me and I panicked. I needed to get out of his room before I bared my soul to him—my naked body to him—even if he didn't ask.

"I must get ready. There is dinner."

He took a couple more steps, closing the distance between us. "It's early afternoon, love." His voice was sultry, deep.

Oh, he was so good at this game and *I was losing.*

"Yes, well, I must go either way. Goodbye."

My brain must have shut down because I had no idea what I was saying. Practically tripping over my feet, I headed toward the door and grabbed the handle. He walked up behind me and put his hand on it, stopping the door from opening.

He was standing so close to me that I could feel his breath on the top of my head. My breathing was heavy and I was feeling hot everywhere. A part of me wished he would just take me.

"Hey, Ember." His voice was powerful, commanding me not to move. I was pretty sure that if he told me to strip naked right there and dance through the gardens with him, I would have done it without hesitation.

"Yes," I said, my voice coming out in a panicked whisper.

"Thank you for the bear," he said in a sensual voice. One that was inviting me to stay, I was pretty sure.

His hand brushed some of my hair away from my shoulder, right before he leaned down and kissed me on the side of my jaw, almost on my neck. Closing my eyes, I enjoyed every second of it as his wet lips grazed my face gently—his hot breath bouncing off my skin. It was so close to my ear that I heard the kiss loudly. I let out a low, breathy moan.

When his body pressed lightly up against mine, I felt his bulge on my butt cheek. I sucked in a hard breath.

Oh, Gods. He's inviting me to stay.

My cheeks flushed as heat ran from my face, all the way down to the apex of my legs. My core tingled as I swallowed the wetness down that was filling my mouth. My panties were equally wet and I needed to get out of here.

His breath was heavy on my body and I could have sworn he blew air toward my ear on purpose. I tilted my head further, showing him more of my neck. I was inviting him to take me . . . but he didn't.

He hesitated for a few seductive breaths before pulling away and finally removing his hand from the door. He was giving me an out—letting me decide what I wanted. Stay or leave. It was clear what he wanted—he wanted me to stay.

Contemplating what I truly desired, I waited for a few more breaths before opening the door.

"You're welcome." I managed to muster myself enough for those two words before I retreated, slamming his door behind me.

Practically running to my room like I was being chased, I went inside and shut the door. The feeling that was flowing through my body was exhilarating. My heart was still racing and I had butterflies in my stomach.

Lust was overflowing—lighting my senses on fire. I wanted to go back to his room so I could rip those gray lounge pants off and see what was trying to show itself to me . . . but I didn't.

Why did I leave? That wasn't what I wanted.

He had kissed me, kissed my jaw. I reached my hand up and placed it to where his lips had been. As I thought of him, I had the biggest smile.

Thinking of his hard chest, I slowly slid my hand down my neck, across my breast, and squeezed it. They were full and achy. My nipples were hard and just as excited as I was.

Continuing my dirty thoughts, I ran my hand across my stomach and slowly down to where I ached. It felt amazing as I rubbed between my legs. I pictured Valarian's hands there, making me feel good—making me feel alive.

My clit twitched with excitement as heat poured through me. I moaned from the pleasure.

Not being able to stand it anymore, I hurriedly undressed, ripping my clothes off as I headed to the bathroom. I spent some alone time in the bathtub with myself and my imagination, easing the pain between my legs. I thought of Valarian the whole time.

Chapter Twelve

The next day, I was happy that I didn't have class. It was my day off from practice, so I had spent the morning writing to my sister. Since I had been here, I had sent several casual notes checking on her. She was still doing well and was loving her job. She said she now has a huge passion for making baked goods. I was extremely happy for her and was grateful she had something to occupy her mind.

In the letter, I told her a little about the people here. I also explained that Vampires weren't as evil as our father made them out to be. I still hadn't asked Valarian what he meant about my father *not* being noble. I left that part out when I wrote to her. But I had, however, decided to come clean and tell her that I had a crush on Val.

Once I read her last note, I got dressed and headed down to the library with my book in my hand. Since I had finished this one, I needed a new one to read. It would hopefully keep my mind off Valarian.

Turning into the hall, my eyes went wide in shock when I saw two Angels standing there shirtless. Their golden tattoos and chiseled chests were eye level to me. I really wished I were taller sometimes.

"Hey, Red," Zayn said with a smile. "We're going swimming. Do you want to come?"

Cash and Zayn both had rock-hard bodies. Cash had bulky thick muscles, and Zayn had leaner ones, but both were sexy. Not as sexy as Valarian, but close. I quickly checked my shield, not knowing if he was around, and remembering to practice. To my surprise, it was still up.

"I don't have a bathing suit," I answered nervously.

"I knew you would say that." Cali came around the corner, smiling and holding up a black bathing suit. It was in two pieces, just like the one she was shamelessly wearing, but hers was blue. It went beautifully with her eye color. "I was just headed to get you."

My mouth about hit the floor. *I don't even want to show my knees, and she thinks I want to show my whole body?*

"It's our day off. We're going and so are you. Here." She handed me the suit. I took it sheepishly. "And I knew you were going to complain, so here's a towel to cover yourself with until we get to the water." She smiled. I cried inside as I yanked it from her hands.

"Hell yeah! Let's go." Cash was super excited.

Quickly heading to the hallway bathroom, I sat my book on a table I had walked past and changed into the bathing suit. For the love of the Gods, this was like a pair of panties and a tiny top. I put the towel around me before I walked out.

"Damn, Ember." Cash let out a whistle.

"To the Gods!" I said, while putting my hands over my face. I dropped them and immediately blushed. "Someone please kill me."

Zayn's eyebrows shot up when he saw my uncomfortable face. He stepped in front of me, blocking my body from sight. "Shut up, Cash."

"Let's go before Ember changes her mind." Cali grabbed my hand and dragged me to the door.

Once we were outside, I fell in stride with Zayn while the others walked ahead.

"So, Zayn . . . who's all going?"

"All seven of us."

Shit! "Oh. I didn't know that."

"It'll be fun, Red."

"I'm going to be embarrassed," I whispered as we rounded the back of the manor.

"Why would you be embarrassed? You look great."

"Well, thank you. I'm just nervous."

He gave me a sympathetic look. "Because Val is coming."

My eyes went wide. "Why would you think that?"

"I don't know. Just an assumption." He smiled teasingly at me and winked a blue eye.

"It's not like that."

"Keep telling yourself that," he said. My mouth dropped open, and he laughed. "It's okay to like him, you know?"

My response was quick. "I don't like him."

"Are you sure? We're friends now. You can be honest with me, even if you can't be honest with yourself."

I sighed. "Is it bad if I do?"

"Not at all," he said sweetly. "Why would it be?"

"What if he doesn't like me?"

"I mean, would you rather not try and miss an opportunity or take a risk and possibly have something magical?"

I scrunched up my nose. "The magical stuff sounds cheesy, Zayn."

"I'm a man and I don't think it's cheesy."

"You read romance novels, so you're not a normal male."

"Hey now!" He ran his hand through his shaggy hair. "I read those for educational purposes."

"Sure you do. You're just a softy, even if you can't be honest with yourself." I threw his own words back to him as I grinned in accomplishment.

"And you're an evil redheaded spawn," he replied. We both laughed hard as I felt the tingle of the edge of the wards.

Once we were past them, we met up with Zila, Asher, and Valarian. I immediately felt embarrassed and wanted to die when I saw them. I made sure my shield was still up.

Asher gave me a surprised face as he cracked his knuckles, then quickly looked away. Valarian looked down at my towel-wrapped body. He raised his eyebrows as one side of his lips curled up. I quickly averted my eyes.

Looking around, my eyes landed on Zila. Since she was in a bathing suit, I could see her King's Guard tattoo on her chest. It was a quarter moon with a wolf's head over it. The wolf had its mouth open like it was howling. It was a beautiful tattoo.

"I love your tattoo, Zila."

"Thank you. It's Strength in Transformation," she said with a smile. "I love yours too, Ember."

"Let's go have some fun!" Cash said and galed away. Then Zila and Asher galed too.

I locked eyes with Valarian and dropped my shield. *I want a female to take me.*

"Cali, can you take Ember?" Valarian galed away, as did Zayn.

"You look amazing. Don't worry. It's just friends having fun." Cali put her arms around me and galed us.

My mouth was immediately agape when we landed. It was not the beachy ocean by the bonfire that we were swimming in. We were standing on rocky terrain and looking down into what looked like a water-filled crater. The view was just as scary as it was phenomenal.

I wondered how we would get down there since we couldn't gale over water, but then Asher ran and jumped off the side. I gasped as he fell through the air, then hit the water. It was a far drop. My heart raced with fear and excitement.

Cash jumped next. He let out a loud "Woo hoo!" as he was falling.

Then, to my surprise, shy, sweet Zila ran and jumped. She pulled her knees up into her body, and as she fell, she let go, rotated, and dove into the water headfirst.

Whoa.

Valarian looked at me with a curious face. I dropped my shields as I met his eyes.

I can't do this.

He prowled toward me. "It's not as high as it seems, only about thirty feet. You can try galing as far as it will let you. You'll be a little closer. Probably about ten feet over the edge, but you'll still be close to this height."

"Come on, Ember." Cali took off running and jumped. She did a somersault, then dove into the water.

"Ember, do you want me to wait for you?" Zayn asked.

"You go ahead, Zayn." I smiled, trying to fake being okay. I was far from it.

Zayn smiled before he took off running and dove into the water.

"You don't have to do this if you don't want to, love." I looked up and met Valarian's breathtaking eyes. "But I have a feeling you're going to love it. You just have to try first."

"I can't physically make myself, Valarian." My body was trembling as he moved in close to me.

"Would you like me to hold you?" The thought of being in his arms did make me feel safer.

"If you don't mind. I mean, you don't have to."

He didn't hesitate as he grabbed my hand. "Come on, before you change your mind." He pulled me over to the edge. "Are you taking the towel?" I looked down at the death grip I had on the towel.

My hands slid to where I had tied it at the top. I pulled it apart and dropped it. Valarian glanced down at my body. His eyes went wide as he quickly observed every part of me.

He ran a hand over the back of his head and cleared his throat. He seemed slightly nervous. It made me smile. "May I?"

He was once again asking permission to touch me. I didn't answer him. Instead, I closed the distance and put my arms around his waist. My body was still shaking, and I hoped that holding onto him would stop it. Plus, I enjoyed being close to him and smelling his skin.

He wrapped his arms around me and met my eyes. I could feel every inch of his warm body on mine as I looked up at him. My lungs suddenly felt like I couldn't get enough air.

"Ready?"

I laid my cheek against his chest and closed my eyes. His heart was beating fast—just as fast as mine, surprisingly. "Yes."

He galed us about ten feet out over the edge, and then we dropped. The rush was exhilarating—the wind flying past my body and then a splash into the water. Valarian let go of me and I let go of him. I had sunk about ten or fifteen feet before I started to swim up. I broke the surface of the water and took a breath. Valarian swam up next to me as I was wiping water from my face.

"Well?"

"That was amazing! Even better than killing a bear!"

"Good job, Red. I'm proud!" Zayn said excitedly.

"Woo hoo! Go, Ember!" Cash yelled from about twenty feet away from me. He was the most excited, carefree person I had ever met. Cali was clapping.

I laughed at my friends and then looked into Valarian's eyes. "Thank you."

"Do you want to go again?"

I didn't even have to think about the answer. "Absolutely," I said with a huge smile on my face.

We swam up to the rocky area along the edge. I climbed out of the water first, then slid and almost fell back into Valarian. He assisted me by pushing up on my butt, right before it almost smacked him in the face. I didn't even feel embarrassed about it. I had a curvy ass, and the thrill of his hands there had me excited.

Once we were standing up on the small rocks next to the water, I caught Valarian looking at me again. It felt good being the one who was looked at instead of being the looker. Okay, I was looking too. Every chance I got, I was checking out his chest and stomach muscles. I was also looking at other things lower that seemed impressive behind wet shorts. For once, I was doing good at being stealthy, making sure he didn't notice me. He, on the other hand, wasn't being as subtle. I locked eyes with him after he looked at my breasts.

"I'm sorry about touching your . . ." He suddenly seemed shy as he ran his hand across the stubble on his face. "Uh, for touching you."

"It's fine." His shyness excited me and I smiled brightly.

He put his arms around me and galed us back up to the top.

"Are you going with me or alone?" I wanted to go with him, but I also wanted to go alone to prove that I could.

Once again, I didn't answer his question. Locked on his eyes, I gave him a mischievous smile, then took off running as fast as I could and jumped off the ledge. I pulled my knees up and flew, then landed in the water. I was swimming up to the surface when there was a splash next to me. Valarian had jumped too. We both resurfaced from the water.

"You did it!" he said while smoothing his black hair back and removing water from his face.

"I did! I can't believe it."

"You're fiercer than you give yourself credit for, Ember." His words did things to me. They made me believe in myself. They also made me excited, hot, vulnerable, and everything in between.

Without even thinking, I threw my hands around his neck and hugged him. Surprising me, he wrapped his hands around my waist under the water and hugged me back.

"Thank you for saying that," I whispered into his neck.

Happiness poured through me as I pulled back and looked at him. He was smiling and so was I.

"Want to see something amazing, love?"

My heart sped up as my eyes wandered curiously around his face. "Always."

"Come on, then." He let go of me and swam off. I followed close behind him.

We swam over to the rocks and he climbed up first this time. He reached down a hand and helped me out of the water. I was a curvy girl, but he barely pulled on me like I weighed nothing. He was so incredibly strong.

"Thank you."

"No problem. It's this way." He nodded his head in the direction we were going.

We walked along the rocks and went into a small cave. I had to duck down to get inside. Once we were in, the air was cooler. There was a small pool of water that was formed from a tiny waterfall. There was moss trickling down and around the stream of water. I gasped at the beauty of it.

"This is amazing," I said, my eyes going wide with wonder.

"Yeah, it is." He smiled as he leaned against a wall, watching me.

Looking at how beautiful it was and unable to contain myself, I carefully made my way over to the small waterfall and went underneath it. My breath caught and I gasped at how cold it was. I didn't realize the water would be colder inside of here than it was out there. I ran out from under the waterfall and almost fell as I headed back toward Valarian.

Goosebumps formed on my skin and I was shivering. "I didn't know it would be that cold."

"Here, this might help." He ran his hands up and down my arms, trying to warm me. As I looked up at his gorgeous face, Zayn's words replayed in my head and I decided to be brave.

Holding his gaze, I stepped in closer. I lightly licked my lips, preparing them for what I was about to do.

Placing my palms on his chest, I ran my hands up slowly as I stared into his beautiful eyes. He leaned down slightly toward me like he was offering. My lips were mere inches from his, both of our breaths rapid.

His facial expression showed me that he wanted this just as much as I did. My heart thundered against my chest as I felt his breath on my face.

This was my moment to be fierce like he said I was. To be brave and do what I wanted to do without thinking of the consequences. So I did. I slid my hands around his neck, stood on my tippy toes to close in on his mouth, and kissed him.

Nervousness filled my body from my actions, but it eased when he kissed me back. One of his hands went into my wet hair and grabbed it, pulling me closer to his mouth as he consumed me.

My body was on fire as I ran my hands down his hard muscles and around to his back, pulling him even closer. We were both into it, and it started getting extremely passionate. At that moment, I would have laid myself on the cave floor, bare for him, if he asked me to.

He slid his tongue into my mouth, it was warm and wet, and felt amazing. I decided to add a little bit of tongue too, so I slid mine into his mouth and rolled it around. A slight moan left my body. Shock hit me when I felt a fang lightly graze my tongue, so I pulled away.

"I'm sorry." I was breathless and scared, but somehow, the danger was exciting.

"For what?" He looked confused. His breathing was just as heavy as mine was. His hands were still on me, still entangled in my hair.

"For kissing you, I didn't mean to. I shouldn't have done that." I was scared. Not because I feared him or his fangs. I was afraid because I liked it. I reminded myself to make sure my shield was tight.

"Don't ever be sorry for that," he whispered.

The hand on my lower back pulled me in and the other tightened in my hair as he leaned toward my face. My mouth slightly parted, ready for him to kiss me again. My body willed itself closer to his. I would never be able to resist him, I realized. His lips barely brushed against mine when I heard Cash speak.

"What are you guys doing in there?" I jumped in shock and pulled out of Valarian's arms as I glanced toward the opening of the cave. Cash's shadow was cast across the cave floor as he squatted down. I quickly stepped further away from Valarian as the Angel entered the cave.

"Nothing, just talking to my buddy, that's all," I said.

Valarian's eyebrows furrowed together in confusion as he looked at my panicked face.

"Yep, just talking to *my buddy*." He smiled at Cash, bent down, and left the cave. He didn't even look back at me.

Fuck.

"So, Ember." Cash stood there grinning mischievously. "Do you want to go skinny dipping?"

I sighed. I had a love-hate relationship with that Angel.

"Shut up, Cash." I punched him in the arm and laughed.

"Ow, you hit pretty hard for a trainee." He rubbed his arm as I bent down to leave the cave. "I was being serious, though."

"To the Gods, Cash. I will stab you!"

"That might be fun too," he said as we emerged into the sunlight once again.

I shook my head at him. "Not going to happen."

Cash grinned before he ran and jumped into the water. I made my way back to the edge and took a seat. I sat there quietly for a while as I watched everyone having fun.

Valarian swam around with the other men, who were all goofing off—taking turns jumping, and trying to dunk each other. Asher was using his air magic to make the water rise like mist. It was amazing to see. Zila and Cali got out and were sunbathing.

After a while, I got back in the water but mainly stayed away from the group of males. I was swimming alone for a while, then I floated around thinking about everything. I wasn't sure if I should have kissed Valarian or not, but no matter what happens from here, I wouldn't regret it.

We swam for a little longer and then gathered to leave. I didn't converse with Valarian again—I also tried not to look at him, either. I knew where I was going, so when everyone started galing home, I galed myself.

Confusion was eating me from the inside out. I liked him, but I didn't want to make things awkward. I would have to live in the same house as him for many years. We don't mate where we live, that's what Cali said.

Everyone stood outside of the manor, talking and laughing when we arrived home. I secretly took off and walked back to my room. I couldn't stop thinking about the kiss.

Once I was back, I took off my wet bathing suit and hung it in the bathroom to dry. I threw on some lounge clothes and plopped on my bed. Since I had left my book downstairs on the hall table, I had nothing to do. I guess I would have to visit the library.

My heart raced in fear or hope that Valarian was at my door when I heard a knock. Hopping out of bed, I quickly walked over and opened it.

"Oh, hey, Zayn. Come in."

"What happened?" he asked before he was even in the room.

I quickly shut the door so no one could hear. "What do you mean?"

"You were having fun and then you went into a cave with Val. When you came out, you clammed up. You avoided everyone, and swam alone, and—"

"Okay, okay." I put my hand up. "I get it."

"So, what happened, Red?" he asked with a concerned look on his face.

"I kissed Valarian."

"Oh." His face was surprised, then he smiled.

"Yeah." I looked down at my feet.

"Well, did you like it?"

"Maybe a little too much." I blushed when I looked up at the Angel.

"Did he like it?"

"Yes, I think so."

His eyebrows furrowed together. "Then what's the problem?"

"Well, for one, Cash came in and interrupted us, so I practically ran away."

"Why would you run away?"

I sighed and shook my head. "I don't know. I just don't think it's anyone's business."

"Okay. What else?"

"I felt a fang against my tongue."

"Oh. Well . . ." He stood there in contemplation, like he was carefully choosing his words. "I haven't kissed a Vampire yet, but I think that's to be expected."

"That wasn't the real problem." I bit my lip.

"Did it scare you?"

"No, completely the opposite." I could feel my face flush as my cheeks got hot. "I liked it a lot."

"That may not be a bad thing." Zayn winked, and we both laughed.

"Shut up. I'm being vulnerable here."

"I'm sorry, Red. I'm just teasing."

"I know." I let out a slow breath. "I'm just confused."

"That's understandable. Val is one of my best friends, I'm sure if you tell him how you feel—"

"I will *not* and neither can you! Promise me."

"Of course, I won't. I don't want you after me. You're mean."

I went to punch his arm, but he grabbed my wrist before I made contact and pulled me close. He hugged me like a sibling would, crushing me in a headlock. I laughed and wiggled away.

"Don't be hard on my friend, Ember! We don't need a Vampire running around with a broken heart."

"Maybe you two can read romance novels and cry together."

"Evil, pure evil. I love it." Zayn put his hand up and I high-fived it. "I have stuff to do. We'll talk later."

"Later, Softy."

"Later, Demon Spawn."

After he left, I went down and finally exchanged my book. I ran back up to my room and engulfed myself in a new world of romance and passion for the rest of the evening.

Chapter Thirteen

I t was a gloomy day as I sat on my bed, reading my sister's latest letter. The rain was beating against the window when I glanced up and noticed the time. I had to meet Valarian for practice, so I wouldn't have time to write her back until later.

The kiss was all I could think about last night and this morning. As I jogged down to the training center, I was still thinking about it while getting soaked with rain. It was almost surreal that I kissed him, and I still couldn't believe that I had done it.

We don't mate where we live . . . that's what Cali said. As I continued to replay her words, I had convinced myself that she was right. It would be awkward afterward if we decided to part ways, especially since he was my trainer.

When I walked into the training center, Valarian was standing there with his arms crossed. He noticed how rain-soaked I was and immediately grabbed a towel and threw it at me.

"You're soaking wet, Ember." I blushed at his words as I caught the towel.

"You must have heightened senses. I didn't think that you would notice," I said, sarcasm lining my voice.

"I always notice when a woman is wet." He smiled big and I could see his fangs. Needing to hide my lust-filled expression, I quickly ran the towel over my face.

"We're going to try something new today. Take a seat on the floor."

"Oh, really now." I laid the towel out on the floor and took a seat, crossing my legs. The taste and feel of his lips were all I could think about and it had me grinning like a fool.

"You keep dropping your shield to speak to me. Now that you can keep it up for longer, it's time to learn this."

"Okay."

Are you ready?

"Wait, what? What was that?" I was confused by hearing Val's voice, but not seeing his mouth move.

He had an excited smile on his face. *Don't talk. Use your mind to speak to me, Ember.*

I dropped my shield. *This is weird.*

Shield up, I heard in my head.

"I can't talk to you with it up."

Yes, you can if you wield the thought to me. If you let your shield drop, other Vampires will be able to hear you. If you keep it intact, we can converse like this in private. No one will be able to hear our conversation but us. When you think of a thought that you want me to hear, just think about saying it to me. It's easy. Try it.

I put my shield back up. *Can you hear me?* I thought while thinking about saying it to Valarian.

Yes, I can. He took a seat on the floor in front of me and crossed his legs.

Can you hear my other thoughts this way? I was hoping he knew what I meant.

I can't. I can only hear what you want me to hear when you wield your thoughts to me. Any other thoughts you have, stay unheard. Your secrets are safe if your shield stays up. He smiled again.

"Whoa," I said aloud.

Ember, focus.

I love the way he says my name. I checked to make sure my shield was tight. It was. *Did you hear that?* I wielded the question to him.

Maybe. What did you say again? He looked at me suspiciously and I smiled.

Nope, I can't tell my secrets. He shook his head with a light laugh. *Can I talk to Zayn like this?*

You can't, but I can. Only Vampires can do this with others. It's a good thing to have if we are ever in a situation where we cannot speak. This is how you can communicate with me. If you are ever in danger and I'm nearby, you can inform me.

Or if we are at the dinner table and I want to make fun of you without the others knowing, I teased.

He laughed. *That too.*

"Alright, time is up for today," he spoke aloud as he stood up off the ground.

"That is the coolest thing I have learned since I learned to wield a dagger!" I said as excitement filled me. He extended his hand to me and helped me off the floor.

"Do you get out much?"

"Hush your mouth." I punched his arm. "Do you?"

"Nah, and I'm okay with it."

Worry about the kiss filled me and I knew I had to bring it up. "So, Valarian."

"Yes, Ember?" He tilted his head like he was waiting for the conversation.

"Are we going to talk about what happened?"

"I assumed you didn't want to, since you didn't *mean* to kiss me."

"Oh, so we are good, then?"

"Sure. We're good, buddy." He turned and quickly walked away.

Did he just call me buddy?

The rain was a light sprinkle now as I walked back toward the manor. My morning class with Val was usually my favorite part of the day but I had a feeling he was mad at me. Especially since today's class was *extremely* short. I didn't know what I did or said. Maybe he was mad because I kissed him or it could have been because I freaked out when Cash came into the cave. I sighed. It was probably because I was sending mixed signals, since I didn't even know what I wanted.

When I got back to my room, I changed into dry pajamas and hung out for a while. I was trying to read my book, but I barely got a few chapters in because I kept wondering about the kiss.

Once it was evening, Cali and Zila came down. They were both ready to go and were now waiting for me to come out of the bathroom to show them what my outfit looked like—an outfit Cali had brought down and *insisted* I wear.

"You have got to be kidding me!" I said through the bathroom door.

"It's not that bad, Ember," Cali said.

"I look like I should be going to a brothel!"

"We may do that."

I let out a hard breath. "Not funny, Cali."

"I wasn't kidding. It's been a while since I visited those sexy ladies."

"I don't mind going to one, but I don't want to look like I work at one," I said as I slung the bathroom door open.

"Sexy!" Cali clapped her hands excitedly.

"You actually do look sexy, Ember." Zila gave me the sweetest smile as her luminous silver eyes showed kindness.

"Thanks."

All three of us girls were dressed similarly. Cali had on a pink lace top that showed off her Angel tattoo, paired with a short black skirt and low-cut matching boots. She also had a dagger strapped to the belt on her hip. She looked very sexy and underdressed.

Zila had on a tan shirt, a longer skirt that went to her knees, and a cute pair of flats. She was sexy too, but in a more modest way. She didn't seem to have a weapon on her. I guess you don't need one when you can transform into a wolf.

Currently, I was wearing a knee-length skirt, but mine hugged my thighs. It had a slit about halfway up one of them. I did strap my dagger onto my leg—the one with the slit—since I never left home without it. My top was gray and semi-low-cut and my boots were black and went to my mid-calf. I quickly threw a black leather jacket over it.

Cali sighed. "Don't do that, it throws off the aesthetics of the whole outfit."

"I'm at least taking it in case I get uncomfortable!"

"Fine. Let's go, ladies."

Zila and I followed Cali out of the manor and I was glad the rain had stopped. I was under the assumption that this was an all-girls trip, so I was completely caught off guard when I saw all four of my guy friends standing there. Each of them wore trousers and button-up shirts, except Valarian. He was wearing a short-sleeved black cotton shirt and I could see his muscles.

"Damn, we're going with the finest women around," Cash said, grinning like the fool he was.

"It's about time. Come on, ladies." Zayn said with a big smile on his face. "You all look lovely, by the way."

Locking eyes with Valarian, his face was pleasantly surprised. I bit my lip to keep from smiling as I stepped onto the portal. He moved over to me and leaned in close to my face.

"You look delicious, love."

"As do you. Oh, I mean . . ." I smiled nervously at him.

"I'd rather you be in a bathing suit, but this is sexy, too." My mouth dropped open as the portal was willed to go.

Valarian had distracted me so much that I completely forgot how much the portal makes me sick. My body started to sway and I slammed my eyes shut. I felt a hand touch my lower back to help steady me. Nausea rose as the hand rubbed up and down soothing me. Then we landed.

"Are you okay?" Valarian asked with his hand still on my back.

Opening my eyes, they met him. "I'm fine." I let out a slow breath, trying to push the nausea down.

"Just breathe." He rubbed his hand up and down once more.

"I can soothe you, Red. But, if I do, you'll never get used to it."

"No, I will be fine. You all go ahead. I'll catch up."

We exited the portal and I walked to the side of it by some trees and leaned against one, using it to hold my body up. My group walked about twenty feet away to give me room, but they didn't leave me. Everyone except for Valarian. He walked over to the trees with me.

"I'm fine. You don't have to stand with me." I didn't want him near me in case I got sick.

"I don't mind." He crossed his arms in that lazy stance of his. His muscles tightened under his shirt and I looked away as I made sure my shield was up. After taking a couple of deep breaths, I felt good enough to continue our journey.

"I'm good now."

He walked quietly next to me while we caught up with our friends. Taking in the sights of the land around us, I noticed there was an abundance of pine trees. It was hard to see much since nightfall had come, but it was beautiful from what I saw in the moonlight.

"Alright, we're all here. We're going to gale outside Hallowshade's wards." Zayn's eyes met mine. "Do you want me to gale you since you don't know where we're going?"

I glanced at Valarian and then back to Zayn. "Sure."

Zayn put his arms around my waist and we landed at the edge of Hallowshade.

As we walked through town, I noticed that all the little shops had closed for the evening. They had an active town, from what I could see.

We stopped at a busy building. It was a saloon that was made entirely of wood logs. Little lanterns were hanging at the entrance. The sound of music, talking, and laughter was pouring out from the establishment.

After we went through the saloon doors, my eyes immediately did a sweep of the room. Everything inside was also made of wood. There were people playing games and drinking beer while others danced to a live band. It looked like they served food as well. The place looked fun.

A man whistled loudly and the music stopped. The entire bar went quiet as everyone turned toward us. I froze, my eyes darting around. I noticed there were a lot of Lycan here, but I also saw the eyes of Fae, Elven, and Casters.

An older gentleman, a Lycan, went up onto the stage area and I confusedly looked at my friends. Each of them were smiling like they were expecting what was going to happen.

"Everyone, please welcome back the King's Guard!" he yelled, and everyone clapped and some started howling.

Then the band started playing again. The older Lycan made his way over to us, went straight up to Zila, and kissed her on the cheek. "Hi, sis. Are you faring well?"

"I am, brother."

His eyes landed on me. "Who is this?"

"Kage, this is Ember Lavaris, our newest King's Guard member. Ember, this is my older brother."

"Kage Moonfall. Nice to make your acquaintance. Welcome to my place, the Howling Moon Saloon." He gracefully took my hand and placed a gentle kiss on the back of it. "You are one gorgeous woman. I swear the King's Guard has the most beautiful females from all the lands in one spot."

"Aww, thank you." I giggled slightly as I blushed. "It's nice to meet you too."

"I need a drink." Valarian strolled off toward the bar and Cash followed him.

"You ladies and gentlemen enjoy yourselves tonight. We'll catch up later, sis. Nice to see you again, Cali." He kissed her hand, and for once, the Angel blushed. She stayed quiet as she smiled. Her blue eyes seemed to sparkle at the Lycan male. "A pleasure, as always, Zayn and Asher." He smiled as he headed toward the stage, grabbed a guitar, and started playing with the band.

"Let's drink and eat!" Asher cracked his knuckles, then walked toward the bar. I followed everyone.

"Here." Val handed me a drink as soon as I got to the bar. "I got you this."

"Oh. Thank you." I took a big swig of it and the burning sensation made me cough.

Val shook his head with a laugh. "Easy there, killer."

"What is this?" I made a disgusting face as shivers went through my body.

"It's whiskey."

"Ember is a girl, V. She needs wine!" Cali reached for my drink to take it and I pulled it closer to me.

"No, I'm fine with whiskey!" I smiled and took another sip, then coughed again. Val laughed as I made another face and shivered.

"I ordered four pizzas, wings, and fries." Cash smiled proudly.

"That's a lot of food," Cali said.

"That's just mine. Did you guys want something?" Cash teased with a wink and Cali rolled her eyes at him.

"Good, I'm starving." Asher rubbed his stomach.

"I got us a table," Zila said as she walked up, so we followed her.

The night went by fast. We ate food, drank liquor, and laughed. After our friends took off, I was sitting at a table alone with Valarian.

Deciding to see what everyone was up to, I glanced around. Cash was climbing the stairs to the stage and I wondered what he was doing. My eyes went wide when he picked up a guitar and started playing with the band. I was shocked at how beautiful it sounded; he played exceptionally well. It was weird it was to see this big, bulky man playing the tiny, thin strings.

"I didn't know that Cash played guitar," I said as I glanced at Val.

"He learned to play because of a bet."

My face scrunched up in confusion. "What do you mean?"

"We were at a bonfire one night and Cash was fiddling around with a guitar. Zayn bet he couldn't learn to play because of his big hands. Being the man he is, Cash took the bet to prove Zayn wrong. Obviously, Zayn lost."

"How much did Zayn have to pay?"

"Oh, they didn't bet money. The loser had to run around the outside of the manor, all the way to the garden and back, naked."

My mouth dropped open. "No way. To the Gods?"

"To the Gods. Zayn did it proudly. All of us guards, the servants, and even the king watched the event." Val laughed hard.

"Are you serious? The king?" I threw my hand over my mouth as I giggled.

"Dead serious. Those two will bet anything."

"I'll keep that in mind."

Locking eyes with him, he smiled. It sent shivers through my body, and I quickly looked away. My eyes landed on the dance floor and I noticed some of our friends were dancing. Asher was dancing with Zila and they were acting like fools. I smiled at their silliness. Cali was dancing with a girl, then they kissed.

"I didn't know Cali liked women."

"She likes people for who they are, not what they are. She's a free spirit."

"I think that's fantastic." Watching my friends, they seemed to be enjoying themselves. "They look like they're having fun."

"Why don't you go dance?"

Meeting his eyes, I smiled. "I may in a bit, Val."

"Val?"

"Is that not your name?" I downed the last of my glass of whiskey. I was feeling good. Maybe a little too good.

Picking up his glass, Val smiled before downing it. He put his hand up and made a gesture at the bartender. That was his second glass, mine was only my first.

"You usually call me Valarian, I was just caught off guard."

"Well, I assumed, since we're civil now, that you would be okay with me calling you Val." I gave him a flirtatious smile and for the love of the Gods, I decided to bat my eyelashes at him.

"Civil? Is that what we are?" A teasing grin spread across his face.

"Yes, very civil." As I smiled widely and leaned in closer to him. Alcohol had me completely letting my guard down.

The bartender came up and set two glasses on the table. I saw Val stiffen slightly. Wondering why, I looked up.

"Thank you, Libby."

"Yes, thank you." I smiled at her. She was a beautiful blonde-haired Lycan.

"You're welcome," she said to us. "What are you doing after this, Val? Do you want to come by?" She gave him a flirtatious smile.

Oh. So they had . . . Oh.

Val looked at me nervously and I smiled at him as I stood up.

"I think I shall dance." I picked up my fresh glass of whiskey and downed the whole thing.

To the God's, it burned. I slammed the glass back down and slowly wiped my lips off with my fingers while staring at Valarian.

Asshole, I said, knowing only he could hear it. Then I strolled off onto the dance floor.

Once I left the table, I didn't look back. The music was enjoyable, so I started dancing like I didn't have a care in the world. It was probably because I'd had *way* too much whiskey—that and I was angry.

Forgetting my worries, I was having fun dancing alone when a male Fae came up and started dancing with me. It was a fast song and he never touched me, so I didn't care. Two songs later, it turned slow. He moved in close to me. Shaking my head, I turned to walk away. He grabbed my arm and held me there.

"Just one song," he said.

"No. I would like to sit down now."

He pulled me closer to him, completely making my body touch his. "Oh, come on." He gave me a seductive smile.

My hand went to reach for my dagger, but as soon as I touched it, the male was whipped away from me.

"She said no!" Valarian was in the Fae's face. "Do you understand what it means when a woman tells you no?" Shock filled me when a loud growl left him.

What the hell was that?

"Are you mated to her?" the Fae asked.

"She's a King's Guard and my friend. She also said no!"

"If you aren't mated, then it's not your business, Valarian!"

The Fae turned toward me and before he had a chance even to make eye contact, I punched him in his face—just like Val taught me. His hand went up to his nose in shock. Val had a sexy smirk on his face as he watched the blood pour out of the Fae's nose.

Yanking my dagger from its sheath, I held it up to his neck.

"I said no!" The Fae took two steps back and bumped into a smiling Val. He looked between us, trying to figure out which one of us was scarier.

"You are starting trouble again, Morgan!" Kage walked up between us. "You know what I told you last time. Get out of my bar and don't come back!"

The Fae puffed his chest like he was going to challenge the Lycan. I heard a low rumbling growl come from Kage. Within seconds, Zila and two other Lycans were standing next to him.

So, now everyone growls?

Two other Fae males came running up and stood next to Morgan. Their faces were shocked, like they had no clue what their friend was doing.

Valarian let out a whistle, and Cash, Zayn, Cali, and Asher immediately flanked us.

Morgan shook his head. "Fuck the King's Guard!"

"I bet you would like to," Cash said as he took two steps toward Morgan. His friends both looked scared as Cash went nose to nose with him.

"Leave now!" Kage commanded.

"Screw this place." The Fae turned and his friends followed him out of the bar.

"Morgan is such a dick!" Cali said.

"Indeed." Zayn turned toward me. "Are you good, Red?"

"I'm fine." I smiled as I sheathed my dagger.

"Nice punch, Ember!" Kage said and I smiled proudly.

"Thanks."

"Damn, I missed a punch?" Cash asked with a grin.

"Come on." Val grabbed my hand.

"Where are we going?" I asked as he dragged me out of the bar.

"Outside to talk."

Chapter Fourteen

Val pulled me around the building and stopped under some trees in the back. His violet eyes were staring at me as he crossed his arms.

"Why are we out here, Valarian?"

"Oh, I'm Valarian again?" He tilted his head in amusement.

"Oh, excuse me! Why are we out here, *Val*?"

"I just wanted to make sure you were okay . . . that your hand was okay. That was a great punch."

"My hand is fine and no concern of yours!" Even if I was angry, my curiosity got the best of me. "Why did you growl at that Fae?"

"He pissed me off. Vampires growl when we get angry."

"Whatever." I turned to walk away.

"Ember, wait!"

"What?" I stopped and glanced over my shoulder.

"Why are you mad at me?"

"Why don't you go ask your bartender friend!?"

You're lucky I didn't punch her too, I thought and his eyes went wide.

"Are you jealous, love?"

My body turned completely toward him. "Why would I be jealous of a stupid bartender?"

He tilted his head with a knowing smile. "You tell me."

Maybe because I want you, you idiot.

An arrogant grin spread across his face. "Someone can't keep their shield up when they're drinking."

"You don't know anything, Valarian!"

He leaned in close to my face. "I know that you want me," he whispered, mere inches from my lips. "And you have since you met me. I also know what you did . . . punching that fucking asshole and then holding a dagger to his throat was the sexiest thing I've ever seen."

Not being able to resist him, not being able to look away, I stared into his beautiful violet eyes. The alcohol made me extremely brave. Reaching up, I grabbed his shirt with a tight fist and pulled him into me as hard as I could.

He leaned his face down, his lips only an inch from mine, leaving an open invitation. He stayed there, just breathing into my mouth. My lips were parted as I breathed back into his.

Heat rose in my core and my entire body yearned for him. My breasts were pressed against his chest as my heart raced uncontrollably. Taking the invite, I slammed my lips onto his.

We kissed hard and wildly. It was overly passionate, making me claw and pull at his shirt—at his body.

Touch me, please.

He pulled back slightly, breaking away from our kiss. I ran my hand up the front of his shirt, over the muscles of his stomach. He had a look of contemplation on his face as he stared back at me.

"Don't stop," I whispered. He grabbed a piece of my hair in his hands and twirled it around his finger while he looked at it. "Please don't stop, Val." He looked back at me and I bit my lip.

He ran his hand down my right leg, the one hanging out the slit in the skirt. He lifted it and held it up by his thigh. I leaned back against the wall to help keep my balance as he pressed his hard cock against my core.

He ran his thumb lightly over my lips and I tilted my head back at the fantastic feeling. His fingers trailed slowly down my neck until his hand wrapped around my throat, willing my face to look at him. Then he smashed a kiss onto my mouth.

As he kissed me hard, he continued running his hand down my body and onto my chest. He stopped at my breast and squeezed. He then ran his thumb over my nipple and lightly pinched it. I sucked in a hard breath through my nose at the feeling.

His hand left my breast as it continued its journey down onto my flat stomach, lifting my shirt slightly until he felt my bare skin. His fingers grazed lightly across my stomach, giving me goosebumps as he circled them around.

Trailing his hand down onto my thigh, he found the edge of my skirt and slid under it. He broke away from the kiss and I swallowed, panting at the sensation.

He ran his fingers up the front of my panties, sending pulsating shivers through me. I let out a gasp. He leaned in close to my ear.

"Is this what you want, love?"

"Yes," I whispered back. I wanted it more than he knew. I'd had orgasms before, but unfortunately the man I was with didn't care about my pleasure, so I had never had an orgasm with anyone other than myself.

Sliding his hands around me, he grabbed my ass hard, lifting me off the ground, pinning me between him and the outside wall of the Howling Moon Saloon.

"Hold on to me," he said with a seductive smile. His hard cock pressed against me as I wrapped my legs around his body and grabbed onto his neck.

He slid his fingers up and down the front of my silky panties, making me pant. Then they slowly slid up under the edge and onto my bare skin. Gently, his finger slid between my lips, spreading them open. I whimpered when one slid inside of me.

"Oh, you're ready," he said as he felt my wetness. He licked his lips like he was ready to taste me. I wouldn't have said no.

Pulling his finger out of me, he ran it up, bringing wetness to where I ached. My clit was pulsating, and when he touched it, I became breathless. I couldn't take much more of what he was doing and it had only been a minute.

Oh, Gods!

"Not yet, love," he whispered into my ear. He could tell I was about ready to lose it.

Gripping his neck tighter, I pulled him into me. I tilted my head, exposing my neck to him. Leaning in, he kissed my throat while he continued rubbing on me.

A fang grazed my skin and I about came unglued. He kept dipping his fingers inside me, bringing more wetness up to my clit. A fire was building between my legs as he continued kissing and sucking hard.

As he repeatedly circled his fingers, I felt the pressure building, and it was too late to turn back. I was about to come. A fang grazed my skin again and I gasped at the feeling as the orgasm spread through my body.

"Oh, Gods!" I cried out.

He slammed his mouth onto mine as I came, silencing the loud moans I was about to release into the darkness. My whole body tensed and was in total bliss. The fire spread through all my nerves as I got my release.

Once I was done, he gently removed his hand. He held me there, looking into my eyes as my breathing slowed. Setting me on the ground, my legs were shaking from what had just happened.

"Feel better, love?" He had a sultry grin on his face. I couldn't talk, I just nodded as I tried to catch my breath. "Are you ready to go back inside?" I nodded again. He grinned, trying to keep from laughing. Grabbing my hand with the one he hadn't used, he escorted me back into the bar.

"I'm going to clean up. Be right back." He smiled, and once again, I nodded.

Heading into the bathroom, I cleaned up as well. Once I was done, I went back to the table. Val was sitting there waiting for me and I noticed he had gotten me another drink. I made sure my shields were up.

"I got you some water so you can sober up," he said as I took a seat. I nodded. "Are you okay, Ember?" I nodded again. He shook his head and laughed. "You will have to talk eventually, you know."

"I'm fine, Val." I took a big swig of my water. My buzz was almost gone after the raging orgasm I'd had.

"What are you thinking about?"

"I was just wondering if you come here often?" He tilted his head at my question.

He leaned in close across the table and whispered in my ear. "I just made you come, Ember. I don't want to make small talk."

I swallowed hard at his words. "What do you want, then?"

"The important question is, what do *you* want, love?"

"I don't know, Val."

He took a big chug of his drink as Cash and Zayn walked up.

"I think we should head home," Zayn said. "Tomorrow is our day off and I want to enjoy it, not be hungover."

"Yeah, it's kind of boring here tonight." Cash sighed and grabbed a piece of pizza.

"I don't think it's boring." Val gave me a teasing smile. I grabbed a piece of pizza and started eating it, ignoring him as my cheeks blushed.

"I'm going to go get the ladies." Zayn walked off to find Cali and Zila.

Once we had everyone, we galed back to the portal. Zayn galed me. We hopped on, and the effects weren't as bad, but I think it was because of how good my mood was. We landed back in Ashbern and we all headed into the manor.

I turned right at the top of the stairs and headed to my room. Someone walked up next to me. I looked up and it was Valarian.

"Just making sure you made it to your room." We stopped right outside my door.

"I did manage to make it through the treacherous halls alone."

He smiled at my sarcasm. "May I kiss you goodnight?"

"Well, after what you just did to me, it would only be proper," I teased.

He leaned in close to me and kissed me. I ran my hands down his back and gripped him tightly.

After about a minute, he pulled away. "Goodnight, Ember."

I wasn't ready to go to bed so I opened the door to my room—my whole body was inviting him in. He hesitated for a second.

"Do you want to come in?" I asked, making sure he understood.

His eyes narrowed as he tilted his head in contemplation. "Are you still feeling the effects of the alcohol?"

"I'm not." I shook my head and a slow smile spread across his face.

"Then, hell yes." He walked into my room and I shut the door behind him.

The fireplace crackled as the light flickered across his face. It was burning low and needed a little more wood. I stood there, not knowing what to do now. I was a lot braver before the door shut. Where was whiskey when you needed it?

"I have to put wood on," I said.

"I got it." He went toward the fireplace as I walked over and took a seat in the chair. My heart raced as I took off my boots and placed my hands nervously on my knees.

"Are you okay?" he asked as he walked up to me. "I can go if you want."

"No." I reached up and grabbed his hand. Gripping it tight, he ran his thumb across it as he smiled at me. "Please don't go, Val."

My breaths were heavy as he kneeled in front of the chair between my legs. Grabbing my hips, he scooted my butt until I was sitting on the edge of the chair and then he spread my knees apart.

Leaning his head down between my legs, he kissed my thigh. I had never been kissed there before and it felt amazing. Giving him room to move closer, I spread my knees wider. Deep, wet kisses were placed on my skin, all the way to the apex of my legs.

Once he got to the top, he slid my skirt up and kissed me through my panties. My hands slid into his hair and gripped it tight as I moaned. Pulling back, he moved my panties to the side and ran a finger down my slit.

"You're already ready again." His violet eyes sparkled in the light of the fire under his long, plush lashes. As he looked at me hungrily, I needed him—needed him now.

Not able to wait, I pulled his head up to my face and kissed him hard. Reaching around his body, I dug my nails into his back as I drew him in closer.

I want more.

He pulled away and met my eyes. "Are you sure this is what you want, love?"

"I have never been this sure of anything in my life," I said in a sultry voice that I didn't recognize as my own.

Hugging my body, he lifted me off the chair. His hard cock pressed against my core as I wrapped my legs around him. He laid me gently on the bed, then took his shirt off. I couldn't help but stare at the fantastic hard muscles he had.

"I'm not a virgin," I said quickly. I was nervous that would turn him off.

"There's nothing wrong with that, love. And for the record, neither am I." After kicking off his boots, he dropped his pants. His eyes wandered over my face. "You're so beautiful."

I smiled. He then slid his shorts off and I sucked in a breath.

As he stood there shamelessly naked, I got to see the hard cock that had been rubbing on me. I wasn't too embarrassed to look. It was undoubtedly larger than the one I had before.

Reaching up, I slid my shirt off and my nipples tightened at the exposure to the cold air.

"I will get these." He slid his hands up my thighs and pulled my panties off.

I reached down to unbutton the skirt.

"Leave it." He smiled and yanked it up around my waist.

My legs collapsed open, inviting him in. He hesitated for a few seconds as he stared at me—at my body.

"Scratch the beautiful part, you're fucking gorgeous." I blushed at his words.

He finally accepted my invitation and slowly crawled on top of me, settling between my legs. The warmth of his cock pressing against my core felt amazing.

Parting his lips, he pressed them against mine. I moaned loudly as his cock slid easily up the wetness of my slit. Valarian growled, making me gasp and pull away.

"What's wrong, love?"

"You growled. Are you mad?" He smiled broadly, showing me his fangs. They seemed to have gotten a little longer.

"That's what Vampires do when we're angry, but it's also what we do when we're extremely turned on."

"Oh. Why are your fangs longer?"

"They get longer with arousal."

My eyes widened. "Oh."

"Any more questions, Ember? Or can I continue devouring you?"

"Devour me, please."

He moved to my neck and kissed it. When his fang grazed my skin, I moaned loudly. For a split second, I wondered what it would feel like to be bitten. I was surprised that I was willing to let him bite me; I really wanted him to. He kissed up to my ear and sucked on my earlobe.

"Are you ready?" he whispered.

"Yes," I moaned as I spread my legs further apart.

He slid inside of me and I gasped at how full he made my insides feel. I was dripping wet, so the entrance should have been smooth, but his cock was large. He slowly went in a few more inches. I dug my nails into his back, trying to get him closer to me. My clit was twitching again, ready to take off. I didn't know where it wanted to go, but I wanted to go with it.

He bent his head down and sucked on my nipple, making it even harder. His mouth was warm and wet. His hand slid between my legs and he rubbed on me. His cock finally went in all the way and I moaned.

He continued thrusting into me while his finger circled my clit. My breaths got ragged and fast as the feeling was building. I was going to have my first orgasm during sex and it was the best feeling in the world.

Looking up from my breast, he met my eyes. The fire crackled as the flames blazed, making the sweat on his skin glisten. I couldn't help but admire how beautiful he was.

He started going harder inside of me, continually moving his finger around as he stared back into my face.

My muscles tensed and my body felt warm all over. I was hungry for him. I needed him. "Kiss me!"

As he slammed a kiss onto my mouth, I exploded. My heart threatened to beat out of my chest. It was like electricity ran through my veins, and every muscle in my body was shivering, clenching at the goodness they felt. The earth stood still, leaving our entangled bodies together as one. I moaned loudly at the height of my orgasm.

My heart was thundering inside of my chest and throughout my body. Val pulled back from my mouth, giving me a chance to catch my breath. He looked at my face with a prideful smile.

"Oh my Gods," I said breathlessly. "That's what I have been missing."

He laughed. "Not anymore, love." He stared into my eyes as he said the words and I could feel my heart open up more.

He ran his tongue over the outside of my lips as he moved slowly inside of me. He sucked in my bottom lip and then bit it lightly. I moaned. After lifting my leg, he slammed another kiss on me as he went in deeper.

Grinding into me, he continued moving until his breaths got ragged. He moaned in ecstasy as wetness filled me. He stopped moving as our breathing slowed down and his eyes met mine.

"Are you okay, love?"

"I've never been better." We both smiled and laughed.

Placing a gentle kiss on my lips, he slid off the bed and went to the bathroom. As he walked away in the light of the fire, I watched his butt muscles. I also noticed he grabbed his shorts on the way out.

When he returned, I assumed he would leave, since he had his shorts on. I noticed he had a towel in his hand and I wondered what he was doing. He wiped up the mess that he left behind on me, then took the towel back to the bathroom. *Well, that was nice of him.* He came back into the room and I heard crackling as he messed around with the fireplace.

Hopping out of bed, I stumbled to the bathroom with shaky legs so I could relieve myself. After peeing and cleaning up a little more, I came out and crawled back into bed naked. I figured I would throw a nightgown on after he left. I was super confused about what the proper sex etiquette was because, usually, I just parted ways. But I wasn't going to ask him to leave. At that moment, I realized that I didn't want him to go.

Val was picking his clothes up off the floor as I laid there on my back, quietly watching him. He threw them on the chair and crawled in bed next to me with nothing but his shorts on. He had something in his hand, a piece of clothing, I wasn't sure what it was.

"Here's your nightgown, in case you would feel more comfortable sleeping in something."

"Thanks," I took it and laid it next to me.

"That was fun," he said, making me laugh.

"Indeed, it truly was."

He slid up next to my side and laid there with his head propped up on his hand while he watched me. "Do you mind if I stay?"

"I would love it if you stayed."

He smiled brightly. "Goodnight, Ember." He laid his head down flat on the pillow and got comfortable.

"Goodnight, Val."

Taking in his features, I watched him as he closed his eyes. He was the most perfect man I had ever met—kind, gentle, fierce, and drop-dead gorgeous. Deciding I couldn't stare at him all night because I needed sleep, I rolled away from him and curled up on my side. The bed moved as he curled up behind me, hugging my body and pulling me close to him. He placed a gentle kiss on my shoulder before he snuggled in.

I had never been cuddled before and the feeling was weird at first, but I ended up loving it. It was comforting. I had never felt safer in my life.

We laid in comfortable silence. His chest rose and fell against my back as I watched the light flickering from the fireplace. My breathing became slow as my body relaxed. Sleep came to us both not long after that.

Chapter Fifteen

The sun was coming through the window and awakened me from the best night of sleep I had ever had. As soon as I opened my eyes, I had a smiling Valarian in my face. I realized that I was still naked.

"Good morning, love," he said.

"Good morning," I whimpered as I buried my face in my pillow, making him laugh at me. Now that the night had worn off, I felt embarrassed.

There was a knock on the door and Val got up to answer it. I cringed at the thought of it being one of our friends. He said something to the person and then shut the door. He had a tray in his hands, still wearing only his shorts, when he returned.

"I had the servants bring you breakfast." He set the tray on the bed next to me. "I'm going to head down and get cleaned up. Since we have the day off, would you like to hang out?"

"I would enjoy that, thank you."

"I'll be back soon." He leaned down and kissed my cheek. I smiled at him as he grabbed his clothes off the chair and left.

Is he just going to walk down the hall shamelessly, with only a pair of shorts on, showing his sexy body to the servants or anyone else around? Of course, he was.

I shoved my head into my pillow and let out a happy squeal as the entire night's events ran through my head.

Sitting up, I pulled the tray toward me and ate my breakfast. As soon as I was done, I took a shower and got ready for the day. I had a permanent smile plastered on my face.

A knock at the door brought me back from all the sexy memories I was replaying and I wondered if Val was back.

I opened the door to a smiling Angel—my friend, Zayn.

"Oh. Hey, Softy."

He strolled in. "You have any plans, Red?"

I couldn't tell him I planned on hanging out with Val. "Not much, just reading."

"Good, because we got a mission and you're on the order." He handed me a piece of paper. My heart skipped as I read my name. I had my first *real* mission. "I know it's our day off from classes, but when missions come up, we have to take them. Don't look so surprised, Ember." Hearing him say my actual name brought my attention back up to him.

"I just didn't think it would be so soon."

"The first one always makes you nervous. I got mine on my second day here, so yours is not soon at all. Just like the portal, it gets easier with time."

"Your name isn't on the order, I noticed."

"Nope, you'll be going with Val and Cash. You'll be well cared for."

"Do you know what the mission is? It says DS on here."

"I do and if I tell you, you can't freak out."

I nodded in acknowledgment.

"There's been a Demon spotting. You have to go and collect information."

"Where?"

He ran his hands through his hair, and I looked back down at the paper.

"MZ." My hand went to my mouth.

"Mazuria."

"What of my sister?" I asked while trying to keep my promise and not panic, but I was sure my heart stopped working.

"She's perfectly well, I checked on her this morning, unbeknownst to her or anyone else. I flew in and quickly returned after I was made aware of the sighting."

"You flew to Mazuria?"

"Not the whole way, that would have taken a week or more. I took a portal to my homeland and flew across from there. I knew you would have questions and I wanted to have answers for you without being seen." He smiled lightly.

"Thank you, Zayn." My heart ached at the love I had for my friend. I pulled him in and hugged him.

"Now, get ready and meet me at the bottom of the stairs."

I swallowed and then nodded. I was nervous.

After I changed into my fighting leathers, I strapped on my dagger and headed down to meet Zayn. We met by the front door and he took me down to the armory.

"Do you know how to use a sword?" Zayn asked as I looked at the walls lined with weapons.

"I don't. I only know how to use a bow and my dagger."

"You can bring a bow if you would like. I see you have your dagger."

I nodded. "I would like a bow."

"Take whichever pleases you."

I grabbed the bow I used for hunting with Val. "This one will do."

Zayn grabbed some arrows and a quiver, handing them to me. Cash strolled in and the look on his face said he was ready for this mission.

He had on a deep brown shirt with leather armbands for fighting. He also had a dark brown leather gorget hanging on his chest, which had leather shoulder caps attached. There were small, rounded leather scales decorating the chest piece. They almost looked like dragon scales. In the center of the gorget was an embossed emblem. It was a sword with a wing on each side—the same symbol as the Angel's tattoo. He also wore brown trousers, boots, and his blonde hair was in a bun.

"Are you ready for this, Ember?" Cash asked with a huge smile. He grabbed two battle-axes and stuck them in his belt. I nodded. I was, indeed, not ready.

I'm not ready.

"She's ready," Valarian said as he walked in, and my attention turned to him. He smiled at me. I smiled back, trying not to blush at the last memories I had of him.

Valarian had a single leather pauldron that was black. It was attached to the leather harness belt he was wearing.

He walked around, picking out his weapon as I watched closely. He chose a short sword for his harness.

Since I saw him rip that wolf's jaws apart with his bare hands, I was unsure why he needed a weapon.

I didn't know violence could be so sexy, I wielded to him.

I think the same thing when I look at you, love. He winked at me and I flushed.

"Alright, troops, let's go!" Cash was too excited.

We headed out of the manor and to the outside.

"Since the mission is on Mazuria, we'll have to portal over there." Cash looked apologetically at me and nodded at the portal guard as we entered.

I hate portals, I wielded the thought to Val.

Just breathe. It gets easier each time. Valarian smiled sympathetically.

We stepped onto the portal and were whipped through air and life. The rush was intense. I tried to keep my eyes open this time, but it was like everything was going by so fast. As the nausea rose, I felt as if I was going to get sick, so I closed my eyes. I started to sway.

Oh no.

Two hands went around my waist and hugged me, and I steadied. The warmth of the skin felt lovely. I knew it was Valarian by his scent, so I laid my head against his chest. Then we landed. I opened my eyes, and we were in the country of Mazuria.

Cash glanced back and forth between our faces in surprise by our hug. He said nothing as he smoothed his beard.

Glancing up, I met Valarian's eyes. He grabbed my chin, looking over my face. "Are you okay, love?"

"I'm fine." *He's so sexy.*

"Shield." He grinned and dropped his hands.

I threw my shield up in confusion. "What happened? My shield was up when we left."

"It fell. Always check them after galing, any large emotional response, and especially after using a portal."

Once we left the portal, we started walking toward my town, Pyreland. Seeing everything was weird. I hadn't been gone long, but it felt like forever ago. Since my new daily routine had taken over, I had forgotten how different my life used to be.

Cash stopped walking, so we came to a halt with him. "We're meeting the Duke of Mazuria, so we have to go to Spellchild Castle first."

"I don't need anyone to gale me, I know the way." I smiled.

"I don't know the way," Valarian said sheepishly.

I prowled over to him the way he does to me and wrapped my arms around his waist. I deepened my voice to sound like a male.

"I'll take you," I said to him, trying not to laugh.

"To the Gods!" Cash shook his head and laughed before he galed.

"I like your arms around me." I completely froze at his words.

My heart raced and I swallowed hard as I looked into his beautiful violet eyes. We might have something more than just sex.

"Don't get used to it," I quickly said, trying to hide my emotions. He laughed and I galed us right outside the castle wards.

Chapter Sixteen

Spellchild Castle was as impressive as I remembered. It wasn't as big as the king's castle, but it was still gorgeous, even on a smaller scale. It was a light-colored brick with sharp, pointy, red towers on the outside. Ivy leaves were growing up most of the castle.

Cash walked up to us and I let go of Valarian.

"Ember, Zayn said that you are going to take the lead today since you know the Duke of Mazuria, and you need to practice," Cash informed me. "I'll start it off and you follow suit."

I cringed on the inside at the mention of the duke. I found him to be not to my liking.

"Of course." I politely smiled.

"Lead the way." Cash gestured with a slight bow.

We met our escort and a few of the guards outside the castle. Something was odd about them. There weren't as many of them as there usually were and the ones here didn't seem friendly. They treated us more like enemies than they did fellow guards, which I found extremely strange.

We walked inside and I looked around at the castle. It was the same as when I was younger. There was a touch of soft blue color everywhere. It was on the curtains, the rugs, and the flags. They were the duke's color. I squished up my nose at the thought. The duke was never a friend of mine—he was a mean asshole—so I now hated the color.

We were escorted to the duke's quarters where he was sitting impatiently waiting for us. He had a scowl on his face from the minute he laid his emerald-green eyes on me. The duke never liked me much either, and I honestly didn't know or care to understand why.

"It is about time. I was worried I was going to have to manage the situation myself!" the duke said, rather snottily.

"We apologize, Your Grace," Cash said sincerely. "We came as soon as we got word."

Glancing over, I noticed that Valarian had gone stone-faced. His eyes were narrowed at the duke.

"There were Demons on my land. They came after nightfall last night. How are you going to manage this situation?"

Cash nudged my arm, reminding me to talk.

"Was anyone injured, Your Grace?" I was worried about the people I knew.

"No, they were not, female!" he spat the words like I was evil and I went still.

Val stiffened. *I don't like the duke.*

That makes two of us, Val. I let out a slow breath.

"What exactly happened, Your Grace?" Cash was giving me time to recover from the duke's response.

"They came up on the beach, close to the edge of town. A woman saw them and warned *everyone*. People were hysterical!"

"What happened to the Demons, Your Grace?"

"Nothing happened. They left." He looked like he was ready for this conversation to be over. I decided to try and speak again.

"A Demon has not entered these lands in years, Your Grace."

"Leave the talking for the males, dear. Learn your place." I took a deep breath and exhaled slowly, trying to calm myself.

I will rip his throat out if he speaks to you that way again. Val's words shocked me and, as I glanced up at him, he looked angry.

Don't do that. I'm fine. I nudged his arm, trying to relax or distract him—I was unsure which.

"So, what are you going to do about this?"

"We will talk to the town folk and get as much information as possible. We will manage it, Your Grace." Cash was good at being nice. He was an elegant speaker.

The duke stood up. "You're dismissed." He waved his hand and quickly walked away before we had a chance to bow.

We hurried out of the castle. I could feel the anxiety and anger coming off my friends. I hated the duke. I didn't know why, but he was always snarky with me, even when I was little.

"Who the hell does he think he is?" Val let out a low growl that sent shivers down me. Good thing we were out of earshot of the castle.

"He's the worst duke I have ever had to deal with, out of all the lands." Cash rubbed a hand across his forehead.

"I should rip his heart out for how he treated you!" Valarian touched my arm. I met his eyes.

"You can't do that and don't say that!"

"Why? It's true. I have no qualms about ripping his fucking heart out!" Val had a stone-cold face.

"Val, calm down," Cash chimed in. "He just has superiority issues."

"That I can quickly relieve him of when I drain him of his blood!" Val let out another growl. My eyes went wide at the sound and the fierceness on his face.

Why is he so angry?

"I will wield your emotions to calm you if I have to, buddy."

Val went still at Cash's words. "That will not be necessary." Val cracked his neck and his face softened. I felt relieved when I saw him relax slightly.

"All right, let's head to the entrance of Pyreland."

After taking a deep breath, I walked over to Val and put my arms around him so we could gale. "Are you okay?"

"I'm fine, love. Let's go."

He didn't look fine to me. I laid my head on his chest and galed us to the edge of town, outside the wards. He kissed the top of my head as we landed. Cash galed in right behind us and I immediately dropped my hands from Valarian.

We started walking—all of us remaining quiet. We got to town and my house was in the first row of homes at the edge. I glanced over at it longingly, hoping we could stop and see my sister.

"She's at work until late this afternoon. Zayn informed me." Cash smiled and sighed.

They're keeping watch on my sister, I thought to myself, feeling grateful.

I smiled and nodded, and we continued walking. We strolled into the center of town, and all eyes were on us—all eyes were on *me*. Some people waved to me and called out my name, while others gasped at the sight of us. Most of the older townsfolk looked concerned about the recent events, but a lot of the younger ones watched us in awe. It was weird to see their faces filled with such wonder.

We walked past the bakery where my sister now worked. I peeped in the window and saw her waving her hands and smiling while talking to a customer. I stopped walking as I looked at her beautiful face.

"What are you looking at?" Cash stared into the store and his eyes found my sister. The expression on his face was pure longing. "Oh."

"Can we stop?" He didn't acknowledge me. His eyes seemed to glaze over as he kept staring at her.

Cinder looked toward the window, her eyes going wide when she saw me. She clapped a hand over her mouth and ran through the door, slamming into me with the biggest hug I have ever had.

"What are you doing here?" her voice cracked.

"We're on a mission." I let go of the hug.

Cinder noticed the others and her face looked slightly shocked.

"Oh. Hi," she said sweetly, while blushing at Cash.

"Hello. Nice to see you again, Cinder." Cash smiled big at her. His blue eyes were sparkling with excitement.

"Cinder, this is Valarian Grey." Her eyes went wide at the recognition of his name.

Since I had told her some things about Val, I was sure she was running through those memories. I hope she didn't think any bad thoughts or he would hear them.

"Nice to meet you." She smiled as she held out her hand and Val shook it.

Since this was the first Vampire she had ever met, I was proud of her reaction. It was better than my reaction had been.

"Likewise." Val smiled kindly at her. Which means she kept her thoughts in check, or so I hoped.

"How are you, Cin?" I asked.

"I'm doing well. Are you here because of the Demons?"

"We are and we can't stay and chat, unfortunately."

"I understand. Should I be worried?"

"You shouldn't be," Cash interrupted. "We are particularly well trained and strong. We can manage Demons, my lady." He winked at her, still grinning like a fool.

She smiled at him as they locked eyes. I looked between the two as my eyebrows furled together.

A perfect love match. I looked over at Valarian, shocked at his words.

Shut up, Val. He smiled at me.

Looking back at the happy couple, I had a feeling he was right. "Well, we have to get going, Cinder." I was hoping to break their eye contact.

"Okay. I have to go back to work before Ms. Delaney relieves me of my job." She gave me one last hug. "I miss you."

"I miss you too." I spoke the words into her hair before letting go.

"Nice meeting you, Valarian. Bye, Cash." She blushed and quickly walked off, and we continued strolling through town.

We talked to some people and got little information. It mainly was a retelling of the same stories. None of them had seen anything, but almost everyone said the same thing—the name of the person who did. The local jewelry store owner was the one who saw the Demon on the beach, so we stopped and talked to her.

She was a shorter woman who was thinner in build. She had long, wispy black hair and rings on every finger of her pale hands.

"I was on the beach gathering seashells for some jewelry I'm making when he came out of the water!" she was saying. "He was taller than me and had gray skin!"

"What happened next?" I asked. Cash let me take the lead on this one since I knew her.

"I screamed, ran off, and alerted everyone! The guards were dispatched to check it out, but found nothing. I don't think some people believed me, but I know what I saw!"

"I'm sorry you had to deal with that." I touched her arm, comforting her. "And I'm glad you weren't harmed."

"Thank you for letting us know. We appreciate your help." Cash reached out and shook her hand.

"Thank you for protecting us." She hurried off.

"This is odd, gentlemen. I don't understand why only one Demon would come to Mazuria."

"Profoundly odd," Valarian added.

"Nothing more we can do. Let's get back so we can report our findings to the king." Cash sighed as he raked his hand through his beard.

We walked back to the portal and stepped on. The ride was just as nauseating. Val held me in his arms again on the way home.

Chapter Seventeen

Two weeks had gone by without a Demon sighting. I had been at Castleva for over a month and had finally come out of my shell. I was attending every meal regularly with the people I now considered my friends.

At least once a week, I took trips into the woods to hunt and learn more about the lands. Val was always with me, so he could feed. He preferred deer, but he would eat anything I caught, even rabbit. We had sex in random places a couple of times and made out every chance we were alone.

I had woken up late today and was running out of the manor, heading down to my training class when Cali caught me just outside.

"Hey, Ember."

"Hi, Cali."

"There's a bonfire tonight. I want to make sure you are coming."

"I may skip it again." I wasn't feeling up to hanging out.

"You must come, I have to have you there." She gave me a sad face. How could I say no to the lovely Angel? I sighed.

"Fine, I'll be there." I had to say whatever would get me out of this conversation quickly or I was going to be late.

"Yay, I'm so excited!" She clapped her hands together. "I'll see you tonight. Wear something nice."

"Okay." I walked off, wondering what I would wear. I hated dressing up.

Valarian was patiently waiting for me as I strolled into the training center. He had his arms crossed and was wearing a tight black, short-sleeve shirt, and tan trousers. I quickly checked my shield while I looked at how sexy he was.

"You are late," he said, but the smile he gave me told me he wasn't actually mad.

"I am not." I smiled big. "I'm right on time."

"If you aren't early, then you are late."

I snickered at his logic. He closed the distance between us and kissed me. I broke away from the kiss more quickly than I wanted to. He immediately noticed me looking around, making sure no one saw.

"I don't know why you insist on hiding us from everyone."

"I just don't want anyone in my business, Val." He sighed, so I quickly changed the subject. "What are we doing today?"

"Weapons training. Come on."

He took my hand as we walked through the training center. Once we were outside, I let go. He gave me a disapproving face but didn't say anything.

We leisurely strolled towards the back of the grounds to the outdoor training area. I was happy about working with weapons and wondered what type we would be using.

As soon as I saw what he had already set up, I got super excited.

"You're going to learn to throw an axe today, love."

"Magnificent!" I was so excited that I clapped my hands together as Cali does. I quickly dropped them, feeling dumb. He smiled at my excitement.

"I have some logs set up here so you can practice." He handed me an axe and continued talking. "You're going to start by learning how to throw it properly until it sticks. Then we will mess around with the diverse ways to throw them. I will demonstrate first." I nodded as he grabbed another axe and walked about fifteen feet away from the target.

He raised it above his head and in one swift move, released it and it landed directly in the center of the target. He quickly removed his axe.

"Your turn. Come here." He smiled as I headed over to him.

"Shouldn't Cash be training me? Isn't he the axe professional?"

He looked appalled at my question. "Who the hell do you think trained him?"

"Of course you did." I shook my head. I was so proud of him, of my man.

He put his arms around me, reaching out to show me how to hold the axe properly.

"Now, you are going to raise it above your head and throw it toward the target," he said close to my ear, sending chills down my spine.

My body was warm from the closeness, so I very lightly rubbed my butt against him. He let out a low growl into my ear and it turned me on even more.

"If you don't want people to know, then you shouldn't do that outside, love." Every time he called me *love*, I melted inside.

"No one can see. They'll just think we're training."

"What kind of training will they think it is when I throw you on the ground and take you right here?"

I smiled at his words. "Sorry." Indeed, I was not sorry.

He stepped away from me so I could wield the axe. "Now throw it."

I did exactly like he said—I raised the axe and released it. The handle of it hit the target.

"You are too stiff, Ember."

"And here I thought you were the one who was stiff," I retorted.

His eyes went wide before he grinned. "Do you want to see?" He prowled toward me and I glanced nervously around.

Once he saw the uneasiness on my face, he shook his head in disappointment before retrieving my axe.

"Get loose with it this time," he said as he handed it to me. All playfulness had left his face.

I threw again, the axe hit but didn't stick. He retrieved it.

"Don't let the axe go when you want to, let it go when it's ready. Stay loose in your grip and let it slide out on its own."

I did as he said. I hit the edge of the target and the axe stuck in it this time.

"Good job." He retrieved my axe once more. "Try again."

I threw axes until I was sweaty and my arm was slightly sore. He was supportive and corrective the whole time.

"That's enough for now. You did an excellent job. You're a quick learner."

"Thanks! That was fun."

"It is fun, but it can be lethal too, Ember. It can save your life or someone else's, just remember that."

"I understand, Val."

"Are you going to the bonfire?" he asked while wiping down the axes with a rag.

"Yes, Cali insists that I go."

"Perfect. I'll pick you up around eight."

"You are escorting me?"

He tilted his head. "Is that a problem, love?"

"No, not at all, I just . . . I didn't know you were taking me."

"Since you have only been there once, I figured you would need a ride."

Oh, I need a ride all right, but not the kind you are thinking. I quickly checked my shield—it had stayed up the whole training session.

A huge grin slowly spread across my face. The look he gave told me that he knew I had thought something bad but hadn't heard it.

"I know that look." He had an irresistible smile plastered on his face. "Excellent job on your shield today, it didn't drop once, as you know already."

"Thanks," I said proudly as we headed back to the manor.

"So, what did you say?"

"Oh, just something about needing a ride from you,"

Without hesitation, his lips pressed against mine. Before the kiss got too wild, I pulled away. He sighed at my actions.

"I'll see you at eight. I'm going to go hunting." Then he galed away. I stood there in shock for a minute, blinking at where he once stood.

I was surprised he left so quickly. I started walking back toward the manor with only my thoughts for company. I was sure I was putting strain on our relationship by wanting to be secretive and he was upset about it.

I honestly didn't even know why I wanted to be secretive. I wasn't embarrassed or anything, I loved him . . .

I stopped walking as the realization hit me.

I love him. Oh no. When did that happen?

I looked around at the trees and the lands, wondering if they heard my thoughts. My heart started racing and I couldn't breathe. I very quickly went to my room, unable to stop thinking about this new revelation. I couldn't even read because my brain wouldn't shut up. After a while, I did manage to take a shower and get dressed.

It was almost eight and I was ready to go. I wore black leggings with a pair of knee-high boots that lace all the way up the front. Of course, I strapped my dagger to my thigh. I wore a nice, black, low-cut tank top that had lace at the top. Cali had brought it down earlier and insisted I wear it. I threw a leather jacket over it. I braided the back of my hair. It was long, falling to my waist now.

Are you ready, love? Val wielded from the hallway.

My heart raced at the sound of his voice in my head. *One second.*

When I opened the door, he stood there looking sexy as ever. This was the first time I had seen him since I realized I was in love with him. As I took in his handsome features, I swallowed hard.

He had dressed up nicely, with black pants and a black button-up shirt with the top few buttons undone. He looked sophisticated and sexy as hell.

"You look exceptionally beautiful and a little badass too," he said as he kissed my cheek.

"Thank you, Val. So do you." I blushed, thinking about the secret that I was holding.

"Shall we?" He held out his arm and I took it.

He escorted me out of the manor and we walked toward the back of the grounds. We stopped once we were far enough away from the wards. Letting go of my arm, he turned to me.

He slid his hands around my waist and whispered in my ear. "You smell good enough to eat. It's very intoxicating."

He kissed my neck as he galed us to the beach, and my heart was racing at the feeling. I looked up into his bright violet eyes when we landed.

"Come on, someone wants to see you." He took me by the hand, and for once, I let him.

We walked onto the beach and the bonfire was already blazing. My eyes bounced from Zayn to Cali, Zila, Asher, Cash, and . . . my sister. My hands flew up to my mouth. She ran to me and practically knocked me down with her embrace.

"Cinder, what are you doing here?" The look of shock was still on my face.

"Cash and Zayn brought me. I have missed you so much, Em."

"What? How?" She let go of the hug, looking at my face with love.

"Don't worry, we spoke with the king and got permission first. It was Val's idea." Cash was grinning proudly as he patted my shoulder with his hand. "You're welcome."

I couldn't stop smiling. "Thank you guys."

"I'm so happy to be here, even though using the portal was bad," Cinder made an uneasy face before she smiled. "Cash helped ease me." I looked over at the Angel, who was still grinning.

"Well, I am glad you are here. I guess you've already met everyone."

"I have." she said excitedly.

"Let's get drinks!" Cash held his arm out for Cinder to take. "Shall we, my lady?"

Cinder did a small curtsy and politely took his arm. "Thank you, sir."

Everyone followed them, leaving me standing there alone with Val.

"Oh, geez." I shook my head.

"I told you, a perfect love match."

"And I told you to hush your mouth, Val."

"Shall we, my lady?" Val held out his arm, mocking Cash. I sighed and took it. "Try not to throw up this time."

"Didn't I tell you to shut up?" He busted out a laugh as he escorted me to the drink area.

We were hanging out at the bonfire when I noticed my sister was talking up a storm with Cash. I watched them carefully from a distance when Valarian's voice brought my attention from them.

"He's an exceptionally good male."

"I know, it's not that. I love Cash. It's just . . ." I took a deep breath and sighed.

"You have to actually use your words now, Ember, since you've been keeping your shield up."

"He's a King's Guard and she wasn't born with the mark. She lives on different lands."

"And that is a problem?"

"I don't know. It can be, I guess." I shrugged. "I just want her to be happy, Val."

I looked over at my sister, who was laughing and smiling at Cash. She had love in her dazzling emerald-green eyes.

Val placed his hand on top of mine, drawing my attention away once more. "She looks happy to me."

"She does." I sighed again, my concerns were confused.

Going into deep thought, I stared at the bonfire. My feelings were torn. I would be happy for her and Cash if they decided to be mated in the eyes of the kingdom. But I didn't know how they would be together if they lived on different lands. I didn't want her to be mated and yet still be alone.

The music that was playing turned slow. Cash bowed to Cinder and then reached his hand out for hers. She politely took it as he led her to the dance floor. He put one hand on her hip, the other in her hand, and she placed one hand on his shoulder. A perfect, proper slow dance. That Angel is nothing but a gentleman.

"If they get mated, the king will offer Cinder to live at Castleva," Val said, getting my attention. "There are bigger rooms for couples."

I checked my shields, and they were up. He just knew me too well.

"I didn't know that." I relaxed, feeling a little better about everything.

I smiled as Asher and Cali joined them on the dance floor. Then Zayn led Zila out there.

"You need a distraction." Val stood up and reached his hands out to me. I didn't hesitate to take it. I would follow this male anywhere at this point.

"Do you have an axe-throwing area set up? Because that would be distracting." He shook his head and gave me a look of adoration. I felt my heart speed up at his stare. Love threatened to pour out from my heart . . . and my mouth.

"Come on." He led me out onto the dance floor.

I shook my head at him in shock. "I can't dance."

"Oh, believe me, you can." He gave me a flirtatious smile and laid his hands upon my hips.

"Not without alcohol," I mumbled.

"You can try. Plus, you owe me." I raised my arms up and placed my hands on his shoulders. I made sure to keep my body from touching his while we danced.

Looking over at Cash and Cinder, I watched them dance. Val let go of one of my hips and put his hand on my chin, forcing me to look up at him.

"Keep your eyes here." He let go and stared deeply into my eyes.

We fell into a peaceful sway together. I felt warm and happy. We danced the whole song in comfortable silence, just staring into each other's eyes. Another slow song immediately followed that one and I did not want to leave Val's arms.

Again?

Absolutely. He slid his hands onto my lower back, pressing my body against his. *Is this allowed?*

I had been thinking about it all day. I loved this man, so there was no reason to keep our relationship a secret anymore.

"At this point, anything is fair game, Val." He smiled happily at my words.

"Just let go of everything," he whispered into my ear before kissing my neck. "It's just you and me, my love."

Wait, did he just say my love? He never says *my,* he just calls me love. Did he have feelings for me, too? I decided that it didn't matter. If he did, he would tell me, and I wasn't going to wreck myself worrying about it.

Wanting to hide my relationship was stupid, and not telling him how I felt was even more stupid. I decided I was going to stop hiding from everyone and not care, so I laid my head on his chest as the night drifted away.

I stayed in his arms for three more songs, and I didn't care if anyone saw. When the time was right, I was going to tell him that I loved him.

Listening to the sound of the ocean crashing against the shores in one ear and Val's heartbeat thundering in the other made the whole night calm and peaceful.

After the bonfire, Val walked Cinder and myself back to my room.

"Goodnight, Valarian, it was nice seeing you again. I will wait inside, Ember." Cinder went into my room and shut the door.

"I had a wonderful time tonight, Val. Thank you." I smiled up at him as he stepped closer to me. I took a step back, afraid that I would pour my heart out to him.

My back brushed up against the wall and I couldn't go any further. He took another step forward, his body now touching the front of mine as he leaned down into my face.

"I had a wonderful night too, love," he whispered and my heart started racing. He leaned in and kissed my cheek. He pulled slightly away, keeping his lips close to my face. "Is anything fair game?"

"I meant what I said."

"Good."

He moved slowly in to kiss me and I parted my lips. I had one hand on his lower back, pulling him as close to me as possible, the other hand I had tightened in his hair. I couldn't get close enough to him. If I could have, I would have crawled inside of his body.

He kissed away from my mouth and down my chin. I tilted my head slightly, offering for him to move further down. He kissed down my jawline and onto my neck. I tilted my head as far as it would go as his kisses got deeper. I was practically panting.

A fang scraped my neck and I moaned. I quickly jerked away and threw a hand over my mouth.

"I'm sorry. I didn't mean to make that sound."

"Don't ever be sorry for making that sound, love." He growled low. "I want to make you make that sound every day."

I smiled at his words. I wanted to go to his room, but I couldn't leave my sister. "I have to go, Val."

"Can we hang out after lunch tomorrow?"

"I would enjoy that."

He leaned down and kissed me gently one last time. "Goodnight, love."

I should have told him my feelings, but I didn't. "Goodnight, Val."

I swallowed the love that threatened to leave my mouth back down and went into my room. I quickly shut the door before I changed my mind and chased after him.

Cinder was sitting in my chair waiting for me. Her eyes went wide when she saw my face.

"Tell me everything!" she said as I fell back against the door, my heart racing with excitement.

So, I did. I told her everything that happened with Val until that point. I also broke down and told her that I was in love with him. She was so excited for me and said I should tell him soon.

Cinder then told me all about her feelings for Cash. She liked him more than I thought. We talked all night long, only getting a couple hours of sleep before the sun came up. Seeing how happy Cash made her made my heart swell.

Chapter Eighteen

The morning was spent relaxing with Cinder in my room before we said our goodbyes. The Angels escorted her home after breakfast and I already missed her. After showering, I got dressed for the day and headed downstairs. I sat in the dining room eating lunch with Calista, Zila, and Asher.

Cali laughed, bringing me from my thoughts.

"You cannot make a whole tornado out of dirt, Asher," Zila said to the air wielder.

Asher cracked his knuckles with a sly smile. "I bet you I could!"

"I got money on that one!" Valarian said as he walked into the dining room. He took a seat next to me and gave me a wink.

Cali clapped her hands together. "I got money on it, too!"

"I wonder if I can make a fire tornado?" Everyone busted up laughing at me.

"No way can you do that, Ember." Asher shook his head, and I shrugged.

I have faith in you. You can master anything, Val wielded. I smiled proudly at his confidence in me.

Are we spending time together after this?

Absolutely, love.

I met his eyes. *Naked?*

Even better. He smiled excitedly.

Zayn entered the room with a somber look on his face, running a hand through his hair as he approached. He had on the same fighting leathers that Cash wore, but his were solid black. I instantly knew that there was a mission. Cash came strolling in right behind him.

"Ember and Val, we have a mission." He nodded his head toward the doors.

Cash sat down and started grabbing food, only briefly meeting my eyes. He smiled briefly before returning to his plate. That Angel loved to eat.

Val, Zayn, and I quickly headed out of the dining room.

"What's the mission?" I asked.

"There was a Demon attack. The Duke of Mayhem has requested our assistance. Throw on your gear and meet me downstairs."

"Mayhem." I turned toward Val. "Your home?" I said the words like I didn't already know the answer.

He nodded.

I hope I see snow, I wielded to him and he smiled.

We quickly changed and went to the armory. I grabbed the same bow I had before. Val holstered his short sword and Zayn grabbed twin blades for his back. We left the manor without saying much and headed toward the portal, making my anxiety rise.

Zayn looked at me with a silent question as we stepped onto it. I nodded in acknowledgment, letting him know I was ready. Val put his arms around me before Zayn willed the portal.

The rush came and it was intense, but being in his arms made the feeling not as bad. As my body pressed into his, I rested my head on his chest. He put his chin on top of my head as he rubbed his hands up and down my back, easing me. Then we landed. I quickly put my shield up and looked into his eyes.

"Are you okay?" Valarian ran his thumb over my lips. I thought about how much I loved him and tried to throw the thought out immediately.

"Yes. It was a little better this time."

"Make sure you keep your shield up since we'll be in a town of Vampires, my love."

We broke free and I watched Val walk away, enjoying seeing those muscles move under his clothes. My heart was overwhelmed by my feelings for him. Glancing up, I noticed Zayn watching me with wide eyes.

"What, Softy?"

The Angel gave me a knowing smile. "Nothing, *my love.*"

Zayn had become my closest friend since I came to Castleva. I adored him, but sometimes I wanted to punch him. My cheeks flushed as we exited the portal.

This was my first time in the stark lands of Mayhem. There was a lot of dirt with roots protruding out of the ground. Some trees looked dead, but somehow, they were still alive.

We walked a bit before reaching a desolate town. There were a couple of shops here and there, but not much to see. When we got to a large manor at the end of the city, a guard with violet eyes was waiting for us.

"Valarian Grey, aren't you a sight for sore eyes!" The two Vampires hugged before he turned his attention to Zayn. "Welcome back!"

Zayn smiled and shook the Vampire's hand. "Nice to see you again, Lazul."

The Vampire was a plumper man who had a friendly smile. His violet eyes stopped on me. "Who is your beautiful friend?"

"Lazul Shadowmend, this is Ember Lavaris. Our newest King's Guard back at Castleva." The man seemed to stiffen at Zayn's words, but recovered quickly.

He held out his hand and I made sure my shield was strong as I shook it.

"Nice to meet you, young lady. Welcome to Vanhall City. I'm this fool's uncle." He patted Val on the back. "I have known many casters in my life. Let me guess, you wield fire magic?"

"Yes, sir, I do." I smiled, concentrating on my shield.

"I knew it!" He let out a boisterous laugh. "I'm good at this game."

"It's not a fair game, uncle. You cheat." Valarian snitched on him. "You know all the surnames of each Caster family and what they wield."

"Don't be telling people my secrets, boy!" He busted out another laugh. Zayn and I both giggled. Lazul had a great personality and I found it pleasing.

Lazul's face got serious with the next words he spoke. "The duke's waiting inside for us."

"Why aren't we meeting at Blackveil Castle?" Zayn asked, running a hand through his shaggy hair.

"That's part of the problem and not my place to say, son."

"My sister?" Val asked. I looked up at his face in shock, he never talked about his family. But honestly, neither did I.

"She's safe," Lazul said, and Valarian nodded.

We stepped inside the manor, which was immensely ruinous. Lazul escorted us to the duke's quarters.

Ember, keep your shield up. You are about to be in a room full of Vampires. Don't let it fall.

I'll be fine, Val. I'm getting better with my shield.

You are. You have come an amazingly long way. He smiled proudly at me. *Just make sure you don't wield your thoughts to others.*

I know. I smiled, reassuring him that I understood.

And if anyone other than me wields their thoughts to you, let me know at once so I can rip their heart out.

That may be a little bit uncalled for.

He grinned, showing me his fangs, and I giggled.

"Are you two talking again?" Zayn broke the silence.

"She needs to practice."

"Jealous you can't talk to me, Softy?" I teased.

"Actually, yes." He frowned. "At least I can talk to Val." He patted Valarian on the back, who winked in return.

We continued walking until we got to a massive set of iron double doors. Once we entered the large room, we were met with three guards, a servant, and an older gentleman, who I believed to be the duke.

Violet Vampire eyes everywhere. I checked my shield, still intact.

"Thank you for coming." Two of us gave a slight bow to the duke. Valarian didn't.

"What is to be the problem, Your Grace?" Zayn spoke elegantly.

"A Demon entered our lands in the middle of the night. He came up on Winter's Peak, by the mountains. The guards swiftly took him out. At the same time, four other Demons attacked Blackveil Castle. They killed one of my guards before three of the Demons were ended. I am now to stay here in Vanhall until the situation is rectified."

"Where's the last Demon?" Valarian dropped formalities.

"Imprisoned in the castle. We figured you may want to get some information out of him, son."

"We do, Your Grace," Zayn informed him. "We will go there and report back to the king with any findings."

Val said nothing as he turned away and left.

"Thank you all." The duke walked away as well. There seemed to be a conflict between him and Val. I didn't know why, since the duke seemed nice to me.

We headed outside and stopped a few feet away from the castle.

"Mountains first, then prison?" Zayn asked and Valarian nodded in response. "Okay, we can gale there."

"Good job on your shield. It didn't fall one time." Val gave me a congratulatory smile.

"You galing with me?" Zayn asked.

"I got her," Val said before I had a chance to answer.

Zayn gave us an evil insinuating smile before he galed away.

Valarian crept up to me slowly and put his hands around my waist. He bent his head down until his face was close to mine, making my heart speed up. "Do you still want to see snow?"

My eyes lit up with excitement. "Absolutely!"

He kissed my neck, and I practically melted in his arms as he galed us away. We landed on a snowbank at the edge of the continent near the ocean. The mountains were blocking where we once stood. I tried to pretend like Val didn't just kiss my neck, even though my heart was racing.

Looking down at the beautiful white of our surroundings, it smelled like a fresh, cool breeze, but different. As I inhaled the cold air, I realized that I had smelled that scent a hundred times before. It was the same scent I smelled on Valarian daily.

You smell just like snow.

Valarian's face looked confused. *What?*

It's not a terrible thing at all, you just smell like it. You smell good. His face now looked amused at my confession.

You smell delicious too, he said back with a wink.

I didn't want to seem childish in front of Zayn, but I really wanted to feel the snow. *Can I touch it?*

Are we still talking about snow? Val asked as he tilted his head.

My mouth dropped open. "Valarian!"

He laughed and Zayn furrowed his eyebrows again, not hearing any other part of the conversation.

You can touch it if you wish . . . the snow, that is. I blushed. *Well, I mean, if you want to touch—*

That's enough! I put my hand up, stopping him. He smiled playfully and I turned my attention back to the snow.

Val watched me attentively as I reached down and grabbed a handful of it. He was right, it was cold. Colder than I imagined. I looked up and saw a distant piece of my land—the country of Mazuria. I saw what could have been the sandy beach, but I couldn't make out my town.

I was on the exact opposite of this view over a month ago, I thought I dropped the snow.

How is it?

I met Val's eyes. *It's cold.*

I told you! He laughed. "Zayn, did you know that this is Ember's first time seeing snow?"

"Oh, we have to do it then!" Valarian nodded his head in agreement.

"Do what?" I curiously looked between the two men. They ignored me.

Zayn pulled his swords from his back and dropped them in front of him. They both fell backward onto the ground and started moving their arms up and down and their legs in and out.

I gasped. "What are you doing? Are you both senseless?"

"Making snow angels." Valarian laughed.

"I'm making a snow angel Angel, since I'm an Angel." Zayn stood up to look at his masterpiece. He ran his hand through his hair, brushing the snow away.

"That doesn't even make sense, Zayn." Val stood and looked at his work. "You should try it, Ember."

The way he said my name gave me goosebumps.

I looked down at the two figures they'd made on the ground.

Wow, now this is amazing! They really did look like angels and I smiled widely. Looking around at the snow, I wondered if I should.

"Come on, live a little," Zayn pleaded. "Be an angel with us!"

I dropped my bow and quiver of arrows onto the ground and held my breath as I fell backwards.

"Oomph." It wasn't as soft as the men acted like it was.

I repeated the motions they did. Val reached down and quickly helped me off the cold ground to look at my work. The snow had three perfect angel figures in it. It was beautiful and I smiled at the happiness I felt.

"Good job for a beginner," Zayn teased.

"I think it's perfect!" Val gave me an irresistible smile.

"Okay, we have work to do." Zayn started walking toward the guard tower. "My snow angel is the best, by the way." He laughed and I shook my head.

"This is the happiest I've been in years. Thank you, Val." I picked up my quiver and bow.

He smiled as he gestured with his head. "Come on, love."

We headed to the guard tower where we stopped and spoke to the guards on duty last night. We found out where the entry point was, which the Demon used to come onto the land. The guards believed that he was a distraction from the other attack at the castle.

Val?

Yes, my love?

I was thinking about the guards and how they acted. I didn't understand why and wondered if it was something the duke had said to them about me.

The guards here are much nicer than the ones in Mazuria.

Indeed, the guards here are always nice. The few that were in Mazuria were standoffish. I found it odd.

I met his eyes. *Me too.*

We decided there wasn't anything more there for us to investigate, so we galed to the outskirts of the Blackveil Castle. I was in Val's arms when we landed.

My eyes went wide as we walked up. "Whoa."

It was a picture of authentic beauty and terror at the same time. I tilted my head and examined it. The stone of the castle was so dark it almost looked black. It had brownish-red vines growing all over it with thorns everywhere and weird rust-colored flowers that were surprisingly pretty for their color.

This castle amazes me, Val. It's a perfect blend of beauty and danger.

He glanced over at me. *Since you feel the need to tell me I smell like snow, I need to tell you something.*

Go on, I'm intrigued. I smiled encouragingly at him.

You're like this castle, Ember. Dangerous, yet beautifully intriguing. His face filled with adoration.

My heart swelled with love, so of course I covered it with a joke.

That's funny, Val. I was going to tell Zayn the same thing.

We both laughed and Zayn furrowed his eyebrows, silently reminding us that we were on a mission.

We stepped into the castle and it was gorgeous. The floor was a shiny black marble and there were gold and deep purple touches everywhere—the duke's colors. I didn't have time to take it all in because a guard swiftly led us down to the prison cells.

As we headed two floors underground, I reminded myself to keep my shield up. Once we entered the dungeon, I was officially creeped out. It was dark and smelled musty. Only two torches were lit on the wall.

The guard stopped by the door as we walked four cells down and went up to the Demon's cell. My eyes widened since I had never seen one before. He was about six feet tall with gray skin and very little hair. He looked at me with his penetrating red eyes.

"Hello, Ember," the Demon spoke with a voice that gave me chills. My heart sped up and I quit breathing.

Chapter Nineteen

I f anyone had told me that I would be standing in front of a cell staring at a Demon who knew my name, I would have laughed. Now it was *too real*. I didn't even have time to respond before my friends reacted.

"Don't speak to her!" Valarian spat. He let out a growl as he moved between me and the Demon's cell.

"Only talk to us, Demon. You aren't worthy of her attention!" Zayn moved too. Both men were now in front of me, blocking the Demon from my sight.

Ember, keep your shields tight! He's an Introspector. I can feel him trying to get into me. Zayn can too!

The Introspector is a thought reader, right?

Yes. He can read your thoughts and your feelings. He can read the deepest part of your soul if you let him in. He can also take hold of your brain and turn you into a living puppet.

I froze in response, willing my shield to be thicker than the mountains.

The Demon was calm and didn't look fearful. "I wish to speak to the girl alone."

"That won't happen." Zayn shifted to the left slightly and my heart thundered in my chest as I locked eyes with the Demon.

Speak with me, girl. I know things. Things you don't know but will wish to. I was in shock hearing him in my head, even after Val's warning.

Zayn stared down the Demon. "Who sent you to attack?"

Talk with me, Ember. Ember Lavaris. The Demon wasn't backing down. *Your pretty little sister may not be safe.*

My cheeks got red hot as my anger took over. "You don't know my sister or me! Stop your lies!"

Val let out a low, rumbling growl. *Don't answer him, it's not safe.*

I placed my hand on his shoulder, trying to soothe his uneasiness.

"We have told you not to speak to her, Demon. Not aloud or in her thoughts. We won't warn you again." Zayn stood taller, ready to stand by his threats. "Who sent you?" The Demon ignored Zayn's questions, still trying to bait me.

"Your mother *was not* killed by Vampires, Ember."

I sucked in a breath as we all froze.

"What do you mean?" My voice came out in a whisper as my chest filled with utter pain.

The Demon's face was empathetic as he tried to gain my trust. "The comrades you are with, they know what happened. So does the king."

"Stop this now or I will rip your heart out!" I didn't doubt that Valarian would stand true to his words.

Talk to me through your thoughts and I will tell you the truth. The truth that no one else is ready to say to you.

I knew I was going to instantly regret the decision I made, but curiosity got the best of me. *What is the truth?*

You've been fed lies for the last two years. Your father is more than he says. He is a Debaser. A soul-taker. He did not kill your mother, but her fate was in his hands.

How do you know this? His evil red eyes stared hard into mine. I had this tremendous feeling telling me the Demon was harmless. My shoulders relaxed and I felt my shield drop.

Attack the guard, get the key to the cell, and open the door. Then we will discuss it. His voice sounded like music in my head. Beautiful. Trustworthy.

I dropped my quiver and bow and turned around.

"Ember?" Val said but I completely ignored him.

"Where are you going, Red?"

Heading toward the exit, I immediately attacked the guard. After punching him in his face, I grabbed the cell keys from his hand. He was in such shock that his instincts took a second to kick in. I had to be fast, so I brought my knee up and hit him in his groin, causing him to fall to the ground.

Zayn and Valarian were on me in an instant. I whipped around and shot a fireball at Valarian, who fell to the floor while dodging it. Zayn was too close, so I elbowed him in the face and sprinted past him toward the Demon's cell.

I must open the door. I must do it now.

"Ember, stop!" Valarian grabbed me by the waist, holding me as tight as he could without hurting me. "Put your shields up."

He was keeping me from my task, so I flailed in his arms, kicking and screaming. There was an overpowering need to complete my tasks—at any cost.

I must open the cell door! I must open it now!

With all the fighting going on, the keys fell from my hand. Valarian let go of me and reached down to pick them up. Looking over, I noticed the Angel had recovered from the hit I had given him. He had blood dripping down his face and was headed toward us. Time was running out.

Stab him! Stab the one you love in the heart. Stab him and then open the door!

Taking my dagger from its sheath, Valarian raised up with the keys in his hand. He met my eyes and, in an instant, I stabbed him in the chest—right between the leather straps of his harness. His eyes went wide with shock and then sadness.

Zayn lunged forward, trying to disarm me, and his arm was cut in the process. He tightened his hands around my wrists, making the dagger fall to the ground.

"Look at me." His angelic words were beautiful as I met his eyes.

He moved his hands to my cheeks and an overpowering feeling took over my body as his magic surged through my veins.

"You are in control, Ember! Push him out and then put your shield up."

The magic he was wielding finally knocked some sense into me. In the moment of clarity, I threw my shield up hard and felt a force get shoved out of my head—out of my body. The darkness I didn't know was in me disappeared.

Zayn looked relieved as he let go of my cheeks. He grabbed the keys off the floor and then knelt by Val, who was bleeding.

"It's okay, buddy," Zayn's voice was sad as he placed his hand over the gaping wound I had caused.

What have I done? Valarian coughed up blood and I threw myself onto my knees next to him. "I'm so sorry." I sobbed as I grabbed Val's hand.

"He's not healing, Ember!" Hearing Zayn scream my name made me jump. He had pure fear in his eyes as I looked at him . "Call a healer!" Zayn shouted to the guard, and the guard disappeared.

"Why is he not healing, Zayn?"

"When did he feed last?"

I blinked tears from my eyes. "He just fed yesterday."

"Hand me your dagger." I let go of Val's hand and grabbed the dagger off the floor.

I handed it to Zayn and then quickly threw my hands on Val's wound. As Zayn pressed the dagger between his hands, the blade started to glow. I had never seen it do that before.

"Whoever gave you this dagger spelled it with Demon magic. It can kill any being with a fatal blow . . . including vampires." Zayn threw my dagger across the room in anger before he put his hands back on Val's wound. His eyes filled with tears. "No magic will help him now."

My father had given me that dagger right after my mother died. I had stabbed him with it. I had stabbed Valarian in the heart.

Looking at my blood-soaked hands, I whimpered. It was *his* blood—the blood of the man that I was in love with.

My eyes met Zayn's with a pleading question. It was a silent sentence he said with his blue eyes as he shook his head. Valarian was going to die and I was the one that gave the final blow. Pain burned through my body, threatening to eat me alive.

"We have to do something, Zayn!" My heart was breaking, my voice cracked. "I am in love with him!" Zayn's eyes blinked as tears ran down my face.

A wailing cry of pain shot through the room. Zayn looked at me in shock and I realized the sound came from my own body. It came from somewhere deep in my soul.

I started bawling and fell against Val's chest, where I could faintly hear a heartbeat. I couldn't make out his face anymore through my stinging eyes.

"I love him!" I screamed. My whole body trembled as tears streamed down my cheeks.

"Put your hands here." Zayn moved his hands off the wound, and I covered it with mine, placing my chest on top of my hands, willing the blood to stay in. I wasn't going to give it a choice.

Zayn went in front of the Demon's cell and pleaded with him. "How can we fix this? I know you know!" The Demon didn't respond. "Please!" Zayn screamed as he shook the bars of the cell.

"The wielder of the Demon blade must sacrifice a part of themselves for the one who was stabbed if she wills for him to live," the Demon said bluntly.

"I will do anything," I whimpered. I would sacrifice anything at this point to save his life—including my soul.

"Feed him your blood, girl and he will heal. If it is not too late, that is." The Demon had a creepy smile and I paled at the thought of feeding someone my blood.

Zayn slid back onto his knees on the other side of Val, ready to do what was necessary. "I can feed him."

"Only the one who truly tried to end him can bring him back. Time is almost up." The Demon looked bored as he shrugged.

Valarian had gone completely still and I didn't hesitate. I crawled over and grabbed my dagger off the ground, then scrambled back next to Val.

"It's a Demon blade so you can't cut too deep," Zayn reminded me. "You will die."

Burning pain radiated through me as I took the dagger upon my wrist and sliced it open. I looked at Zayn, confused about what to do.

"Put your wrist up to his mouth."

Drops of blood dripped into Val's mouth as I held my wrist up to it. He didn't move, nor did he swallow. Zayn shook his head, eyebrows furrowing together like he didn't have any information.

Genuine fear ran through my body at the thought of this *not* working. My heart ached and my eyes burned as the fear threatened to rip me from the inside out. I was choking on air from crying so hard.

"Drink, Val!" I pleaded. "Please, love."

Unsure if he had heard me or if it was just the timing, but he immediately swallowed. I pushed my wrist closer to his lips and he started sucking. Whimpering sounds of relief fell from my lips. Glancing at Zayn, he relaxed as he wiped tears from his face.

Then everything changed.

Valarian moved with such lightning-fast speed that I didn't even know what was happening when he scrambled to his knees. His face had veins running through it—he didn't look like himself anymore. I only saw it for a second before he landed on top of me. He grabbed the back of my head and sunk his teeth into the left side of my neck.

Chapter Twenty

Before I could even recognize the split second of pain, a blissful feeling fell upon me. My entire body was on fire, but in an exceptionally fantastic way.

The warmth spread from my head and down to my toes. The fire moved between my thighs and settled at my core. I wrapped my legs around Valarian, pulling his body closer to mine as he fed from me. The world fell away as he drank my blood, leaving only him and I intertwined as one.

I could die in this man's arms right now and be happy about it.

My blissful moment was interrupted when Val was ripped away from my arms—coldness now filling the warmth that was once there. My breathing was heavy and my chest ached as I missed the feeling of his body on me. I needed him back . . . needed his body to complete me.

Zayn had his arms around Val, dragging him away from me. The guard came back, rushing in with a healer right behind him. The guard tried grabbing for Val but he was too strong. I blinked a couple of times before coming back to reality. The blood from the bite tickled as it ran down my neck. I reached up and put my hand over the wound.

The daze had finally worn off and I realized what had happened.

Valarian was in bloodlust and I was his target.

Come in here with me, where it is safe, girl.

"Fuck you, Demon." I made sure my shield was up and strong. I felt utterly betrayed as anger filled my body.

After grabbing my bow, I nocked an arrow and shot it through the bars of the cell. It hit the Demon in his right eye.

He flailed his arms, thrashing and screaming in pain as he fell to the floor. The arrow wouldn't kill him, but it felt good to see his agony since he had no remorse for the pain he caused.

"Help me hold him down!" Zayn's voice brought my attention away from the Demon.

I wasn't sure if he was talking to the guard or me, but we were both there to help. Once we had Val contained, Zayn grabbed his cheeks and locked onto his eyes, willing him to stop fighting.

"You are okay, buddy. You are fine. Come back to us." He spoke the words so gently they sounded like music dancing on a spring breeze.

Valarian stopped thrashing and his body finally went limp. The healer took the opportunity to run up and touch his arm. Valarian's whole body radiated with pure goldenness before the light disappeared. We slowly eased off, giving him room to breathe.

The healer grasped my arm and I watched as the wound on my wrist closed. Reaching up to the one on my neck, it was also gone. The healer then did the same to Zayn's arm. I had forgotten that he got cut from my dagger and I felt terrible.

Zayn reached down and offered his hand to Val, helping him up. Valarian locked eyes on me and I took a step back in fear. I didn't want the man I loved to hate me forever.

He quickly closed the distance between us and grabbed my face, staring deeply at me. I swallowed as tears fell from my eyes.

"Are you okay, my *hertis rote*? I didn't mean to hurt you."

I nodded. I didn't know what the other words he said meant, but it wasn't important right now.

Val looked me over to see if I was truly okay and then he turned his attention to the cell. The Demon had pulled the arrow out of his eye and had gone still on the floor. He watched us curiously with one red eye as dark green blood oozed from the other.

Val glanced around the room, his eyes finding the keys that Zayn had dropped at some point. He yanked them off the floor and unlocked the cell door. None of us bothered to stop him as hc entered.

Valarian grabbed the Demon by the neck, lifting him off the ground with ease before pinning him against the wall. The Demon smiled in response.

"You are now life-bonded to the female," the Demon's voice was calm as he spoke the words. "How does it feel to have her life in your hands?"

Even though I had no clue what he meant, my breathing became shallow as my chest tightened in fear. *What have I done?*

Valarian's response was quick. He punched his fist into the Demon's chest cavity and yanked his heart out before letting the limp body fall to the floor.

We all watched him in shock as he strolled out of the cell and yanked the dagger off the ground. He prowled up to me and held it out hilt first.

"Would you like to do the honors, bond-mate?" He held the heart out to me as an offering.

Taking the dagger from him with shaking hands, I stabbed the heart right in the center and dark green slime oozed from its insides. The heart wilted and turned to black mush in his hand. The slimy gooiness ran through his fingers, melting away to the floor.

Everyone stood there silently, looking at each other as we tried to slow our heartbeats. I glanced at Zayn, who ran a hand through his hair and let out a sigh.

My attention was brought back to Val when he put his arms around my waist. My body willed itself closer, pressing against him.

"I'm so sorry," my voice crackled with genuine sorrow as I trembled in his arms.

He lowered his head to my mouth and placed a gentle kiss on my lips. The warmth and the softness of his lips were thrilling. The world could melt away and leave us standing there alone and I wouldn't have noticed.

"Ahem." Zayn cleared his voice, making us break free from our blissful encounter. "We need to report to the king immediately."

Valarian pointed his head toward my bow. "Grab your stuff."

After sheathing my dagger, I picked up my bow and quiver. Val grabbed my hand as we all headed up the stairs and out of the castle. None of us spoke or even looked at each other. The silence was a blessing and a curse. Once we got away from the castle, we stopped.

"I don't even know what to say." Zayn scrubbed his hands over his face before he looked between us with a sigh. "Welcome back, buddy." Val dropped my hand as Zayn hugged him. As soon as they were done, Zayn embraced me. "I'm glad you're both okay." As soon as we had finished hugging, Val immediately grabbed my hand again. "I'm going to fly back to the portal so I can calm down. You two take some time to process and talk. I'll see you both before we see the king."

A gust of wind hit me as Zayn released his raven black wings. My breath caught at the beauty of them, every feather was perfect. I would never get acclimated to seeing them. With quickness, he took off into the sky.

We were completely alone as my eyes met Val's. We both stood there with very little to say. It was awkward, to say the least. Feeling uneasy now that the adrenaline was wearing off, I dropped his hand.

"I was going to thank you for saving me but since you killed me before that, I'm not sure if I should."

I averted my eyes to the ground, not wanting to show him the shame on my face. Val laid his hands upon my arms and I lost it.

The tears were coming hard as I placed my face into my hands. I tried to hold my crying back, but it wouldn't listen.

I felt the warmth of him as he slid his hands around my body, pulling me in.

"I was kidding." He spoke the words into the top of my head, placing his cheek upon it. "Thank you for saving me."

"I killed you, Val." I broke free from the hug and started pacing. "I fucking stabbed you with a spelled dagger!"

"But I'm still here, Ember." He watched me as I went back and forth in front of him.

I couldn't process everything that was flowing through me. "A dagger my Vampire-hating father gave to me!"

"It's okay, love." He tried to soothe me, but the shame I felt for letting that Demon in was too much to manage.

"It's not okay, I let him in! He said things to me, Val, and I let him in!"

He grabbed my arm, halting my pacing. "I'm alive because of you, Ember!"

"You could have been dead because of me!" I sobbed, hiding my face in my hands again. He pulled them away and placed his palms upon my cheeks, willing me to look at him.

"Do you understand what you did, giving me blood? It's the highest honor you can give to a Vampire. We only feed from animals and mates."

Tears were rolling down my face because I was *not* his mate, so I shouldn't have fed him. Even though I had no choice at the time, I felt like I had violated him. If I wouldn't have let the Demon in, none of this would have happened.

"I'm sorry," I whispered as I looked at the ground in shame.

"For what?"

"Stabbing you and then forcing you to feed."

"You didn't stab me, the Demon did. He just used your hands." He grabbed my chin and made me meet his eyes again. "Don't ever be sorry for feeding me. It truly is an honor—one I'm not worthy of. I'm the one who should be apologizing. I'm terribly sorry I bit you. I needed the blood after I had lost so much and I didn't realize what I was doing."

"What does life-bonded mean?"

He let go of my face and sighed. "You paid the price for my life with yours. You're bonded to me forever. You won't die until I die and we will always have a strong connection, even if we aren't mated in the eyes of the kingdom. Even if we are just friends."

I wanted to be more than friends. I needed him like I needed air or food. He kept me alive. I quickly recovered from the thought.

"But you're a Vampire, you can live . . . forever."

He laughed. "About a thousand years, but close." He smiled, tilting his head at me.

"And how long will I live?"

"You can still be killed, but your lifespan is now the same as mine. You'll be alive as long as I'm still breathing, love."

"How old are you now?" I assumed he was much older since he was a Vampire.

"I'm only twenty-six."

I was more worried about him than myself. "What if I die? Do you die too?"

"No, you paid the price, not me. I would still be alive. I would just be a shell of a person with a broken bond."

"That is so much to take in." I wiped the tears from my cheeks. "I'll try not to die, I guess."

"I know it's a lot, but we're going to have to finish this conversation later. We have to get back and report to the king. I can't wait to see the look on his face when he hears this story. He loves some good action."

Val seemed happy for someone who had just died and been resurrected. I had a feeling I was about to ruin that good mood.

"What do you know about my mother's death?" His face went still as his body tensed. "Did a Vampire kill her?"

"No."

Confusion settled in me. "Then who did?"

"Demons."

"Why?" The Demon failed to mention that part.

"I cannot say. It's best to let the king explain." He gave me an empathetic look.

"If you knew, why didn't you tell me?" I was getting upset and he could sense it.

He brushed his thumb down my cheek to wipe away a tear. "King's orders."

I couldn't be angry with him because I knew how dedicated he was to his job. He would never go against the king's orders.

I started walking toward the direction of the portal—or at least, I thought so. "Then let's go talk to him!"

Not giving a shit where I was going, I stomped through the dirt of the lands. I was mad, tired, and needed answers . . . and I needed them now.

My emotions were in overdrive. I had just killed the man I loved and brought him back to life *and then* bonded with him until death. I found out Demons killed my mother and my father was a Debaser—whatever that meant—and this was all within the last hour. My mind couldn't take it all in.

"Stop walking, love." Val came up from behind and put his hands around my waist. "We can gale from here." My anger stilled slightly at his touch.

"I'm sorry, I'm just upset. So much has happened today. My dad isn't the person I thought he was, and now I'm life-bonded, and . . ." I stopped myself from rambling on and looked up into his eyes.

"Are you upset about being bonded to me?"

"I don't know, Val." I shook my head. "Everything just happened so fast."

The wrong words may have come out of my mouth. I should've told him about the feelings I had for him. The feelings that were stronger than friendship, stronger than just sex. I should've told him that I was madly in love with him and he was my everything, but I didn't. I stayed quiet.

Val also stayed silent as he galed us back. Once we landed, we walked past the guards and stepped onto the portal. Prowling up to me, he put both hands behind my head and locked eyes with me. He smelled so delicious, like snow and the woods. Heat rose in my body, making my cheeks flush.

Val willed the portal to go. I closed my eyes when I felt the rush of air. Soft lips moved gently against mine, taking my attention away from the feelings of the portal. They felt and tasted delicious. The sensation of being whipped through air while being kissed at the same time was a fantastic combination. My body wanted his. Wanted it like it was a missing piece of mine. He was the blood in my veins. The strength I needed when I was scared. The only thing I wanted was to lie beside him and tell him my feelings while I handed him the keys to my entire heart.

Val broke the kiss as we landed back in the country of Ashbern, leaving me panting.

"Thank you for sacrificing yourself to save me." Letting go of my waist, he grabbed my hand as we stepped off the portal.

Zayn strolled up with a concerned face. "You guys good?"

"Yeah." Val had the courage to speak, I didn't. I nodded as Zayn looked between us. I was worried my voice would give away all the feelings I was holding in. Shame. Love. Fear. My body was trying to cool off and calm itself.

"The king has already been warned that an incident occurred and he knows we're on our way."

Angering the king was something I never wanted to do. Now, I had killed one of his guards, even if he didn't die. I would be lucky if I didn't get a death sentence after today's events. I hoped he would at least tell me the secrets he knew about my family before he has me killed.

Chapter Twenty-One

We were all tense as we galed outside the wards of Castle Elderfall. None of us spoke as we made our way to the king. The walk down the halls seemed to go on forever. I didn't even speak to Valarian in my mind; he didn't speak to me either. The silence was deafening. When we finally reached the large double doors, they opened on their own, and we stepped inside. The king was sitting upon his throne, looking relieved to see us. Then his eyes went wide.

"Welcome to Castle Elder—"

"We have no time for formalities, Meyers." The king interrupted the servant who stepped forward. "Thank you, you are dismissed." The servant hurried off. "What happened to you three? You're all covered in blood and soaked in healer magic."

I looked at us, and there was a lot of blood, but I didn't see any magic.

"We went to investigate the Demon attack on Mayhem, Your Majesty."

"I know the details. Drop the formalities," the king said with true power. His eyes went to Val. "What of your father?"

Val stiffened and my breath caught. "The duke is unharmed and residing at Vanhall City for now."

The duke's Valarian's father. I kept that thought to myself.

"What else happened?"

"We went to question a Demon that was held in the prison." Zayn ran a worried hand over his chin. "A lot happened after that, sir."

"Ember, come here and give me your hand so I can see for myself."

Not knowing what he meant, I walked up and gave the king my hand. He took it and looked into my eyes as a gust of air blew through the room. The king's blue eyes went wide in surprise as they turned silver, then completely gold. He smiled, then he looked confused. He gasped before he went still. His eyebrows furrowed and he gasped again. Then he smiled and dropped my hand.

"You got to make snow angels." He smiled longingly, with a reminiscing look on his face. "I haven't done that in years. Nice shot to the Demon's eye, Ember, you make me proud."

"Thank you," I said softly as tears threatened me.

"You stabbed Val? And then fed him?"

"I didn't mean to. I'm sorry." *I'm going to be executed.*

"Why would I execute you?" I checked my shield and it was still up.

"You can hear thoughts?" I said without thinking. *Oh, no.*

"Of course, my child. I can do everything." He beamed radiantly. "And you are still going hunting with me, I don't care how nervous you are." He laughed.

"I'm sorry, I did not mean to offend—"

"There is truly no need to apologize, my child. Valarian is alive and well, thanks to the sacrifice you made."

What about my father? My mother?

"There is a lot to discuss. Questions that you need answered." He shifted in his seat, resting his chin on his fist as his face went blank.

I walked back over to Zayn and Val.

"The Demon told you the truth, Ember. Vampires did *not* kill your mother. Your father was the one who made up that excuse two years ago. We never believed him, but we didn't know the truth until recently."

"I don't understand."

"We caught a Demon on your lands a few months before your arrival here and he gave us some valuable information in exchange for his life. We have been investigating your father since."

"What are you investigating him for?"

"We were informed that your father is a Debaser."

"That's what the Demon said, but I don't know what that is."

"It's a person who trades souls to Erebus, King of the Demons, in exchange for money and other things. Your father has taken varied species. Casters, Lycans. There is even a young Angel missing. He takes them and sells their souls to Erebus."

Confusion filled me as I shook my head. "But why would he do that?"

"To help Erebus build his army. Each soul that is taken gets turned into a Demon. We have been contemplating a way to save them, but have yet to develop a good plan."

"Did he trade my mother's soul?" I asked as tears formed in my eyes. Valarian reached down and grabbed my hand.

"Technically, yes. From my understanding, she was given to Erebus."

Tears broke free from my eyes. I let go of Valarian's and put both of my hands on my face, trying to block the tears from coming out. Zayn put a hand on my back to soothe me and I dropped my hands. I had many questions, and I didn't know where to start.

"Is that why you brought me here?"

The king looked empathetic and sighed.

"Every guard gets summoned at the age of twenty-two. You'd just had a birthday a week before your arrival. It was bad timing. You already know this information. You are merely upset and it makes it hard to think. But I assure you, it had nothing to do with the events or your father."

"If my father is a Debaser, why hasn't he been imprisoned?"

"That is a particularly good question. We have laws to abide by, Ember. The laws state that we cannot imprison him because we cannot prosecute someone solely on the word of a Demon. Numerous species have been coming up missing for more than two years now. It had been few and far between, but it has become more frequent. Once we found out that it was your father a few months ago, we started investigating and biding time, waiting to catch him in the act. Unfortunately, he is a clever man." The king frowned.

"What of my sister? Will she be safe?"

"For now, she is. I cannot put around-the-clock guards on her without her noticing. I have guards checking on her three times a day and reporting back for the next couple of days. She is currently safe at work right now."

"Thank you for telling me about my mother." All emotions left my body. I felt numb.

"I wish it were not true. I am sorry for the pain you have to face with this information. With that being said, I must retire." The king stood, and we all bowed our heads.

He started to walk away and stopped. His eyes met ours.

"Magnificent work today from all of you. You make an effective team. And thank you, Ember, for saving Val. You are a true King's Guard and I am proud to have you."

"Thank you, Your Majesty."

"Congratulations to you both on your life-bond." He gave us an affectionate smile and walked away.

We all quickly left the castle and walked past the wards.

Zayn stopped a few feet in front of me. "We can gale from here."

"Can we go somewhere first?" I couldn't go back to my room yet.

"Where?" Val looked at me with concern, tilting his head slightly.

"To the beautiful place." I gave him a sad smile. He walked up to me and grabbed my face.

"Of course, my *hertis rote*."

"I will meet you back at the manor." Zayn quickly galed away.

Val wrapped his arms around my body and laid his cheek on top of my head before we galed away.

I knew that he knew exactly where I wanted to be when we landed right next to the wisteria trees. He let go of my waist and I quickly walked over to a tree with excessively long limbs brushing the ground. Valarian strolled up next to me and moved the branches aside. I walked underneath and turned toward him.

"Can I be alone, please?"

"Of course. I'll stay close by. Just wield me your thoughts when you're ready to go back." He smiled kindly, understanding that I needed my space to process things. I nodded, and he disappeared.

As I walked over to the tree, I noticed the magic wasn't dancing around. They were slow-moving and gentle. They were caressing me as if they knew I was sad. I raised my hand and ran a finger down the tree, feeling its smooth bark. The magic scattered away from where I touched.

The day's events were taking hold of my heart and squeezing it. The pressure was building to the point where I thought I would die if I didn't let it out. Starting to sob, I covered my face with my hands, unable to hold back anymore. I fell to my knees as pain radiated through my body making my heart hurt. My shield dropped as I cried hard.

As I fell to my side and laid there, the magic seemed to come to a standstill with me. The pain became unbearable and my brain wouldn't shut off. I started screaming and punching the ground I lay upon, trying to release the sadness and anger from my veins and my thoughts.

The magic scattered away. I was wailing emotions so deep that I didn't know if I could come back after that. I was afraid of losing the happiness I had gained. I scared myself. I needed him—needed Val. He was what made me happy.

I need you. I wielded to my bond-mate.

He was there in an instant. He laid down beside me and wrapped his big arms around me as I cried. There was nothing sexual about it. He was just there for me in my time of need. I turned in his arms and faced him.

Closing my eyes, I laid my head on his chest. We cuddled up under the tree until the sun had set. Neither of us ever spoke a word. It was getting cold outside and I started to shiver. Valarian scooped me up into his arms and carried me out from under the trees as I stared unfocused into the world.

He galed us back to Castleva Manor, carried me upstairs to my room where he laid me on my bed. He reached down and untied my boots and removed them, then pulled the blankets up over me.

Laying there quietly, I stared at the curtains that were slightly swaying in front of my window from the night air. They were a pretty, gray color—the same color as the flowers on my blanket.

Val walked over and threw a piece of wood into the fireplace and then shut the window. I heard two thuds as he removed his boots.

He crawled into bed and scooted up behind me, once again wrapping his arms around me. He must have taken his shirt off at some point, because I could feel the warmth of his bare skin next to my body.

There were no sexual feelings towards the situation from either of us, which made me feel comforted and content. We laid there in blissful silence. I was done crying. I didn't have any tears left.

With his arms wrapped around my body and exhaustion hitting me hard, sleep took over. I slept all night and morning.

Val left my room at some point, I didn't know what time, but he wasn't there when I woke up in the afternoon. I wasn't going down for practice today because I didn't want to. Somehow, I was still tired, so I covered my head with my blanket and went back to sleep.

Chapter Twenty-Two

S leeping deep all night and day did nothing for me. I was still tired when a knock woke me early in the evening.

It's probably Zayn, I thought to myself as I opened the door.

"Not Zayn and shield." Val smiled playfully. He leaned in and kissed my cheek.

"I am too tired to shield or care if you hear my thoughts. So, unless there is a group of Vampires running around, you're just going to have to deal with it," I said as he walked inside and shut the door.

"I missed you at practice and am glad to see that you're still breathing." Val strolled over and took a seat in my chair.

I decided that I did need my shield up because my emotions were overwhelming and I didn't want him to know. So, I put it up and then crawled back into bed. "I didn't feel like going."

"That's fine, the king gave you three days off to process things. I persuaded him not to count today. So, you technically have four days off." He looked at me tenderly.

"You're the best." I covered my head with my blanket, hiding from him and the world.

"Do you want to talk? Or would you like me to leave?" I didn't answer. He sat there quietly for a minute before I heard him stand. "I'll let you rest, love."

"No, wait . . . " I sighed and uncovered my head. "I need to talk. I just don't know what to say."

"I'll try and help as much as possible." He sat on the edge of my bed.

"So, I'm insanely upset about my father and the role he played in my mother's death."

He nodded. "I understand that you need time to process."

"Yeah, so that's all I should be thinking about . . . but it isn't." I nervously bit my lip.

"What else are you thinking about?"

"I don't know what to say."

"Take your time." He rested a hand on my leg through the blanket. I felt that touch and knew what I needed to do.

"Can we go to Amethyst Falls? I need a place to think."

"Of course, get dressed and meet me downstairs."

He left me sitting there, the questions in my head swarming. I got ready and hurried down to find him standing just outside the wards. He immediately wrapped his arms around me.

"You don't have to gale me. I can gale myself now that I know the way."

"What fun would that be?" He smiled. I smiled lightly since I was nervous. He galed us and we landed at Amethyst Falls.

It was almost sunset when I walked up to the trees. Val lifted the branches for me and I stepped inside. The magic was dancing around happily, as if it knew what I was going to do.

"I'll give you some privacy."

"That's not what I want."

He looked at me curiously. "What do you want, Ember?"

I took a deep breath, then slowly let it out, deciding I had nothing to lose. My heart was racing from the words I was about to say. I was worried that he didn't have feelings for me. I just needed to know how he felt, and I needed to know now.

"I want you, Val. That's what I want."

"You have me, my love."

"I'm not sure you want me in the same way I want you."

His hands gripped my cheeks lightly, willing me to look at him. "You have *no idea* how bad I want you."

"No." I pulled away from him, putting distance between us. "I mean, do you want more than sex?"

"I have wanted more than sex since the beginning. You were the one wanting to hide what we were doing."

"I was confused. I didn't know what I wanted, Val!"

The overwhelming feeling in my chest was too much to bear. I walked over by the tree trunk and sat on a bed of fallen flowers.

"Well, I knew what I wanted. I have wanted you since the day I met you. I have wanted you more than I have ever wanted anything in my life. To the Gods, Ember!"

"Oh," was all I managed to say in response.

"I have been wanting to talk about something too, love." He slowly prowled over to me as I looked up at him with tears in my eyes. "You're like a force that is always pulling me in. A force that I'm scared will break me one day if I can't have you. I can't stop thinking about you and it was like this before the bond. The bond has just made it even stronger." My breathing was deep and fast from his words as he kneeled on the ground next to me. "I didn't want you to know about this force because I didn't want to scare you. I was giving you the time to think about what *you* wanted. That was more important to me than anything I wanted. You were more important."

Tears escaped my eyes, and I looked down at my hands. He sat flat and crossed his legs. Grabbing my chin, he made me meet his eyes.

"So, if you're still wondering, yes, I want more than sex. I want to be with you more than anything, my love. I would die for you. Hell, I already did. Because you are my *hertis rote*."

"You have said that twice before. What does it mean?"

He wiped the tears from my face. "It means, heart's root. That's what you are. My heart's root. You keep the blood pumping through my veins. You keep me alive."

My chest swelled with the overwhelming number of feelings I had for the gorgeous man in front of me. I leaned over toward him and placed my hands upon his cheeks, pressing my forehead against his.

"You are my *hertis rote* too, Val." I ran a hand through his long hair.

The realization that he had the same feeling hit me when I saw that his eyes looked relieved. He moved his head and placed a gentle kiss on my eyelid. "I am the luckiest man in the world."

He kissed down my cheeks until he found my lips. The kiss was sweet and tender. His hands traveled down my arms and it gave me goosebumps. My breathing was heavy and I had an ache between my legs as I leaned deeper into the kiss.

Pulling back, he stopped the gentle kissing, but I didn't want to stop.

The kiss made me yearn for more. It heated that area between my thighs, making me crave him. Needing him close to me, needing him inside of me, I crawled onto his lap and wrapped my legs around his waist.

Eagerly digging my hands into his back, I pulled him in tighter. Trying to cure the cravings, I slammed a kiss onto his mouth.

My fingers traveled up and I tightened them in his long hair. Heat took over my body as he moaned in my mouth. The vibrations from it tickled my tongue.

My body moved in ways I didn't know it could as I rubbed my core on him. Needing him even closer, I shoved him down onto the bed of flowers. As he laid on his back, I shifted until I was on my knees on top of him. He growled and yanked my face down to his, making me moan in excitement.

Wetness filled my panties as I rubbed my core on his cock. He squeezed my ass, assisting my grinding.

Moving to his ear, I gently pulled his earlobe into my mouth and sucked it. Running my tongue around it, I blew a light breath into his ear as he shivered.

Kissing down to his neck while I still grinded on him, I decided to be brave. Opening my mouth and baring my teeth, I bit him. He growled and rolled me over, my legs spread open and his body landed on top of mine.

His scent was intoxicating, smelling of lust and danger as his body was heavy against mine. I was panting with pure excitement as he stared into my eyes.

"That was sexy as hell," he said, then slammed a kiss onto me.

His tongue rolled seductively around mine as we kissed. When he sucked on my tongue, I about came unglued. Every time I felt a fang graze me, I got wetter. Taking his bottom lip into my mouth, I sucked it lightly, then nipped it between my teeth. His head fell back, as he let out a moaning growl.

Slowly pulling back, he kissed next to my mouth, trailing further away, heading toward my jaw. I moaned in ecstasy as he sucked on my chin and slightly nibbled it, never piercing my skin.

My heart threatened to beat out of my chest as he continued kissing me, moving down to the front of my throat. Seeing the sunset through the trees as I tilted my head, inviting him to take all of me that he wanted, I felt a fang scrape against my neck and it sent shivers down my entire body.

"Take me," I moaned.

"I am, my love."

"No." I said breathlessly. "I mean feed from me."

"Are you sure?" He continued kissing my neck. I let out a loud moan as a fang scraped my skin again, giving him his answer, but he didn't bite me.

He stopped the kissing and gently pulled my shirt off, releasing my breasts from their prison. My nipples were standing high, waiting for their turn.

"You're so beautiful." He ran his fingers slowly across my chest, tracing the outline of my tattoo. Leaning his face in, he kissed my chest and then ran his tongue across it.

Feeling how rock-hard he was between my legs, I raised my hips to press against him. He moaned into my chest from what I did, and I felt his hot breath blowing against my skin.

Continuing kissing, he worked his way back up to my neck and onto my shoulder. My clit was sensitive and twitched with excitement as I continued rubbing the aching pain between my legs onto his hard cock.

Putting his mouth back on mine, he silenced the moan I released as my clit screamed to be let loose.

Running his thumb over my hard nipple, he growled as he broke away from the kiss. His mouth went straight to my breast. Making a pulsating pattern as he sucked in my nipple had me squirming with excitement. He swirled his tongue around, and it sent a spasm through me, all the way down to where I ached, willing the heat at my core to rise further.

Shifting up onto his knees, I instantly missed the warmth and heaviness of his body. It was worth it when he pulled his shirt off, showing me his rock-hard muscles.

With the sunset behind him and the trees all around, it was the most perfect picture of beauty I had ever seen.

Sliding his hand down my thigh and slowly to the top of my boots, he unlaced each one and pulled them off. He slid his hands back up to the top of my pants and untied them. I lifted my hips in assistance as he pulled them off next. He then reached up and ran his finger along the waistband of my panties before pulling them off.

Going still, he took in every inch of my naked body and made a slight growling sound that sent shivers through me. He pulled his boots and pants off, leaving himself dressed in nothing but a pair of shorts as he eased himself back on top of me.

Reaching his hand between my legs, he slid a finger down my slit until he found my wetness. His eyes closed as he growled again. With his mouth wide open, I could see the last bit of sunset glistening off his wet, now elongated fangs.

Sliding down me, he used his hands to spread my legs further apart so he could look at my wetness—the wetness he proudly made.

With a single finger, he reached out and slid it between my lips, spreading them open. He ran it around slowly, taking his time and dragging some of the wetness up to my clit, which was twitching and wanting attention. My body jerked at the feeling as he circled his finger around. This was the highest pleasure one could ever dream of. I felt like I was folded inside out.

"You're so wet." He looked at my core like it was inviting him in. "I want to taste you."

I moaned at his words, completely breathless and willing to let him do anything he wanted to me. "Do it."

He gave me a sultry grin that showed the eagerness and excitement he had. Easing himself down slowly, he put his mouth close to my core. I could feel the heat from his breath bouncing off my center as he blew slightly, making me jump with anticipation. I was about to come unleashed.

Slowly running his tongue from my entrance up to my clit, I moaned loudly as the uncontrollable feeling kept building. He went down again and licked at my opening, bringing the wetness up to the bundle of nerves that were now screaming. I had never felt anything more wonderful in my entire life.

His tongue darted inside of me, proudly licking every drop of me that he could find. He came back up to my clit and licked in circles. Reaching down, I twined my fingers into his hair, using it to press him closer to my core. He moaned loudly, the vibrations bouncing off me as he continued licking.

Placing a finger inside me, he curled it forward as his tongue continued the job it started. Sucking my clit into his mouth, I tensed as the feeling built to the point that I couldn't take it anymore.

Raising my hips, I grinded on his face. The overwhelming feeling exploded inside of me and I moaned loud as I rode the ride of ecstasy he had been giving me.

Feeling like a million stars burst from my skin, a fire burned through my veins as I melted into his face. My orgasm sent me on a journey of pure bliss as I fell through space and time. The magic of the lands danced around us excitedly as my orgasm ended.

My breaths were uncontrolled, ragged, but my yearning pain had finally eased. I had never had an orgasm even close to the feeling of that one. They were good and relieving, but this one was magical. Valarian raised up with a proud look on his face.

"Are you ready?" he whispered with a seductive voice.

"Yes, please," I moaned.

As he pulled his shorts off, I got to see the rock-hard manliness that was ready for me. He slowly laid back on top of me, and I felt the warmth of his entire body. I also felt the warmth of his hard cock as it laid upon my wetness and slid up between my lips.

"I'm sorry, love. This will hurt, but only for a second."

My face must have looked confused because he smiled as I locked eyes with him. He leaned in to kiss my neck, but he didn't.

Val bit into my skin, his sharp fangs piercing the flesh on my neck. I gasped as a flood of raw emotions filled my body. Warmth spread through me, the feeling settling in my core, heating me and threatening to burn me from the inside out. I shivered with pleasure while he drank from me. He let out a light growl of approval when I dug my claws into his back.

A deep moan of pure pleasure fell from his lips and into my neck as he slid inside of me. Continuing my hands down his back, I caressed his muscles, feeling them move beneath my hands. My legs started to shake the more he thrusted into me.

Grabbing the back of my knee, he lifted my leg higher to make more room for him. Running his manly hands slowly up my thighs, he went deeper inside of me, making me moan.

The endorphins from the bite were still flooding my veins as his tongue licked up the blood that I felt running down my neck. He lowered his hand to my clit and circled his finger on it, priming me for another orgasm.

Feeling high at the multiple sensations going on, he bent his head down as he sucked on my nipple, making my nerve endings twitch again—begging to be let loose. He went deeper inside of me, moving his hips in a circular motion while his fingers were rubbing me.

Scratching my nails down his back, he moaned with pleasure. He slammed his mouth onto mine, taking me higher. I raised my knees as high as I could, letting him explore the deepest parts of me as the feeling kept building. The feeling was almost overbearing as I gave him every piece of me and bared my entire soul to him.

Running my hands flat over his chest, I could feel every rigid muscle he had. All of them were working hard under my hands, moving to please me.

We fell into a rhythm, our bodies becoming one as the magic danced around us, cheering us on. This wasn't sex, I realized. We were making love. Magical, passionate, soul-consuming love.

Sweat glistened in the moonlight across his chest and arms as I stared at him. Glancing up into his face, pure joy, and love spread through me. Not being able to hold back how happy I was, I smiled at him. He gave me a loving, seductive smile back, his eyes saying he loved me, too.

Moving my face to kiss his neck, I opened my mouth wide and bit him again. He sped up, rotating his hips, and grinded into me as he moaned.

Grabbing a handful of his hair, I moved my mouth to his lips, kissing him harder as I rode the wave again. The flooding sensation took over, and I moaned loudly into his mouth as he moaned back into mine, riding the wave of ecstasy with me this time. Wetness filled me as we came together.

Our bodies slowed as our heartbeats became one. Sweat poured off both of us. The magic came alive even more and was now dancing around us in swirls as our breathing slowed. The sparkles seemed to have multiplied as millions of them danced around us in celebration.

"My *hertis rote*," he whispered. I looked into his face with tears in my eyes and swallowed hard, almost choking on my own emotions as magic danced behind him.

"My *hertis rote*," I whispered back. He locked eyes with me and placed a slow, passionate kiss upon my lips.

I love you, Val. I thought to myself, but couldn't make myself say it. We made love again immediately after.

Chapter Twenty-Three

Today was my first day back to practice after the four days off the king had granted me. We had no additional information on my father. I was in the dining hall eating lunch and listening to everyone chat, not paying attention to the conversation after a hand slid onto my thigh.

Stop that. There are people around. I met Valarian's eyes. I absolutely didn't want him to stop.

That's what makes it so fun. He grinned and continued moving his hand slowly.

I'm going to stab you one of these days. I shook my head, my breathing getting heavy as his hand slid closer to my core.

Didn't you already stab me once?

I whipped my head over to him and frowned at the memory. He smirked.

Bite me, I teased.

And I have already done that twice so far. He winked at me.

Val and I had been sparring and making out all morning, and he was in an extremely good mood because of it.

Where did the bite go, Val? I noticed it disappeared.

The magic of my venom makes you heal within minutes, love.

I rolled my eyes. *Of course it's magic.*

He leaned in and gave me a brief kiss and I let him—even though we were in front of our friends. He smelled so good and tasted good, too.

"Yuck, not at the dinner table!" I glanced up as I heard Zayn speak, his nose crinkled up before he grinned.

"I knew it!" Cash's face was shocked as he pointed to Val and me. "I knew you guys were going to get together!"

Cali giggled. "Did you just figure this out, Cash?"

"You guys didn't know?" Cash shook his head, doubting the others.

"Oh, I most definitely knew. I had a front-row seat for most of it." Zayn winked at Val and me.

Cali raised her hand. "I knew too."

Cash looked at the beautiful Lycan as he ran a hand through his beard. "Did you, Zila?"

"Absolutely! I smelled the lust coming off them at the first bonfire, when we were swimming, when he was chopping wood, at the second bonfire, and the—"

"Okay, show off," Asher teased.

"Sorry, it's a Lycan thing." Zila grinned with pride as she winked at Asher.

He chuckled before turning his attention to Cash. "I think everyone knew but you, buddy."

"I'm pretty sure that I knew first." Cali smiled at Val and me. "Even before they did."

I looked at her beautiful face, wondering how. "When did you know, Cali?"

"It was obvious the day you arrived . . . after V came to my room."

"Lies! No way you knew on day one!" Cash said, not buying her story.

"I absolutely did! No one throws V off balance and you most definitely did that, Ember. That's why I gave you a sexy dress. I knew what I was doing." She laughed and clapped her hands together.

"Cali!" My mouth fell open. She had sent me to the lion's den wrapped up in a pretty package, and even though I was in shock, I was never more grateful to have met that lion.

"Okay, okay. Enough about my love life." I whipped my head toward Val, my eyes going wide at his use of the word love. Everyone went quiet.

"What?" He smiled at me. "You know what I meant."

"Ha-ha, you're going to have your hands full with this one, buddy," Cash said while shaking his head.

A messenger Imp arrived in the dining room, grabbing all of our attention. Since it wasn't a private room, he didn't need an invitation to come in.

"Greetings." His twinkling orange eyes locked on Zayn as he held up a letter. I assumed it was a mission.

With a sigh, Zayn took the paper. "Thank you."

"Salutations." He disappeared as fast as he came.

I wonder if the Imp knows any other words, Val.

I have never thought about it before. Val had a look of contemplation on his face. He was thinking about it now and it made me giggle.

Zayn sighed after he finished reading. "We have a mission."

"Where and who is going?" Cash asked. The look on his face told me he hoped it was him.

"Asher, Zila, and Ember. It's on Tessalone."

Locking eyes with Val, I knew he was going to be concerned that he wasn't going with me. When he clenched his jaw, my thoughts were confirmed.

"What's the mission?" I asked, looking back to Zayn.

"Looks like another Demon attack. There's a missing Fae. Grab weapons and get to the portal." Zayn was in commander mode now and it suited him. I immediately stood and headed for the armory as Val followed right next to me.

As soon as we got out of the dining room, I grabbed his hand, trying to soothe him. He gripped mine back.

We were both quiet as we headed downstairs. I immediately filled my quiver with arrows. Turning to look at Val, I noticed he was deep in thought as he watched me.

"What's wrong, Val?"

"I don't want you going without me. If I leave now, I can ask the king and—"

"No," I said, cutting him off.

Val looked surprised, like he wasn't expecting to hear that from me. "What do you mean *no*?"

"I know you don't want me going without you, but I can protect myself. We won't always get to go on missions together, so this will be good for practice. I need to know how to not rely on someone to always be there for me. I need to learn to survive on my own."

"Wow." He slowly nodded his head in surprise.

"Are you mad?"

"No, I was trying to produce an excuse to counterbalance your reasoning, but I don't have one." He prowled toward me in that sexy way of his. "You're strong and I know you can protect yourself, love."

Leaning down, he kissed me deeply and it started to get a little heated. We had sex early this morning, but I was ready to go again. I would have been happy having my way with him all day, every day.

"Oh, don't mind me. Continue." We broke free from our fantastic kiss as Cash grinned brightly at us.

"Why are you even down here?" Val asked, looking frustrated that the Angel just ruined our kiss. "You aren't even on the mission."

I giggled at the men as I grabbed my bow.

"I was making sure that everyone got all their weapons." Cash ran his hand through his beard. A look of anticipation and excitement filled his face. "I was too excited to stay up there."

A shadow caught my attention and when I glanced up, it was Asher. He grabbed two small scythes and attached them to his belt. Zila walked in behind him, grabbed two sai, and put them in hers.

"Do you use weapons, Zila?" I had been curious since she fought in wolf form in the forest the day I met her.

"Rarely, but sometimes. I prefer mauling people." She smiled sweetly, and I smiled back at her. She was extremely fierce for someone so kind and gentle.

"I have another question. It's kind of odd."

Zila smiled at me knowingly. "Go ahead, Ember."

"What happens to your weapons and clothes when you change into your wolf form?"

"They disappear, then when I transform back, they reappear, thankfully."

"How?" I was so confused.

"How does fire shoot from your hands?" she asked.

"I don't know." I shrugged. "It's just magic."

"Exactly." She smiled. "It's magic for me too."

I glanced up at Cash with a question in my eyes. He knew before I even spoke.

"It's the same with our wings. They don't rip our clothes or anything." He grinned. "Just magic."

"Wow, that's amazing, guys!"

Zila giggled at my excited words. "That's how we feel about your fire hands and his wind." She pointed at Asher. He made a breeze come through the room that blew back our hair.

Never in my life did I think or feel like I was special, but her saying it like that made me realize that we were all special in our own way—even Casters.

We left the armory and walked out to the portal. Val leaned down and gave me a long, passionate kiss goodbye. Asher and Zila were both smiling at me as I stepped onto the portal.

"Stop that," I said, and they both laughed.

Zila stood next to me and grabbed my hand. I was so grateful for the friends I had. Someone wielded the portal to go and I tensed. Trying to make my body relax, I took deep breaths and slowly blew them out. It helped.

Starting to sway, I tried locking my body tight. Zila leaned into me, trying to assist. Then we landed in the country of Tessalone. The portal was getting more manageable, but it was *still* miserable.

My heart was beating fast and my stomach was uneasy as we stepped off the platform.

"Do you want to sit?" Asher asked.

"No, I'll be fine."

They strolled next to me for a little bit, giving me time to feel better. Once we got over the beautiful bridge, we galed the rest of the way. Since I didn't know where we were going, Zila galed me. We landed right outside the wards of Gailshire and walked for about a mile before the castle came into sight.

My eyes widened as I looked up at it. "Whoa! It's so gorgeous."

The castle was phenomenal. The brick of the structure was an off-white color with several towers, each of them with a green top.

We headed across a drawbridge and up to the gate, where the portcullis opened for us. A bronze-skin male with short black hair greeted us. He had beautiful amber-colored eyes, which meant he was a Fae.

"Welcome to Gailshire Castle. The Duke of Tessalone is expecting you. My name is Tobias and I will be your guide for the day. Please, follow me and I will show you to the duke's quarters."

We did as we were told and followed Tobias. The interior of the castle was even more gorgeous than the exterior. Everything was a creamy white color, with touches of emerald green everywhere. My eyes were the same color. There was a beautiful crystal chandelier in the foyer and fresh flowers lining the hallways.

As we entered the duke's quarters, a mahogany-skinned man sat in a chair with his legs crossed, reading a book. He had a patient and pleasant smile on his face when he saw us. I already liked this duke better than the Duke of Mazuria.

We bowed our heads.

"Welcome. I hope you found your journey pleasant."

"We did, Your Grace, thank you." Zila's sweet tone suddenly sounded refined and elegant.

"I am delighted to hear that." His amber eyes sparkled as he smiled.

"What is the issue at hand, Your Grace?" Asher sounded equally refined.

"A half a dozen Demons came onto my lands in the middle of the night. No one was injured since the guards quickly killed most of them."

"That is good news."

"Yes, vastly so, Zila. The sad news in this situation is that we now have a missing Fae."

"Do you have information on them, Your Grace?" Asher asked.

"Yes. Tobias has all the info you need, Asher. He is going to escort you while you talk to witnesses and the family of the missing girl."

"Thank you, Your Grace," Asher said. We all bowed our heads and followed Tobias out of the castle.

"We can gale to Magecrest from here," Tobias said once we got outside the wards. He galed away and we followed. I went with Zila again.

We landed right outside of Magecrest Market. The town was hopping with people even after the attack last night. Many of the stores were packed with customers buying fruits, vegetables, and other items.

There were species from different lands that came here to go shopping. I saw a male Angel shopping for fruit at the first stand we passed. Further into town, I saw a female Elven. She was beautiful and had enchanting, deep brown eyes.

"We will talk to the family first." Tobias led us through town.

We made it through the shopping area and were now at the edge of the housing community. The parents of the missing Fae were standing outside their home, waiting for us. There was also a familiar Fae standing with them. I saw Zila stiffen when she saw her crush, Natsu, standing with the family.

"Hello, Mr. and Mrs. Amata, this is the King's Guard that is investigating the Demon attack. They have a few questions for you."

"Zila, my darling." The mother came forward and gave Zila a big hug.

"I'm sorry to hear what happened. Who is missing?"

"It's Primavera." The mother started crying and a small gust of wind hit me when her wings popped out.

I had never seen the wings of a Fae before. They were blue and green with an iridescent sheen to them, remarkably like the wings of a dragonfly. No one else around me reacted to it, so I tried my best to keep the look of shock off my face.

"Oh, no." Zila gasped as her silver eyes filled with fear. "Not Prim!"

"Where was she when she was taken?" Asher asked, taking the lead.

"The guards were down on Fairy Beach, which was where the Demons came up," Natsu said. "Once the warning bells rang, my sister galed down to the site. I didn't know she had left until twenty minutes later. My mother was hysterical when I got home, so I grabbed my bow and headed out, myself. She was nowhere to be seen."

"Why would she go to the beach during a Demon attack?"

Natsu's stunning amber eyes looked at me. "My sister is a fighter, Ember. She was trying to help the guards, which she did because she killed a Demon. They lost track of her somehow during the altercation."

"I'm so sorry, Natsu." Zila stepped up and hugged him. He took it gracefully.

"We will do whatever we can to help get Primavera back," Asher said confidently.

"Thank you all." Natsu bowed, as did his father.

"Come back and see us soon, Zila," the mother said, still crying.

"I will try." She smiled kindly before we left.

Tobias led us around town while we took statements from witnesses. We didn't get any helpful information, so we headed back toward the portal. We thanked Tobias for his escort and parted ways. Once we galed to the bridge, we stopped to talk.

"Do you think she's still alive?" I asked with a concerned face.

"One can only hope," Asher answered.

Zila took a seat on a wooden bench and sighed. "The Demons are going to keep taking people until there is no one left."

"We can't let that happen!"

Asher's green eyes met mine, ready to fight. "Agreed."

"Is there a dungeon on the Demon lands?" I was willing to help rescue everyone.

"I have never been to the country of Mistlaven, but there's a map in the library." Zila eyed me curiously. "I'm sure we can find out."

"Why do you want to know, Ember?" Asher asked. I met his eyes, and his face told me he already knew what I wanted to do.

"Because I want to go there and save as many people as we can. The king said others are missing as well. Who knows how many they have taken over the years."

"That sounds dangerous." Zila looked uneasy. "But I'm one hundred percent in."

"Me too." Asher nodded. "We'll have to talk to Zayn and get the king's permission."

"We should head back and arrange that." I was nervous about the plans I had just started.

"Hold on. I have an idea." Zila stood up. "You two stay here, I'll be right back." She galed away.

As I stood there with Asher, my brain wouldn't stop thinking about what happened with the Fae.

"I have a question."

"Yes, Ember?"

"Why did Mrs. Amata's wings come out?"

"Cash told me that happens sometimes when Fae or Angels have a strong emotional response."

My eyes widened. "That would kind of suck!"

Asher laughed. "It most definitely would."

The conversation stopped as his mind seemed to be somewhere else.

"Is everything okay?" I asked and he sighed loudly.

"Not really." His emerald-green eyes looked at me before glancing away.

"Do you want to talk about it?" He bit his lip like he was trying to keep himself from talking. "You don't have to if you don't want to." I wasn't trying to pry—it was just an observation.

"I'm having relationship issues," he said as he cracked his knuckles.

"That's never good."

"She is always upset that she doesn't get to see me as much as she would like."

His face was sad and my heart hurt for him. "How long have you been with her?"

He took a seat on a nearby bench. "Two years."

"How long have you been a King's Guard?" I asked as I sat down next to him.

"Only six months."

My mouth was slightly agape. "Oh. I assumed it was longer."

"It seems like forever ago. It wouldn't feel as long if I weren't in love with someone from another land." He leaned his elbows on his knees.

"Have you thought about mating her and seeing if you can bring her to Castleva?"

"We've had that conversation. She's not willing to leave her family."

"What will you do?" I was super concerned that he was going to get his heart broken.

"I don't know. I was hoping you would tell me." We both laughed.

"You don't want relationship advice from me." I shook my head and looked at the ground. I barely had my life and relationship figured out.

"I'm sure it wouldn't be that bad. You seem to be understanding in situations. She isn't. She knew that I would have to come here when we started our relationship, but didn't care at the time."

My eyebrows furrowed. "Then it changed?"

"Yeah. She was under the assumption that I would be seeing her more. We only get a weekend home every six weeks once we're trained. Well, seven weeks, now that you're here."

"I'm sorry." It could probably stay every six weeks. I only really needed to see Cinder, and I'm sure she would be happy to come stay with me for a weekend.

"It's all good. It's not your fault, Ember."

"Can she come and visit you?" I asked.

"I have invited her to visit multiple times, but she doesn't like portals."

I snickered. "Who does?"

"I can feel her pulling away and it scares me."

"I'm sorry, Asher." I laid my hand on his shoulder, feeling awful for him.

"It comes with the job, I guess." He sighed. "Sorry to put all this on you. I just don't like talking to the guys about it."

"You can talk to me anytime. Can I hug you?"

He snickered and then saw that my face was serious. "Oh. Sure." I reached over and embraced him. "Thanks, Ember."

"I don't think I did anything to help."

He gave me a sad smile. "Just talking about it helps sometimes."

Zila galed right in front of us, scaring the shit out of me.

"Okay, here's the plan!" she said excitedly.

She told us what she had done and I was pleasantly surprised. Now we had to tell Zayn and I wasn't sure he was going to like it.

Chapter Twenty-Four

We arrived back at the manor and dropped our weapons off in the armory. We found Zayn, Cash, Cali, and Valarian, and brought them to the study. I wasn't sure they were ready for what we were about to say.

"Go ahead, Ember. Since it was your idea." Asher smiled excitedly at me.

"I want to sneak into the dungeon in the country of Mistlaven and free the missing people they have taken." I stood there with my hands clasped together in front of me, waiting to hear everyone disagree with my plan.

"How would we get there? Their portal has been closed for centuries," Zayn said, running a hand through his hair.

"I already thought of that," Zila said. "I talked to Natsu and he's willing to sail us there. His sister Prim is missing, so he's hoping we find her. I also got permission from the duke to use one of the Fae ships."

"That's a two-day sail, Zila, and then another two days back."

"We don't have to sail all the way, Zayn. Natsu said he could pick us up at Mayhem harbor after they drop off food on Mazuria. That would limit our time on the seas. Then

Natsu would drop us back off on Mayhem afterward. We would need permission from your father first, Val." We all looked at Val.

"He will allow it, I'm sure."

"Where would we enter Mistlaven?" Cash asked.

"Let's go to the library and look at the map," Zayn said before he left the study.

When we walked into the library, I wasn't expecting what I saw. Zayn headed straight for the eight-foot table in the middle of the room and yanked the crimson tablecloth from it. Below it was a massive, detailed map of all the landmasses in our world.

"Wow," I said and Val looked at me with pure adoration.

"We would have to come up here." Zayn pointed to a place called Nebulous Forest.

"How will we enter by boat without being seen?" I asked.

"Fly," both male Angels said in unison.

"There are only three of us with wings." Cali pointed at us. "There are four of them without."

"Since Natsu is coming, he could fly one of us in," Zila said with a blush. I assumed she had thought about her being in Natsu's arms.

"We would have to sail as close as we could, then fly from there," Zayn said. I glanced up at Val as he shifted uncomfortably.

"Perfect. That would work," Cash said.

"Does anyone want to stay behind?" Zayn asked. No one responded. "Then it's settled. I'll talk to the king and we'll all meet back here in an hour."

"Sounds like a plan. I'm going to go eat," Asher said before leaving.

"Me too," Zila added.

"Zila, send an Imp to the Duke of Tessalone after you eat, asking what day we could leave."

"Of course, Zayn. I'll let you know as soon as I get an answer." She smiled before leaving the room.

"I'll be back later." Zayn headed for the door, Cash following.

Cali sighed. "Wait for me!"

Now that we were alone, Valarian closed the door.

"So, you went on one mission without me and decided to take on Demons on their lands?" He narrowed his eyes on me.

"That *is* kind of what happened." I bit my lip nervously as he headed toward me.

He put his hands around my waist and pulled me into him. He pressed his lips against mine, making the heat immediately rise in my body before he pulled away. "This mission sounds like a crazy idea."

"Are you mad at me for suggesting it?"

"Of course not, Ember. I'm proud of your bravery." He kissed my neck. "And your kindness." He kissed again. "And of your loyalty." Another kiss.

"Is there anything you don't like about me?"

"Yes."

I giggled. "Like what?"

"I don't like the fact that you still have clothes on." The sultry look on his face heated my body even more.

In one swift motion, I pulled my shirt over my head revealing my naked breasts to him.

His eyes widened as he grinned. "I appreciate you being spontaneous, but we should go somewhere else, love."

"What's wrong with here?" I pressed my body against his front.

"There are people . . ." He moaned loudly when I ran my hand down his hardness.

"I don't care about the others, Val," I whispered into his ear.

As I lowered myself to my knees in front of him, he growled before I even touched him. It brought a smile to my face. Pulling his pants down enough that his cock sprang free, I wrapped my fingers around it and he moaned again. It was extremely soft for something so hard.

Gently running my tongue down his cock made it jerk in my hand. Val growled again. I continued to lick it up and down until it was wet and juicy. Then I slid it into my mouth and sucked. He let out a tremendous growl and I felt the rumble in my mouth. I continued licking and sucking for a bit until he stopped me.

"You can't do that here. I will roar this whole house down." I looked up at his face from under my eyelashes and licked my lips. He growled again.

Reaching down, he slid his hands under my arms and picked me up. I wrapped my legs around him. We kissed as he carried me to the map table and sat me down. He stopped and quickly removed my boots. I lifted my butt as he removed my pants and panties.

"Don't move, love." Val walked over to the door and shoved a chair in front of it. "Sorry, but I would have to kill any man that sees you naked and I kind of like my friends alive." I laughed as he headed back to me.

Pressing his hand against my torso, he pushed me back onto the table. I gasped when he grabbed my thighs and yanked my ass to the edge of it. He immediately started kissing my inner thigh, working his way up as I moaned in pleasure. My hands squeezed into fists as he kissed up to my core and stopped. He blew a light breath of air onto the hotness between my legs and I almost came unglued as I moaned.

"Can you be a good girl and be quiet, love?"

"Yes," I whispered, but we both knew I wasn't going to be quiet.

He spread my lips open, making room for his mouth to enter. Not wasting time, his tongue went straight to my clit. My hands gripped the edges of the map table as he sucked and licked. He ran his tongue down to my entrance and stuck it inside me. I let out another moan and he growled. The vibrations of his growl had my back arching.

He pulled his tongue out of me and inserted a finger. I moaned again, this time louder.

"Quiet, love."

Lowering his mouth again, he licked my clit while his finger worked its magic. His other arm wrapped around my thigh, holding it tight. He knew I wasn't going to last long with the multiple sensations going on. Every muscle in my body tightened as I went over the edge.

"Oh, Val," I moaned.

As the amazing release flooded my body, I tried to squirm away but he gripped my thigh harder, holding me in place until the sensations calmed. Once my body went lax, he raised up and wiped my juices from his face with the back of his hand. Val picked me up and laid me atop the crimson tablecloth that was spread on the floor. The velvety softness against my bare back felt amazing. He removed his boots and clothes before he laid down on top of me. As he kissed all over my body, he paid incredibly close attention to my breasts. I felt a fang brush against them and moaned loudly.

Bite me! Raising his hand, he laid it over my mouth and for a split second, I wondered why.

In one quick motion, he bit into my breast, and the flooding sensations from the venom ran through my body. I moaned as loud as I could, the sound coming only out of my nose. I now knew why he covered my mouth.

Once I quieted enough, he let go and brought his mouth up to meet mine. He slowly slid inside of me while we kissed. My clit pulsed with every stroke he took. He rotated his hips as his hard cock hit the best spots. After a while, he stopped.

Grabbing me, he flipped me onto my belly. Placing kisses on my back, he worked his way down my body, kissing every part of me. He kissed the cheeks of my ass while his hand was between my legs and I thought I was going to explode again.

Pulling back, he grabbed my hips and raised me onto my knees before sliding inside of me from behind. The feeling was incredible. His hand reached down around my stomach and he circled his finger on my clit while thrusting into me. I arched my back up, letting him deeper inside of me.

The feeling was building and I was ready to explode again. I moved my hips in unison with his. The soft moan he let out told me he liked it, so I continued.

"Harder," I cried out.

Val stopped rubbing my clit and grabbed both of my hips as he thrusted harder into me.

The feeling intensified and I came again. My orgasm made the walls inside of me squeeze and brought him to pure bliss with me. He grabbed my shoulder and moaned as his wetness filled me.

Falling flat on my stomach, I was panting hard. He laid on top of my backside and kissed me gently on my shoulders.

"Let's get cleaned up before the others come back, love." He grabbed his shirt and cleaned up the mess he'd left on me.

After he pulled his pants up, he handed me my clothes. I quickly got dressed as he put the chair back in place. Then he went into the hall and threw the tablecloth and his shirt down the laundry chute.

As he came back into the library, he stood bare chested in front of me and my heat rose again.

"I should run and get a shirt," he said as he leaned in to kiss me.

The door flung open as Zayn and Cash entered. Their eyes darted back and forth between me and a shirtless Val. Cash grinned and nodded his head in approval.

"Umm." Zayn hesitated as he eyed us. "We spoke with the king."

"What did he say?" Val asked.

"He approved, as do I." Cash's grin couldn't have gotten any bigger. I immediately blushed.

Asher and Zila walked in and both went wide eyed.

"What's the word?" Asher asked as he cracked his knuckles.

"The king approved." Zayn looked at Zila. "Did the Duke of Tessalone respond?"

"He said the ship left this afternoon. We'll meet them in Mayhem the day after tomorrow. We'll have to get permission from the Duke of Mayhem first." Zila looked at Val.

"Ember and I will go talk to him tomorrow." I glanced up at Val. This was surprising news to me.

Cali walked in. Her eyes went wide and I sighed.

"That's all the info we know for now. The king canceled all classes until we get back from this mission. We need to rest as much as possible." Zayn ran a hand through his hair. "Cover the table and let's get out of here."

Zila looked around. "Where's the tablecloth?"

Val smiled proudly as he crossed his arms. "It got wet so I put it in the laundry." I shriveled up inside.

"Nice!" Cash grinned, nodding his head in approval once again. My face was red hot with embarrassment as Cali giggled.

"Okay, everyone is dismissed." Zayn rubbed his hand along his beard like he was trying to keep from laughing. "Unless anyone has anything else to say?"

Cash raised his hand. "I have something to say!"

"No, you don't, Cash!" Val said, while grabbing my hand. Everyone laughed as we left the library.

As soon as I got back to my room, I took a shower. After Val got cleaned up, he brought food up for us. He finally had a shirt again. We ate while we chatted about the plans. Not long after, I fell asleep in his arms.

Chapter Twenty-Five

Val was lying on his back and I was in the crook of his arm. He was running his fingers through my hair when I opened my eyes.

"Good morning, my love." He kissed my forehead.

"Good morning, Val." My palm was lying flat on his chest, so I took the opportunity and slid it down his stomach. Before I got to his shorts, he grabbed my wrist.

"Stop that. We have an errand to run."

"I just want you." Turning my face, I kissed his chest.

"When we get back, you can have me. I have to head down to my room to shower and gear up." I rolled over with a sigh, and he moved with me, placing kisses on my shoulder. "You will be fine until then, love."

With a yawn, I stretched while purposely arching my back, making my butt rub against a very hard part of him. He quickly sprang off the bed.

"We have stuff to do." He adjusted his cock and I giggled. He leaned down and kissed my forehead. "I'll be back."

After I showered, I threw on my fighting leathers and braided my hair. Val wasn't back yet, so I figured I would take the time to catch up with Cinder.

Hey Cin,

I hope all is well. I know I have not written to you in a week. I have some important things that I need to tell you. I am going to ask the king to let you visit. Take care.

Love, Em

I folded the letter and stuck it in an envelope. As soon as I sealed it, the silver circle appeared.

"You may enter."

"Greetings," the Imp said, his orange eyes dazzling.

"Thank you." I handed him the letter with a smile.

"Salutations." The Imp disappeared.

A minute later, the shiny circle reappeared on the floor. Unless Cinder had already written a letter for me, there was no way she finished one that fast.

That is odd. "You may enter."

"Greetings." He handed the letter I wrote back to me. "Undeliverable."

"Why?" I asked, my face filled with concern.

He blinked his orange eyes as he repeated the words. "Undeliverable."

I sighed because I knew I wasn't getting any more words out of him. "Okay, thank you."

"Salutations." He disappeared.

Val returned to my room with a tray of food for us. He set it on the little table in the corner and I quickly took a seat.

"The Imp says other things, Val."

His eyebrows raised in surprise. "How do you know?"

"Because I wrote a letter to my sister and he came back and said it was undeliverable. What does that mean? Do you think she's okay?"

"Maybe she was in the bath." He uncovered my plate and set it in front of me. My eyes widened at the bacon, eggs, sausage, and toast.

I immediately glanced at the clock. "You're probably right. This would be about the time she would be getting ready for work."

"I'm sure she's fine. You can try sending it again later."

We both ate our breakfast, then went down to the armory and got what we needed. Of course, I got my bow.

As we stepped onto the portal, Val pulled me into his body. I closed my eyes and laid my head on his chest as I prayed these portals would get easier soon. The feeling wasn't as bad as the previous times, but it still wasn't good. We landed in Mayhem and headed to Blackveil Castle. It was just as creepy and gorgeous as I remember.

Val took my hand as we walked up the steps. We went inside and he escorted me down to the duke's private quarters. He knocked lightly and a servant answered the door.

"How can I help you?" Val didn't even acknowledge him as he pulled me into the room.

"Everything okay, son?" the duke asked with a concerned look on his face.

"Can we have privacy, please?"

The duke glanced at the servant and nodded. He quickly left, shutting the door behind him.

"Please sit," the duke said, nodding his head toward the small dining table. Val and I both took a seat. "Would you like some tea?"

"No." Val's tone was flat, unwelcoming.

I ignored him as I smiled at the duke. "I would enjoy some, Your Grace."

"No need to use formalities here, my dear." He poured me a cup and handed it to me. "What was your name again?"

"Ember Lavaris."

"Nice to officially meet you, Ember. You can call me Ryker."

Even though it made me slightly uncomfortable to drop formalities, I nodded. "Nice to meet you, Ryker."

Val shifted uncomfortably and the duke's eyes went to him. "So, what is it you need, son?"

"We need to ask you something."

"I knew this day would come. She is a lovely choice for you. Have you set a date yet?"

"For what?" I asked with wide eyes.

"The mating ritual, of course. I am assuming you are here to ask for my blessing?"

My face went pale as I glanced at Val. He smiled at my nervousness.

"We aren't here for that, Father."

"My apologies, my lady." Ryker bowed his head to me before meeting Val's eyes. "What is it that I can help with?"

"We need your permission to have a ship docked at the harbor. We'll board here before we set sail for Mistlaven, then we'll need to dock again after the mission."

"You came all the way here for that? You could have sent an Imp."

Val's eyebrows furrowed. "Yes or no, Father?"

Ryker sighed. "Of course you can, son."

"That is all we need." Val stood up and reached a hand down to help me stand. I shook my head as I met his eyes.

"Why in such a rush?" the duke asked as he poured himself more tea.

Val, sit down and try to be nice. For me, please. Val sighed as he retook his seat.

"I'm glad you decided to stay." Val said nothing so Ryker turned his attention toward me. "Ember, you are the newest guard, correct?"

"Yes, Your Grace."

"Please call me Ryker. I insist." The duke smiled. He seemed nice to me. I felt like the issues between father and son could use some work. "I heard what happened in the dungeon. I was terribly upset that my son didn't come see me after he was stabbed."

I swallowed hard, wanting to shrink into myself. "I'm sorry about that."

"You have nothing to be sorry for, my dear." Ryker laid his hand on top of mine and smiled. "The guards told me everything. I am grateful you saved his life."

Val cleared his throat, pulling my attention to him. He impatiently clenched his jaw. "Where is my sister?"

"She is around here somewhere. Would you like me to send for her?"

"Yes." Val shifted in his seat, still looking uncomfortable.

The duke didn't move for a few seconds. I realized he was having a silent conversation with someone before he turned his attention back to me.

"How are you enjoying being a King's Guard?"

"I thoroughly enjoy it, Your... umm, Ryker." I smiled politely and he smiled back with amusement.

"It is a tough job, but imperative. You must be a powerful woman."

I shook my head. "I am stronger than no other."

"If my son has fallen for you, then I respectfully disagree."

My eyes went to Val, who glowered at his father. "My relationship is none of your concern."

"I am not saying anything bad, son." Ryker met my eyes. "I noticed the way he looks at you is not emblematic of friendship, Ember. It truly pleases me to see him happy."

"She already knows how I feel. She doesn't need you to tell her." We became silent for a few short breaths before Val stood up. "There's my sister."

As I glanced at the door, it opened. A beautiful young woman with long black hair gasped when she saw us.

"Brother." She ran straight to Val for a big hug. Her eyes drifted to me with a curious face. "Valarian, is this Ember?"

"Yes, this is my mate." He had a genuinely sweet smile on his face.

His mate? At first I panicked, but then I realized he probably meant bond-mate. I guess we're telling people now.

"Nice to meet you. My name is Wynter. I have heard so much about you!" She gave me her hand and I shook it before she turned back to Val. "Were you mated before the eyes of the king without me there?"

My eyes went wide in shock and Val laughed. "We haven't been, no. She is my bond-mate."

"She is the one that stabbed you, correct?" I got nervous when she looked back at me.

"She did." Val smiled brightly. He seemed almost prideful that I stabbed him. Currently, I wanted someone to stab me.

She slid in the seat next to me and leaned in. "What did it feel like to stab him? I have been telling him I'm going to stab him since I was ten." I giggled and threw my hand over my mouth.

"That is true," Ryker said with a laugh.

Wynter laid her hand upon mine. "Valarian has told me such wonderful things about you. We *must* be friends. I have so many stories about him as a child that I can share with you."

Val crossed his arm. "Okay, Wynter, that's enough."

Wynter rolled her eyes. "We will talk at a different time when *he* is not around." I already loved his sister.

Val locked eyes with his father who nodded slightly. *A secret conversation*, I thought to myself.

"We have to get going soon. Wynter, can you take Ember for a walk? I need to talk to Father alone. I will meet you by the front door in a bit."

"Of course, Val. Let's leave the men to their boring chatter." Wynter stood up, and I followed. "Come on, Ember."

"It was nice meeting you, Ryker."

"The pleasure is all mine, my dear." He smiled politely as we left.

"So, have you and my brother officially mated yet?"

"We haven't had a mating ceremony, no. I don't think that's what he wants. I'm happy just being his bond-mate." I answered her even though I knew Val had already told her as much. I was now concerned about where this conversation was going.

"No, Ember. I mean, have you had sex?"

"Oh, I, umm . . . "

"That means yes." She giggled and my face turned beet red. "Which means you must truly like him."

I smiled at the thought. "I do."

"Is it *more* than like?"

"I'm not sure yet, but possibly," I lied. I was madly in love with him, but I hadn't said it yet. But neither had he.

She stopped walking and turned toward me. Her eyes were a beautiful violet and the same shape as Val's. She made me *so* comfortable, I was afraid of her asking more questions as I might answer her honestly.

"Well, I know my brother. He has never brought a lady here and has *never* called one his mate. So, just remember those feelings you are having are the same ones he is." She smiled big. "It only takes three little words to let someone know you care. It is better to say what you want than to die not saying what you feel."

I nodded as I swallowed down fear. "That is true."

"Just know, I truly approve of this mating." I smiled at her beautiful face. "Well, now that I have said my piece, I would like to show you something."

I followed her down a few halls until we came to one I hadn't been in yet. It was lined with paintings.

"These are family portraits. This one here is of Valarian and me when we were young."

Looking up at the perfect painting of my mate made my heart swell. They both looked like they were happy children with a great childhood. I couldn't help but wonder what went wrong with him and his father.

"And this one here is of my mother, Leona. She was so gorgeous."

The painting depicted a dark-haired beauty, just like Valarian and Wynter.

Then a realization hit me. "Did you say, was?"

"Yes." Her face became sad as she peered up at the painting. "She died when I was only five years old. She was the most amazing person, from what I can remember."

My heart was hurting thinking about them losing their mother when they were only children. I felt a similar pain.

"I'm so sorry." I glanced back at her picture. "She was gorgeous. You look just like her." She blushed at my words and we continued walking.

We made it to the front of the castle where we talked for a good thirty minutes before Val found us.

"What are you two hens clucking about?"

"I was just telling Ember about the snowball fight we had in the castle." Wynter giggled.

Val grinned mischievously. "Father was furious with us, but mother wasn't!"

"She most definitely was not. She even participated and hit father with a snowball." They both busted up laughing. Wynter sniffed and wiped a single tear from her eye.

"We have to get going, Wynter. I'll send an Imp soon."

"You must visit more, Val. You too, Ember." She pulled me into a hug.

"I would love that."

We said our goodbyes and left.

"I'm sorry you had to deal with my family," Val said once we were outside.

"Don't apologize. I thoroughly enjoyed meeting them. Your father was nice and I absolutely adore your sister. I think I might have fallen in love with her today." He stopped walking and looked deeply into my eyes.

"She wielded the same thought to me about you, right before we left." I smiled as he leaned down to kiss me. "Let's go home, love."

We took our time going back to the portal. Val's arm was around me the whole way.

Home, that was where we were going. It truly was my home now.

Chapter Twenty-Six

We woke up the next day and got ready for the potentially dangerous rescue mission ahead of us. We were all quiet as we geared up and walked to the portal after lunch.

"If we time this correctly, it will be nightfall when we arrive," Zayn said to us as we went onto the platform.

All seven of us were going on this rescue mission together. I had an uneasy feeling when I thought about the possibility of some of us not coming back. As if he could feel my anxiety, Val immediately put his arms around my waist, pulling me in.

Zayn willed the portal to go and, as we were whipped through the air, I felt a kiss on the tip of my nose, then on my lips. This man could kiss me a hundred times an hour for the rest of my life and I would never get tired of it. We landed in Mayhem and I was barely nauseous.

"Thank you, Val."

"For what, my love?"

"For being you," I said before I placed a small kiss on his lips.

Cash's voice drew my attention away from Val. "I can't wait until I am mated! How is Cinder doing, by the way?" He was grinning from ear to ear. I just shook my head and walked off the portal.

A realization hit me when Cash mentioned my sister. I forgot to resend the letter last night and would have to try again when I get back home.

If we survive, that is.

We galed to the docks and found Natsu waiting for us. I had never been on a ship before and was slightly nervous about sailing. I didn't want to get sick in front of everyone, even though it wouldn't be my first time.

"Welcome!" Natsu waved his hand toward the ship. "Come on aboard Miss Conduct."

"You named your ship Misconduct?" I asked.

"Her name is *Miss* Conduct." Natsu smiled proudly.

Cash grinned and nodded. "That's an impressive name."

Of course, he would love it.

"Wait!" A female's voice called out. I turned around and saw Wynter and Ryker approaching us.

"You aren't going, Wynter," Val said immediately.

"I know, father already said as much." She made a sad face and then smiled mischievously. "You won't be able to stop me once I become a King's Guard."

My eyes widened with excitement. "You have the mark?"

"I do! Strength in blood." She pulled the top of her shirt down and showed me her tattoo—one battle-axe, a shield, and a drop of blood. A replica of Val's Guardian Mark, but hers was still black.

"Wynter, that is not appropriate." The duke looked appalled.

"I cannot wait until I come next year. We will be such good friends, Ember!"

"Hi, Wynter." Zayn smiled at the black-haired beauty, in a way I had never seen from him before. Wynter's cheeks blushed. There seemed to be a mutual crush.

"Hi, Zaynith." I almost forgot that it was his real name since I hadn't used it in so long.

"What are you both doing here?" Val asked, breaking the eye contact between Zayn and Wynter.

"We have come to see you off, son," Ryker said. "I have the guards keeping an eye out. They are going to notify us immediately when you return."

"It'll be the middle of the night, maybe even morning when we get back."

"That's fine, son. We will be here, either way. Good luck to all of you."

"Yes, good luck, and be careful." Wynter pulled Val into a hug and then me. She put her hand on my cheek. "Take care of my brother, Ember. He will be too busy taking care of you to watch out for himself."

I smiled. "I will."

"Goodbye, Zaynith and everyone else." Wynter waved at our crew as we boarded the ship.

Val held me in his arms as the ship moved. We watched his sister and father standing on the shore until they were tiny, then found a seat. Val sat behind me and pulled me in close to him. We didn't talk much—most of us just stared out at the ocean and watched the water move. The nerves were keeping us quiet. I wanted to ask Val about his father, but it wasn't an appropriate time.

"Oh, Gods," Asher yelled and took off running. Horrible sounds filled the air as he vomited over the side of the ship.

Cash immediately got up and eased him with some magic. A few minutes later, Asher sat back down. I hoped he felt better for the rest of the trip. I was grateful when I realized that the sea wouldn't make me sick.

Six and a half hours later, we were close to the Demon's land. We were far enough out to sea that they couldn't see us, especially since the sun had set.

"Alright, guys, it's time," Zayn said as the ship stopped.

"I'm coming with you." Natsu hurriedly lowered an anchor over the side.

"You can come to the shore to drop one of us off and then you will come back to the ship." Zayn was now in commander mode.

"Zayn." Natsu's eyes were pleading.

"You are *not* a King's Guard yet."

"No, but I have the mark and will be at Castleva in eight months. My sister is in there!"

Zayn shook his head. "We can't let you go."

"What if it was Calista in there, Zayn? Would you go? Or what if it were Wynter? Would you, Val?"

Zayn ran a hand through his hair. He looked around at us. Val nodded, then Cash, Zila, Cali, and Asher. His eyes stopped on me.

Zayn wants to know if you approve of him going. We all must vote, love.

A thought hit me as I looked at Natsu's pleading amber eyes. I would do *anything* for Cinder. I would fight for her and die for her. He had a sword on his back, and I was grateful for it. I sighed as I met Zayn's eyes and nodded.

"Okay, you can come, but you better not die. I don't know how I'd explain that to the king." Zayn ran his hand down his face and scrubbed his eyes. "Alright, partner up with someone with wings. Cash, you're going to have to carry Val since you're the only one strong enough."

Val shifted uncomfortably next to me. I ran a hand down his arm to soothe him.

Natsu walked up to the Lycan. "I've got Zila." Her silver eyes blinked with surprise before she blushed.

"I'll go with Cali. I would prefer a girl." Asher walked over to her and started cracking his knuckles.

"I've got Ember." Zayn strolled up to me. "Let's do this."

Zayn reached over and picked me up like a baby. He was strong, so it took little effort. I put my hands around his neck to help hold on.

Natsu picked Zila up the same way, and she blushed as she put her arms around his neck. Cali grabbed Asher and almost dropped him.

"Are you good, Cali?" Zayn looked concerned. "We could switch."

"I got him." She had a smile on her face, but it was slightly red as she struggled.

Surprisingly, Cash picked up Val easier than I thought he would. The look of discomfort on Val's face had me giggling inside.

Cash grinned proudly. "Don't worry, buddy, I won't drop you."

"Just keep your hands where they are supposed to be, pretty boy." Cash laughed at Val's response.

A large gust of wind flowed between us when everyone's wings popped out. Before I even had a chance to look at the beautiful wings and their glory, Zayn took off into the air. My breath caught at the feeling of flying. The sky was dark and there were a thousand stars above my head. It was amazing. My breathing got heavy as I looked down at the now tiny ship. I laid my head against Zayn's chest. It wasn't sexual at all. Val may have torn the throat out of anyone else I tried that with, I wasn't sure.

Zayn seemed to get higher and higher so I squealed. "How are you doing, Red?"

"I have never felt more alive in my life!" I giggled. A portal I couldn't handle, but flying wasn't so bad.

He laughed. "Anytime you want a ride, let me know."

We flew for about ten minutes before we started descending into the darkness. The tree line was coming up quickly and I flinched. We were going too fast and I was worried we would crash, so I tensed my body. Zayn slowed down at the last minute, straightened his body out, and landed us gently on the ground.

"How was it?" Zayn asked as his raven black wings disappeared.

"That was fun, Softy!" He laughed as he sat me down.

Natsu came flying in fast. Zila looked content being held in his arms and I smiled at the sight. In my opinion, they would make a perfect couple. They landed right next to me and he set her down. My eyes immediately went to his beautiful wings. They were blue and iridescent—just like his mother's.

Then Cali came in with Asher. Her face was red as she ascended. Her creamy white wings flapped hard. I wondered if they were a different color because she was a female. She practically threw Asher when they got close to the ground.

"I almost died, Asher! You have to ride back with Zayn. "

"You mean you almost killed me!" he retorted. His face was sweaty and filled with fear.

"That too!" She took a few deep breaths before her wings disappeared.

Cash came down next and I tried my hardest not to laugh when I saw the scowl on Val's face. Cash was grinning with pride, as per usual.

After they landed, Cash set Val down and he practically plowed through the people to get to me. He leaned me back and kissed me as hard and passionately as he could. We broke free from the kiss and stared into my eyes.

"I missed you, my love." I blushed. "That Angel is handsy."

"You're welcome, buddy!" Cash said as he smacked Val on the butt.

"I'm going to kill him one of these days." Val smiled at me and pressed one last sweet kiss on my lips. "Are you ready for this?" I nodded but I was, indeed, not ready.

"Alright, Natsu. We're going to sneak into the dungeon as quietly as possible. If we find any captives, we will produce a plan to release them. I'm overseeing this mission, so you take orders from me. Val and Cash are my second and third.

Honestly, you take orders from any of us. If you don't, I'll make sure the first year of your life at Castleva is spent cleaning toilets."

Natsu gave a slight bow of the head. "Understood, Zayn."

Cash pulled his axe out of his waistband. "Let's do this!"

We wandered through a dense area of woods, the fog in the air made it incredibly creepy. Val held my hand while we walked, keeping me slightly behind him. He told me to step where he stepped so I didn't trip and fall over anything I couldn't see. Vampires had better night vision than us Casters.

We finally came upon a large brick building, so Zayn commanded us to all squat down.

"I believe this is it," he said.

"It does look like the one on the map. What's the plan?" Cash asked.

"I think the girls should investigate first. We are smaller, quicker, and therefore, stealthier," I waited for the men to disagree with my suggestion.

"I could fly up overhead and check the perimeter while Zila and Ember investigate the building," Cali said and Val let out a low growl. "Stop growling at me, V. I'm not afraid to hit a Vampire." Cali's blue eyes looked fierce. Val just smirked at her.

"I think that plan sounds great," Zila added.

"Of course you all do. Us men will just play cards until you come back." Cash frowned and looked at his axe.

Cali rolled her eyes. "Crybaby."

"Enough, all of you. I think Ember is right." Zayn looked into my eyes. "You ladies get in and out. No stopping to help anyone, no matter what the situation is." I nodded.

Val quickly kissed me. "Be careful, love."

Cali didn't hesitate. She flew over the trees and I lost sight of her in the darkness.

"Zila, you come up that side and check out that window. I'm going to go around the back and see what's there." She nodded.

We quickly left the forest, staying as close to the ground as possible before parting in the darkness. I was all alone now. As I rounded the backside of the building, I found a pile of wood in front of a window, so I climbed onto it. When I peeked inside, there were cells and a couple of Demon guards.

Hearing a slight thud, I looked up. Cali put her finger over her lips to quiet me. She held up two fingers and pointed to the right. Okay, so there were two more Demon guards over there. She crouched down on the roof as I crawled off the top of the wood and squatted.

Hearing someone walking, I withdrew my dagger. I had it ready when I sprung up into the intruder's face. I halted my blade mere inches from Zila's chest.

"I'm sorry," I whispered. She smiled and nodded.

Cali landed on the ground next to us. "Let's report back."

We hunkered low to the ground and worked our way slowly back to the woods. As soon as we were near, I could see the relief on their faces.

"There are two Demon guards inside at the back of the dungeon. I could see some cell bars in the moonlight, but I couldn't see any prisoners. It's dark in there."

"I saw two Demons standing guard by the road," Cali added.

"There are three in the front of the building," Zila said. "So, there are at least seven."

"We can easily take that many," Cash said.

Val nodded. "Agreed."

My eyes went wide. Could we take on seven? That was less than one Demon per person or one for each King's Guard, and Natsu could watch. I really hoped I could do this. I have only killed one Demon in my life, and it was only last week—and technically, Val killed him. I just stabbed the heart.

"Was there a back door, Ember?"

"There was, Zayn. Maybe we should breach both doors at the same time."

"That works." Zayn went into commander mode once more. "Cash and Cali, fly up and take out the two guards posted by the road. Ember and Val will go through the back door. Zila and I will go through the front. Once we are all in, Asher, you come in and help us take out these Demons. Natsu, you can stay here."

"Come on, Zayn!"

"You heard me. Unless you see one of us struggling, you stay here."

Natsu's face hardened. "Will do."

"Alright, team. Don't get yourselves killed."

Zayn slowly crawled out of the woods with Zila right behind him. Cash and Cali took off flying. Val crawled out next and I stayed right on his tail. When we got to our destination, Val kicked in the door at the exact same second that Zayn kicked in the other side.

Val quickly grabbed the Demon in front of him and squeezed his throat. I went under Val's arm and thrusted my dagger up into the other Demon's neck. As soon as he fell, I turned and stabbed the Demon Val was holding in the back. He fell to the ground, dead.

Walking toward the cells, I met Zayn and Zila. Asher was right behind them. They had already taken out the other three Demons.

"Excellent job. The alarms didn't sound." Zayn pointed at the cells. "Let's check these out."

"How? There's no light. I can barely see with my wolf vision."

"I got it." I held a fireball out with my hand and lightly lit the room.

"Zila?" I heard a girl's voice I didn't know.

Zila ran to the first cell. "Prim! Where are the keys?"

"Found them." Asher unlocked the cell door and Primavera ran into Zila's arms.

Asher started unlocking the cells as quickly as possible.

"That one's empty," Val said, and Asher skipped it.

He unlocked another cell and I went in. It was an incredibly young boy, only about ten, with bright blue eyes.

"Come on, it's okay." The young boy ran and hugged me. "Zayn, I found the Angel."

"Everest, your mother and father will be so happy to see you." The boy ran to Zayn and hugged him.

"And I found a young Elven girl," Val said.

"I have a Caster," Asher added.

We had half the cells left when suddenly the alarm sounded.

"Shit, let's get out of here now," Zayn ordered.

"We can't leave anyone, Zayn." I was panicking. "Hurry, Asher!"

I quickly used my fireball to look in the last few cells.

"Zila, take the prisoners to the forest, now!" Zayn commanded.

"Come on, everyone. Follow me." She led them out the backdoor and disappeared.

"There's one in here, Asher!" He quickly ran to me and got the last occupied cell opened. It had another Caster in it. I felt a hand grab mine, I looked down and it was the young Angel. He hadn't gone with Zila.

"Let's go, now!" Zayn yelled, and we all piled out the backdoor.

We were only about ten feet from the exit when we were met by half a dozen Demons. I pushed the little Angel and the Caster running next to me down to the ground as a Demon plowed into me. I already had my dagger out, so I stabbed him in the chest as soon as I had the chance. Val used his sword to slice a Demon's head clean off. Zayn and Asher were tag-teaming two others.

"Run to the woods!" I screamed at the prisoners.

Zila came out of the edge of the forest and escorted the last of the prisoners away as Cash and Cali landed in front of us. All the Demons around us were dead.

"Four Demons attacked us and the alarms went off. We took them all out." Cash had dark green Demon blood dripping from his axe.

"Let's get out of here." As soon as Zayn said the words, Cash was swiped off his feet.

Chapter Twenty-Seven

s Cash was flung into the air, his wings opened, helping him land. One of his hands went to the ground as he hit hard. When I saw what knocked him off feet, my mouth dropped open. It was a Basilisk that was about thirty or forty feet long.

The exceptionally large snake shot out and almost nipped Cali in the face. She was swift and dodged it like a pro, but fell to the ground in the process. It wrapped its tail around her and started squeezing.

We immediately attacked, but unfortunately the snake was just as quick with its dodges. Val lunged and grabbed its head. I sprang out and tried to stab it with my dagger. It whipped its body and knocked both Val and I to the ground.

Zayn sliced at its tail with his sword and landed a blow. Cash mirrored the same actions with his axe. The snake dropped Cali and she hit the ground with a thud. Val quickly yanked her out of the way.

The Basilisk opened its mouth and I could see its enormous fangs. With its head so close to me, I could see sharp scales on the side of its neck and made a mental note not to go near them.

Immediately making a fireball, I threw it at his face, but he quickly dodged it. The fireball slowed, boomeranged back, and hit the snake in the back of the head. I looked at Asher and knew he had used his wind magic to maneuver my wayward fireball.

Carelessly and impatiently, I threw out three more fireballs at the snake and they all missed. I didn't contemplate using my bow. There was no way I would hit a target moving that fast.

Asher used his air magic to make a small dirt tornado to block the snake's vision. The tornado helped for a few seconds, and I was impressed by his magic skills. I made another mental note that we owed him money now. Val, Zayn, and Cash seized the opportunity to attack and slice as much as they could.

Zayn flew up in the air and came down hard with his sword, stabbing its back. The Basilisk screamed and wailed.

My heart raced with fear and adrenaline as I seized my opportunity and lunged forward with my dagger. The Basilisk quickly knocked me to the ground and wrapped its body around me. I was being suffocated as the air was expelled from my lungs.

The three men kept slashing with their weapons while Asher picked up a large rock with his wind magic and threw it at the snake.

Cali threw a couple of throwing daggers at it, but the snake was too fast—they all missed. As she pulled out her katana, the snake smacked her with his tail, sending her and the sword flying to the ground. It kept knocking everyone down, one by one, and fear hit me. I was going to be squeezed to death

With a loud roar, Val went primal. He dropped his sword and jumped on the snake. He bit into its side while simultaneously punching through its skin and ripping out some of its innards. The snake finally threw me loose and I gasped for air as I hit the ground with a thud.

Cash shot up into the sky and came down hard with both of his axes. Everyone was attacking it, but the Basilisk wasn't going down.

Thunder cracked loudly, bringing my attention to Zila and Natsu who had come running out of the woods. A flash of lightning sparked in the sky.

"Get down!" Zila screamed. Everyone hit the ground. I was already there.

Natsu put his arms in the air and brought them down hard. A bolt of lightning hit the Basilisk in the back. It squealed and jumped around. He threw another lightning bolt, and the Basilisk dropped his head flat.

As I saw my opportunity, I hoped the dagger had the same effect as it did on other species. Hopping off the ground, I took off running as fast as I could, jumped up and slammed my dagger down into his head.

The Basilisk screamed out a weird cry and flung me away from it before it began to still.

Another bolt of lightning hit the Basilisk and its breathing became erratic. Valarian raised his sword and chopped into his neck three times before his head finally popped off. I took a deep breath as I realized the snake was dead.

"Ready the ship!" Zayn shouted and Natsu shot into the sky. "Let's get these people as close to the shore as possible!"

We ran as fast as we could without tripping over the brush. Val held my hand the whole time. Someone grabbed my other hand—it was the Angel boy again.

We finally made it to the sand after about twenty minutes of running. Most of us were panting as we tried to catch our breaths.

"Anyone with wings, get to that boat immediately! Carry someone if you can," Val commanded.

"Guards with wings, grab a prisoner that doesn't have them!" Zayn ordered.

Primavera didn't need to be told twice. "Can you fly?" she asked the tiny Angel, who nodded his head. "Then follow me." She grabbed the Elven girl and shot into the air. The Angel boy released his black wings and followed close behind her. Cash grabbed Asher while Zayn grabbed the male Caster.

"We'll be right back." Zayn flew off.

Cali grabbed the female Caster and followed the rest. Natsu landed in front of us and grabbed Zila.

Everyone was gone but me and my mate.

"Are you okay, my love?" Val grabbed my cheeks and looked my face over.

"I'm a little sore. Are you okay?"

"The snake's scales got me." He lifted his bloody shirt and I gasped. There were three large gashes in his stomach. "It'll heal soon."

"Will blood help?" I tilted my head to the side, offering him my neck.

He quickly leaned in and sunk his teeth into me. Even with the fear, the feeling was incredible. He only drank for a few seconds before he pulled back and wiped his mouth.

"Thank you." He lifted his shirt again and I watched the wounds disappear.

Zayn and Cash landed in front of us. Zayn grabbed me, and Cash grabbed Val. We flew back to the ship as it was sailing away. Once we landed, I looked around. All seven guards were safe. We saved five prisoners, but Natsu was the real lifesaver. I was amazed by his powers. It was a great mission overall.

Primavera brought blankets out as everyone found spots to lie down. It was the middle of the night and cold on the sea, so people were huddled up with each other for warmth. Val was behind me and the Angel boy in front of me. I held my arms around him, keeping him warm. He fell asleep during the ship ride.

You are the kindest, most amazing person I know, Ember.

And you are as well, Val. I should have told him I loved him, but I didn't. I figured it should be a more private moment.

Most of the prisoners had fallen asleep so it was pretty quiet. Zila was standing with Natsu at the helm of the ship. He was rubbing his hands up and down her arms, trying to keep her warm. My heart filled with love while I watched them.

Cash and Zayn had their wings wrapped around their bodies to stay warm. They were both pacing the ship, keeping watch. Cali had her wings wrapped around Asher. I smiled at the family I now had before I laid my head against Val and tried to get some sleep. It never came.

Chapter Twenty-Eight

We finally made it back to Mayhem at daybreak. Wynter and Ryker were waiting for us along with about ten of the duke's guards. Once we were docked, we piled off the ship.

"Is everyone okay, son?" Ryker asked.

"We saved five prisoners."

"We need to figure out what to do with them." Zayn was back in leadership mode. "How do you think we should handle it, Your Grace?"

"I see that there is a variety of species here. I believe we should send an Imp to each duke and ask them how they would like to handle their citizens."

Zayn nodded. "Good call, Your Grace."

"I am glad you are both safe." Wynter pulled Val and me in for a group hug.

The duke and his guards escorted the saved prisoners up to the castle. Wynter followed them, holding hands with the young Angel boy. The King's Guard was standing there talking when I saw Val meet Zayn's eyes. Zayn nodded. Another silent conversation. After that, Val took my hand and led me away.

"Where are we going?" I asked and he smiled.

"To kiss the snow, love."

Once we had walked for a few minutes, he wrapped his arms around me and galed us to the snowbank. As soon as we landed, Val let go of me, dropped his sword, and fell back into the snow. There was love in my eyes as I watched him with a winsome smile. With a laugh, I threw down my bow, and joined him. I moved my arms up and down and made a perfect snow angel.

Once we were done, Val got up and offered me his hand. "What we did was dangerous," he whispered as he pulled me from the ground. "The cold reminds me that I'm alive." As his eyes locked on the snow angels, the look on his face was far away—almost inscrutable. That was the moment I realized the snow had a deeper meaning to him than he led on. Whatever his connection with it was, I knew I was adding memories. He put his arms around me from behind and laid his chin on my shoulder. "I want to show you something." I didn't ask where we were going this time. As long as I was with him, I didn't care.

Val galed us away and we landed outside of an entrance to a cave. He grabbed a torch off the cave wall. "Can you light this for me?"

I wielded a small fireball and held my hand up to the torch to light it. Val stepped inside and hung the torch on the wall. The cave was empty except for a couple of animal hide blankets on the floor.

"What is this place?"

"It's a cave, Ember."

I rolled my eyes. "I know that, Val."

He laughed for a split second before his demeanor changed. "I used to come here when I missed my mother or when my father made me angry, which was often."

I should have asked him about his mother, but I didn't want to upset him. "I could see why you would come here." I looked around, it was kind of boring, but it seemed peaceful.

"After spending a whole night with you and not being able to touch you, I just needed a moment alone. Plus, I wanted you to see how stunning this was."

I wouldn't have considered it stunning. It was dark and damp. Before I had a chance to respond, he slid his arms around my waist and lifted me off my feet. He kissed me as he walked us over to the blankets and set me down beside them.

"Hold on." Val walked further into the cave, where I could no longer see. I took the opportunity to remove my snow-covered boots. The fur pelts felt nice against my bare feet as I stepped onto them. Taking off my bow and quiver, I laid them on the ground.

A few minutes later, Val returned with a bundle of firewood and arranged it in a small pile in the corner.

"Can you help again? Then quickly close your eyes."

Val could have asked me to swim to the edge of the realm and back and I would have. I would do anything for him. Once again, I wielded a small fireball and threw it at the pile of wood. As soon as it started catching on fire, I quickly closed my eyes.

His footsteps were light as he strolled toward me. He was shuffling around when I heard two thuds. He had taken his boots off. His warm hand pressed into mine before he gently pulled me down next to him, lying down on his back before helping me do the same.

"Now, make sure you're looking up."

After I opened my eyes, my mouth went agape in shock. When he said the cave was stunning, this must have been the exquisiteness he was referring to. As the fire flickered, my eyes took in the sights of the beautiful, delicate white crystals hanging from the ceiling. The light glinted off them, making them sparkle. It was phenomenal and I was mesmerized.

"Wow, what are those?"

"That is gypsum." He pointed his finger at the different ethereal drippings as he spoke. "The crystalline forms you see there are what happens when it turns to selenite. My mother taught me that."

"It's extravagantly beautiful."

He tipped his face toward me and whispered, "Almost as beautiful as you." After he said those words, my heart ached with fear—I never wanted to be alive without this man.

As I stared into those gorgeous violet eyes of his, I wanted to bare my soul to him. Open my chest, yank out my heart, and hand it to him on a silver platter. Now would have been the perfect time to tell him how much I loved him—but I couldn't do it. The fear of him not feeling as deeply as me was stronger than the need to tell him.

Instead, I reached over, grabbed his cheeks, and pulled him in for a kiss. One that quickly got heated when he rolled over on top of me. The coolness of the cave air hit my bare skin as he lifted my shirt and immediately started sucking on my breast. As the fire crackled, the light danced across the crystalized ceiling making it sparkle with beauty. The only thought I had was that I could stay here forever with this man.

During the battle with the Basilisk, I feared losing Val. Shit, I had a fear of dying myself. Letting that fear take over now, I was getting anxious, and wanted to rip his clothes off.

Reaching down to the front of him, I frantically unbuttoned his pants and slid them down, releasing his ass and hard cock from their prison. I was trying to get to his warmth quicker so my body would know that he was okay—that I was okay. Like Val, I needed to feel alive.

This would be fear sex—the kind of sex you have after a battle. When the thought of dying or losing the person you love hits hard and a good release is the only way to cure it.

In one quick motion, he yanked off my pants and underwear before his hard cock slid inside me. My moans echoed loudly through the cave. The flicker of the fire on the crystals seemed to go with our rhythm as he pounded into me.

Holding onto him as tightly as I could, I dug my nails into his back, never wanting to be without him. Opening my mouth, I bit into his neck. Not hard enough to puncture it, but hard enough for him to let out a huge growl of approval.

In a flash, he yanked me off the ground. My legs still were still wrapped around him when he slammed me against the cave wall. The coldness of it pressed against my back was exhilarating and I gasped at the sensation.

Needing him more than ever, I squeezed his ass with one hand, while the fingers on the other tightened in his hair, pulling him closer. He growled deeply into my mouth, as I smashed a kiss onto his lips.

As his thrusts became harder, he hit a fantastic spot inside of me and I almost came unglued. My impatience was building and I realized he wasn't going to bite me until I asked. I needed the bite now because my orgasm was about to take over my body and I wanted the biggest release possible.

"Bite me!" I screamed.

His hands squeezed my ass cheeks hard, digging his nails into them as he struck out and sunk his fangs into my neck. Loud moans fell from my lips as the warmth of the bite ran through my veins like a stream running for the ocean.

The blissful rush lit every nerve I had on fire sending me over the edge. Moans of ecstasy left his nose as he took hungry gulps of my blood. His cock pulsed before a stream of warm cum shot inside of me.

Our bodies slowed as the rush left us. His forehead sunk forward onto my chest in exhaustion. I slowly trailed my fingers over the back of his head while we both caught our breath. Once all of my muscles relaxed and my heart regulated itself, he carried me back to the blanket.

We only cuddled for a few minutes before we had to get up. Unfortunately, we had things we had to accomplish, so we got dressed and said goodbye to the beautiful cave.

Val galed us back to just outside the wards of the castle. The smile he was wearing was huge as he grabbed my hand. By the look he was giving me, I could tell that not only did he adore me, but he also loved me. He would lie down and die for me if I asked him to—of course I would do the same for him. Since that look told me all I needed to know, I couldn't wait to get home and finally admit that I was in love with him. The thought warmed my body as we started walking quietly toward the castle. We didn't have much to say—we had already said it with our bodies.

Once we were inside the castle, he headed down to the duke's quarters. My heart grew slightly when I saw Ryker chatting away with all the prisoners and King's Guards.

"There you two are. Where have you been?"

"We went to see the snow, Father."

"I had a feeling that is where you went." Ryker's smile dropped as a mournful expression filled his face. He quickly took a sip of his tea before he continued. "While you were gone, we wrote letters to the dukes. We are waiting to hear back from each of them."

"Once they write back, we can figure out a plan and go from there," Zayn added.

"Until then, indulge yourselves with a cup of tea and some food," Ryker smiled, and for a split second, I could see where Val had gotten some of his characteristics from.

The thought quickly dropped when Val pulled me over to a table filled with breakfast food.

"Eat something. You need to regain your strength." *I have fed on you twice in a short period,* he said privately.

Before I had a chance to oblige him, someone tugged on my shirt. When I looked down, the little Angel boy was grinning from ear to ear.

"Well, hello."

"My name is Everest. Thank you for saving me!"

"You are very welcome, Everest. My name is Ember."

His eyes grew wide as he sucked in an excited gasp. "Like the embers of a fire?!"

"Yes, exactly." I couldn't help but giggle at how cute and adorable he was.

"Did you see me fly?!" he asked with the proudest smile I had ever seen.

"Yes. You did an excellent job!"

"I am in Mr. Zaynith and Mr. Cashmere's class! They taught me!" My heart ached at how sweet he still was, even after being imprisoned. I hoped he wouldn't be traumatized from what he had been through.

He smiled and ran off before I had a chance to answer him.

"You want one of those someday?" I froze entirely at Val's question.

"Uh, maybe." I picked up a pair of tongs that was resting in a tray of bacon. "You know, a long time from now, when I'm ready to quit and raise a family." Val smiled and kissed me on the cheek before he continued filling his plate with food.

Standing there in utter shock, I wondered what Val wanted—what I wanted. Did Val want children? *Did I* want children? I had never even thought about it before but now I was going to overthink it. Until yesterday, I hadn't even thought about us getting mated in the eyes of the kingdom, either. I was perfectly content with what we had.

Now I was left wondering . . . did I want more?

Are you okay, Ember?

I met his eyes. *Yes, Val. Why?*

You have been standing in front of a tray of bacon for a few minutes now.

Oh. I looked down at the tongs and then back at him before I lied. *I was deciding if I wanted bacon.*

Well, I definitely want some bacon. He took the tongs and started scooping the meat onto his plate.

So, you do want bacon? I asked with a confused face.

He titled his head as his eyebrows furrowed. *Is this one of those things you do, like the chair thing, where you're talking about one thing, but you really just want to have sex with me?*

Hush your mouth, Val. I just couldn't decide if I wanted bacon.

He laughed aloud as he shook his head. *Okay.*

But I thought about it and I think I may want bacon too.

Without hesitation, he put some bacon on my plate and smiled. *Happy now, love?*

Yes, thank you for your bacon.

Val chuckled as I yanked up a biscuit and quickly turned away. My heart was pounding against my chest as I wandered to the nearest table. I tried to put the thoughts of marriage and children out of my head as I took a seat close to Ryker.

"Ember, my dear. How are you after that hard mission?" Ryker asked.

"I am a little sore from being slammed on the ground by a Basilisk, but I will be fine." I was also a little sore from being mated exceptionally hard in a cave, but I let that part stay secret.

"Yes, Zayn told me the story. All of you King's Guards are powerful warriors. I could not be prouder," he said, making me smile.

A hand touched my arm seconds before warmth flooded through me. My eyes widened with shock as I glanced up and saw that Cali had healed me.

"I didn't know you were a Blessed Angel!"

"Did you not see my wings?" She wagged her eyebrows.

"Is that why they're white?"

"Emotional healers have black wings, like those two idiots," she nodded her head toward Zayn and Cash, "and physical healers, like my beautiful self, have white wings."

My eyebrows furrowed in confusion. "But you fight."

"I'm a fighting healer, Ember. It's rare, but it's my destiny." She winked a beautiful blue eye.

"That's amazing, Cali. Thank you for healing me."

"You're welcome." The brown-haired beauty smiled proudly before she walked away.

We ate our breakfast while in full discussion. After about an hour, we had notes from all the dukes. The two Casters were Water Casters from the country of Cerulean. Each of the dukes were sending King's Guards to get their citizens so we were free to go. Natsu had left on his ship with his sister right after breakfast. Zila looked sad after that and it broke my heart.

After we said our goodbyes to Ryker, Wynter, and the freed prisoners, we headed to the portal. Since none of us slept on the ship, exhaustion played on all our faces.

As soon as we landed back in the country of Ashbern, Zayn stopped us.

"I have to go report to the king, but first I wanted to congratulate everyone for doing an amazing job. I couldn't be prouder than I am right now. You guys should get some rest. Classes will resume in a few days."

After parting ways, everyone went straight to their rooms. Of course Val came with me. I quickly changed into pajamas and got into bed. Neither of us could hold our eyes open long enough to take a shower. As we cuddled, sleep came quickly to us both.

Chapter Twenty-Nine

We woke up not long before dinner. Val and I took showers and dressed in our regular clothes, then we strolled leisurely to the dining room. The food smelled amazing as we took seats next to each other.

"Where's Asher?" I asked.

"It's his weekend home so he went straight there when we returned this morning. He said he would sleep when he got there." Zayn sighed as he ran a hand through his shaggy hair. "I slept all day and I'm still tired."

"Me too," Zila said after she stifled a yawn.

After making plates, we became silent as we started to eat. I was sure it was due to exhaustion. Most of us were probably going back to bed once we were done.

I had only had a few bites of my food when the door flung open, startling me. We all froze in shock when the king entered the room. We rose quickly, practically falling out of our chairs as we bowed our heads.

"Don't look so surprised. This was quicker than an Imp." He looked furious as his eyes quickly bounced across each one of us. "Where is Asher?"

"It is his weekend home, Your—"

"No time, Zayn. There is an attack!"

Is? Not was? I thought to Valarian. He shrugged, his face looking concerned.

The king waved his hands and galed all of us to the armory. I was so confused about what had just happened, but my instincts kicked in and I immediately went for my favorite bow. Everyone scrambled in different directions as they grabbed weapons. Everyone wasn't ready yet because they had grabbed more weapons than I did so I snatched up a small throwing axe and shoved it in my belt.

"Everyone ready?"

We all said yes simultaneously. The king waved his hand and all of us landed next to the portal. We immediately ran onto it.

"Val and Zayn, you're in charge," the king said before he gave me a look of empathy. "The attack is on Mazuria."

My heart ached as we were swished through time and space. My adrenaline was pumping so hard that I didn't even feel uneasy on the portal. A hand grabbed mine and squeezed. Knowing it was Val's, I squeezed back, unsure if I was calming him or myself. We landed in my homeland and it was . . . bad.

There were no guards as we ran off the portal, but there were red eyes everywhere. Screaming and crying came from all directions as the citizens tried to defend themselves against the Demons. Most commoners never learned how to fight and rarely wielded their magic past anything simple like lighting a fire. Most of the townsfolk of Pyreland couldn't even gale further than two feet.

Without hesitation, we all went in separate directions as we engaged in the brawl. The first altercation I saw was a lady trying to fight off a Demon so I galed to her. When I landed, there were two Casters on the ground, already dead. My chest filled with sadness seeing their bodies but I had no time to mourn. The Demon bit into the woman's face and tore off a piece of her cheek. As her hand frantically clasped over it, she fell to the ground, screaming in pain. I pulled an arrow from my back and used my magic to light it on fire. A loud whistle rang from my puckered lips as I nocked it and pulled the bowstring taut. The Demon immediately turned, his red eyes locking on me. Releasing the string, the fire arrow shot straight into his chest. I didn't see what happened after that because another Demon slammed into me, knocking me to the ground. As he fell on top of me, my bow got crushed between us. With my only free hand, I pushed up on his throat, trying to keep his snarling face from mine.

Valarian yanked the Demon off me, bit into his neck, and ripped a chunk of his throat out. As the Demon thrashed around, I jumped up and immediately stabbed him in the chest with my dagger. The Demon stilled and Valarian dropped him.

"Are you okay, love?" he asked but I didn't have time to respond.

Over his shoulder, I noticed three more Demons running toward us so I shoved Val out of the way and pulled an arrow from my quiver. I shot a fire arrow at the second Demon, hitting him in the stomach. Val grabbed the Demon that got to us first and twisted his neck. Quickly nocking my arrow, I released the bowstring, hitting the second Demon in the face. He pulled on the Demon's head until it popped off. As I reached back for another arrow, Zila came out of nowhere in her wolf form. She lunged for the third Demon knocking him to the ground. Snarling and biting was coming from them both as they fought. Her jaws locked on his neck, and as she shook hard, he stopped moving.

Turning my attention back to Val, I caught the last second of him ripping a Demon's head clean off his shoulders.

You make murder look sexy. He smirked at my words as he dropped the head to the ground.

The sound of more fighting came from behind me, and as I turned toward it, I saw Zayn and Cash tag-teaming a trio of Demons over by my house. Fear for my sister's life filled me as I galed there to assess the situation.

Cash was repeatedly burying an axe into the side of a Demon's neck. He chopped until his head came off. Too close to utilize it, I threw my bow on my back and immediately stabbed another Demon in its chest. He stilled instantly and melted away.

"We need more Demon blades!" I said to no one in particular. "They die quicker with them!"

Zayn sliced the last standing Demon in the stomach with his sword. "Indeed."

I tossed him my dagger and he used it to stab the Demon in the chest.

"Where's Cali?" he asked breathlessly, handing me back my dagger.

There weren't any more Demons as I glanced around, but a glowing caught my attention. Cali was kneeled on the ground next to the woman that got bit on her cheek, healing her.

"Right there." I pointed.

"Since everyone is safe and I don't see any Demons, I'm going to get an aerial view." Zayn shot up into the sky.

"I'm going to check on Cinder." Cash galed up by my house door and went inside.

"What do we do now?" I asked.

Valarian pulled me into him and rubbed his hands down my back as he kissed the side of my head. "Find Demons to kill."

"I don't see anymore, Val."

Zayn landed next to us. "We need to split up. There are Demons throughout the town. We need to find as many as we can and kill them!"

"And find your sister!" Cash said as he cracked his neck. He had a look of anger mixed with concern. "The house is empty."

I had no time to even think about where Cinder was because Cali appeared in front of us with the woman in her arms.

"Find a place to hide!" Zayn commanded and the woman took off running. "Cash, you fly up with Cali and head toward the middle of town. You can look for Cinder and defend the area while Cali heals people. Val, you and Ember gale to the backside and come in through there. I'm going with Zila straight into the front. If we hit it from both ends, we can meet in the middle, at the town square. Everyone clear on their orders?"

I had a realization . . . "Zayn, where are all the Royal guards?"

Everyone squinted their faces and looked around in confusion.

Zayn's jaw clenched as his face angered. "The duke must not have sent them."

"That fucking asshole," Cash said as he released his raven black wings.

Cali followed suit and released her creamy ivory ones. "Everyone, be careful," she said before they took off into the sky.

"Let's go, Zila." Zayn galed closer to the entrance of town and Zila trotted after him, a prowling nature in her posture.

Val stepped in close to me. I wrapped my arms around him and galed us to the backside of town. It was eerily quiet when we landed, so we entered with caution.

"Should we look somewhere else?" I asked, noticing there were no Demons around.

"No. We'll keep walking until we meet the others. Just keep a good lookout. The sun is almost set so it'll be completely dark soon."

Val and I walked slowly, stumbling across one dead body after another. He pulled me close to him when we came across the body of a young boy. My heart ached at the sight. These were people I knew. People I grew up with.

As I tried to calm my aching chest, a Demon with wings like a bat landed in front of us, and three more came up from behind. I had my dagger in my hand, ready to go.

Valarian pulled his sword from his waist. We stood there in a standoff, waiting for one of them to make a move first.

The Demon in front of us lunged for me. Val intercepted the blow and shoved him away from me. He swung his blade, decapitating him instantly, then swung at another, completely slicing the Demon in half. I was mesmerized by how lethal my bond-mate was. Raising my blade, I stabbed into the neck of the Demon closest to me. A second later, pain radiated through my back, so I swung around, instantly stabbing the Demon that scratched me. Since I hit his shoulder, I wasn't sure if he was dead when he fell to the ground.

Reaching down, I yanked the axe from my belt, and threw it at a Demon that was going for Valarian. It got him in the chest, stunning him enough for Val to rip his head off.

Thanks. He immediately turned and started ripping more enemies apart as they ran up one by one.

A Demon came at me and I dodged his grasps. I swung out sloppily with my dagger and hit him in the arm. Everything was going so fast—my brain could barely keep up as I stabbed anything that moved.

The Demon on the ground wasn't dead, I realized when he started crawling up my leg. While my attention was on kicking him off, another one grabbed me from behind. A third came up, pinning me between the three.

It's hard to gale when your adrenaline is pumping. Even harder when someone is holding onto you. But it wouldn't have mattered if I had the opportunity to gale away.

We were inside the town wards so the magical barriers wouldn't have allowed it.

When two more Demons appeared in front of me, I immediately tried to get my mate's attention.

Val! Glancing away from his murdering spree, we locked eyes.

An enormous growl of anger left him seconds before Demons started flying everywhere. Valarian ripped through the ones in front of me as if they were thin as paper, tearing them limb from limb. One Demon was still holding me from behind when a blade went to my neck.

"Don't move or you're dead."

My body shriveled up after he spoke. "Father?"

Chapter Thirty

My heart was about to fall out of my chest at the sound of my father's voice. Locking eyes on Valarian, he ripped a Demon's arm off and threw it at another one that was headed toward him. There were over a dozen Demons on the ground. He was quickly ending them all. Once he finished, his eyes locked on mine.

When he saw my situation, his face angered, going completely feral. With bared fangs, a thunderous growl escaped his mouth. Veins ran down his face like they did when he was in bloodlust.

"Let her go!" Val growled.

"You move and she dies."

Val took two steps forward, calling his bluff. I winced as my father inched the blade into my neck sending blood dripping down my throat.

Ember! Val screamed, and I ignored him.

"Why are you doing this, Father?"

Father? Val asked me silently. His face looked confused but still extremely angry.

"To have a better life for us."

Confusion filled me. "So, killing me will make your life better?"

"I have no intention of killing you. The Vampire, yes."

"You touch him and I will rip your heart out myself!" I spat.

Valarian growled in approval. The blade went slightly further into my throat, causing more pain and I winced.

Val sucked in a breath, his violet eyes filled with fear. *Stay still, Ember.*

"Oh, you like him? How sweet." He snapped his tongue and sighed. "Look how many of my soldiers you killed, Vampire!"

"So, you're working for the Demons?" I asked, hoping to distract him so I could come up with a plan.

"I like to think of it more like collaborating with them, my dear."

"For what purpose?" Another growl came from the side of me and this time, it was Zila.

"Don't move, wolf, or you will be dead right after the Vampire!"

Zila growled again, baring her blood-stained teeth.

"If you kill him, I will literally die!"

"Don't be so dramatic, Ember. You will be sad but your life will go on. In our new home, nonetheless."

I got completely distracted by this new revelation. "Our new home?"

"Yes, on Mistlaven."

Valarian and Zila both growled with disapproval.

"She's mine. She's not going anywhere with you!" Val practically growled the words at my father.

I'm sorry, but I'm going to fucking kill your father. I ignored Val as I tried to keep him talking.

"Mistlaven? Why would you even think I would live on the Demon land?"

"Because your new life awaits you there."

"I don't want a new life! I already have a life on Ashbern." My blade was still in my hands, but with his arm around me, it was caught underneath it, so it was useless to me.

"Doing the king's bidding is not a happy life. Why take orders when you can give them?"

More confusion filled me. "Why the hell would I give orders?"

He laughed and it sent chills down my spine. "Because that's what queens do, Ember."

"I'm not a queen!"

"You will be once you mate Erebus."

"Over my dead body!" Valarian growled.

"That can be arranged," my father said with another laugh.

"Why would you think I would marry the King of the Demons?" I asked.

"Because you have been promised to him. I made a deal when you were ten. The Duke of Mazuria was distraught because he wanted you for himself, but he has since gotten over it. Especially since I gave him your sister."

"You didn't! You are a sick bastard! I'm going to fucking kill you!"

"Oh, hush, Ember! You will be happy once you see the life we will have. We can have everything!"

Zila has a plan, Val wielded bringing my attention to him.

Don't get yourselves killed, Val!

She'll attack him when he is least expecting it so I can rip his head off. We just need a distraction, love.

I swallowed hard. *I can try and do that.*

"What are you two saying? Did I not teach you that we don't associate with Vampires, Ember? They are the reason—"

"Lies! You have been lying to me for the last two years! I know you're the reason my mother died. I know you're a Debaser!"

My father faltered for just one second and Zila lunged for his leg. Valarian sprung forward to grab me, but was met by a Demon that he quickly stabbed. My father kicked Zila in the side and she yelped. Valarian stopped a mere foot from my face as my father dug the dagger in deeper. I winced as I felt more blood roll down my throat.

Don't move, love. Val went stiff with fear and held his hand out in a peaceful manner. "Let her go. Please." I had never seen Val beg before but the fear in his eyes proved that he would do anything to save me.

"You still have the dagger I gave you, Ember? Because I'm going to use it to kill this Vampire!"

"You cannot kill him, Father!"

"Yes, I can. Even Vampires won't heal from a Demon blade!"

Anger filled me and I was now clenching my teeth. "No, you can't, because it will kill me!"

My father sighed. "Ember, I told you to stop being dramatic!"

"Shut up and listen to me!" I screamed. "If you kill him, I will die! We are life-bonded and he is my bond-mate!"

My father's body stiffened at the revelation. "Did you consummate the bond?"

"That is none of your concern," I spat through gritted teeth.

"If you did not consummate the bond, then it doesn't matter. King Erebus will still want you as long as you're intact."

I let out an almost manic laugh before I screamed, "In that case, I fucked him repeatedly!"

Severe pain radiated through me as my father shoved the blade entirely into my neck.

I always thought that death wouldn't hurt. I figured our bodies would release endorphins that would make us not feel the pain.

I was wrong. . .

Valarian let out a loud, roaring scream of pain as I gasped for air. The Demons were on him instantly, making it impossible for him to come to my aid. My only free hand went up to cover the wound on my neck trying to hold in the blood that was gushing out of it. Zila was growling and biting at my father and he let go of my other arm to defend himself. Now that my other hand was free, I seized the opportunity.

With my last remaining ounce of energy, I raised my dagger over my head and stabbed him in the face. He let out a scream of pain as he fell down and Zila started mauling him. As I fell to my knees, Val caught me and gently laid me on the ground.

The two black winged Angels landed next to us. "Calista! Come here now!" Zayn frantically called for his sister.

Val kneeled beside me and placed his hand on top of mine, trying to cover the wound. His face pained, but gentle. "It's okay, love, I've got you."

"Cash, find Cali!" Zayn commanded, before kneeling next to us. "What the hell happened?"

"If she dies, I will die!"

Zayn's eyes left me and went to Val. "That's not what you said?"

"I will die on the inside, Zayn! You'll have to kill me! Promise me!" Val's bottom lip trembled with fear and even though I was dying, I wanted nothing more than to comfort him.

Zayn shook his head frantically. "Val . . . I can't."

"Promise me, Zayn!" he growled, his voice rumbling through to my soul.

"I promise, buddy." Zayn's voice cracked as he closed his eyes tight.

The pain was so unbearable that I couldn't speak. Blood pooled in my throat and I was choking on it. A large amount of the disgusting wetness was spreading fast, pouring down my body. I was dying . . . and I was okay with it.

I was okay with it because I got to feel what the true meaning of happiness was.

I fell in love.

The words Wynter said to me came back to my mind.

It is better to say what you want than to die not saying what you feel.

I knew what I had to do before it was too late.

Val.

He put his hand on my cheek as tears rolled down his face. "Yes, my *hertis rote*?"

I love you. I always have.

"I love you too, Ember." He sobbed as he leaned forward, pressing his lips gently against mine.

The pain finally left my body with the kiss—nothing hurt anymore when Val pulled away. Looking up, the stars above my head were beautiful. They flickered as my eyes fluttered shut one last time.

Chapter Thirty-One

Valarian

They say when a bond-mate dies, the other person goes insane. I was kneeling on the ground next to the person I loved most in this world, the person for whom I would die. My bond-mate. There was no way of saving her—no way of giving her life back. I would become a shell of a person soon.

Zayn better stick by his words and kill me. . .

"Where is Calista?" I screamed as Ember's eyes closed.

"I don't know, Val!"

"She is dying, Zayn!" I pulled her into my lap and pushed her hair out of her face. I stroked her head while her breathing slowed. She had gone quiet.

One way or another, I was going to die today if she died. If Zayn doesn't kill me, I will offer myself to the Demon King.

"Hold her wound!" I lifted my wrist and bit into it as Zayn frantically threw his hands over her wound.

"Will that work at this stage?" he asked.

"Vampire blood only heals non-lethal wounds, it doesn't stop death, but I have to try." I watched Ember, waiting for her to swallow, waiting for any recognition that she was still here. "Come on, love. Drink for me, please."

She is too far gone, Zayn thought loudly.

Zila's thoughts were also loud. *To the Gods, please let this work.*

I knew they were having trouble keeping their shields up because of the emotional stress, but having to listen to multiple thoughts from people's heads was distracting me. "Shut up, all of you!"

Zayn laid his hand on me and I felt a slight tingle as he used his magic to calm me.

Oh, no! Cali thought as she landed and fell to her knees next to me. "To the Gods!" She placed her hands on Ember's body as I watched.

Calista's skin started glowing extremely bright and then went dark. Nothing happened. The wound didn't close.

"I don't understand. I wielded my magic with full force." Cali sobbed, tears running down her cheeks.

"It is too late, sis." Zayn's voice cracked. Cali started wailing out a cry of pain. Cash lifted her off the ground and hugged her.

This cannot be real! Tears ran down my face as I blinked. I locked my gaze on Ember's beautiful face as she took her last breath.

My bond-mate, my *hertis rote*, was dead in my arms.

A sharp pain radiated from my heart, spreading through my veins. I gritted my teeth as the burning agony spanned across every inch of my body.

Our bond was now broken . . . and I wanted to die.

The pain started eating me from the inside out, moving through my veins like lava. It threatened to take every piece of who I was. It threatened to take *me*.

My heart seemed to shatter into tiny pieces as it filled with sorrow.

A loud scream left my mouth without me even realizing it. The haunting sound lasted so long that the realm started to shake.

The vibrations underneath me made me stop screaming. The ground cracked slightly open as dirt scattered.

"What was that?" Zayn asked.

"I don't know, did his scream—" Cali was interrupted as the realm shook again, tremendously.

The ground split wide open, leaving a gaping hole. With a thunderous clap, a six-foot wall of flames burst out of the pit. The fire crackled and spat higher and higher before it finally simmered down.

Wide eyed and breathless, I watched as a large hand came out of the crater and slammed onto the dirt, and then a second hand did the same. An enormous man pulled his body out of the pit of fire. There were gasps from all around me as he crawled to his feet

This giant was extremely tall, over seven feet. He had emerald-green eyes and fire red hair, just like Ember. I realized that he wasn't a large *man* at all—he was, indeed, a God. It would have been a marvelous sight if I wasn't holding my dead mate.

"My child," the man spoke, looking at Ember with a saddened face. I remained quiet as I pulled her closer to me, trying to keep her safe. He tilted his head slightly, his face filled with concern. "My name is Volcanis. I am the God of Fire. This woman is a direct descendant of my bloodline."

Neither me nor my friends spoke.

Volcanis narrowed his teary eyes on me. "Do you truly love this woman?"

I nodded frantically before I finally mustered myself enough to say something. "I truly do."

"If I asked you to die for her, would you?"

I didn't even have to think of that answer. I would die for her and regret nothing. "Yes. I would do anything to see her happy and alive."

"If I offered to exchange your life *right now* for hers, you would do it?"

"Yes, I would!" My voice cracked with pain. "I love her."

The God of Fire sighed as his eyes traveled curiously over Ember and I. "You are life-bonded to this female? She saved you? She paid the price for your life?"

I nodded as tears streamed down my face. "She did."

"Then you owe her." He raised his hands and the ground rumbled, making rocks and dirt pop off it. Ember's body left my lap and floated about a foot off the earth.

Her entire body was illuminated with a golden glow. The beams of light encased her body, shrouding her like a blanket. She was then raised higher, above my head. The brightness radiating off her lit the night sky as if the sun had come out. Then the fire appeared. Flames crackled and flickered around her, encasing her body like a tomb. The heat from the fire was almost unbearable.

My heart raced as I wanted to stop him. I was afraid he was going to hurt Ember even more. I wanted her back, I needed her back. But I didn't know what to do. I glanced at my friends for guidance, but they were all mesmerized in wonder and fear.

After a few minutes, the flames slowly died down and then disappeared. The golden radiance was still shining brightly as her body was slowly laid back on the ground.

"It is done." As soon as Volcanis said the words, the light encasing her body disappeared. I peered down into her beautiful, freckled face.

"Is she . . . is she . . ." I couldn't speak. Her colorless skin started to turn creamy again, her cheeks turning pink.

"She is alive. I brought her back to life. Brought her back for you."

"Why?" I wasn't trying to be rude, I just needed to understand.

"I felt her pain when she was dying and heard her thoughts. She said she was okay with dying because she found the true meaning of happiness. She found love. Then I heard your unbearable scream and I could not stand idly by any longer."

Tears ran down my face. *I'm not worthy of this beautiful woman.*

"I had that feeling once upon a time, many years ago. I felt I was not worthy enough for a woman. She left this world long ago. . ." He had a wistful, longing smile. "Ember will recover soon. You have paid the price for her life."

"Are you going to kill me now?" I was ready. It was worth it.

"No, son. You are now mirror-bonded to her. It is the strongest bond one could ever have. It has only happened once before in history. She paid the price for your life and you paid the price back."

"What does mirror-bonded mean?"

"It means you will both stay alive if the other does. With a life-bond, if one of you dies, the other would die on the inside, becoming a shell of a person. With a mirror-bond, you both go together. Your lives mirror each other. The bond will keep you together for eternity. In this world and beyond."

I pulled Ember back into my lap as more tears streamed down my face. I was a sobbing mess in front of a God. "Thank you."

"I must rest now." He walked a few feet away from me and stopped. Looking back over his shoulder, his eyes locked on Zayn. "Tell my brother to wake me when it is time."

Volcanis crawled back into the earth. The flames shooting twenty feet high in a glorious wall of fire. Our world shook once more, dirt bouncing off the vibrating ground. With a thunderous clap, the flames diminished back into the ground and the hole sucked closed.

Before I had a chance to stop her, Ember moved quickly, grabbing at her neck. I tried to calm her as she sucked in deep breaths. She was scratching and pulling at her throat and me. When her eyes opened, I think I stopped breathing.

Chapter Thirty-Two

Ember

I was suffocating—I couldn't breathe.

Reaching up, I grabbed for my neck, right where my father had stabbed me. It felt like I was going to choke to death on my blood. Val was in my face, trying to hold my arms down as I gasped for air.

"Sit still, Ember." Val sounded panicky as he tried to soothe me. I kept fighting him because I needed my hands to cover the wound before I bled to death. "You're okay, my love!"

Zayn came into my field of vision as he knelt next to me and grabbed my cheeks. Cash kneeled right next to him.

"You are okay. You can breathe," Zayn whispered to me.

Magic took hold of my body as both Angels surged a large amount into me. It willed me to stop thrashing—to stop panicking. I relaxed and dropped my hands. I swallowed what tasted like blood. A few of my friends let out a sigh and some let out sobs.

"What happened?" I asked. My voice was hoarse and cracking.

"You're alive, my love. That's all that matters."

"Welcome back, my truest friend," Zayn said in a sad voice.

Cali was off to the side hysterically crying. Cash got up and threw his arm around her, trying to soothe her. He still had an axe in his other hand as he gave me a sad smile.

Wondering why everyone was emotional, I sat up and looked around. There were no more Demons—not alive, anyway. Glancing behind me, I saw Zila still in her wolf form, her mouth on my father's throat. He was alive and staying exceptionally still. My own father had stabbed me.

Zayn saw where I was looking. "Cash, tie him up."

"What happened?" I asked again, not understanding.

"We have to get you home. We can talk then." Val placed his hands on my cheek, rubbing his thumb around.

"No," I squeaked out. "Tell me!"

Val sighed as he blinked tears out of his eyes. "It's a long story, but basically, the God of Fire brought you back to life."

I sucked in a large breath. "What?"

"It's a lot to take in. But I need to get you out of here now, my love."

I looked at my father with pure hatred in my heart. "What of him?"

"That's for King Reign to decide." Val swooped me into his arms before he stood up. His eyes met Zayn's. "It looks to me like they have all fled. Are you good without us?"

"Yep. We'll manage everything from here." Zayn smiled at me before going into commander mode. "Cash, Cali, make a perimeter sweep and see if there are any Demons left."

Valarian galed us over to the portal. When he carried me on, I noticed the guard was still missing. He willed it to go and we landed back in the country of Ashbern. I was too shocked to care about the feelings the portal gave me. I laid my head onto Val's chest as we walked inside the manor and up to my room.

He sat me on my bed before he went into the bathroom and turned on the water. A minute later, he came out and went to my dresser. After digging through the drawers, he pulled out a pair of underwear and a nightgown. He held the panties up with a smirk on his face. I gave him a slight smile. He set my clothes in the bathroom, turned the water off, and then returned to me.

Kneeling in front of the bed, he nestled between my legs and took my hand. "How are you feeling?"

"I'm not sure, Val. I think I may be in shock or something."

He pressed a kiss upon my hand. "How about you take a hot bath while I go update the king?" I nodded my head.

He rose off the floor, pulling me off the bed by my hand. He gently took me into the bathroom. I stood next to the tub and stared at it.

"May I undress you?" I nodded again.

He slowly lifted my blood-soaked shirt off me and threw it down, then kneeled to the ground and slipped off my boots. A heated rush flew through my body as he reached up and unbuttoned my pants, then pulled them off. After he slid my panties down, I stood there, completely naked, not feeling ashamed or embarrassed.

He rose from the ground and looked into my eyes as the heat once again filled me. "Are you ready to get in, my *hertis rote?*"

There was this weird, overpowering feeling that said I needed him so I grabbed his face and pulled it down to me. I slammed my mouth onto his, kissing him hard. His strong arms went around me, holding me tight as he kissed me back, before he pulled away.

"I can feel the lust coming off you, Ember. I want you, I truly do, but I must talk to the king. You get cleaned up and I'll be back soon." I nodded again.

Taking my hand, he held it while I stepped into the bath. It felt good as I sank into the hot water. Val quietly walked out of the bathroom and shut the door. I leaned back into the bathtub and closed my eyes.

> *Walking in Ethereal Pastures, the large field of magic seemed to go on forever. I was running through the fields alone because Valarian wasn't with me. Confusion filled me because I didn't know how to get out of the fields. I stopped running and looked down at the blowing rose buds. The magic had disappeared.*

> *The beautiful flowers started to shrink before my eyes as the blooms dripped with blood. The once vibrant red flowers turned black and*

wilted away to nothing. A new bud arose from the plant. It almost looked like the roses, but deadlier. It had spikes on it—ones that could practically gut you if you got too close to them.

A creeping black fog started rolling across the ground toward me. I turned to run and was met with the same thorny flowers that seem to move like they were alive.

'No one will save you. No one can save you, Ember!' I heard in my head. 'No one can save you from this, from the darkness. You will be mine, for eternity!'

Vines curled around my ankles and held me in place. They felt like cold, dead fingers against my skin as they crawled up my legs. I thrashed and screamed as I tried to fight them off, but they were too strong.

A large bud appeared out of one of the vines and it almost looked like a face. It shifted slightly and grinned its blood-soaked fangs at me. It wasn't a flower . . . it was a Demon.

'Ember,' it whispered.

A Demon that knew my name . . .

'Valarian!' I screamed, hoping that he would come to my rescue. The flower Demon quickly grew arms and wrapped them around me. I kicked, screamed, and tried to draw blood to the already bloody disfigured flower face.

Valarian rose behind the flower Demon and sliced him with a sword. The flower Demon put a leaf-looking hand over his face and screamed as he wilted . . . then I started screaming.

Chapter Thirty-Three

"**W**ake up, Ember!" Val was in my face and shaking me when my eyes popped open. "Are you okay?"

I gasped for air as I tried to control my racing heart. "I had . . . a nightmare."

"I heard you screaming in my head. I felt your fear and the pain of the thorns scratched you. I don't even know how it is possible, but I did!"

"What?" I shook my head in confusion. "Were you close by?"

"No, I was at the king's castle." He let out a hard breath. "It has to be a part of the mirror-bond."

"What bond?"

He laid his hand gently on my cheek. "We have a lot to talk about. You may want to get dressed first."

Val helped me out of the bathtub and got me dressed before he escorted me to my bed. He was treating me like I was glass and was going to break.

"I changed your sheets right before I left to see the king because they had blood on them."

With a sigh, he kneeled before me once more. Taking my hand in his, he told the story of how I died and was brought back to life. He also explained to me that Volcanis had mirror-bonded us.

By the time he was done reliving the tragic events, we both had tears streaming down our faces. "I'm sorry, I couldn't save you from your father."

I placed my palms on his cheeks, willing him to look at me. "It's okay, Val. I'm alive and now we will be together for eternity."

"That's the best part of all of this." We both chuckled as we wiped away tears.

Pulling him toward me, I pressed my lips against his. He put one of his hands on the back of my head and curled his fingers in my hair, making the heat rise in me once again. When he tried to pull away from me, I gripped his shirt, refusing to let him go. He finally turned his head to break free.

"You should rest, love. You have had a rough day." He shook his head. "Shit, you literally died . . ."

"I'm fine, Val." I pulled him back in, kissing him again. He let me ravish him a little longer this time. We were both panting when he pulled away.

"Zayn just asked me to come into the hall. I'll be right back." I sighed as he stood up. "You really should get some sleep, Ember."

Valarian left the room, dimming the oil lamp on his way out. As I was waiting for him, I started thinking about how hard his body was. The yearning pain in between my legs didn't stop. I tried to will it to, but it was controlling me.

It had never been like this before. I had a feeling that the new bond was doing it. It was like I needed to make love to complete it.

After a few minutes, Val came back with a frustrated face. "You're killing me, Ember!"

My eyebrows furrowed. "What do you mean?"

"This mirror-bond has me all messed up. I felt your pain earlier when you had a nightmare. Just now, I was talking to Zayn in the hall and I felt your lust radiating to me and . . ."

"And what?"

Val did something I had *never* seen him do before . . . he blushed. "And my cock got hard from it. I was so glad when Zayn stopped talking. I have never been happier to have a conversation end in my life!"

I put my hand over my mouth, trying to stifle a laugh.

"Everyone is back and safe, by the way."

"My father?"

"He's locked away on Mayhem. My father had him put in the cells there. There was too much of a risk to bring him here."

That was a clever idea. "What about my sister?"

Val sighed and shook his head. "We can't find her."

"We must go look!" I jumped off the bed and started heading toward the closet. Valarian grabbed me around my waist before I made it there.

"We can't go until morning, my love. The king has shut down all the portals until daylight. So, unless you want Zayn and Cash to fly us there, we must wait."

My eyebrows rose. That didn't sound like that bad of an idea.

"Don't even think about it." He purred. He knew me too well. "We need to sleep so we'll be rested for tomorrow. If what your father said is true, and the Duke of Mazuria has Cinder, we'll be fighting again."

"I can't sleep knowing my sister may not be safe!"

"What do you want to do, then?" Still holding me from behind, Val laid his chin on my shoulder. "Are you hungry?"

"I am genuinely hungry," I glanced over my shoulder and met his eyes, "just not for food." The minute I said the words, my heat rose again.

His entire facial expression changed as I felt his cock harden against my butt. "You can never get heated around the king or I will die of embarrassment."

His fingers grazed my shoulder as he pushed my hair to one side. I instantly tilted my head, ready for him to kiss me—bite me. I didn't care either way.

"You need to sleep, love," he whispered.

"I need *you*, Val."

Placing his lips upon my neck, he started kissing. His hand left my waist, cupped my breast, and squeezed. I moaned as I pressed my butt against him. Val let out some incredibly sexy noises as I rubbed on him, paying attention and learning what he liked. That made me eager to get more moans out of him.

Swinging me around to face him, his arms wrapped me in a big hug. I started to get on my tippy toes to kiss him, but he picked me up so my face met his. We locked lips and it was terrific. I would never get tired of kissing him.

Setting me back on my feet, he slowly took off my nightgown. Both of my breasts were cold, and my nipples were hard. He knelt in front of me and slid my panties down. I stepped out of them one foot at a time. He ran both hands up the side of my thighs and onto my butt. He squeezed my ass and pulled me toward his face, placing a single kiss at the apex of my legs. My head fell back as I let out a breathy moan.

Moving his hands to my knees, he spread my legs open. Reaching up between them, he spread the sensitive lips apart and ran his tongue slowly over my clit. He had complete control over me and my body, and I was okay with giving him that kind of power. He suddenly stopped, and I whimpered.

He looked up at me and smiled, his lips glistening in the moonlight from my wetness. He pushed on my stomach, and I fell back on the bed. He stayed down on his knees and scooted forward. Lifting both my legs, he put them over his shoulders.

Consuming me like I was his last meal, he swirled his tongue slowly, licking every drop of wetness I had, stopping occasionally to suck on me, making me twitch. He licked from my entrance up to my throbbing clit.

My thighs were shaking from the feeling and my body was hot all over. I reached down and pulled his hair as I moaned. I attempted to squirm away from him, but he held on to my thighs, not letting me go. He licked harder as I rode the wave of ecstasy once more.

Once I was done and my breathing was heavy, he ran his tongue down my thigh. He stopped and kissed it.

May I feed from here? he asked as he continued to kiss the inside of my thigh.

"To the Gods, yes!" I screamed and he growled in approval.

Valarian sank his fangs into my thigh, eliciting a split second of pain before my body went into pure bliss mode. The euphoria radiated through me and I could swear I saw stars, magic, and love while he sucked. He crawled off the floor, standing while I was still in my blissful state.

After dropping his pants, his hard cock sprung out, ready for me. He grabbed my hips and picked me up, moving me more towards the center of the bed.

As he laid on top of me, he entered me immediately with a loud moan. I pulled my knees back, willing him to go deep inside me. He pulled one of my legs up and threw it over his shoulder. My clit was pulsating with pleasure and excitement.

"Let's finish what you were doing under the trees."

He dropped my leg and hugged my body, then rolled over and pulled me on top of him. I hesitated for a second before he grabbed my hips and started moving them forward and backward.

"I don't know what to do." I had only had sex in one position until I met Val.

"Just move however you want. Do whatever you think feels good because it all feels good to me." I immediately started thinking about how sex was described in some of my books.

Starting to move slowly, I slid up and down, forward and backward. I circled my hips one way and then another. I rotated them in different directions until I found the spot that felt the best. He moaned at all my movements and it made me go faster.

The feeling was building in me again. As I was grinding on his hardness, he held onto my hips. My breaths were coming out ragged as I felt the rush coming. The throbbing in my core was so hard that I fell forward slightly.

Putting my hands on his chest, I dug my nails into it, using him to keep me upright. The climax that came was intense.

"Oh, Gods!" I screamed out as the blissful feeling took over me. He went tense and moaned, squeezing my hips hard. Wetness filled me as he got his release right after mine.

With panting breaths, I fell onto his chest and he put his arms around me. I closed my eyes for a brief second while I listened to his heart race. My breathing slowed as he caressed my back.

I finally felt complete—the bond was sealed.

Chapter Thirty-Four

The next day I woke up in Valarian's arms with him breathing on my neck. He was cuddled up close to my back, sound asleep. My heart ached with the amount of love I could have for this man. A sudden knock at the door startled me.

Shit.

I slid out of bed and quickly threw on my nightgown, then pulled the blanket back over Val's extremely sexy and extremely naked body.

When I opened the door, Zayn was staring at me with a worried face. "Have you seen Val? He's not . . ." He glanced toward my bed. "Oh. Well, that makes me feel better. I was starting to worry."

Val turned toward us and blinked his sleepy eyes. "What's going on, buddy?"

"It's almost time to go. You have enough time for a quick shower if needed."

"Alright." Valarian hopped out of bed, completely naked, and strolled into the bathroom. My eyes went wide and I blushed as I looked back at Zayn.

"Congratulations." He smiled in approval and nodded his head.

I giggled and swatted his arm. "Stop that!"

"Are you staying here?" He tilted his head in a pleading manner.

"I will do no such thing."

He sighed. "You better go get cleaned up, then. Meet me by the portal in twenty minutes. Don't forget to arm yourself."

"I won't."

"I'm glad you're alive, Ember. I may not have the same kind of feelings for you as Val does, but you're particularly important to me. You're like a sister and I do love you. I would have died if . . ." His beautiful blue eyes filled with tears as he choked up.

"I know. I love you too." I reached out and hugged the Angel.

"I'm glad you're okay. Now, let's get your sister back." He let go of the hug and left.

I wiped tears from my eyes and then quickly got out my fighting leathers and laid them on the chair. I went into the bathroom to hop in the shower with Valarian.

"Hello, bond-mate."

"Hi," I said to him as I stepped into the stream.

His hands instantly slid around my waist and yanked me into him. Then his luscious lips gently pressed against mine.

Since time was of the essence, the kiss didn't last long. Val pulled away and grabbed the soap. The heat rose inside of me as he washed the front of my chest and then headed down my stomach.

"Okay, you better do that." He handed me the soap and I giggled.

"Just so you know, Val, you never have to ask permission to feed from me."

He smiled with pure pride. "That is truly an honor."

We both washed up quickly and got out. I was standing in the bedroom drying off as Valarian strolled to the door and opened it, wearing nothing but a towel.

My eyes widened. "What are you doing, Val?"

"My leathers are in my room."

"To the Gods, keep that towel on. You're going to scare the servants!" I shook my head as he laughed and left my room.

Ten minutes later, I was standing outside of the portal with Val, Zayn, and Cash. We were all armed and ready to go, waiting for the rest of our party. To my surprise, Asher came strolling up. He gave us a fake smile.

"It's your weekend home, Asher. Why are you here?" I asked.

"Zayn told me what happened. I insisted on coming back and finding your sister." His emerald-green eyes looked concerned as he cracked his knuckles.

None of us were happy about what we had to do, but I was grateful everyone would risk their lives for my sister. I smiled at him as tears welled up in my eyes. "Thank you."

A few minutes later, Zila and Cali came strolling onto the portal. Val slid his arms around me and I had just enough time to take in one breath before Zayn willed the portal to go.

I realized the portal had finally gotten easier when we landed in Mazuria. It was quiet, unlike it had been during the battle. I was grateful to see that there was a guard stationed here now, but I couldn't help but worry what happened to the ones that were on duty last night.

All seven of us slowly walked off the portal and headed toward Pyreland. It was dead calm. Cash galed up to my house and went inside.

A minute later he came out, but I didn't see Cinder with him. He galed back to us and shook his head.

"He does have her!" he said, looking completely heartbroken and angry.

"Alright, guys, this isn't going to be pleasant or fun. If anyone wants to stay here in town and check on the people, go now."

"I actually would like to stay back and make sure no one needs healing," Cali said with a look of worry plastered all over her face. "I can catch up with you in a bit."

"That's fine. Anyone else?" Zayn asked.

"One of you should stay with her." The way Cash said it, meant he wasn't staying. He was ready to fight for Cinder.

"It's my sister, I will *not* stay behind."

"If my mate goes, I go." Valarian pulled me close to him.

"I'll stay and help her," Asher said with a wry smile.

"Alright, it's settled. Asher and Cali will stay here. The rest of us will head to Spellchild Castle. You two catch up with us as soon as you can." Zayn was such a born leader and I smiled with pride at the thought.

"Let's go then," Cash said as he strolled ahead of us. He was getting impatient.

We walked for a bit on the outside of town. I didn't see a single person and it bothered me.

Zayn stopped in front of us. None of us were ready to storm the castle, per se, but we didn't have a choice. "We can gale from here."

Zayn galed and everyone followed. Val and I were the only ones left standing there. I walked up to him and put my arms around him so I could gale us.

"I want to tell you something." Val's violet eyes sparkled as he looked down at me. "I love you, Ember Lavaris. I just wanted to make sure you knew that. I didn't say it because you were dying. I meant it and I should have said it sooner."

"I love you too, Valarian Carter Grey." I smiled before leaning in to kiss him, but he stopped me.

"Hold on. Who told you my middle name?"

"Why do you need to know?" I asked with a mischievous grin.

"So I can rip their heart out, my love."

I giggled before I decided to give up the secret. "It was Cash."

"I knew it." We both laughed. Before I galed us away, he leaned my head back and put a long, beautiful kiss upon my lips. A kiss that also said I love you.

We finally broke free and galed to meet the others. When we landed outside of the castle wards, Zayn, Cash, and Zila were nowhere to be seen.

Valarian grabbed my hand. *Crouch down, Zayn needs us.* He dragged me over to the tree line in a half-crouch, where my friends were hiding.

"What's wrong?" Val asked Zayn as he pulled me to a squat.

"There are no guards or movement anywhere." Zayn's eyes narrowed on the castle in deep thought.

"What do you think's going on?" Cash asked as he ran a hand through his beard.

"I don't know, but it can't be good," Val stated.

"Did anyone check on the duke after the attack last night?" I asked.

"I tried to, but I was met by guards right over there." Zila pointed, her face concerned. "The guards said that the duke had put the castle on lockdown and he wasn't taking any visitors until later. I told Zayn about it."

"And I told her there's nothing we can do if he doesn't want to accept our visit." Zayn ran a hand nervously through his hair. "I told the king when we got back."

Cash said what we were all thinking. "I have a bad feeling about this."

"We need a plan." Zayn looked around at us, waiting for any suggestions.

"I know a way into the castle without being seen." Everyone's face turned toward me.

"How?" Zayn asked.

"A secret hole in the wall."

"And we can get into the castle through a hole?" Zayn asked with a surprised look.

"We all can't . . . well, you men can't. Only Zila and I will be able to fit through. It's a small hole." I nervously bit my lip, waiting for disapproval.

Val looked concerned as he grabbed my hand. "I don't want you going in without me."

"I'll be fine, Val." I kissed his hand, trying to calm his nervousness.

"That seems like a plan, though not one that I'm completely comfortable with." Zayn had a somber face while he looked at Zila and I.

"We can get in and get out, Zayn. No one would even know. We can assess the situation and come straight back when we're done. If Zila wants to go with me, she can. Otherwise, I'll go alone."

"I'm in," Zila said without hesitation.

"Alright. You've got about twenty minutes. If you don't come out, we're coming in for you." We both nodded, acknowledging Zayn's orders.

I leaned over and kissed Val on the lips.

"Be safe, my love," he said.

"Always." I gave him a quick hug before I took my bow and quiver off and set them on the ground.

Valarian's eyebrows furrowed. "Ember, you need—"

"It won't fit through the hole." I smiled. "We'll be right back."

Zila and I were stealthy with our actions as we hunkered to the ground and headed through the trees. We got to the side of the castle that had the thickest forest and I pointed to the tree closest to the castle.

"The large tree did damage to the structure a long time ago, so there's a small hole right behind it. We have to squeeze through, but it'll be fine. I used to do it all the time when I was younger." Zila nodded in acknowledgement.

We crept up to the castle and quickly went behind the tree. The fear of being caught was rushing through me and my heart was racing from the silence. I hadn't heard or seen a guard, or anyone, for that matter.

Since we needed to stay quiet, I was hoping Zila understood what I was about to do. Holding my hand up, I pointed to myself, then pointed to the hole. I pointed to Zila, then pointed to the opening again. She nodded in acknowledgement before I climbed inside. My breasts and bottom were much bigger than they were last time, so when I say I squeezed into it, I mean it. Once I got to the end of the hole, it came out into a random room with supplies in it. I climbed out and dusted off my clothes. Zila came in right behind me and did the same.

Quietly walking over to the door, I opened it about an inch, looked through the slit, and saw nothing. I opened it a little further and stuck my head out. No one was in sight as I shut the door.

"There's no one out there," I whispered to Zila.

"So, what do we do?" she whispered back to me.

"I think we should look further, otherwise, we don't have any information for Zayn."

"True." She nodded. "Let's go."

Cracking the door open again, the halls were still empty. Since I knew this castle like the back of my hand, I knew where the duke's quarters and private rooms were. As soon as we stepped out, I went right.

We crept through the passage, peeking around every new corridor before we entered it. Nothing. We continued to the duke's private quarters and stopped at the door. I was afraid to open it, afraid he would be in there, or worse . . . that Demons would be.

I slowly opened the door and peeked inside. It was empty. I motioned for Zila to follow me in.

"I don't know what to think about this. It's odd." I looked at Zila and her face was as confused as mine.

"I'm assuming they didn't all die in last night's attack because there are no bodies." She had a good point.

"It's been about ten minutes. We should head back."

Walking over, I peeked out the door and didn't see anything. I motioned for Zila to follow me, she did.

We were turning down the last corridor to the supply room when Zila grabbed my arm. She put her finger to her mouth, telling me to stay quiet. A few seconds later, I heard footsteps. They were getting louder, coming toward us. We doubled back and went through the first door we saw.

It was dark inside the room when we closed the door behind us. After hearing the footsteps go by, I opened the door and looked out, seeing the back of the duke walking down the hall. I had to follow him.

"It's the duke! I think we should follow him."

Zila nodded, agreeing with me.

We exited the room and slowly followed him, only going into a hallway that he had already passed through. He stopped at the end of a corridor and we waited to see which way he would go. As soon as he turned left, we started heading down the hallway. We got to the end and I went to peek down it . . .

"Hello, Ember!" His evil voice sent shivers down my spine.

Zila had twins sai on her and she unsheathed them as I grabbed my dagger.

"Don't move! If you do, Cinder dies."

I halted my dagger, which was already raised up and was ready to come down.

"That's what I thought. Follow me. You too, Lycan."

"We will do no such thing," I said to the duke with an angry look on my face.

"You will or Cinder dies. Do you not see how the game works, Ember?"

As I stood there, I had to weigh my options. I could either go with him and die, or not go with him and my sister dies. My mind was made up.

"I'll come with you, but you will let the Lycan go."

"And I will do no such thing, female," he spat the words out at me like I asked him to give us his first-born child. "You *do not* give me ultimatums. Are we clear?" The fiery girl in me wanted to stab him and burn his remains. The cool-headed part of me that loved my sister knew I should listen. So I nodded.

"Good, now that is settled." Three Demons walked up behind us.

One grabbed my arm, one grabbed Zila's and the other went between us. We were now captured. I hoped my friends would find us quickly.

We were escorted down a few corridors. I realized we were going into the banquet hall as soon as we stopped in front of the huge double doors.

The third Demon opened the doors for the duke. Apparently, the duke was like my father and had no qualms about working with Demons.

We were shoved into the room and thrown to the ground. I wished I could wield my thoughts to Zila so we could devise a plan.

Looking up, I was completely brought away from the thoughts I had. "No!"

"Ahh, there is my mate!"

Chapter Thirty-Five

My mouth was agape as I looked up from the floor. The man from my dreams last night was real and he was standing right in front of me.

He was slightly taller than Val, with dull black hair and gray skin. He had on a tunic that was untied and open at the top, which let me see his Demon tattoo. It was an inverted star made up of multiple lines and had a circle around it, with fire intertwined around the star.

'No one will save you. No one can save you, Ember!' I recalled the words he spoke in my dream. *'No one can save you from this, from the darkness. You will be mine, for eternity.'*

"No! I am *not* your mate. I have a mate. I am taken!" I screamed.

Val, it's Erebus, the Demon King. We are in the banquet hall. I wielded the thought to Val, not knowing if he would hear it. I got no response.

Erebus' intimidating red eyes narrowed on me. "You were promised to me long before that wretched Vampire ever came into the picture!"

"Do *not* talk about my mate, Erebus!"

"So, you know who I am, which means you know my plans. Valarian will soon be ended and you and I will be united in a mating ceremony."

"Don't speak his name, either!"

"He will be just a memory. A memory I can remove from your mind." His voice was low and wicked, sending chills down my spine.

"If you kill him, I die with him, and then we will live in blissful eternity together, so go ahead and kill us both!"

"You won't die, Ember." His smile was more nefarious than his voice.

"Yes, I will! We're bonded." I decided not to mention that it was a mirror-bond.

"You won't die from a broken bond, Ember, you'll just want to. Luckily for you, I am the King of the Demons. I can break the bond cleanly to make sure you don't feel the pain. Once it is done, we will be mated."

My heart sped up at the thought of having my bond broken. Tears were swelling in my eyes, but the anger and fear for my bond-mate was stronger. "I will kill myself before I ever let that happen!"

"You will be mine, my dear." His evil laugh sent chills through me. The fear of losing my connection to Val made it hard to breathe.

The door flung open, bringing my attention away from Erebus. Cinder was dragged in by Demons and thrown to her knees next to me. She scrambled across the floor and collapsed into my arms. My fear spiked, making my heart race faster when around twenty Demons stomped in and surrounded us.

Valarian, I need you!

"And there is your mate!" Erebus looked at the Duke of Mazuria as he pointed to my sister. My face filled with pure anger as I glared at the smile on the duke's face.

"You touch her and I will rip your heart out!" The words I screamed echoed through the dining hall. My anger is now much stronger than my fear.

"This is unquestionably entertaining. Our little Ember here thinks she is a warrior. I find that sexy in a mate." Erebus had an evil smile that matched the duke's.

"We should take the Lycan too. I'm sure we can find someone to mate the wolf and turn her." The duke looked proud of his statement.

Meeting Zila's silver eyes, I hoped she understood my stare. Her head just slightly nodded, the smallest movement, only noticeable to me. My silent request was answered. We would *die* before we let them take any of us.

Keeping an arm around Cinder, I raised my other hand and wielded a fireball at Erebus' head. My fireballs were usually about the size of my hand but this time, it was ten, twenty times bigger. It was the largest and hottest fireball I had ever wielded. As the flames traveled through the air, I knew he was going to dodge it, but that was my plan. I needed to distract them. It flew to the side of the room with both the evil males. They fell to the ground to keep from getting hit.

Now was our chance.

Zila transitioned into a wolf right before my eyes and went for the Demon standing closest to her, mauling him. Without hesitation, I jumped up and stabbed the Demon closest to me with my dagger. I immediately lunged for another one, slamming my dagger into it. Zila and I quickly took out five Demons before we were halted.

"Stop or she is dead!" I looked up from my battle fever and saw the Duke of Mazuria holding my sister with a short knife to her throat. Cinder whimpered and I froze in fear.

"Let her go!" I screamed.

"That is going to be a no." He gave me an evil smirk and I lost control.

Dropping my dagger, I balled my hands into fists and let out a primal scream. Fire burst out of my skin before my entire body burst into flames. Even though it engulfed me, it didn't hurt.

Small fireballs shot in random directions—they seemed to be motivated by the anger I was feeling. The duke stumbled back away from the hellish fire, with my sister still in his grasp as I furiously headed toward him. I was going to end him with my bare hands.

An arrow shot past me and went straight into the duke's head. His arms dropped away from my sister as he fell to the ground, dead. Looking toward the door, Asher had my bow and he knew how to use it.

Valarian's growl echoed in the room mere seconds before he started tearing into Demons. He punched a hole into one and ripped his heart out, then another.

Cash was axing his way through the Demons, trying to get to Cinder. Zayn took one's head off with one slice of his sword. Cali stabbed another under his chin with her katana as Zila ripped the throat out of one. Asher pulled out two scythes and started chopping into any enemy that moved.

A Demon stepped in front of me, so I grabbed him by the throat and squeezed. He caught on fire and screeched out a horrific scream before he dropped to the floor. My eyes widened as flames disintegrated him to nothing but ash.

Cash had made his way over to my sister and helped her off the ground. Now that I knew she was safe, it was time for me to take on Erebus. Hopefully, my new fire skin stayed with me for a few more minutes because I was going to *kill* the King of the Demons.

The flames flickered over my skin when I locked eyes with Val for just a second. His eyes went wide with surprise and fear.

It doesn't hurt, I quickly wielded to him as I grabbed my dagger off the floor and turned away. Erebus was mine.

My feet slammed against the marble floor as I ran toward him. He wasn't expecting me to run into him and only had a split second to brace for the impact.

Plowing straight into his body, he fell and I landed on top of him. Ready to kill him, my flames shot higher, more intense, and I was hoping he would burn to death under my body. With a battle cry, I pulled my dagger up into the air and slammed it down, hitting the . . . ground. Erebus had disappeared into thin air.

What the fuck?

Ember?

Hearing my name, I turned my attention away, now trying to find my mate. The look on his face told me that he was afraid to touch my body, which was still covered in flames. Hopping to my feet, I glanced around. Almost all the Demons were dead—at least, the ones that hadn't run. Zayn, Cali, and Zila were finishing off the last three.

"Are you okay, my love?" Val's eyes traveled over my body with fear and fascination.

"I'm fine." Glancing around, all of my friends were staring at me with confused or fearful faces. "Where's Erebus?"

"Ember, why are you covered in flames, but not dying?" an out of breath Zayn asked.

"Where did Erebus go?" I yelled. I didn't have time for other questions.

"He disappeared." Cali had a scared look on her face when she spoke.

"We need to find him. I have to kill him!" My adrenaline pushed me forward as I started to run past my friends. I had to kill Erebus before he came back for me or my sister.

Zayn stepped into my path, halting me—his beautiful blue eyes locked onto mine.

"You are safe, you are fine. Calm down." I felt the magic, but it wasn't strong enough to stop me.

"No . . . I . . . I have to kill him."

Zayn held my stare. I tried to move my body, but it felt sluggish. "Calm down, Ember."

"I can't, I have to kill him!"

Cash stepped next to Zayn, his blue eyes now piercing mine. A double surge of magic from the Angels hit me at once and my heartbeat slowed. I felt at ease. Comforted. Calm. The flames died down and disappeared.

Valarian instantly hugged as tight as he could. I eased into his arms and laid my head on his chest as I took deep breaths. It felt like it was the first one I had taken in the last thirty minutes.

He rubbed his hand up and down my back. "You're safe, my love. You're safe."

"We need to retreat now." Zayn started for the door and we all followed.

"We can't go yet." We stopped and stared at my sister.

"Why not, Cinder?" Zayn asked.

"I wasn't the only one who was captured. There's a young girl downstairs in the dungeon. We have to save her," Cinder said, stifling back a cry.

"Just one?" Zayn asked.

"Yes, that I know of."

"Let's go," Zayn ordered. "Ember, lead the way."

Chapter Thirty-Six

We quickly made our way down to the dungeon underneath the castle. Taking all the people I loved in this world down there made me uneasy.

When we got to the cells, they appeared to be empty.

"The last one." Cinder pointed to the end. Cash had his arm around her, soothing her.

Val, Zayn, and I walked to where she'd indicated while the rest of our party remained at the entrance. We got to the end of the cells and it was too dark to see, but then I heard a whimpering cry.

"It's okay. We're here to save you." I spoke as softly as I could, hoping that the fire skin didn't come back. That would freak her out. Shit, it freaked *me* out.

"I don't know you. Why am I here?" the girl asked, fear lining her voice.

"I don't know. We came here to save my sister. She was locked down here with you. The Demons are gone for now, but we have to hurry and get out of here."

After hearing a shifting sound, I saw the outline of a small girl. She stayed in the shadows, so I couldn't make out her features.

"What is your name?"

"Silvaria," she whimpered.

"Nice to meet you, Silvaria. My name is Ember."

"Ember, she's a Lycan. I can smell her," Zila said from behind me.

"Are you a Lycan, my dear?"

"I am. I was taken a long time ago. I think."

"We're a part of the King's Guard. We vow not to hurt you if you come out of the cell," Zayn said as he unlocked the cell.

The Lycan took a few steps back into the blackness.

Zayn locked eyes with me. "Hold on," I whispered. I turned toward Zila and nodded my head in the direction of the cell.

"It's okay. I'm like you." Zila's voice was calm as she stepped into the cell. "Can you smell me?"

The girl peaked out of the darkness before she ran into Zila's arms and hugged her. Trying to hide my reaction so I didn't scare her, I threw a hand over my mouth at how the girl looked.

She was a little over five feet tall. The clothes she was wearing were torn-up, ratty. I didn't know how long she had been down here, but she looked like she hadn't bathed in weeks . . . months.

Zila ran her hands down the girl's matted hair, soothing her. Val's hand went to mine and held it as tears formed in my eyes. The pain this girl must have felt was unbearable to think about.

"We have to hurry, Zila," Zayn said, trying to get us out of the castle as soon as possible.

"If you want out of here, you have to come with us," Zila said sweetly and the girl nodded.

Zila turned toward us and walked into the light, the girl under her arm. Her eyes were silver-gray, just like Zila's. Her hair was solid black, halfway down her back, and incredibly tangled. The girl's skin was creamy ivory, except for the dirt covering her. She was gorgeous, to say the least—or would be after she had a bath.

"Come on, everyone, let's get back so we can talk to the king." Zayn headed for the door, leading the way.

We made our way out of the castle with no altercations. It was like the Demons had all disappeared, and there was no sign of Erebus anywhere.

As soon as we were outside, I ran over to my sister and hugged her.

"I love you, Cin! I'm so glad you're safe."

"I love you too, Em." I let go of the hug, and Cash was right there, taking Cinder back into his arms.

"We need to gale to the portal and get back," Zayn said to the group.

"I would like to fly and get an overhead view of the grounds. Will you wait for me?" Cali asked Zayn.

"I'll actually fly with you. Everyone else, gale to the portal and we'll meet you there." Zayn looked at Val and he nodded. I didn't know what the men were saying in their minds.

Cali released her soft ivory wings and flapped away into the sky. Zayn released his raven black wings and did the same. It was a magnificent sight to see in the bright sunlight.

"I'll go first," Asher said, before disappearing.

"I'll gale with Silvaria," Zila said before both Lycans disappeared.

Cash held Cinder as they galed away next. That left me standing alone with Val.

I sighed. "This has been a day."

"It truly has." Val pulled me into him. My heart sped up at the nearness. This man was my whole life and I couldn't imagine being without him. "Since I know the way, I don't need you to gale me anymore," he whispered before he kissed my nose.

"What was it that you said to me when I said the same thing? Oh, yes . . . what fun would that be?"

Wrapping my arms around his hard body, I galed us back to the portal. We waited about ten minutes for Zayn, then we went back to Ashbern.

Outside Castleva Manor, one by one, we slowly stepped off the portal with a sigh. Each of us was covered in Demon blood, tired and could barely move.

"Thank you all for helping me save my sister."

"She's our sister now too," Zayn said with a smile. Cash's eyebrows furrowed together at the thought and I almost laughed. His feelings obviously differed from Zayn's.

"Why is Meyers here?" Asher asked while cracking his knuckles.

My eyes shot in the direction he was looking as the king's personal servant strolled up to us.

"King Reign would like to see all seven," his eyes darted around, "nine of you in exactly thirty minutes."

"Thank you, Meyers," Zayn said. The servant bowed and galed away.

"I'm going to make a sandwich. Are you hungry, Cinder?" Cash asked.

"Yes. I haven't eaten in days." Her face was polite and pleasant as they strolled off toward the manor.

How can she come out of being held captive and still be so sane?

I don't know, Ember. Is it love? Val placed a kiss upon my neck.

I hope so, Val, I said and smiled at him.

"Are you hungry, Silvaria?" Zila asked.

"I haven't eaten in over a week." In the light of the day, I could tell how dirty she was. She was also very underfed.

"Come on," Zila said as she took her hand.

"I'm hungry too." Asher followed both Lycans.

My heart ached at the thought of Silvaria and my sister not being fed.

"I'm going to wash up," Zayn announced.

"Same," Cali said, and the two Angels followed the rest into the manor.

I looked up at Val, waiting to see if he was hungry or needed a bathroom break.

"Are you hungry?" he asked.

"No."

"Do you have any plans for the next twenty minutes?" I shook my head. "Want to come with me?"

"I absolutely do." I smiled as Val wrapped his arms around me and galed us away.

We landed in Amethyst Falls. The waterfall was loud and running fast. The magic was dancing around in pure bliss and excitement. He held my hand as he lifted the branches and stepped underneath the biggest purple wisteria tree.

"Are we here to mate?" I blurted out and Val laughed.

"The next time I mate with you, it will be slow and proper." He kissed me gently on the lips. My heat rose at the thought of mating with him again. *Next time* couldn't come soon enough.

"Okay, I can feel your lust again. No more kissing." He pulled away from me and I laughed. "I have something I need to say."

His face went serious—a look of fear in his eyes. "No, don't give me sad news. I cannot handle any more right now."

"I... uhm."

"What is it, Val? What's wrong?" I stepped in closer to him and placed my hand on his cheek, feeling the light stubble of his facial hair.

"I just want you to know that every time I said your name or smiled at you, every time I growled in anger or lust, and every time I called you *love* or my *hertis rote*, I was saying *I love you.*"

My heart warmed at his confession, making tears form in my eyes. "Oh, Val. I love you too."

"I know you do, so . . ." He held his hand out to me, his fist clenched shut. "I have a question to ask." He opened his hand and there was a silver ring with a big, beautiful amethyst in the middle with smaller stones on each side. I gasped and threw my hands over my mouth.

"This was my mother's ring. I . . ." he hesitated and cleared his throat. "I wanted to know if you would do me the honor of being mated to me, formally, in front of the eyes of the king and our family and friends?"

"Of course, I will." I cried as he slid the ring onto my finger. He leaned down and kissed me gently. My heart swelled with love when I looked into his beautiful violet eyes that matched my ring.

"Wynter told me your mother had passed. What happened to her, Val?" My face filled with concern. I shouldn't have ruined the moment by asking. He never talked about his parents and I never pushed it. "I'm sorry, you don't have to tell me."

"We are bond-mates, I'll tell you anything you want to know."

"And I will do the same." I ran my hand down his arm, caressing him.

"For Vampires, one birth is rare, two is amazing, and three is unheard of. My parents already had Wynter and myself." He looked down at the ground, trying to calm himself. I stayed quiet and gave him the time he needed. "My father wanted another son so badly, he pushed until my mother gave in. She died giving birth to my brother. Unfortunately, he was stillborn . . . a common thing for Vampires. I was only ten years old when it happened. I haven't forgiven my father since."

"I'm so sorry." Tears were rolling down my cheeks as I took in the saddened features of the beautiful man before me.

"You remind me of my mother. I mean, you look nothing like her, but she was fierce. She liked to take my sister and me to do exciting stuff. She didn't let anyone control her and was a free spirit. She also cared for others deeply, like you." I wiped the tears off my face as he continued. "She was the one who taught me how to make snow angels. I taught Zayn and Cash on our first mission to Mayhem together. They know about my mother, every time we go there, we do it out of honor for her."

My heart was filled with utter despair. My mate had been through pain, like me. I now knew why the snow meant so much to him.

"Val, I want to say something without you getting mad."

"I could never be mad at you, my love."

"I believe, in my heart, that it's time for you to forgive your father." He stiffened and swallowed. "After you died, and then I died, it's just . . . we don't know when it's truly our time to go. He could be gone on any normal day. You would be devastated if you didn't forgive him first."

"I know. I think about it all the time."

"He knows you hate him, yet he still loves you. He has shown that in just the few times I have met him. I can tell that he's a good man, Val. You get it from him."

A tear escaped his eye and I wiped it away.

"How did I get so lucky? You're the most perfect woman I have ever met."

Me? Perfect? I was nowhere near that. The fact that someone could love me with the amount of flaws I had was scary, yet somehow, amazing.

"I love you so much, Valarian." I kissed him gently. "I don't think you understand the amount of love I have for you."

"I love you too, my *hertis rote.*" He gave me a compassionate smile. "And if anyone understands, it would be me."

He pulled me into him and placed a gentle kiss upon my cheek before slowly moving to my lips. We broke free to avoid it getting too passionate. It was extremely easy for us to get lost in the moment.

"So, I have a question, love?"

"Yes, Val?"

"Why were you on fire?"

"I wish I knew the answer to that. I got mad and it just happened. It's never happened before."

I swallowed hard. My newfound fire skin may have been pretty amazing, but the fact that it could happen when I angered scared the shit out of me.

"Promise me something, Ember."

"What is it?"

"If you ever get mad at me, you will sleep in Cali's room."

My eyebrows furrowed together. "Why?"

"Because I don't like to be hot when I'm sleeping. Your fiery skin would make it unbearable to get any rest."

I playfully pushed him away from me and laughed. "Who said we're going to share a room?"

He recovered quickly, pulling me close to him as he growled. "If you think I'll spend even one night in bed *without you*, you're completely mistaken, my love."

I threw my arms up around his neck and he picked me up off the ground. His lips met mine for a minute before he set me back down with a sigh.

"We have to go talk to the king." He took my hand and escorted me away.

Chapter Thirty-Seven

We galed to the outside of the wards of the king's castle. Most of our party was already there. I looked around to see who was missing.

"Where are Zila and Silvaria?"

"They'll be here in just a second. Zila wanted to wash her face and arms first," Zayn said with a sympathetic look on his face and I frowned.

We stood there for a few more minutes before they finally arrived. Zayn headed into the castle and we followed. Valarian was holding my hand.

We walked into the throne room and I heard a gasp coming from the new Lycan. Silvaria's eyes were wide—mesmerized by the king, whose face looked overly concerned. We quickly made our way up to him and bowed our heads.

Meyers stepped forward. "Welcome to Castle Elderfall, currently residing is Your Majesty, King Reign, the God of the Sun."

The king sighed impatiently. "Thank you, Meyers. Zila, you and the other Lycan come forward, please."

Zila grabbed Silvaria's hand and stepped up to the king and bowed. The other Lycan bowed seconds later. I could tell that Zila had tried to clean her up, but it didn't help much.

"What's your name, child?" the king asked.

"My name's Silvaria."

Zila leaned over and whispered something in her ear.

"Oh. My name is Silvaria Timberland, Your Majesty."

The king smiled kindly before turning his attention to Zila. "Did you know this Lycan before her capture?"

"I did not, Your Majesty."

"Give me your hand, little wolf."

Silvaria walked forward and the king took her hand before a gust of wind went through the room. The king's eyes went silver, then completely gold as they went wide in surprise, then confusion . . . then sadness. Val grabbed my hand when my breathing got heavier. After a minute, the king dropped her hand.

"I am so sorry, Silvaria," King Reign said as tears rolled down his face. "I will not mention all the pain and sorrow you have gone through, since it is not my story to tell. But I am terribly sorry for the length of time you were in there and the things you went through. How old were you when you were taken?"

"I was nine." I think all of us gasped.

Dropping Val's hand, I put both my hands over my face to try and keep from crying. My mate immediately pulled me close to his side and ran his hand up and down my back.

After composing myself, I looked over and Zayn held Cali on one side, while Asher was on her other, and Cash was consoling Cinder. It was utterly amazing to know we had people here who cared for each other.

"My senses tell me that you are now twenty-three. So, you have been locked up for fourteen years." She gasped. I don't think she realized how long it had been. She whimpered slightly.

How? I don't understand.

I know, my love. Val hugged me tighter.

"I saw that your parents were killed when you were taken. Do you have any other family?"

"I don't, Your Majesty."

This just keeps getting worse, Val. He rubbed his hand up and down my back.

"You are welcome to stay here as long as you like or for eternity. We can also send you back to Direbreak if you choose. We will talk more about that once you are settled in."

"Thank you, Your Majesty." Zila bowed.

"Thank you, Your Majesty." Silvaria followed suit and bowed too. Her bow was more like a quick nod. I could tell that she hadn't had formal training and assumed she had had little to no education past the age of nine.

Zila quickly grabbed her hand and returned to our group. My heart ached for the little Lycan.

"Ember, I am assuming the red-headed beauty is your sister?"

"Yes, Your Majesty."

"What is your name?"

"My name is Cinder Lavaris, Your Majesty."

"Come forward, my child, so I can see what happened to you."

Cinder slowly strolled forward, holding her chin up high. She was particularly regal in her movements and speech when around royalty—just like our mother had been. If there were ever a queen's position available, she would be the perfect woman for it. I smiled proudly.

She gently held her hand out to him and he took it. Another gust of wind blew through the room. His eyes turned gold and his eyebrows furrowed in anger and sadness. When his eyes returned to normal, he let go.

"I'm sorry for the way you were treated, and I am grateful it was not worse. You can stay here if you like as well. If you decide to go back home, you will have to wait until we recheck the town to ensure your safety."

"Your Majesty?"

"Yes, Asher."

"Calista and I already checked on the town, and she healed the people that survived. We do need some people sent there to oversee . . . um."

"To manage the bodies of the ones that did *not* survive, sir," Cali finished. I cringed at the thought.

"I will send a crew." The king's face was sad as he blew out a deep breath. He gave a look to one of his guards and they quickly left the room. He then turned his attention back to my sister. "You can decide whenever you're ready, Cinder."

"Thank you, Your Majesty." She bowed her head and quickly made her way back to the group.

"Ember, come here, my dear."

I walked up to the king and held my hand out. I knew what he wanted.

Another gust of wind, and his eyes changed colors again. They looked proud, then scared, then shocked. They looked compassionate and then happy. He dropped my hand and threw his hand over his mouth. He had tears in his eyes and I was slightly confused.

"You were blessed by my brother? By Volcanis?"

His brother? I nodded.

"Zayn told me but I had to see for myself. You have been through a lot in the last forty-eight hours."

"I have, Your Majesty. We all have."

"Indeed." He sighed before his eyes went to my mate. "Valarian, step forward."

Valarian stepped forward and stood next to me. I had never seen him look prouder or more regal than he did right now.

"Valarian Grey, you have asked Ember Lavaris to be mated for life in the eyes of the kingdom." I heard gasps from behind us and a woo hoo from Cash. Someone else was clapping—I knew it was Cali. The king chuckled at the responses of our friend.

"I have, Your Majesty." Val smiled with pride.

"I see this mating to be fit and proper. It is the strongest bond I have seen in five hundred years. I will honor the mating ceremony. Set a date and it will be done."

"Thank you, Your Majesty," Val said.

"You may return." We both bowed and quickly went back to our friends.

"Back to business. Ember, your skin caught on fire. Do you know why?"

"I do not, Your Majesty."

"You died and were brought back, and because of that, your body has changed." I glanced back at Cinder as she threw a hand over her mouth. She didn't know that I had died.

"It has, Your Majesty."

"Since the God of Fire blessed you, your powers are stronger. You are considered a Demi-God now. Your powers will far outweigh any others you will ever meet." My mouth dropped open in shock. I looked at Val, and he had a similar face.

"Whoa," was all I could say and the king laughed.

"I am going to call in an expert to help you be able to control your newfound powers."

"Thank you, Your Majesty." I bowed.

"I would like you all to know, seeing what I saw tonight, through different eyes, I have never been prouder of a group of King's Guards. You seven are far superior to any I have seen in my twelve thousand years."

Whoa! I looked at Val and he smiled brightly at me.

"Get cleaned up and get some tasty food in your bellies. You deserve to celebrate this victory. You are all dismissed." The king smiled proudly.

We all bowed, turned, and left. There were smiles plastered on our faces as we went outside the castle and galed back to the front of the Castleva grounds.

"Congratulations!" Zayn plowed into me with a hug as soon as we landed, then he hugged Val.

My sister congratulated me and hugged me.

Then something weird happened: Zayn got down on one knee in front of Val and I. He looked up at us with his bright blue eyes.

"As a fellow King's Guard, I, Zaynith Storm, will honor this mating by always protecting your mate when you are not around, Valarian Grey. And your mate when you are not around, Ember Lavaris." He pounded his fist on to his heart twice. "Until death." Then bowed his head and stayed there.

Cash kneeled next to him and repeated the same exact words. Asher followed suit and did the same, then Cali and Zila. Tears were rolling down my face by the time they were all done. It was a glorious sight to see.

They rose and spoke in unison. "We are honored."

We all started hugging, laughing, and talking. I noticed Silvaria out of the corner of my eye, staying quiet, so I walked over to her. "Hello!"

"Hi," the little Lycan said.

"This may be weird, but I wanted to know if I could hug you?"

"Uh, sure." She practically fell into my body. As I hugged her tight, I looked up at Val. He had a sincere and proud look on his face.

"If you ever need anything, just know I'm here for you. We all are."

"That is deeply true," Cali said, walking up to us.

"Did you all realize that we outnumber the males now?" Zila asked. It got quiet as all the men looked at us.

Cali clapped her hands together excitedly. "The girls have finally taken over!"

All the men suddenly looked concerned as they stared at us. Zayn ran a hand through his hair, Cash scratched his beard, and Asher looked down at his hands as he cracked his knuckles. Valarian stood there grinning with his arms crossed in that lazy stance of his, shaking his head at me.

Evil women, he wielded, making me laugh.

"Can we eat now?"

"Didn't you just eat, Cash?" Cali asked.

"I'm hungry again!" Everyone laughed as we walked into the manor and headed for the kitchen.

Chapter Thirty-Eight

We entered the dining room and there weren't enough chairs, so a servant quickly went and got more. They had lunch on the table in only minutes: a hearty soup, bread, and fresh fruit. It all looked delicious.

We started sipping soup and grabbing bread. Val filled my glass with iced tea as I looked at the eight other people at the table. Family: that's what they were. I hoped Cinder and Silvaria would decide to stay with us. Glancing at little Lycan, my mouth dropped open.

Oh, Gods, Val! Look!

At what? He followed my gaze. *Oh.*

Silvaria was eating with her hands, which would have been fine if it wasn't soup. As I watched, I couldn't help but feel bad for her. She had no idea what a normal life was.

Glancing at Zayn, we locked eyes. He looked confused. I darted my eyes at Silvaria and back, urging him to look. When he did, his eyes went wide. He looked back at me and I shrugged my shoulders because I didn't know what to do.

"Zila," Zayn said and nodded his head toward Silvaria, who was quickly devouring her soup. She looked ravenous—poor girl.

"Oh no, honey, here." Zila took a napkin, wiped her hands, and handed the Lycan a spoon.

She stared at it, looking embarrassed.

"Like this." Zila scooped soup with her spoon and took a bite.

Silvaria took her spoon and tried to mock what Zila was doing. She slurped up soup, spilling a little. I wanted to run over and help her, but I knew she didn't need everyone in her face, so I let Zila continue to manage the situation. Silvaria looked proud of the bite of soup that she half spilled and it had me smiling at her innocence.

Once lunch was over, we parted ways. I was walking back to my bedroom when Val grabbed my hand with an extremely excited smile on his face.

"What is that smile for?"

"No reason," he said.

"Lies. Tell me."

"I get to mate you. I get to mate a Demi-God!"

He grinned with pure pride and I blushed at his excitement.

"Do you still think I'm going to mate you now that I am a Demi-God? I could have my pick of any male on any land," I teased as I swung my arms through the air.

Val growled and yanked me up off my feet. "I will rip their hearts out, one by one." He kissed me as I dangled in front of him.

"I would expect nothing less from you, Val," I said as he carried me to our room.

Once there, I plopped down in the chair and took my shoes off. Val went into the bathroom and I heard the water turn on as I rubbed the soreness from my feet. A few minutes later he strolled out naked and unashamed.

"Can we finish what you started earlier?"

"I didn't start anything, Val." The heat rose in my body at the thought of us in the tub earlier. Val's naked body shivered and he instantly got hard.

"I can feel your lust again. You're starting it now, Ember!"

"I am not!" I laughed.

He prowled slowly up to me. "Do you think you're funny?"

"Sometimes, yes." I winked at him.

He started tickling me, and while I squirmed away, I fell out of the chair and onto the floor.

"If a light tickle makes you squirm, imagine how much you're going to squirm in the bathroom."

"Oh. Do you promise?"

"I vow to always make you squirm," he said as he lowered himself on top of me.

"I'm not sure I believe you," I whispered as I wrapped my arms around him.

Leaning in, his lips pressed against mine as his hands went between my legs. When the heat rushed through me, I did indeed squirm.

Someone knocked on our door, bringing me from bliss. *Shit!*

"It's Zayn with a mission," Val said as he hopped up. He went into the bathroom and I opened the door.

"Hey, we have a mission."

I sighed. I just wanted an hour alone with my bond-mate. "I know. What is it?"

Zayn's face looked concerned as he ran his hand through his hair. "You aren't on the order, but the king said you can come if you want."

My eyebrows furrowed in confusion. "What's the mission?"

"We have to go to Mayhem to question your father."

"I'm coming," I said as I headed to the chair. "Let me get my boots back on."

"I figured you would, Red."

Val came out of the bathroom, dressed and ready. After throwing my shoes on, I grabbed my purple velvet cloak and draped it across my shoulders.

"Sexy," Val said, making me smile.

Val held my hand as we made our way down and stepped onto the portal. We landed in the land of the Vampires and headed toward the Castle. My heart pounded against my chest as we entered the dungeon and I locked eyes with my father.

"Ember, my dear. Have you come to free me?"

I swallowed hard under his gaze. "You deserve to rot in there, Father."

"Those are awfully harsh words coming out of someone so beautiful."

I shook my head. His compliments meant nothing to me anymore. "Why did you do this?"

"I did this for Erebus and myself."

An aching pain settled in my chest. "What about Cinder and myself? Do we not matter to you?"

"Why would you?"

Tears formed in my eyes as my pain broke free. "Because we're your daughters!"

"Oh, little Ember. You still think I am your father. Hilarious." He grinned wickedly as confusion settled on my face.

"What do you mean?"

"I am a Changeling, my dear. I took over your father's face and his life when you were ten."

My thoughts went in multiple directions: *Why didn't Zila notice his scent? Is that why he never cared much for us? Why did he never buy us things when we got older?*

"Why . . . why would you do that?" I asked.

"Erebus needed some of us on the lands to investigate. To find weaknesses and break through them. We will be stationed everywhere. There are spies in every country, except one because we do not think that Ashbern can be penetrated without notice. We were hoping you would be the one."

Val and Zayn both stiffened at his revelation.

"What do you mean?"

"Plans were set in motion two years ago. I gave you a Demon spelled dagger *and* gave you a reason to learn to use it. We hoped that your hatred toward Vampires would buy us more time. We needed you fully trained and strong before we went forward with the sacrifice."

"What did you do to my mother?"

He smiled. "I gave her to Erebus."

"Why?" I screamed.

"Getting rid of your mother was an effortless way to fuel your hatred and get you where we needed you. Erebus wants you to be strong if you are going to be his mate."

Valarian stepped closer to the bars. "Over my dead body," he growled.

"That can be arranged, Vampire."

My anger rose at the threat to my mate. My skin felt warm, then hot, and out of the corner of my eyes, I saw flickers of fire rolling over it. My eyes scanned my fire-coated arm before they shot to Valarian. His face was filled with wonder and fear once again.

"Magnificent!" my fake father said.

"Shut your mouth, Changeling or I will end you!" Valarian growled. Zayn stepped into my field of vision.

"Ember, you are safe."

I may have been safe, but the Demon wasn't. Visions of me ripping his face off with my bare hands and running through the streets with it flickered through my mind. My fire got higher and hotter at the thought.

"Ember! Look at me."

Locking eyes with Zayn, his magic hit me full force this time and I started to calm down. The fire went to a slow flicker across my skin as I took a deep breath and blew it out slowly, then it vanished.

"Why is Erebus doing this?" Zayn asked the Changeling.

"To rule our world, obviously." He had an evil grin when he spoke the words.

"The entire realm?"

"Of course. The lands will eventually be ours once King Reign is executed. Erebus will have Ember and continue to be second in command." His eyes went to me. "Since he was promised that he could keep the castle on Mistlaven and rule it as his own, you will be the Queen of the Demon lands. Then Tartarus can rise and take over the throne on Ashbern and rule the rest of the entire kingdom. All the landmasses and species will bow to him."

Tartarus? The Primordial God of the Demon lands? I asked Val. His response was a growl.

Zayn narrowed his eyes on the Changeling. "That won't happen. We won't let it!"

"Oh, it will. We have been putting our pieces in place for a hundred years or more. We had to wait until a descendant was born from Volcanis with the most attributes closest to his. She is the only one born in five hundred years with bright red hair. We are ready for this war—you are the ones who are not. That was proven when we attacked Mazuria."

"Why did you attack my homeland?" I asked.

"It was the closest and weakest land. We were making a statement, showing how easy it is to take over. Plus, you attacked us first and stole Erebus's prisoners. He was distraught. He was even more upset when he found out you killed one of his Basilisks. That little attack on Mazuria was just the start of what is coming."

"How, when we took out almost all of your Demon soldiers?" I asked, hoping to pump him for more information.

"If you think that was even *close* to all we have, you are truly mistaken. This world will be ours."

"Why are you so willing to tell us things?"

"If you think I have any actual loyalty to Erebus, you are truly mistaken. Do you see any Demons here to rescue me, Ember? No. He does not care enough to rescue me, therefore, I could not care less about his secretive plans."

I shook my head, then furrowed my brow. "Then why would you go through all the trouble of raising me and my sister?"

"I did what I needed to do for my own gain. Neither of you meant anything to me. Nor your mother."

"I'm done with this conversation," I said as I threw the hood of my cloak up and headed toward the dungeon door.

"Erebus will be coming for you soon, Ember. He will not let a prize like you go."

I stopped walking and whipped around to look at him. "Screw you and Erebus!"

"What did the king say to do with him, Zayn?" Val was ready to kill him.

"Execution after questioning."

Valarian strolled up to the cell door. "My pleasure."

"Wait," I said as I walked back over.

"Oh. My honorable daughter wants to save me."

Zayn unlocked the cell and I entered.

Walking straight up to the Changeling, sadness filled me. Tears threatened to break loose as I stared at his face. After lowering the hood of my cloak, I removed my dagger from its sheath.

"Ember, you have been my daughter for the last twelve years. You cannot kill me." His face tilted as he gave me an evil smile.

"You are *not* my father." My dagger came down hard as I stabbed him in the chest.

His eyes stared into my face as they turned red, then he fell into me. His head laid upon my shoulder for a few seconds before his body slid down onto the floor, dead. It slowly changed back into a Demon. Once he'd transformed completely, I threw my hands over my face. Even though I knew he wasn't my birth father, my heart ached. I had just stabbed someone that looked like the man who raised me.

Arms wrapped around my body. I had smelled him seconds before and knew that it was Val. He hugged my back and pulled me close to his body before turning me around. I put my head on his chest and cried. After a while, I was calm enough to wipe the tears from my face.

I didn't look back at my fake father. Val took my hand and led me out of the dungeon. We headed outside and took the portal back to the country of Ashbern. We were walking up to Castleva Manor when I remembered the previous thoughts I had.

"How did Zila not smell that he was a Changeling?" I asked. "She smelled Silvaria and knew she was a Lycan."

"Well, if you remember, Zila didn't see him until after he already had you in his grips," Val said.

"But even then, it wouldn't have mattered. Changelings change everything about themselves, even their scent. They are an exact copy of a person. Even your mother didn't know about your father," Zayn added.

"Exactly," Val agreed.

"So, they don't take over a body?" I asked, confusedly.

"No, they don't take it over," Val said. "They shapeshift."

My thoughts were overwhelmed with theories and suspicions. "So, my father could still be alive?"

"Technically, yes," Zayn said, running a hand over his chin. He was also in deep thought now.

I let out a large sigh. "I should have asked him before I stabbed him."

"Your father may still be imprisoned somewhere on Mistlaven." Zayn said. "We don't know if they have more people in other prisons there. The country is large."

"My mother could also be a prisoner for all we know. Saying a Vampire killed her was all just a cover-up. The Changeling said she was given to Erebus. He never said what had happened to her."

"That's true. You might be onto something." Zayn nodded his head before he sighed. "I have to go report to the king."

We said our goodbyes and parted ways with him. Val and I quietly headed back to our room.

Chapter Thirty-Nine

Exhaustion had hit me by the time we made it to our room. I immediately plopped into the chair. "I'm so glad to be back." I sighed, quickly taking off my boots.

"I think we should get a new room."

My eyebrows furrowed as I glanced up at Val. "Why do you want a new room?"

"Well, there are these rooms, then there are rooms for mated couples. They're bigger, too. We could move all of our stuff into one, so I would never have to leave your side."

"I would actually love that. Can we get a purple blanket?"

His face looked mortified before he sighed. "You can have whatever you want, my love. That's a sacrifice I will make for you."

Jumping up, I ran into his arms, and he caught me, lifting me off the ground and spinning me around. I tipped my head back and laughed before he set me down.

"You're amazing, Valarian Grey!" I stood on my tippy toes as I kissed him.

"I'm just a man in love with a sensational woman and I want her to have the world. Even if it means I have to sleep under a girly blanket." I smiled and kissed him again.

Heat began to flow through me and I grabbed his neck, pulling him closer to me as an urgency filled my body. I needed him, and I needed him now. Digging his nails into my ass cheeks, he lifted me off my feet again and I immediately wrapped my legs around him.

After a few minutes of hot, passionate kissing, he broke away. "Shit!"

"What?"

"Zayn is coming down the hall with your sister." When he set me on the floor, a sigh of frustration left me.

Val opened the door without even waiting for a knock. "Come on in," he said. Cinder had a shocked look, like she wasn't expecting the door to be whipped open.

"What's going on, guys?" I asked.

"Cinder wanted to talk to you, and I need to talk to Val," Zayn said. Val stepped out of the room and shut the door.

"Hey, sis," I said as soon as they were gone.

"Will I be able to go home and get my stuff?" she asked.

"I'm sure we can arrange that."

"Okay, good."

I narrowed my eyes on her. "Are you planning on staying here?"

She sighed. "I have thought about it hard. It would be safer for me to stay here. For a while at least."

Covering the distance between us quickly, I pulled her into a hug. "I would love that. I'm so happy!"

"Me too. We can have sister time. Plus, I want to be here for your public mating!"

I smiled at the thought of mating Val. "And I want you here, Cin."

"So, now that's settled. I have tons of questions."

"I figured." I swallowed at the thought of all the things I would have to tell her.

"So, you died and were brought back to life, and I need to know what happened because everyone went quiet when I mentioned our father, and then Zayn quickly brought me up here!"

She was rambling. She did that sometimes when she got nervous.

"Take a seat. This is going to take a while." I took my cloak off and laid it on my chair.

We both sat crossed-legged on my huge bed. I told Cinder everything: about our father being a Changeling, me dying, being brought back to life by the God of Fire, and everything in between.

"My Gods, Ember!" Tears were streaming down her face. "This cannot be true!"

"I know, but it is, Cin."

"I understand that, but it's a lot to take in." I handed her a handkerchief, and she wiped her tears away.

"It truly is."

The men walked back into the room, bringing our attention to them.

"Are we all caught up?" Zayn asked.

"Yes, I filled Cinder in on everything," I said with a sad smile on my face.

"Okay, Silvaria has asked to be taken home in the morning. Cash and Zila are going to escort her."

"Where will she live?" I asked. Sadness filled me knowing that she wasn't going to stay here.

"They sent an Imp to an old family friend and they said they would be glad to take her in."

I sighed. "Well, that's good news, even though I was hoping she would stay for a while."

"She's a scared girl who needs to be with her kind, love," my mate said.

I nodded my head. "I understand, Val."

"I would like to get my things and stay there for a few days. I have matters to address," Cinder said.

"I speak for everyone when I say that we would prefer you *not* to go alone. I can ask the king if I can send Cali with you, if that's okay?" Zayn asked. "Ember can't go because someone is going to be helping her with her, umm, fire skin thing."

"I would be delighted to have Cali stay with me if she doesn't mind." Cinder held her head high. She was right back to being regal again.

"I will talk to Cali and the king." Zayn smiled at my sister. "I'll let you know as soon as I know, Cinder."

"Thank you, Zaynith."

"Now that's settled." Zayn turned his attention to me. "Ember, your pedagogue is here."

My eyes widened. "My what?"

Zayn laughed. "Your teacher, your educator, for the Demi-God thing."

An exasperated breath left me. "Oh."

"Can I come with you?" Val asked.

I smiled at my man. "Of course you can."

He walked up and grabbed my hand. "Let's do this."

"Hold on," Zayn interrupted. "Ember has to leave her dagger here."

My brows furrowed. "Why?"

"For the safety of your teacher."

The statement left me a little confused. "Umm, okay." I took my dagger off and set it on the nightstand and I instantly felt naked without it.

"Okay, let's go," Zayn said as he opened the door.

"Come on, Cin," I said as we all left my room.

We headed down to the manor's foyer, turned left, and went into the study. There was a beautiful, tall, brown-haired woman wearing black leather pants and a black shirt. She had emerald-green eyes, which told me she was a Caster and I immediately wondered which kind.

"Hello. Ember, I presume?" She held her hand out to me and I shook it.

"Yes, ma'am."

"My name is Katzia. I will be your educator on all things Demi-God-related. It is a pleasure to meet you."

Even though she sounded extremely formal, she seemed nice, so I smiled. "It's a pleasure to meet you as well."

She glanced at my friends. "I see we have an audience."

"Yes, this is my mate, Val. This is my sister, Cinder, and my best friend, Zayn." I pointed to each person.

"I am pleased to meet you all. Even though I know it is nerve-racking to have your skin catch on fire and have someone teach you how to control it, I do not think it is wise to have all these people around. You will need to focus."

"Oh, I'm sorry." I bit my lip with nervousness.

"If you would like to have one person attend class with you, that would be fine with me. At least until you're comfortable."

I looked around at my family and wondered how the hell I was going to decide who stayed.

"I'll make this easier and bow out." Zayn made a slight bow, smiled at me, and left the room.

As I looked between Cinder and Val, my breathing sped up. How could I choose between the two most important people in my life?

Choose Cinder, Val wielded.

Why?

I can hear her thoughts and she needs to feel important. I'll be fine. He smiled lovingly at me.

"I would like my sister to stay, please." Cinder smiled proudly as a look of relief filled her face.

"Perfect," Katzia said.

"I'll see you after, my love." Val kissed my forehead, met Katzia's eyes for a second, and left.

Was that a secret conversation? Does he know her?

"Shall we get started?" Katzia asked.

"Yes, ma'am. But can I ask you something?"

She grinned at my words. "I already know what you are going to ask. I am a Fire Caster, just like you both. I am also a Demi-God like you, Ember." Flames danced across her skin momentarily, then disappeared as quickly as they'd come.

"Oh, wow." It wasn't my best moment or response, but I was a little shocked. "I have one more question."

"Go ahead."

"Why do my clothes *not* catch on fire when my skin does?"

"Magic," she said.

I snickered. "Magic seems to be the answer to everything."

"Indeed. Let's get started." Katzia met eyes with my sister. "Cinder, do you mind taking a seat over there so you can watch from a distance? It will be safer."

Cinder politely smiled and took a seat over by one of the big windows.

"Ember, how many times has your skin flamed?"

"Twice, ma'am."

"While I do respect the polite address you are using, there is no need to call me ma'am. You can call me Kat or Katzia, whichever you prefer."

I nodded "Okay."

As she strolled up next to me, I saw how tall she was. Almost six feet, I was sure. She took a turn around my body, looking me over. "Each of those times, how did you turn your flames off?"

"My Angel friends helped me."

"Interesting. Do you know what else is interesting? Your mate is an extremely interesting male." I politely smiled, wondering where this conversation was going. "He is also very handsome."

"Oh, well, thank you." I blushed, thinking about him.

"Are you mated in the eyes of the kingdom yet?"

"We aren't, but we will be very soon." I held up my ring for her to see.

"Beautiful. I wonder if Val would have a drink with me later since he is *not* truly mated?"

What the hell? I held her gaze as she stepped back in front of my face. My smile was now gone.

"I'm sure he would decline." I glared at her. I didn't know what kind of crap she was pulling, but I knew Val, and I knew he would never hurt me. She wasn't going to bait me with him.

"What about your sister?"

I glanced over at Cinder. "What about her?"

"She seems really dainty and fragile. I am sure it wouldn't take much to hurt her."

My face whipped back towards Katzia. "Are you deranged?"

"Not that I know of." She tilted her head, locking eyes with me. "Maybe I should just find out for myself." My jaw tightened h in anger as she strolled toward Cinder.

Reaching down for my dagger, I remembered I didn't have it. I gave Katzia a look of pure evil as I headed toward her, ready to kick her ass. My skin started to warm, and I saw the glow out of the corner of my eyes.

"There it is!" She held her hand up to me. "Ah, no, no. Stay put, Ember. You do not want to hurt your sister."

"Do you think this is funny?" I asked her. I was furious and my fire skin proved it.

"I apologize, Ember. I had to get you to show me your ignitus."

"My what?" My skin flamed high as Cinder's eyes went huge with shock.

"Your fire skin, your ignitus. Now you must learn to control your emotions so you can turn your ignitus on and off without the help of your Angel friends."

"I don't know how to," I said through gritted teeth.

"And that is why I am here."

"Make it stop, then!" More anger boiled through my veins as I had visions of grabbing Katzia by the throat.

"I cannot. Only you can do that. It is going to be a long, hard battle to be able to control it, but I have faith in you."

"At least one of us does!" My fire skin, my ignitus, flickered high again. I was getting more agitated by the second.

"I need you to breathe and try to control it."

"I can't!" I started to walk toward Katzia.

"Ember, you do not want to hurt Cinder. Stay put and breathe!"

"Cinder, leave the room!" I screamed as flames flickered around me.

A fireball shot from my skin and headed toward her. Katzia threw her arm out and somehow sucked the fireball up into her hand.

"No, Cinder, stay. You have to fight this, Ember!"

"I can't!" All I could think about was hurting Katzia as the flames flickered higher

"Zayn, Val, now!"

My heart raced out of control as they entered the room. Val headed to stand guard in front of Cinder and Katzia as I sucked in air angrily through my teeth.

"Ember, look at me." Zayn stepped into my field of vision. "I'm going to give you a small dose of magic, but you need to focus and breathe like Kat said."

A little bit of magic hit me as I took deep breaths, trying to calm myself. After a minute, my flames slowed down. Zayn stepped away from me as Val moved out from in front of Katzia.

"You are in control. Stop your ignitus. It listens to you and only you."

I met her eyes and focused as hard as I could. I let out a huge breath of relief when I saw the flames subside.

"Why? Why would you do that to me?" I asked. Exhaustion hit me and it felt like I had run five miles.

"We have to practice, Ember."

"I can't do this every day!"

"You won't have to. I just had to see how strong your ignitus was. It is extremely strong, like mine. I am surprised and intrigued."

"Oh, well, how nice for you!" I shouted.

"Ember!" Val shouted back. I locked eyes with my mate.

Be nice. She is just doing her job, love. I took a deep breath and relaxed.

"So, you were all in on this?"

"I was not," Cinder said, shaking her head. She still seemed in shock.

"They weren't in on anything. I wielded to Valarian to stick around when you chose your sister. I was not sure how strong you were. Once you told me the Angel had helped you, I wielded to him to keep Zayn around, too. I apologize for what I had to do, but it is necessary for you to learn.."

"Whatever. I really don't have a choice, I guess."

Her lips tightened into a line. "Unfortunately not. We are blessed and must learn how to use that blessing."

I shook my head as tears formed in my eyes. "This doesn't feel like a blessing."

"It may not now, but once you can control it, you will be grateful."

"I hope so."

"You are done for today. I have to get back to Cerulean."

My eyebrows furrowed in confusion. "Land of the Water Casters? Why would you live there and not on Mazuria with the rest of the Fire Casters?"

"Because my father was a Fire Caster, but my mother was a Water Caster, like my sister. My mother loved her lands so much, my father moved for her. I was primarily raised there after I graduated from the academy in Mazuria."

"How old are you?" I couldn't help but be nosy.

"I am eighty-six years old." She smiled proudly. "We are done for the day. I have to set up my room and retrieve my things, now that I know I am for sure needed."

"When is the next practice?"

"We are going to take a few days off. We will resume once I am back. If you have any questions, I will be around. Try not to get mad until then." She smiled before leaving the room.

Val strolled up and pulled me in, kissing my forehead."You're amazing."

"That was . . . bewildering, Em," Cinder said with a strained smile.

"Yes, but you did better this time," Zayn added. "I only had to use a small amount of magic."

"I'm tired. Can we go to my room?" I asked Val.

"Of course, love."

"I got a room for Cinder set up," Zayn informed me. "I'll show her to it."

"Thanks, Softy."

We headed up the stairs together and exhaustion hit me—I could barely walk. When we got to the top of the stairs, Val carried me like a baby the rest of the way to our room. He laid me in the bed and snuggled up next to me. As I thought about how different my life was now, I fell asleep.

Chapter Forty

My eyes fluttered open to the feeling of kisses on my shoulder from the love of my life.

"Good morning, my love."

"Good morning, Val." He smiled and continued placing kisses on me. "Wait . . . morning? Did I sleep all day *and* night?"

"You did, baby."

"Oh wow. I must have been tired."

Val slowly trailed his fingers up and down my arm. "Indeed. I didn't want to wake you, but Zayn said we have a mission today."

I stifled a yawn. "What's the mission?"

"We have to go to Mazuria with King Reign so he can elevate a new duke." My eyes widened. "You will need full leathers and your King's Guard pin."

My eyebrows furrowed. "What? I don't have a pin."

"Zayn dropped it off. It's on your nightstand."

Wanting to look at my new jewelry, I immediately pulled away from Val. Grabbing the crimson box off my nightstand, I slowly opened the lid and sucked in a breath at the beauty of it. The bed shifted as Val scooted close to my back and looked over my shoulder.

"Do you like it?" he asked while he nuzzled his face in my neck.

"I love it."

I pulled the solid gold pin out of the box and turned it in my hand, admiring it. It was a shield with two swords behind it, a lion's head in the middle, and the letter R at the bottom.

"Is the R for King Reign?" I asked.

"It is. We all have one."

"That is amazing!"

Val laughed at my excitement. "Okay, dirty girl, shower time."

He hopped over me like he had all the energy in the world. Heading into the bathroom, he turned the shower on. I crawled out of bed with a sigh and got out my leathers.

Val appeared from the bathroom with a smile. He was a morning person, I was not. "You shower here. I'm going to head to my room because my leathers are there."

Prowling up to him, I slid my hands over his chest and peered up at him from under my eyelashes.

"Oh no. Not happening." He grabbed the front of his pants and adjusted his hardness. I gave him a sultry grin.

"Val," I pleaded and licked my lips.

"Stop, Ember."

"Say my name again," I said as I pressed my body against his.

"I love you, but we can't be late to this, my love."

"Fine." I dropped my hands from his chest with a huff and he laughed at my mad face.

He leaned in and kissed my neck, making me let out a light moan. He quickly pulled away and growled.

"Don't growl. It turns me on!"

"You being turned on is making me growl, love. I can feel it." We both laughed. "Go get ready."

"Fine!" I stomped toward the bathroom while making my own growling sound.

"That's sexy. Do it again!"

My head whipped toward him with a mischievous smile.

"I love you, but we can't be late to this, my love," I said, throwing his words back at him. Val laughed as he left the room.

I quickly showered and dressed in black pants and a black shirt. I was in the middle of trying to get my corset tied when Val walked in, and I heard another growl.

"You're so sexy," he said as he shut the door. He had my bow and quiver in his hand and set them on the bed. "I brought this up. I assumed you wanted it."

"Thank you. Can you help me, please?" Val strolled over and tightened the laces on my corset.

"Can you wear nothing but this to bed tonight?" he asked as he pulled the strings tighter.

"Absolutely!" Once he finished lacing me up, he kissed my neck.

"You smell delicious, my love."

"Thanks," I said, turning in his arms to meet his face. He was entirely in black with his leathers on. He had his short sword strapped on his harness. "You look handsome as hell." I stood on my tippy toes and quickly kissed him.

"Are you excited?" he asked.

"I am!"

"Where are the rest of your leathers?"

"Right here." I grabbed the leather vambraces off the dresser and slid them on. Snatching up my dagger, I strapped it to my leg.

"Your gloves," Val reminded me. I slid the black gloves onto my hands. "Are you ready now?"

"Ready as I will ever be."

He opened the door and waited for me to exit. I stopped, grabbed the leather straps to his harness and yanked him toward me as I planted a hard kiss on his lips. The kiss got heated quickly and I wondered if he was going to pull away soon.

"That's a death grip you have on my buddy." I broke away from Val's warm lips and looked up at a smiling Zayn.

"It could be a death grip on your neck," I said as I reached for his throat.

Zayn quickly grabbed my wrist and used it to spin me away from him, tightening his arm on my neck and putting me into a headlock.

"Damn it," I said as Val and Zayn laughed.

"You're never going to one-up me, Red!" I stomped his foot and he let go.

"Ouch!" I was about to lunge for him again when Val grabbed my arm.

"Come on, children, we need to go."

I crossed my arms with a huff. "Fine, but later I'm kicking your ass, Softy!"

Zayn laughed. "Good luck, Demon Spawn!"

We headed down the hall and saw Cinder coming out of her room with Cali. She was dressed in all black and had on one of Cali's leather corsets. My eyes went wide in shock, as Cinder usually only wears dresses.

"Why are you dressed like that, Cin?"

"She's coming with us, so I dressed her up," Cali said excitedly while she clapped her hands together.

"And she needs a weapon?" I asked, noticing the axe hanging from her belt.

Zayn snickered. "After these last few weeks, yes."

"I'm like her living doll," Cinder said with a sigh.

I pfft through my pursed lips. "Believe me, I know all too well!"

"You ladies should appreciate me and my style more," Cali said as she crossed her arms and huffed.

"We appreciate you, Cali. Even if we *are* your dolls," I said with a laugh.

"Okay, enough about dolls. Let's get going," Zayn said, falling into commander mode.

Once outside the manor, we saw Cash, Zila, and Asher all dressed in black leather.

"About time, I was . . . woah. You look amazing, Cinder!"

Cinder's cheeks turned bright red. "Thank you, Cash."

"Ah, don't you all look fantastic," King Reign said, appearing out of nowhere. Everyone immediately bowed their heads. "You may rise."

He was wearing a royal robe that was black with crimson threading. He also had on his crown today, and I had never seen it before. It was solid gold with rubies. I knew he was huge—over seven feet tall—but I felt small with him standing next to me.

"I see eight of you. Where is Silvaria?" he asked.

"She doesn't want to come, Your Majesty," Zayn said.

"We can drop the formalities until the Elevation." He gave us a kingly smile. "Let's go. Zayn, lead the way."

"Yes, sir." Zayn walked and we followed.

The king fell into step next to me, and my heart sped up.

"Don't be nervous, Ember," the king said. "Your lands are fine. Everyone that survived is safe and healed. Once I elevate the new duke, everything will be restored." He had been listening to the thoughts and worries I didn't even realize I had.

"Thank you, sir."

"Nice pin." He gave me a wink. I smiled at him and he smiled back. We fell quiet as we stepped on the golden platform of the portal.

"Cinder, come here, my child," the king said. He grabbed her hand and her skin started to glow. "There, that's better. You will eventually get used to the portals, but today is a day that we can't have you sick."

"Thank you, Your Majesty." She refused to drop formalities. She moved close to Cash and he took her hand.

I felt the rush of warmth and then cool breeze as the portal was wielded to go. Val's hands wrapped around me right before he placed a kiss on my lips. We broke away as soon as we landed and I looked up into his smiling face.

"I love you, Ember."

"I love you too, Val."

Cash cleared his throat, making Val and I look over at our friends. Everyone was watching us. I met the king's eye with an apologetic expression. To my surprise, he had the biggest grin out of everyone.

"Have you set a date for the mating?" he asked. "I think next week will be perfect." My eyes went wide.

"Next week is fine with me," Val said. I whipped my head to meet his eyes and he smiled. "You're already mine, love. No reason to freak out."

"Indeed, it is just an event to show everyone your love for each other," the king added.

The way he said the words eased me. It was just an event. In my eyes, Val and I were already mated for life. No one could change that.

"Next week is perfect!" I agreed with a smile.

Everyone cheered as we stepped off the portal in Mazuria where the king's Royal Guard was waiting for us. There were ten of them, dressed like us. As the king led the way, they fell into step, five on each side of our group.

Once we got to the edge of town, I noticed the streets were lined with people waiting for us. They cheered and clapped as we approached. King Reign nodded and waved as we passed.

Just keep your eyes on any movement and keep your face blank, Val wielded to me.

A little boy ran toward the king, his arm stretched high in the air as he held up a piece of paper. A Royal Guard stepped in front of him before he got close. The rest of the guard stopped walking.

"Let him pass," King Reign commanded. The guard stepped aside and the boy ran right up to the king.

"I made this for you," the boy said as he held up the paper.

"Let me see what we have here." Reign bent down to be closer to the boy's height and took the paper with a massive smile on his face.

"It is me when I am a King's Guard. See." The boy pointed to the picture. "That is my tattoo . . . I made it gold even though it's black now, but that's okay because my mother said that it will be gold someday."

"Your mother is right. It will be gold."

"I can't wait to be a guard!" It took all my power not to smile or laugh.

"I would be honored to have you," Reign said.

"Pyro, come here, son. I am so sorry, Your Majesty." The boy's mother bowed.

"It is quite all right. He is just a curious and excited child. How old are you, son?"

"I'm six!" Pyro said.

Reign smiled at the boy and stood up. "Well, I can't wait to have you join my guard in sixteen years, Pyro. I hope we get by without you until then."

"Thank you, Your Majesty," the mother said as she dragged Pyro off.

The king resumed walking, as did we. Once we got close to the town center, I noticed a wooden stage. The king walked upon it and the Royal Guard followed.

We stay down here in order of rank. I told Cinder to go last, even though she isn't a guard, Val wielded to me.

At the bottom of the stage, Val took a spot on the left side, and Zayn went next to him. I was confused about why Val went first when Zayn was always in charge.

Cali stood next to Zayn and then Cash. On the right side of the stage, Zila stood, then Asher. So, I followed suit and stood next to him. Cinder came and stood next to me.

Stand up straight. Feet shoulder width apart. Hands behind your back. Val must have told Cinder the same thing because she mirrored my stance. *Look straight and don't smile.* I stared straight ahead as the entire town stood before us.

The king's servant walked past us and up onto the stage. He had two guards and a woman with him. He must have been here waiting for us.

"Everyone, please welcome Your Majesty, King Reign, the God of the Sun," Meyers roared. Everyone bowed in unison.

"I would like to address a few things today," King Reign said. "First, I would like to give my condolences to the families of the King's Guard and the Mazuria citizens we lost during the demon attack. My heart goes out to you all. Please do not hesitate to let my personal secretary, Roselyn, know if you need anything. She will be here for the next week, staying in the inn. She will gladly send me a messenger Imp with any requests. Now, let's take a moment of silence for the ones we lost." The crowd bowed their heads. My friends next to me didn't, so I didn't either. It was hard to keep guard and bow, I guess.

"Let's proceed," the king said after a minute of silence. "I'm happy to announce that I am here to elevate a new duke." The crowd cheered and clapped.

"After much deliberation, I have made my choice. Please join us on stage." Everyone was smiling with excitement. I wanted to glance over my shoulder to look and see if I knew the new duke, but I had to keep my eyes on the crowd. "Kneel. Sword, please."

I was dying inside not knowing who it was, so I looked out of the corner of my eye but couldn't see anything.

Don't even think about it, love.

Damn, you know me too well, Val. I kept my head forward as the king continued.

"Rise. Everyone, please welcome your new Duke of Mazuria, Hendrick Lavaris." I sucked in a quick breath of air, then calmed my racing heart as the crowd cheered.

Hendrick was my uncle—my father's brother. I hadn't seen him in years. He was always off exploring the world, and when he was here, he was collaborating closely with the king to make a better world for everyone. I couldn't think of a better person who would make a greater duke and I had to force myself not to smile. I hoped that I would get to see him after the ceremony.

Is this someone we like?

Very much so, Val. He is dear to my heart.

Good. I could hear the happiness in the tone of Val's voice in my head.

"Now that—"

King Reign's words were cut off when some of the crowd started to scream. I reached down for my dagger out of instinct and yanked it out. All the King's Guard had drawn their weapons as well. Half the crowd was looking up and moving back away from us. I followed their eyes and my mouth dropped open.

A large red bird with a black head flew in fast—right above the crowd's heads. It flapped its wings slowly as it lowered itself to the ground and landed. The ground shook slightly under its talons, and wind hit me from its wings as it pulled them in.

The bird stood at least twelve feet tall and resembled an eagle. I glanced at Cinder for a split second, and she had pulled her axe out and was holding it in defense. I was sure she didn't know how to use it, but an axe is an axe.

"Stay behind me. Only fight if you have to," I said before looking back at the giant bird. It was staring straight at my face. It let out a large squawk. Fear went through me, and I froze.

Chapter Forty-One

My heart was racing as I stared into the biggest eyes I'd ever seen. All the King's Guard circled the bird while I was sincerely worried that I was about to be its lunch. It let out another squawk as it began to walk toward me. I pushed the fear aside and lunged forward. It dodged me and I rolled to the ground.

The massive bird stood over me and tilted its head like it was wondering what the hell I was doing. I reached over and sliced at its leg with my dagger and missed. It let out a squeak and stepped back.

Wait, love. Stop! I heard Val say.

Cali flew up into the air and landed on its back. The bird flung her instantly off. Cash rushed forward with his axe and Val jumped in front of him.

"Everyone, stop!" Val screamed. I don't know why he wanted us to stop, but my adrenaline made me push forward. I jumped to my feet and lunged again.

"Ember, stop!" I heard the king say, and I stopped moving, my dagger only inches from the bird.

"It's okay, love." Val ran up to me. He placed his hand gently on my arm, lowering it. I stared at him with a shocked face.

King Reign galed in front of me. "It is okay, Ember," he said before he turned toward the bird. "What is your name? Oh, I see. Who sent you? Oh. When did that happen? Well, that is excellent!" I looked at Val and he was smiling. I was *so* confused.

"Ember, come here." I did as the king bade and walked closer to his side. "This creature does not want to harm anyone. She is here for you." He reached up and ran his hand down her feathers. She seemed to have let out a light purring sound.

"Why?" I asked.

"She is yours now."

"I don't want a pet, Your Majesty." The giant bird let out a protesting squawk and the king laughed.

"She is *not* your pet, Ember. She is your Familiar. She was gifted to you by Volcanis."

"Oh." I looked up at the large bird. *What the hell am I going to do with it?*

"You don't have to do anything. She is self-sufficient and will be there mainly for your needs and to protect you. She said she doesn't have a name, so you must give her one. Valarian can talk to her, so she will let him know if she needs anything from you." The bird squawked in approval.

The king galed back up onto the stage. "Now, where were we? Ah, yes. Now that the new Duke of Mazuria has been announced, let's all head to the town's square. Servants have set up food and refreshments for everyone!"

"Are you okay, love?" Val asked.

"I think I'm in shock," I said as I stared at the bird.

"What are you going to name her?"

"I have no idea." Val laughed, pulled me close, and kissed the side of my head.

"Uncle Hendrick," I heard Cinder say. Glancing over my shoulder, I saw him pull her into a hug.

"Nice to see you again. You're lovely as ever." He locked eyes with mine and we both smiled. "Come here, girl!" He stretched his arms out and I ran into them. "I missed you both," he said as he kissed the tops of our heads.

"I missed you too!"

"Where is this mate of yours? The king told me all about him." I looked over my shoulder at a smiling Val. He stalked forward in that sexy way of his.

"Valarian Grey, sir. It's nice to meet you." He held out his hand and my uncle shook it.

"Hendrick Lavaris. It's a pleasure to meet you too. Reign has told me so many things about you. All good, I might add."

"Of course they are. Valarian is the highest-ranking guard I have," the king said as he walked up. "He hates commanding, so Zayn does most of it, but he is still the commander whether he likes it or not."

So, that's why Zayn was in charge, even though Val was older.

"That's excellent. When is the public mating?" Hendrick asked.

"I will be officiating it next week," the king answered.

"I'm sorry I won't be able to make it. Reign gave me a lot of crap to clean up." My uncle patted the king on his arm. I tensed at the fact that he was touching the king and called him by his first name.

"You're the best person for the job, friend. Hopefully, it will keep you on land. I've missed you over the last few years."

"Maybe we should get some whiskey at the Howling Moon." Hendrick winked at the king and my eyes widened.

"Not if you're going to howl the whole time we are there, again!" the king said as he slapped my uncle on the shoulder. My mouth was agape as I glanced at Val. He was staring at the two and smiling. I seemed to be the only one uncomfortable at their friendliness. Even though I knew they were friends, I didn't think they were *that* close.

"I might howl again!" They both laughed. A squawk from my new pet—umm, Familiar—brought all our attention away.

Asher was petting her and she vibrated lightly as she let out small chirps.

"What?" he said as he looked at us.

"She likes that," Val said. He turned to look at me. "She wants to know when you're going to accept her."

"What do you mean?"

"She wants your attention." The bird squawked like she was agreeing.

"You could start by giving her a name," the king said. He wasn't going to let up on that and I let out a sigh.

"I don't know her, so I don't know what to name her."

"Get to know her." Val nodded his head toward the bird.

Asher removed his hand and stepped aside as I slowly walked up to her.

"Can you relay the conversation, Val?"

"Of course, love."

"Hi," I said and the bird squawked.

"She said hi."

"Do you have a name in mind?"

"She does not."

Taking in her beauty and her strength, she was so big, and her muscles looked strong.

"You're gorgeous." I whispered.

"*So are you*, she said." I smiled as Val relayed her words.

"I will come up with a name for you, but I can't think of one right now."

"She will be patient."

I slowly reached my hand up and brushed it down her feathers. She vibrated lightly, then tilted her head down, and I pet the top of it. She lowered to the ground and laid almost flat. I pulled my hand away, wondering what she was doing.

"I don't know if that's a good idea," Val said.

"I think it's a phenomenal idea," the king said.

I looked back and forth between them. "What?"

"She wants to take you for a ride. That's how you seal the bond," Val said and I gasped.

"I can't do that!"

"You said you loved flying with me," Zayn said.

"That was different. This is an animal!" My heart sped up just thinking about it.

"She's insulted by your lack of faith in her skills," Val said.

"I'm sorry." I looked back at the bird. "I didn't mean it like that." She lowered again, tilting her head more.

"I think that's a great idea, Valarian," the king said.

"Yes, we can go there soon," Val responded.

I hated that they could talk and I couldn't hear. "What idea?"

"I was telling King Reign that we could have a harness made by the blacksmith on Dazeth. He does custom work and is very good at it."

"Is it okay if we wait until then?" I asked my Familiar.

"She would prefer to get the bond going with a small ride." I looked at Val's face. "You need to bond, love. Once you do, you can talk with her through your thoughts."

My eyes widened. "Really?"

"That's what she said." Val smiled.

My eyes wandered over her plush feathers wondering how I would keep from falling off. "How do I hold on?"

"Grip her feathers. They're strong," Cash said. I noticed he was standing close to my sister.

"Hold on," Hendrick said right before he galed away. I stood there in shock. I didn't understand how he galed inside the wards. I knew the king could, but the king could do anything. He returned a minute later with a leather strap in his hand.

"How did you gale inside the wards?"

"I'm the Duke of Mazuria now. I have the power to gale anywhere on this land." He took the long leather strap and tied it around the bird's neck. "This should do."

I took a deep breath and stepped closer to her. I slid my leg over her body and hoisted myself up. Taking the makeshift reins, I gripped them tight. My bird opened her wings and started flapping them. She slowly eased off the ground as I looked down at my friends with wide eyes. They stared back in fascination, except for Val. He looked pained, like he was worried about me. I smiled, trying to reassure him that I would be fine.

Be safe, my love.

Always.

I love you, Ember.

I love you too.

As soon as I thought those last words, we took off quickly into the sky. The wind blew my hair back as I braced myself. We were ascending and we were doing it rather quickly.

"To the Gods," I yelled. We flew away from Pyreland. I looked down and couldn't see my family anymore. *Shit!*

Once we were up as high as she wanted, we glided softly through the air. I was scared at first, but then it felt amazing. When the air slid across my skin and my hair whipped behind me, I felt invisible. I let out a loud whooping sound and my bird squawked.

She continued flying, and I noticed we were going over the ocean. I wanted to ask her where we were headed, but she couldn't answer me yet.

A few minutes later, we started to descend as we headed for the Arna mountains. She glided us down to the top of one of the mountains and slowly flapped her wings as we landed with a light thud. I crawled off her to stretch my legs. I raised my hands over my head with excitement I couldn't contain.

"That was amazing!" I yelled.

It was, I heard a husky, beautiful voice in my head. I threw my hands over my mouth.

"I can hear you!"

Once we landed, the bond must have kicked in.

"It's so weird. You sound like a real person!"

I beg your pardon.

"I'm sorry. I did not mean to offend."

I was joking. I have been known to be sarcastic. She squawked and it almost sounded like a laugh.

"Me too! We will get along beautifully." I had a weird feeling like I knew her well. "Can you hear my thoughts?"

Only if you want me to. Like you do with your mate.

"How do you know he is my mate?"

I saw the way he looks at you. He loves you dearly. Plus, he told me. She let out a cackling screech and I laughed.

"Why did you choose the Arna Mountains?"

I was born here many years ago.

"Do you still have family here?"

Her eyes looked sad. *No. You are my only family, which I am grateful for.* My heart ached at hearing she didn't have a family, and I felt my love for her grow.

"You need a name!"

I would be happy with any you choose.

"Since you chose the Arna mountains, I say we name you Arna." She hung her head down like she was sad. "Do you not like it?"

I love it, and I am honored.

Tears threatened my eyes. "Perfect. I am honored to have you as my Familiar, Arna." I reached up and rubbed her neck.

Thank you, Ember. We must get back. The king told me I couldn't be gone long.

"Let's go!" I threw my leg over her and hoisted myself up. Arna flapped her wings as we took off from the mountains. Ten minutes later, we were back in Pyreland.

Arna slowly lowered us to the ground. I watched the faces of my family as they all looked amused.

"Woo-hoo. Way to go, Ember!" Cash said excitedly. Cali was clapping her hands.

"How was it?" Zila asked.

"Can I go next?" Cali asked.

"No, I want to go," Cash said and my eyes darted to him.

"You have wings, Cash!" Asher said as he pushed him aside.

"Enough! Geez. I haven't even put my feet on the ground yet." Val offered me a hand, and I took it as I slid off Arna.

"You are now bonded," the king said. "I like the name you picked."

"What did you name her, Red?"

"Everyone, I would like you to meet Arna. Arna, all these fools are my family. Don't worry . . . you will grow to love them as I did."

Arna let out a squeaking laugh. *Tell them I am honored to meet them all. Tell the one that keeps petting me that he is hot.* The king laughed at her words.

"I will do no such thing!" I looked up at Asher as he stroked her feathers. "She thinks you are . . . sweet, Asher."

"Aww. She is sweet too."

That's not what I said!

My eyes widened. "Arna, hush."

"Okay. Time to head back," the king said.

"What about Arna? Will she fit on the portal?" I asked.

"I will take her for a ride. Once I have had my fun, we will gale the rest of the way," the king said.

Oh, this will be fun, Arna added.

King Reign threw his large leg over her and hopped on.

He is much heavier than you. The king laughed as Arna started flapping her wings and we watched in awe as they flew away.

"This has been a crazy day," I said to the group.

"Well, I must be off," my uncle said. He hugged Cinder, then me. "I have festivities to partake in. Have a great mating ceremony. I will see you all soon." He strolled off to enjoy his party.

Val smiled. "Ready to go home, love? We have a mating to plan."

"I have to figure out where Arna is going to live! She won't fit in the manor."

"King Reign already did that while you were gone," Cinder said and my eyebrows raised.

"He has some Elven coming to build her a barn," Zayn added.

"Well, that's good." I sighed. It may have been weird since I barely knew her, but I missed Arna already.

"Let's go already," Cash said. "I'm starving."

"Do you ever not eat?" Zila asked.

"It takes a lot of food to keep these muscles strong." Cash held up his arm and made a huge muscle. Cinder's eyes lit up and I shook my head.

"Cinder and I have to get home so we can pack our stuff and then come back tomorrow," Cali said

"Yes. I have things to take care of before the move," Cinder said as Cash pulled her close to him.

"Come on. Let's go home," Zayn said as he threw his arm around Cali.

Val grabbed my hand. We all chatted and laughed as we walked back to the portal with our family.

Chapter Forty-Two

F our months had gone by since I arrived in Ashbern. My sister and Cali just got back yesterday. She decided to stay here at Castleva Manor for a while. I had my sister, Val, and the rest of my friends—who I now considered my family. I also had a new Familiar. Silvaria decided to go and stay with a family friend back on Direbreak, so Zila and Cash took her home a couple of days ago.

I had a thousand thoughts running through my mind. *When were the Demons going to attack again? What lands did they have spies hiding on? Would Erebus come for me? How am I going to control my ignitus?*

But today wasn't the day to answer those questions. Today, I had to focus on myself.

Val and I moved our stuff into a newly upgraded mating room yesterday. I was standing in front of my mirror, looking at myself when I realized that I was a completely different person than I was three months ago.

I had killed the man I loved and died in front of the man I loved. The God of Fire had resurrected me. A piece of my soul had died when I found out my father wasn't my father, he was a Changeling. And the most important thing that happened in what seemed like an eternity ago was . . . I fell in love.

"Come on, Ember. Oh, my Gods," Cali whispered. Turning around, Cali and Zila were standing there with tears in their eyes.

"We're going to be late." Zila sniffed back a cry.

"I'm ready."

I strolled over to the girls and we quickly left the manor. We galed to our meeting spot. Zayn walked up to me and put his hand on my shoulder.

"You got this." He wielded a little bit of magic through me, calming my nerves.

"Thank you, Softy." I quickly hugged him.

"You look beautiful, by the way." I had to stop myself from crying when I saw tears in his eyes. "Are you ready?" I nodded.

Zayn linked his arm with mine and escorted me through the trees. When I came around the corner, I saw everyone I knew and loved. As I walked past them, I smiled. All the servants of Castleva Manor were standing there.

Then I saw my King's Guard family. Cash was standing with Cinder. Zila was standing with Natsu and Primavera. Then Cali and Asher too. I even saw the king's personal guards.

As I walked further, I saw Wynter and Ryker. Wynter was crying. King Reign was standing at the front, under my favorite wisteria tree. He smiled kindly at me.

Then I saw Val.

He was wearing all black and looked extremely handsome. He had his shirt completely unbuttoned so that I could see his chest and tattoo.

My heart sank when I met his eyes. I stopped walking when I saw they were filled with tears. Zayn slowly nudged me forward.

Zayn continued holding my arm until I was next to Valarian. He let go and quickly went to stand with the King's Guard.

"You look gorgeous, my *hertis rote.*"

"Thank you, Val."

I was wearing a violet ball gown with a heart shape at the top and silver embellishments adorning it. Today was my mating ritual. I was going to mate the man I loved.

"We are here to mate Valarian Carter Grey and Ember Violet Lavaris," the king's voice was boisterous and commanding. Val smiled when he heard my middle name. I'd already told him days ago, and he said my middle name meant that I was destined to marry someone with violet eyes. I smiled lovingly at him as I recalled the memory.

"Ember, have you brought your mate a strong and proper weapon?"

"I have, Your Majesty." I had picked it out in a shop on Dazeth. It took me three trips to the Fae land to find the perfect one.

"Ember, please gift your weapon to your mate and say the words of honor." I turned around and Cinder handed me the short sword.

"I, Ember Violet Lavaris, gift you, Valarian Carter Grey, this sword. Will you always protect me with this weapon until death and thereafter?"

I handed Val the sword. It was a gorgeous, strong piece of steel with a leather-wrapped handle, just like Val had always wanted. I had a single large blood drop shape engraved in the sword's steel near the hilt. Strength in Blood. The look on his face told me he loved it.

"I, Valarian Carter Grey, vow to protect you with this weapon until death and thereafter."

"As do we! Until death and thereafter!" All my friends shouted in unison, then pounded their chests twice.

"Valarian, have you brought your mate a strong and proper weapon?"

"I have, Your Majesty."

"Valarian, please gift your weapon to your mate and say the words of honor."

Valarian turned and grabbed a bow from his father. My hand shot over my mouth as tears welled up in my eyes.

"I, Valarian Carter Grey, gift you, Ember Violet Lavaris, this bow. Will you always protect me with this weapon until death and thereafter?"

Tears ran down my face as I took the gorgeous bow from his hands. The perfect weight and size, it had one amethyst stone on each side of the middle, on the handle.

"I, Ember Violet Lavaris, vow to protect you with this weapon until death and thereafter."

"As do we! Until death and thereafter." Our friends once again shouted in unison and pounded their chests twice.

A gust of wind came through, and lightning crossed the sky. The magic of the lands danced, making a sparkly tornado around Val and me. Once the magic died down, I looked at Val's chest as his tattoo glowed brightly, then it changed right before my eyes. His tattoo now had a battle-axe head like mine, along with a shield behind it, a drop of blood in the center of the shield, and fire burning below. It was like our tattoos had merged into one.

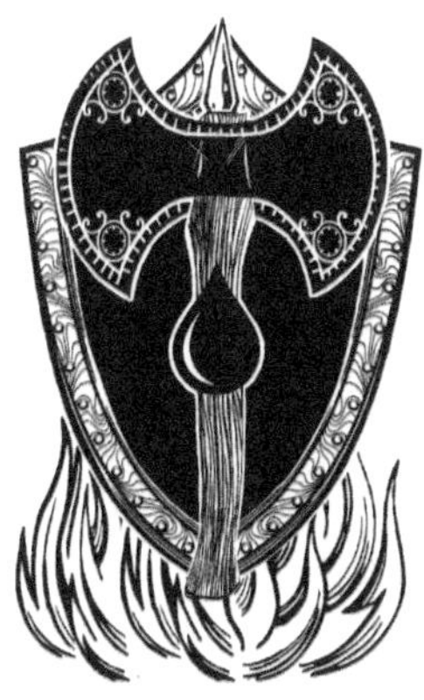

The magic hit me, and my skin started to sparkle as I looked down and watched my tattoo change into the same one he had.

"Strength in Blood and Fire! You are now bonded until death and thereafter!" The king shouted proudly.

A single tear fell from my eye. Val wiped it off with his thumb before he grabbed me, leaned me back, and kissed me deeply. We pulled away from the kiss and everyone started cheering. Cash was making a loud, whooping sound as Cali clapped. My sister was crying, and so was Val's. I guess she was now my sister, too.

"Let's retire to the party!" the king said.

We galed to the beach and the bonfire was already going. The servants quickly started setting out the food, and the band started performing. Everyone came up and congratulated us, one by one.

"Welcome to the family, daughter." Ryker pulled me into a big hug.

"Thank you. I'm grateful to be a part of your family."

He smiled kindly at me. "We are honored to have you. If you need anything, don't hesitate to ask."

Then, to my surprise, Val reached over and hugged his father.

"I am sorry, Father," Val whispered into Ryker's shoulder.

"I know, son, I know." Ryker patted his back, soothing him.

"I love you." The moment brought tears to my eyes once again.

"I love you too, son." The males broke free of their hug, and for the first time, I saw Val smile at his father.

"I finally have a sister," Wynter said as she yanked me into a hug. She let go and wiped away a tear.

"Wynter, this is my sister Cinder."

"Nice to meet you! I now have two sisters." Wynter hugged Cinder.

"Nice to meet you too," Cinder said.

Zayn's face looked nervous as walked past Val. "Wynter, would you like to dance?"

"I would truly love to, Zaynith." He took her arm and led her away. There was a scowl on Val's face.

A perfect love match, I wielded to him.

What is it you say to me? Hush your mouth, Ember. Val smiled widely as he threw my own words back at me.

We might both end up with Angels as brothers, Val.

He shrugged and then smiled. *I see nothing wrong with that.*

"Congratulations to you both," Cali said as walked up, before immediately turning her attention to Ryker. "Duke of Mayhem, would you like to dance?"

"Yes, my dear, but on one condition . . . you must call me Ryker." She took his arm as he escorted her away. She winked over her shoulder at me as they entered the dance floor.

"Cali said we should enjoy some privacy."

"I wish I could talk to others like you, Val."

"Someday, we will have a baby Vampire running around that can't shield their thoughts, and you'll think twice."

My eyes went wide as I looked at his face. "One thing at a time, Val. I want to enjoy my life as a King's Guard for now."

"As do I, but after five or ten years, I'm definitely putting a baby in you." He hugged me tight as he leaned down and kissed me.

"Forty years, maybe fifty. But at least twenty," I corrected.

"You are so indecisive." He laughed. "We can just practice until then." He kissed me, and after a few seconds, a thought hit me, and I pulled back.

"Wait, how do you know it will be a baby Vampire?" I asked.

"I don't. We have a fifty percent chance of having a baby Caster, so you never know." He kissed my neck.

"I don't even know how to hold a baby," I admitted.

"You have forty, fifty, or twenty years to figure it out before we start a family." He laughed, and I rolled my eyes at him. "Until then, those people are our family." He looked out toward the sandy beach.

I turned in his arms and looked out at our friends—our family. Val hugged me as we watched them. Natsu had his hand in Zila's as he led her to the dance floor. To my shock, I saw the king go out onto it with my sister. She looked as elegant as ever. It only lasted about a minute before Cash nervously cut in. The king let him in and laughed.

King Reign grabbed a female servant and whipped her onto the dance floor. She had a shocked look on her face. After a minute, she relaxed and started to smile and have fun.

"Come on, everyone, this is a celebration!" The king's words were strong and powerful in the cool evening air.

The other servants headed onto the dance floor and started dancing. My heart filled with pure happiness.

"What's wrong, Ember?" Val said when he heard me sniff back a cry.

"I am just really happy," I whispered.

"Come on, my love." Val dragged me onto the dance floor. He put his arms around my body, holding me close to him. I looked up into his beautiful eyes.

"How does it feel to be mated to me, Ember Lavaris Grey?"

"Oh, I love the name." I smiled proudly. "And it feels amazing."

"You are finally mine." He kissed my lips softly.

"I have been yours since day one, Val."

He smiled, showing me his fangs. "I love you, my *hertis rote*."

"I love you too, my *hertis rote*." I laid my head on his chest and listened to his heart. It was like it was playing a song only for me—beating for me.

We danced until we were tired and couldn't dance anymore.

Valarian wanted alone time with me, so as our friends were all dancing and having fun, he galed us to my favorite spot.

Sitting on a blanket of lavenders right outside the wisteria trees, I looked up at the stars above us as the moonlight shone on my face. Valarian plucked a flower and put it behind my ear. I smiled as I felt his breath against my skin. He placed a gentle kiss upon my cheek and then on my neck. We made love under the stars. The magic danced and danced around us while he held me for eternity.

Strength in Blood and Fire, until death and thereafter.

Chapter Forty-Three

Erebus

I walked into my quarters and took a seat on my throne. I am the King of Mistlaven so I am in charge until the God of Sulfur, Tartarus, awakens. There were plans in motion that were ruined by the King's Guard so now we had to make new plans.

"We have infiltrated Direbreak, Your Majesty. It has been two days and the Lycans have not noticed yet," one of my guards said to me. I glanced up to a dozen of my soldiers standing in front of me.

"Excellent. We are back to two lands with a spy on them?"

"Yes, it is unfortunate that we lost both of the spies on Mazuria. I just got word that Ember Lavaris killed the Changeling."

"Of course she did. My mate is fierce. The Changeling should have never stabbed her. He deserved more than the quick death she put upon him." The thought of her being so evil brought a smile to my face. "And as for the Duke of Mazuria, he was an imbecile and not even a Demon. We didn't need someone so weak."

"I have other upsetting news, Your Majesty."

"Spit it out then!" Fed up with these idiots, my patience was running thin.

"She has mated the Vampire in the eyes of the kingdom."

"Lies!"

"It is the truth."

"I can break their bond."

"You said you could not break it yourself."

My eyes narrowed on the guard. "No, but once Tartarus has risen, he can break it for me."

"What if he does not?"

"That is multiple times you have doubted me. You have also dropped formalities repeatedly. I will not tolerate disrespect." I waved my hand and five Demons strolled up behind the ignorant fool.

"What shall we do with him, Your Majesty?"

"Feed him to the Chimera. He has not fed this week." I watched them drag the idiot out of the room kicking and screaming. It was pathetic to be honest. I never did like him anyway, he always smelled putrid.

I pointed at a Demon that looked less incompetent. "You are now in charge, Finley."

"I am proud to serve you. Anything else you need, Your Majesty?"

"Yes, I need the King's Guard dead. All but Ember Lavaris and Valarian Grey. Do not harm them. I want to make sure she watches while I rip his heart out and eat it in front of her. Since she decided to mate him and ruin herself, I will need another virgin for the transformation."

"Where shall we find that, Your Majesty?"

"The virgin has to be a Fire Caster. Find her sister, Cinder, and bring her to me. She is not as fierce as Ember, but with the Duke of Mazuria dead, she can hopefully be the virgin that raises Tartarus." The feeling of power flowed through my body as I thought about taking down all these weak, unsuspecting cretins.

"The kingdom will be mine!"

Sneak Peek

CONTINUE READING FOR A
SNEAK PEEK OF
EMERALD SKIES
PRIMORDIAL GODS BOOK TWO

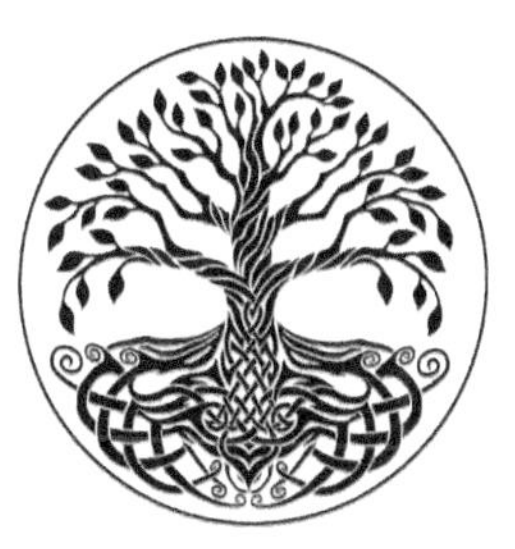

Emerald Skies

Cinder

Hot and sweaty from baking for a couple of hours, I saw an Angel enter the room. I wondered immediately where Cash was. He was usually not far behind Zayn.

"Hey, Cinder," Zayn said to me. He eyeballed the table filled with desserts. "It smells so good in the house."

"Hello, Zayn." I smiled politely at the sweet Angel before I saw Cash come strolling through the door, and my heart raced.

"Oh, I smelled this in my room." His eyes immediately went to the table as he scanned all the baked goods I had made today before he looked at me. "Ha-ha, don't you look adorable with flour on your cheek?" My hand immediately wiped my cheek as he smiled at me.

Cash was always such an upbeat person and always made me smile. My blood boiled at the way he looked at me. Well, that and I was nervous about what I was about to do.

"Hello, Cash." I blushed, looking down and wiping flour off the front of my apron. "I'm glad you're here. I have something for you."

I nervously grabbed the pie I had made for Cash and handed it to him. He looked at it with a confused face and I immediately felt silly for gifting him a dumb pie.

"You made this for me?" He met my eyes, and I looked nervously to the ground.

"Yes, I thought you would like it. Ember said that apple was your favorite."

Why had I done this? And in front of Zayn. My nerves were killing me.

"Wow, this is amazing." Glancing up, Cash had a huge smile on his face. I immediately blushed and swallowed hard. "Thank you, Cinder. It truly is an honor to get to eat your pie." I heard Zayn snicker, and my eyes shot to him.

He looked shamefully away. I didn't understand what was funny. Was he jealous? I turned my attention back to Cash. I stared into those gorgeous blue eyes of his and had to turn my head away.

"You're welcome and please excuse me, but I must finish this cake." I continued mixing up the cake batter when I felt a presence stand close to me.

"It truly is an honor to have you cook for me. Thank you, Cinder." Cash bowed to me. Then he kissed me on my cheek, causing me to blush. I saw him grab a fork and leave the room before I looked up at a frowning Zayn.

"He just took the whole pie. He wasn't even going to offer me one piece."

I giggled at Zayn's reaction.

"I made one for you, too. Ember said cherry was your favorite." I smiled brightly at him.

"Wow. Thank you, Cinder." He smiled as he walked over to me. He laid a sweet kiss on my cheek, then left the room. I shook my head at the two crazy Angels.

My new life at Castleva was going well so far, except for the fact that I had a crush on *two* men.

Unfortunately, it didn't matter what I did, Cash wasn't paying the same attention to me that he once had. I didn't know what I had done wrong.

Maybe Zayn was a more proper fit for me. He was sweet and friendly and always gave me attention. I put the cake in the oven as I sighed before I quickly washed my hands and went to find Noreen.

Also By P.S. Nail

Primordial Gods Series
Violet Flames: Book One
Emerald Skies: Book Two

Argentium Vampire Hunters Trilogy
Raised by Venom: Book One
Scorned by Venom: Book Two

Endless Reels of Thoughts:
Snippets of Poetry from an Unsettled Mind:
Volume One

Dreaming of becoming an author since she was a young girl, P.S. Nail finally took the plunge and decided to self-publish her debut paranormal romance, Violet Flames.

She enjoys playing the guitar, video games, reading, and spending time with friends and family. She currently lives in the United States with her husband, three sons, and pets.

She will continue writing until death, dismissal, or dishonor.

Acknowledgments

Special Thanks

I want to thank my fans, also known as my family and friends, for supporting me. I had the best cheerleaders anyone could ever dream of having while building this fantasy world.

I want to thank my husband, Brian, for letting me hide in the bedroom for months while I wrote and edited this book. Without you giving me the space to do what I needed to do, this book would not have been possible. You will always be my Valarian.

I want to thank my children, Brian Jr, Devin, and Kaden, for letting me read fight scenes with them and bouncing ideas off their young, intelligent minds. I love you! DO NOT READ MOM'S BOOK!

I would also like to thank my Aunt Vicky. By now, I am sure you know that this book was dedicated specifically to you. You better have cried when you saw that dedication page, which is all I am saying—wink, wink. Thank you for letting me geek out and freak out and all the other emotions we went through together. The daily calls, texts, emails, facetimes, and laughing sessions will forever be a part of my soul. You are the best aunt anyone could ask for.

A special thanks to my friend Brock Boyer for all the feedback and ideas on tattoos, maps, and more. Great minds think alike! Thank you, Nicole Ellis Crippen and Rosey Boyd, for letting me ramble for days, and days, and days. You three are excellent friends for putting up with me. I appreciate you!

Finally, I would like to thank my graphic artist, Diletta De Santis, for bringing the images in my head to life! You're amazing! And a special thanks to my editor L.M. Wilkinson. You got my manuscript edited in record time, and it turned out beautifully.

www.ingramcontent.com/pod-product-compliance
Lightning Source LLC
Chambersburg PA
CBHW020856130726
47900CB00014B/820